The Silver Queen

Centered around the mysterious disappearance of Aspen's famous solid silver and gold statue during its return from the 1893 Chicago World's Fair, young Daniel Carrington is forced to deceive his boss and his closest friends in a desperate race to find his missing mother and sister in New York city and elude a murderous bounty hunter only steps behind them.

by

Paul W. Harris

This book is dedicated to all those who enjoyed **Independence Pass** and wanted to know what happens next. Truth be told, I wanted to know too.

I hope you enjoy the adventure.

P W H

This is a work of fiction.

CHAPTER 1

Aspen, Colorado. 1889.

"I'm sorry, son. It's done for. It can't be saved. It's all gone."

And indeed, it appeared so.

The fireman's face was a gruesome mask streaked with sweat and grime, telling of the effort he and his comrades had expended in their efforts to save Harry's cabin from the inferno that was consuming it. The fireman was familiar to Daniel. A kindly face and just one of the dozens of unsung heroes of the young city of Aspen who invariably raced to the call of danger, whether it was a fire threatening someone's home or a mine collapse. He was concerned for Daniel and it showed in the furrows of his brow.

Looking over the fireman's shoulder it was clear that behind the smoke, crackling resins and shooting flames, Harry's cabin truly was all but gone, reduced to flaming timbers and incinerated dreams. Daniel pushed closer to the inferno but found Red Corcoran's hand clamped on his shoulder, restraining him from such foolishness. There came a whoosh and a burst of smoke and flame shot skyward as the roof of the small cabin collapsed.

Daniel's eyes brimmed with tears. The strength abandoned his legs and if it wasn't for Red's grip on his shoulder he would've crumpled. Again the flames flared, forcing them all back, all but Daniel. Peering into the fire, feeling the heat burning his face, it occurred to him that it was not just Harry's cabin or their possessions that were lost; it was his past life that was being consumed. All of it, everything, evaporating in flames and smoke along with physical connections to his mother and sister, all gone forever. He was left with nothing. Nothing, but for the newly purchased wedding suit he wore and the beautiful bride he'd worn it for. Kate was his life now, as well as his wife.

One half-hour prior his world and his prospects had been very different. Daniel, hand in hand with his bride Kate and their bridal party, several dozens in all, had been trooping merrily from the church toward their wedding celebration at the Hotel Jerome when they heard the ascending wail of the emergency siren.

Kate's mother, Shirley, Aspen's most prominent madam and owner of the Paragon Saloon, followed them walking arm in arm with Red Corcoran, the shyest of her suitors and the man most instrumental in Daniel's survival in town. Following them sulked Rachelle, Kate's younger sister and her surprised, soon-to-be-husband Leafy Lane. He wore the guilty look of a child caught stealing since he, as well as Big Shirley and Red, had only minutes before learned that Leafy was the father of Rachelle's baby and Shirley's first grandchild.

At first, the siren caused little alarm but it was soon followed by a cacophony of bells and shouting as the fire crews dashed to their equipment and hitched their fire wagons.

"Where's the fire?" Jerome Wheeler, Aspen's wealthiest mine owner, yelled to a wagon full of firemen racing to the burning building.

"It's on the front of the mountain," the man yelled back.

Daniel looked up toward Aspen Mountain and a shudder ran up his spine. A column of smoke was rising on the lower mountainside, where Harry's cabin stood. Daniel looked at Kate, then Shirley and Red. They read the panic in his eyes.

"Go!" Kate said, her concern erasing the bliss she had worn just moments before. "Go, Daniel! It could be Harry's cabin!"

Reluctantly he released Kate's hand and chased after the fire-wagons racing toward his biggest fear.

"Red, you'd better go too," Shirley said, encouraging him to follow. "You might be able to help." Red also hurried off, hailing a ride on one of the wagons heading to the fire.

Could it really be Harry's cabin that was burning? Daniel thought as he ran. Perhaps it was the cabin up hill, the one owned by Billy Tomb? It was difficult to tell from a distance but the nearer he came, the more probable his fears were indeed becoming a reality.

The first of the fire-wagons was already at the scene when he arrived. The wooden walls of the cabin were hungry tinder for the fire, the pine resins popping and flaring in delight. Firefighters rushed about, uncoiling hoses or pumping water into them, and one volunteer was already spraying a meager stream of water onto the inferno.

Outwardly stone-faced, Daniel could only stand and watch as the small log cabin that he had shared with Harry Rich and had called home for the past six months disappeared in the crackle of flames and smoke. So much of his brief life was being consumed. Letters from his mother and the address in New York where he sent his money to them every month, and that of the uncle he was planning to join in San Francisco. Also, there was all that stolen money.

There came a rush of heat and smoke that engulfed him as a wall of the cabin collapsed, covering them in a shower of sparks that threatened to start more blazes in the trees around them. The firemen responded quickly and trained their hoses on the new fires to save the adjoining nearby cabins, having surrendered the fight to save Daniel's and Harry's.

Daniel's knees trembled and he gathered strength only from Red's reassuring grip on his shoulder. Minutes passed like hours as the fire gradually consumed the cabin. The remaining walls collapsed, falling inward toward each other, slowly reducing the cabin to a pyre of glowing logs and ashes.

But through the smoke and wavering air, one identifiable item stood against the onslaught of the flames, indestructible like a phoenix ready to emerge. The large iron oven under which he and Harry had buried the money stolen from the bank in Leadville. And that was another problem completely.

What if the money was gone? All of it burned, only ashes remaining? It could be a blessing in disguise since it meant that the evidence of their robbery was destroyed. On the other hand, if the cabin was now his and the money was not burned, then what was he going to do about that predicament? Was it truly as safe as Harry said it would be, buried under the oven? Harry had certainly reassured him often enough. It was doubtful that Harry set the cabin on fire. It was his cabin, after all. And the last he'd seen of Harry, he was leaving town hiding under a canvas in the rear of his wives' wagon, trailed by an angry Doc Holliday looking for his money.

"Well, that should kill about half of the bedbugs in town, I should think," boomed the voice of Jerome B. Wheeler, who had wheezed his way up the narrow path from the road to stand beside them. His face was a mix of shock, humor and exertion. "Harry probably knew them all by name." Jerome laughed, ignoring the fact that his humor went unappreciated. "How did it start, son? Any ideas?"

Daniel was pondering the same question. He'd been at the cabin that morning to retrieve Harry's clean clothes and all had been in order then. The only thing amiss at that time was the unexpected appearance of Doc Holliday and Hamlett, the sheriff's deputy from Leadville, the one who hated Harry for disfiguring his face. Could they have burned down Harry's cabin for revenge over his unpaid gambling debts?

Daniel was unaware of the deal that Harry and Doc Holliday had made in the courthouse, whereby Harry had committed Daniel's half of the stolen money to Doc for his untruthful testimony which had exonerated them. If Doc Holliday had burned Harry's cabin down for revenge, then it would be bitter irony that he had also burned his money as well.

Harry would never burn his own cabin unless he had removed the money first and wanted to disappear. But, considering the day's events prior to the wedding, there was really no opportunity for Harry to do this. Or was there?

Could it have been accidental? The oven always had a fire burning in it. It was where Harry cooked the potatoes he sold to the miners. It burned continuously and as far as Daniel knew, there had never been an instance where their enterprise had endangered their living space. That the cabin had never burned down before had led Daniel to believe that it never could. Obviously, that was a fallacy because, as with most things involving Harry Rich, anything was possible. It was a shallow pool of logic that Harry waded in, Daniel reminded himself.

But as they watched, Daniel noticed something odd. With the nearest wall now fallen, he saw more clearly the giant iron oven that had been Harry's lifeline, their business and their treasure trove. In glimpses through the flickering flames and shimmering heat, Daniel was shocked to see the massive iron oven was not upright as it had been just hours before but was tipped onto its back. A chill ran down his spine. What had happened to the money buried beneath it?

The walk back to the Hotel was a somber one. Daniel was buried deep in thought and both Red and Jerome knew when to leave a man alone. Before entering the Hotel's ballroom Wheeler took Daniel's elbow. "If you'll take some advice from an old man. This is only a setback, son. It's not the end of the world, though it might seem that way at the moment. It is these kinds of events that build character in a man. So, I want you to be of good cheer for your bride and your guests." He turned to Red. "Life is full of these types of crises, isn't it, Red?"

Red nodded. "This too shall pass, son."

Wheeler brightened and smiled at Daniel. "I want you to look to the future of our business together and the future of your new family." Daniel managed a smile, mostly for Wheeler's sake. "Now, let's go and celebrate your marriage, shall we?"

After what he'd just witnessed, Daniel was numb to his surroundings, feeling at a distance from reality until he found Kate in his arms. She smiled at him, her eyes full of compassion and love. It was the way she held him that renewed his strength, and once again his smile sprang forth. Kate was his refuge.

She and the wedding party had stood outside the hotel for a short while watching the plume of dark smoke rising. Rumors churned among the thirsty guests. No Problem Joe and others openly speculated on the possibility of the fire being at Harry's cabin as they watched Harry and his wagonload of women fading from view, heading west, trailed by Doc Holliday. After what they had witnessed at the church, the humor and the irony of Harry's departure from Aspen was lost on no one.

Shirley eventually encouraged everyone inside, and most of the guests were gathered around the bar in the dining room when Daniel entered. Kate, took his hands in hers and looked deeply into his eyes. He was honest to a fault, she thought, and had little ability to lie to her. Daniel was an easy read compared to other men, of that she was certain. Though only seventeen, she knew men and how they thought and what they wanted; after all, she did grow up in a brothel.

What she saw in Daniel now, as they held each other amidst the somber crowd, was the deep loss he was suffering. He felt distant and he looked different, also. She smiled at him and he threw his arms about her and clutched her to him, his life-saving raft of love and security. A round of applause for the newlyweds rose as did the clinking of many wine glasses amid many a toast.

After the last of the photographer's powder had flashed, the guests settled in at their tables. Under the brilliant electric lights, which had been such a novelty only months before, and under the gaze of the massive silver and gold statue of The Silver Queen, the couple sat at their bridal table surrounded by her family and their many friends, including the Wheelers.

Jerome had gone to great lengths to make their wedding celebration both sumptuous and memorable. The tables were decorated with huge vases of fresh spring flowers and on the bridal table he had organized a spray of lilacs and orchids. They feasted on fresh quail in wine sauce and loin of veal served with wild mushrooms. Jerome had gone to great lengths to have his chef create a tiered wedding cake in the same colors as the flowers that decorated their table. When the dining had finished and the wine glasses refilled, Jerome called the room to order.

"Friends, ladies and gentlemen!" The room quieted. "Well, I guess you could say it's been an exciting day for our bride and groom." There was a smattering of laughter from those who enjoyed Jerome's sense of understatement. "I do sincerely, as does my family, wish Kate and Daniel the very best of happiness. Also, on behalf of Kate's mother, I also wish them a large family. She'll bother me much less if she has grand-children to chase after." Laughter rose at her expense and Shirley shot Rachelle a quick look while Leafy ardently avoided her gaze.

"I wish to propose a toast to our bride and groom." The assemblage rose as one. "To Daniel and Kate Carrington! To their success as a family and to their family's happiness!" The toast was repeated loudly and merrily and Daniel blushed, embarrassed by the attention and the obvious affection of their gathered friends. He focused on the adoring, sweet face of his new wife, took Kate's face in his hands and kissed her boldly and with love and was applauded loudly by one and by all.

Later, Jerome took Daniel and Kate aside, motioning for Shirley to join them. "I doubt that you'll have to stay with your mother-in-law too long." Pressing an envelope onto Kate's hand, he patted Shirley's bottom but she deflected his hand with a well-practiced gesture. Mrs. Wheeler pursed her lips and with a huff turned her attention elsewhere.

"Mind your manners, Jerome. Your wife's watching."

"That's why I do it," Jerome laughed.

"Oh, really?" Shirley questioned, amused. "Not because you can't keep your hands off me?"

"Well I should mind my manners now that I can see where your affections truly lie." He nodded toward Red Corcoran and Shirley gave him a weak smile. Jerome laughed his big, manly laugh and sauntered off to join his wife and daughter.

It was late when the musicians played their final tune and the exhausted revelers began to fade, nearing midnight when the last of the guests departed. Shirley and Red gathered the wedding gifts and placed them into Shirley's buggy alongside Rachelle, reluctant to leave her soon to be husband Leafy.

Shirley hugged Daniel warmly and happily said goodnight to her daughter, kissing her and wishing them a happy and successful marriage. Together they stood, with Jerome waving Shirley, Red and Rachelle off into the night.

"Well, I guess you two should be turning in." Jerome said with a smile, "I've ordered breakfast to be delivered mid-morning so I don't want to see either one of you before noon, if you get my drift." He laughed and jabbed Daniel in the ribs playfully. "Now, let me escort you two love birds up to your bridal suite." Jerome led them back inside the hotel and up the stairs. "I've taken the liberty of placing a bottle of Champagne next to your bed in case you get thirsty during the night." Jerome winked at Kate. Kate blushed.

"Thank you, Mister Wheeler. You've been very kind to us." Jerome gave Kate a kiss on the cheek and shook Daniel's hand warmly.

"I wish you both a long and happy life." His sincerity was undoubtable, touching them both.

Though not their first time in each other's arms it was this night Daniel would remember as the beginning of a new life. Safe for once, enfolded and entwined in the loving arms of his bride.

Only the coming of the dawn broke their embrace.

Chapter 2

A few years later.

Filling most of the front page of the Aspen Times, dated May 21st. 1893, was a picture of the Silver Queen accompanied by headlines announcing the impending departure of his, "Tribute to the Silver Industry", quoting Mister Wheeler's description directly. An accompanying article glorified the now familiar story that the statue was bound for Chicago and destined to be the centerpiece of the Colorado State Pavilion at the World's Fair.

Daniel lay the newspaper on his cluttered desk and considered the picture for some time. Symbolically meant to represent the value of the Colorado silver industry to the national economy, the massively valuable sculpture stood all of eighteen feet from floor to canopy and the silver alone weighed over five tons. Approximately rendered in the classical Grecian style, she bore regal bearing but was hardly the goddess Diana, a woman of mythical beauty. Seated imperiously on her silver canopied throne she was pulled in a silver boat by two cherubs each bearing cornucopia filled with apple sized nuggets of solid silver and gold.

Daniel smiled inwardly. He was confident the photographer had earnestly tried to do an excellent job, and to be fair, photography had its limits. But, even if one considered kindly the photographer's best intentions, the visage of Mister Jerome B. Wheeler's interpretation of the 'Goddess of Silver' was far from fetching. Unfortunately, or perhaps by intent, during the process of sculpting and casting, her face had developed features more masculine than feminine. To Daniel's eye, in the photograph she looked very much like Mrs. Wheeler.

The statue's very existence, its notoriety and now its relocation, was provoked by reaction to political decisions being considered in Washington that could have far reaching consequences for the owners of silver mines in Colorado and the western states. A movement gaining momentum in Congress was determined to repeal the Sherman Silver Purchase Act which would, effectively destroy the silver mining industry. It was Wheeler's hope, and indeed the hope of all the country's silver miners, that the fame of such an imposing piece of art as The Silver Queen would help sway the US Congress to vote in favor of the industry.

Daniel finished reading the article and turned his attention back to the thick folder open underneath. The invoices and ore manifests were neatly stacked and he went about logging the various entries into a ledger in his neat, precise handwriting. His time spent working in this office for Wheeler's mining company had amounted to very little in the way of mining experience; a filing clerk is how he presently viewed himself. Absently, he picked up the small, silver-framed photograph sitting on his desk, considering it with mixed emotions as he usually did.

It was a somber but pleasant amber-colored photograph. Kate held their daughter Rose on her lap, seated on a couch, both wearing sun bonnets and smiling for the camera. Truthfully, it was only Kate smiling, their daughter Rose, wore the sullen, mystified expression of a one-year old.

He replaced the picture carefully and withdrew an envelope that peeked out from underneath the blotting pad. It was weathered and the writing smeared, but he held it with the same reverence as the picture of his family. "RETURN TO SENDER" was written across the front of the envelope in a bold hand. His breathing quickened as he considered it, as if it would tell him why the letter wasn't delivered and what his mother and sister would do without the small but precious amount of money it held.

With a sigh, he opened a drawer in his desk and placed the envelope on top of several others, all bearing the same salutation and rejection. Peeking out from beneath the stack of letters was a small gold locket on a fine gold chain. Carefully opening the locket, he studied the pictures of his mother and father. The photos were partially singed. Once it had held a lock of his mother's hair, now it only retained the scars and the smell of the cataclysm it had survived. It had been his mother's. Now it was the only object he possessed to remind him of her.

Without warning, everything in the office rattled and shook. The drinking water in the pitcher across the room rocked back and forth, splashing water onto the floor. Daniel grabbed the edges of his desk and prepared for more tremors but the shaking subsided almost immediately.

In the two years that he'd been working for Jerome Wheeler's Smuggler Mining Company, he was familiar with emergencies underground and he knew what the shaking meant. It was a mine collapse. The only questions were: where was it and how bad?

The office had gone silent. Then, the door burst open and John Carter, Wheeler's top manager and most trusted engineer, raced into the room and grabbed his coat and hat.

"That was a cave-in!" he yelled, unnecessarily. "Daniel! Come with me! The rest of you grab stretchers and lanterns and follow us."

Daniel was one step behind Carter as they hurried down the stairs and out into the usually busy street. Curiously, the traffic, both horse-drawn and pedestrian, seemed frozen in place. There was no sound or any movement. The whole town was hushed, as if collectively waiting for something more to happen.

Suddenly, the strange peace was shattered abruptly by the ear-splitting wail of the emergency siren. As if by magic, the still-life tableau burst into a concert of purposeful activity alive with men darting this way and that. Some went to the fire engines, some the ambulances, but invariably, all went toward the danger.

"Which way?" Carter yelled at a group of men. He needn't have asked. He'd guessed already. Two of the men held up their arms pointing east, toward Independence Pass. "Hurry!" he yelled to Daniel, breaking into a run, reacting to the sinking feeling that the greatest of his fears had become real.

They sprinted around the corner onto Galena Street, zig-zagging through the carts and wagons, dodging several horses who reared up, making a fuss, spooked by the trembling in the ground under them. The fire siren continued howling and dozens of men spilled out from bars and offices, donning coats and some still carrying their work shovels, all dashing to rescue their fellow miners. Women stood about in shock, pointing toward a pall of dirty smoke and steam rising from the base of Ajax Mountain.

It took no more than several minutes for Daniel and Carter to reach the entrance to the Glory Hole Mine. All about them was total confusion.

An unrehearsed ensemble of men dashed this way and that, some shouting orders, others assisting survivors stumbling back to the surface dazed and shaken. Chaos reigned above them as remnants of what had been a prosperous mining enterprise of trestles and gantries groaned and tilted steeply.

Carter found the mine foreman staring into a massive depression in the earth which was gasping smoke and steam like the entrance to Hades. Carter grabbed the man roughly.

"What happed here?" Carter yelled. The mine foreman looked back lamely, mouthed something they could not hear and pointed down into the smoking crater. Cautiously, Daniel and Carter stepped to the edge, which crumbled under their feet the nearer they went. Leaning forward they peered into the roiling, vaporous hole.

Steam rose up from the depths. It came in bursts, in time with a rhythmical puffing sound. They moved closer. The steam cleared a little. There, at the bottom of the hole, they saw Jerome Wheeler's steam locomotive laying on its side, smoking and smoldering, its wheels fitfully turning. To their left and right were broken, twisted sections of rail tracks leading into the crater.

"I told you this would happen!" Carter yelled at the man. "How many men are down there?"

"I dunno, forty, fifty … maybe more," he mumbled. "We got some out already."

"You don't know?" Carter screamed into his face. "You're the mine manager, aren't you?" The man shrugged. "I told you that you were too close to our shafts," Carter was red-faced, spitting mad and barely holding his temper in check. John Carter's concern for the miners' safety was renowned and respected in Aspen. "Do you remember me saying that to you, Mister Bishop?" Daniel grabbed Carter's arm, pointing.

Through the smoke and dust-laden air, a gaggle of filthy, bedraggled miners emerged from the mine's entrance carrying two unconscious survivors on stretchers. Leafy Lane appeared among them, laboring under the weight of his human burden. Daniel raced to him, Carter close behind.

Leafy was masked in dirt and dust and suffering a coughing fit. Carter patted him on the back to help clear his lungs and sat him down.

"What happened? Carter asked.

"No one told us they were blasting next to us. The shaft caved in…. it opened up … right into the Glory Hole … that's how I got here."

"Are there any of our men down there?" Daniel asked urgently.

Leafy nodded. Carter and Daniel turned to run into the Glory Hole Mine but Leafy grabbed Daniel's arm. "We have to get them out." Leafy struggled to his feet.

"There's a faster way. I'll show you," Leafy said and ran ahead of them as quickly as he could manage.

"Where are we going?" Daniel gasped when they stopped.

"Grab these lamps and follow me." Leafy said, handing them lamps. He grabbed the two rolled emergency stretchers and together they raced into the mine entrance. "We can get there from this mineshaft and bring them out this way."

The rickety elevator descended at a frustratingly slow rate and then bumped to a halt, throwing them about. Illuminated by the light coming down the shaft from above, they lit their oil lanterns and those on their helmets. "This way," Leafy yelled, pulling up the neckerchief over his mouth and racing ahead of them they followed him down the dark, dusty tunnel.

As they ran in the flickering light, their shadows danced and jogged along the walls keeping pace. The floor was uneven, littered with rubble and rocks, and Daniel tripped more than once. In places where the walls had collapsed, wood mine supports tipped at angles or jutted from the ceiling. Iron spikes and nails projected from them like spear points. Onward they ran, dodging the dangers they could see and damning those they could not.

The tunnel forked more than once but they trusted Leafy's knowledge of the mine. Coughing and choking on the dust, stumbling into the gloom and the danger, they were drawn deeper by the sounds coming from the darkness. Slivers of light appeared ahead. Suddenly they were upon them.

Working frantically in a hell hole of dust and heat, a dozen men were busy clearing rocks and rubble while others assisted injured miners to come through a jagged hole in the rock wall. Shouting encouragement to those trapped under the rubble and using crowbars and shovels, they flailed at the wreckage, heaving away the loose rocks that hampered them. Gasping for air in the toxic atmosphere, illuminated only by weak, constantly shifting shafts of light from their headlamps, they threw themselves into their desperate work. Injured men lay off to the side moaning in pain while the rest frantically dug at the pile of rocks from where the cries of another trapped victim arose. At last, the injured miner emerged and was handed down, man-to-man, to be carried to safety.

Another man then appeared, then another, then another. "Leafy," Carter yelled. "Are these all our men?" Leafy shook his head vigorously. "No!"

"Are our men safe?" Daniel asked.

"Not sure." Leafy helped another miner through the rubble. "I'll check when we get back up."

"I want everyone accounted for," Carter yelled, frustrated and angry at the fool Bishop, who had disregarded his advice and caused this catastrophe. He slung an unconscious man over his shoulders and carried him off down the mine shaft.

"Take that man and go with him, Daniel," Leafy gasped. "I'll stay and help get the rest of them out of here." Leafy helped a survivor to his feet. "And bring stretchers!" Daniel nodded and took the man under the arms and half dragged him down the shaft chasing Carter. With the failing of the electric pumps, water was filling the shafts, ankle-deep in places, adding to the discomfort and danger.

The casualties they were carrying were dead weights. Carter's man was unconscious and Daniel's could not let go of his crushed knee, making it difficult to step over some of the fallen rocks that made the footing treacherous. The elevator arrived overloaded with rescuers carrying lamps, shovels and more equipment.

"Where are they?" One of the rescuers shouted as they poured out. Daniel pointed down the shaft.

"Two minutes if you run," he wheezed. The rescuers hurried off while Carter and Daniel loaded their casualties into the flimsy metal crib and pushed the lever for it to ascend.

When the elevator reached the surface, Daniel's eyes were assaulted by the brightness. Off in the distance a church bell bonged. The cage door was pulled open and many hands reached in to help them. Still partially blind as his eyes adjusted to the daylight, Daniel felt someone take him firmly by the arm and he instantly recognized the booming voice of Jerome Wheeler.

"Mister Carter. What happened down there?" Carter ignored him. He was busy assisting the injured man onto the ambulance and into the capable hands of a white-clad nurse.

"How is it down there? Is everyone alright?" Wheeler bellowed. "Who else is down there? Is anyone dead?" Wheeler's questions came at him like a military assault. Eyes tearing, Daniel fought a coughing spasm. Wheeler took the injured man from him and with the help of several others, carried the man into the shade of a strangely tilted building. Daniel was still gasping for air when he was lifted to his feet. Wheeler's face was barely inches from his.

"Who's in charge down there?" Wheeler demanded, his face flushed and drawn taut. Daniel took as deep a breath as he could manage before answering. All around him doctors and nurses dashed about, loading injured miners onto waiting wagons for the trip to the hospital. Another painful breath.

"Leafy Lane … and some of his crew." Daniel gasped, "Maybe… a dozen men."

"What happened?" Wheeler yelled as Carter returned.

"The Glory Hole undermined us," Carter spat out in disgust. "I warned them they were getting too close to our shafts, but they wouldn't listen."

"So, it wasn't our fault then?" Wheeler asked, his business sense gaining traction.

"Not so far as I can tell."

"Well, I guess that's good news on top of bad. How is it down there, John?"

"It's bad, but I've seen worse. I need the shift roster," Carter said as he raced off.

"I want you to make sure that we get all of our men out of there, Daniel. I'm counting on you." Jerome took hold of Daniel's hand. He grasped it tightly, sincerely. "But you be careful, son," Wheeler said, as Daniel stepped into the elevator. "I need you alive, and so does your family."

"I'll be careful, Mister Wheeler," Daniel said and smiled, dropping from sight in the elevator. It wasn't long before things went wrong.

*   *   *

When the lift bumped to a halt Daniel jumped out and injured men took his place. Heading back the way he'd come, he raced down the shaft, making a mental note of the number of men he'd seen leave the mine. Several times he stumbled, picked himself up and ran on again. Abruptly, he stopped running and stood still. He heard it again. A groan seemed to come from the rock and then a low rumble trembled through the walls. The floor shook, he fell sideways and the narrow shaft filled with dust.

"Leafy!" he called out. "Leafy!" he called again into the dusty blackness. No answer returned. He raced on and almost immediately ran into an overhanging beam. His head rang like a gong, he felt nauseous and his balance was unreliable but in other regards he was mostly unhurt.

He gathered what strength he could muster and stumbled along the tunnel following the thin beam of his lamp's light. Sounds of men toiling grew louder and the lights from their lamps flashed this way and that in the dust filled tunnel, as if it was under siege.

Daniel called out, "Leafy, where are you?"

"Here!" A shout returned from somewhere in the gloom. Daniel made for the sound, tripping and falling over the debris. He kept moving toward where he thought the sounds came from but they faded and then the lights disappeared, as if he had been abandoned on purpose.

Without warning the tiny flame in his headlamp died out and all light evaporated as if a hood had been pulled over his head. Enveloped in total darkness he began to panic. His breath came in short gasps, his forehead tingled and his hands went cold and his fingers numb. He reached for the security of the wall but misjudged the distance and fell sideways into a pool of freezing water. On his hands and knees, he cursed loudly, hoping that he would be heard. But nothing came in reply. Pushing himself up to a kneeling position he called out again.

"Leafy! Anyone! Help!" He struggled to his feet and freezing water rushed down his sodden pant legs, filling his boots. It was a miserable feeling topping off a miserable situation. "Where are you?" But no answer returned. "Leafy," he called out again. Still no answer. He moved cautiously back the way he thought he'd come but ran into a wall. In the pitch blackness it was impossible to find either his way out or his bearings. "Leafy!"

His head throbbed and his vision played tricks on his brain. He felt nauseous as his claustrophobia threatened to overwhelm him. He hated being under the ground. It was his worst nightmare, being buried alive. He sat on a rock, considered his predicament and tried to think clearly.

He picked up two rocks and banged them together. He listened. The clacking sound echoed down the tunnel. He listened as intently as he ever had in his life. Clacking sounds returned to him, faintly. He turned his head back and forth. The sounds he heard were probably not far off, but the convolutions of the tunnels made distance abstract at best, and confusing.

His options were obvious and limited. He could stay where he was, shivering with the creeping cold and in the dark. Or he could attempt to retrace his path back to the main tunnel. He shivered again while he tried to remember the way he had come and the layout of the mine shaft. His freezing clothes were draining the heat from his body at an alarming rate and if he didn't find warmth soon, he was sure he would freeze to death. He decided to move, so walking cautiously, his hands and arms stretched before him, he advanced.

He heard voices again and his heart rose. "Leafy, I'm here!" he yelled, surprised that his voice had become hoarse and virtually useless. "Over here!" he called out again. Fighting the panic that rose unbidden he saw a tiny flash of light and hurried toward the faint glimmer of rescue and stumbled against a leaning timber. He remembered later the sound of the tumbling rocks that came loose above him and the pain when a large stone crashed down onto his skull.

Chapter 3

The light shone on Kate's face as her mother's new electric lighting illuminated her in the most charming way. "We're here," she said, and Shirley rushed to them, beaming, her arms outstretched to take the child. "Come in, come in," she said, kissing Kate's cheek. "Here, let me hold my darling Rose." She took the infant and tickled her while Kate leaned her cane against the hall chair and removed her coat. "Where's Daniel? Leafy was telling us about the problem at the mine today."

"He's washing up," Kate replied. "He was filthy when he came home from the hospital." Kate wore a look of tired exasperation. "I'm sorry, but he's not in a very good mood," Kate confided to her mother. "You know what I mean?" Shirley nodded and drew nearer.

"You look like you could use a good night's sleep," she whispered. "Why not let me take Rose tonight?" Shirley smiled deviously, holding the smiling Rose high in the air leading the way into the dining room. "Guess who's here?" she said merrily.

The table was set for six. Red was seated with Rachelle, Kate's younger sister, and her husband Leafy Lane. Red stood as Kate entered, always the gentleman. He still did the same every time Shirley entered the room even though they had been married for more than a year. He smiled broadly, and for a large man didn't shy away from giving Rose a gentle finger pat on the nose, sending the infant into a fit of giggles. His big, bearded, smiling face always made her laugh.

"Is Daniel with you?" he asked.

Shirley said, "He'll be along," and she gave Red a warning glance "He's washing up." She carried Rose over to a red velvet couch where Rachelle's children played with Maisie, Shirley's long-time housekeeper and confidant. Maisie doted on the children and though she'd had no children of her own, they always calmed in her soft, brown arms. Perpetually prepared, Maisie had warm blankets and a cozy, warm lap ready for them and they quieted down instantly, magically.

Shirley sat when Red had pulled back her chair for her. She smiled for him and he beamed back. "Leafy's been telling us about the cave-in."

Avoiding their gaze Leafy peered into his glass. "How long were you down there, Leafy?" Shirley prompted.

"I don't know." Leafy said, uncomfortable that Daniel was absent for the retelling of the day's events. "I only know that Mister Wheeler's going to have to buy himself a new locomotive." He smiled briefly at Rachelle. They'd been married two years and their marriage had been a rocky affair. It had helped that Leafy and Daniel were the same age and since now they were both parents, they had even more in common. What he and Daniel did share was that they were in love with the same woman, Kate.

"Were you scared?" Shirley asked.

Leafy's eyes closed and for the moment he was back underground in the collapsing mine. The smoke, the dust and the darkness were the things he remembered most clearly. He shuddered recalling the shouts and cries of men injured, scared, groaning in the darkness and the halos from small lanterns that swung from the ceiling timbers, darting shadows on the walls of the tunnel. And then the frantic search to locate his missing men, and Daniel.

*　　　　　*　　　　　*

The reflection looking back at him in the mirror was not of the man he'd seen there that morning. Where had his youth gone? Daniel sighed, rinsed the soap from his face and used the small towel to clean dirt from his ears and dry his face. Rubbing his bristled chin, he looked more closely at his reflection. He had aged, so his reflection told him. There were lines about his mouth that he had never noticed before, and dark circles were forming under his eyes.

Thoughts of his near demise, and the good fortune that his friend came looking for him, had somehow renewed his sense of purpose. He had a family now, a wife and a child to take care of. He was tall and fair-skinned and his hair had darkened, gone from tawny to a deep brown. He squared his shoulders and forced himself to smile at his reflection. There appeared to be an aspect of maturity about him he'd not noticed before today, if one was to ignore the bruising on his face and cheek and the bandage around his head.

But the collapse today may have changed all of that. He gingerly touched the swelling on his head and winced. It was sore to the touch, but other than the inconvenience of not being able to wear his hat it was a minor injury. He put on his coat and straightened his tie. He was changed, but for better or worse, he knew not.

"Oh, Daniel! Why do you always knock? This is your house too, you know." Shirley kissed him on the cheek as she ushered him inside. "Come on in. We've just fed the children. You'll have some wine, won't you?" She reached out to touch his forehead, he winced as she gently touched it, smoothing it. "Does it hurt?" He nodded and she pursed her lips sympathetically. She took his coat and hung it up on the coat tree. "Come and have a glass of wine, you look like you could use one."

Daniel hesitated, looking around the room at those who had become so much a part of his life. It was a complete family. His new family. Separate and distinct from the family he had lost contact with. The tremble of his guilt, at his lies and his deceitfulness threatened to overwhelm him again. He swallowed hard and silently asked again for God's forgiveness.

Kate was looking at him sternly, so he arranged his face into a suitable smile and braced for the evening ahead. He barely remembered sitting. Didn't remember Red pouring wine for him, but there was something decidedly beautiful in how the light reflected through the crystal glasses. The flashes of rainbow color were mesmerizing. A soft hand rested on his. When he looked up it was the ocean of redemption in Kate's eyes that drew him back to shore.

Chapter 4

A tall, well-dressed man alighted from a horse-drawn cab opening his umbrella as he did, careful not to step into a puddle.

"How much?" he asked, his speech crisp, his accent less Irish than most.

"'alf a crown, for you." The driver replied, in an accent a knife could cut. Over the man's shoulder was the Dublin Metropolitan Police headquarters building.

"You could be in there one day, you know?" The man said plainly, and the cabby's grin faded. The man handed over the coins, his face impassive. "What with these prices you charge. It's extortion, is what it is." The cab driver took the money and flicked the reins, the horse moved forward.

Briefly the cabby looked over his shoulder at the man standing in the street. He raised his middle finger and smiled. The man pointed a finger at him, pistol like, and smiled back. They knew each other well, he was the detective's ears on the streets of Dublin. The detective turned and avoiding the pools of water, strode quickly into the Dublin Police Headquarters, climbing the wet steps two at a time.

As he reached the top steps two young constables emerged and touched their fingers to their hats in salute. One officer hurried to open the door for him.

"It's noice to 'ave ye back, Detective Killeen," the young officer said.

"Nicer for you than for me I think, constable." He rewarded the eager young officer with a rare smile. "But, t'anks all the same." Inside he shook his umbrella into a brass bucket by the door and removed his distinctive bowler hat, smoothing his thinning, dark hair.

The reception area was not particularly large by government building standards, but its design lent weighty heaviness to its volume. Already the gloom was closing in on him again, a pervasive feeling he had tried to forget during his holiday. The wide stone staircase, possibly the remnant of the long-passed architect's first and hopefully last, public commission stood before him as it had always. Where once the ascending staircase had been symbolic of his career advancement, now it was more akin to climbing steps to a prison cell on a higher level.

He pulled his trouser legs from his boots, squared his shoulders and held his bowler hat purposefully. This style of headwear marked his rank and he bore it rather than wore it. Always well turned out as a matter of personal pride, he never appeared in public without his hat. He felt undressed if he was bare-headed.

His countenance darkened even more as he crossed the foyer, his steps echoing with each footfall. Pale light creeping in through the dirty leaded windows did little to enhance the prevailing gloom of the place. To his right the desk sergeant was busy, deftly parrying the questions of several persistent men. His intuition told him that they were newspaper reporters, so he avoided eye contact with any of them as he passed. The sergeant acknowledged the detective's arrival with a brief nod and a shrug before turning his threadbare attention back on his tormentors.

A dour, red-haired constable manned the desk at the top of the stairs. He nodded at the detective, displaying no deference.

"Why are you still here, Ivers?" the detective said, in passing. "Not by choice, sir."

"Anything I should know about while I was gone on holiday?"

The young constable shrugged. More conversation would be pointless.

The door to his office was marked with his name and he took a moment before he opened it as if to reconfirm that it was indeed his office.

Detective Inspector M. Killeen, the embossed signage declared.

He opened the door and entered the darkened office, headed directly for the window and pulled the heavy curtains apart. Irish daylight, for want of a better name, sneaked about the room exposing his desk and the stack of mail that awaited him. He rolled his umbrella and placed it on a hook to leak into a small waste basket, then hung his coat and hat on the wooden coat stand by the door.

Taking a clean, pressed, white handkerchief from his coat pocket he wiped it across the desk, sending a shower of dust particles scurrying into the wan beam of sunlight. For a moment, they held his attention. So many individual motes of dust, all set in motion by one man's hand, he thought, turning his attention to the stack of mail.

Leafing through the mostly inter-departmental litter, he saw at the bottom of the stack the familiar fawn envelope of an official telegraph message. With a sudden sense of urgency, a presage of unwelcome news, he tore open the envelope and his heart quickened as he read the message. He hurried from the office carrying the single sheet of paper out to the constable at the desk and shoved it under his nose.

"Do you know anything about this, Ivers?"

Ivers looked at the telegram, looked up blankly and shook his head. "It came right after you left on holidays is all I know, sir."

Killeen shoved the envelope under Constable Ivers' nose, forcing him to read it. "What does it say on the envelope?"

The morose constable looked up. "It says: URGENT, for Detective Inspector M. Killeen, sir."

"So, you just put it on my desk without telling anyone about it?"

"Well it was addressed to you, sir. I don't go about reading other people's mail if that's what you're inferring, sir." Killeen gave the moron a withering glance as he hurried down the stairs and over to the sergeant's desk.

"Welcome back, sir," the older police officer said, smiling as Killeen approached.

"Thank you, sergeant." He darted a smile that came reluctantly. Sergeant Callahan smiled in return. He had been Michael Killeen's mentor through the years and there existed a strong bond of camaraderie between them. The sergeant frowned, noticing Killeen's concern.

He stepped from behind his desk. "What's troubling you, Michael?"

"Do you remember a few years back, when the Fenians tried to rob the Bank of England? They blew it up and then ran away. Do you remember that?" The sergeant nodded and took the telegram the detective handed him.

"I remember. Didn't the father die in prison?"

Killeen nodded. "Well, now it seems that the English, who were so keen on keeping them both in prison for the rest of their lives, have gone and let the remaining one escape."

The sergeant looked up after reading the cable. "Didn't some of them get away to America?"

Killeen felt as if an old wound had been poked. He remembered the night well, had relived it often in these intervening few years. The last he'd seen of the remaining Shadlow family they were dissolving into the fog onboard a ship headed to America. It still irked him that the authorities in New York, whom he had alerted via the Atlantic Telegraph, had failed to apprehend them, though he had sent them a comprehensive description.

"Do you remember the man who led us to them?"

The sergeant's face darkened as he approached a similar conclusion. "You don't think he'd come back to Dublin?" The sergeant paused. "Hold on. I think I have something here," he said, handing the telegram back to the detective. "Them reporters who were just here were here asking about a ruckus down by the river night before last. I thought I remembered the name from somewhere." He took out a thick folder containing a sheaf of papers. "Reagan was his name, wasn't it? Clive Reagan." He ruffled some papers until he found what he was looking for. "Ahhh! Here it is. This report came across my desk last night." He read from the paper in his hand.

"Man assaulted, found unconscious. Name of Clive Reagan. Next of kin notified. Admitted to Trinity Hospital. Condition unknown."

He looked up, but the detective was already running for the stairs. Moments later he returned at a run, pulling on his coat and clutching his hat.

"Sergeant, would you let the Constabulary know to look out for Patrick Shadlow? Do it quietly. It may be a coincidence, but I don't believe in them. I'm going to the hospital."

"Right you are, sir," the sergeant said, touching his finger to his forehead. "I'll put out the word."

Out in the street it was still raining. The detective waved his arms to attract a cab and boarded it before it had come to a stop. "Trinity Hospital, driver. And hurry!"

The driver had done his bidding and they had clattered along the cobbled and muddy streets at breakneck speed. While bumping around in the back, he'd tried to remind himself of the facts concerning the Shadlow affair. As clearly as he could recall, after the Fenian attack on the Dublin Bank of England, the police on the streets did their job as zealously as usual and followed a trail of rumors to Mister Clive Reagan, who was most cooperative. In confessing all he knew, Mister Reagan incriminated other members of the group and named Paddy Shadlow as the principle organizer.

The Fenians were familiar to Killeen. They were a loosely knit collection of drunks who espoused the eviction of the occupying English and the return of Irish independence. Though most often involved in various acts of mischief, occasionally they perpetrated larger acts of political vandalism, sabotage and assorted acts of terrorism against the government. To Killeen and his men, they were simply a nuisance. But now they had become wanted terrorists responsible for viciously attacking a policeman and the subsequent detonation of an explosive device at the front door of the Bank of England in a simple-minded attempt to rob it.

Tierney was the name of the man who fingered Clive Reagan. He had unfortunately died during his non-voluntary interview, but prior to that he had confessed that he was the one who had provided the Shadlow family with tickets on a ship headed for America. He even volunteered the name of the ship and its departure time and date.

The fact that Killeen had caught two of the three fugitives mattered little to either him or the Constabulary. The younger one was who he truly wanted. Daniel was his name and he had escaped arrest, along with his mother and his sister. He was the vicious one, the one who had beaten the night constable near to death and practically blew him to pieces with explosives.

It was irksome in the extreme to the respect for the Constabulary and they were determined to find young Daniel Shadlow and return him to Ireland to stand trial for what he had done.

The hospital ward was long and as he followed the matron down the rows of beds, their heels clacked loudly on the wooden floors resonating off the white scrubbed walls. On either side of the room patients received ministrations from attentive nurses, dressed in white like swans, dealing out medicines and sympathy. Intermittently the hush of the ward was broken by the moan of a patient or clatter of instruments into metal trays.

They approached an area of the ward where the beds were curtained off for patient privacy, the detective assumed. The matron slowed as they neared the last of these cubicles and she drew him closer so that they could speak in whispers.

"Detective," she took a tight hold of his forearm, "don't alarm him." She was a kindly woman and her sincerity for the care and well-being of her patients was obvious. "I know you have questions of the man, but I beg of you, please be brief. He's gravely injured and I don't hold out much hope, if you know what I mean?" she cautioned. "His wife is with him, so please try not to upset her."

The detective removed his hat to signal his grasp of the gravity of the situation. The matron pulled apart the curtain, and as seasoned a policeman as he was and considering the number of victims he had seen over the years, he still gasped.

*   *   *

Clive had been drunkenly staggering his way home after a day working as a stevedore, unloading ships at the docks. It was demanding work, especially at his age but it was the only job he could find since his trouble with the police. Arrested back then regarding the Bank explosion, he had volunteered information in the hope of forgiveness. He was never actually beaten, but he was viciously threatened and they had forced him to betray his friends and comrades-in-arms, the Shadlows.

It was late and the streets were muddy and uneven with pot holes scattered about like a battlefield gone silent. He'd stopped to relieve himself in a shadowed corner of a building when he heard a noise behind him. It was an unusual noise, a weighty noise, a thud of wood against stone. He stopped peeing but hearing nothing more continued relieving himself, until he heard it again. It was closer this time, but when he turned around, he saw nothing moving at all. Thud. The sound came again. He'd heard that sound before, back in the garden of memories. A splash came from somewhere near. Someone had stepped in a puddle.

He stood corpse-still, placed his hand against the reassuring brick wall of a building, his heart beating a tattoo, eyes wide, waiting for something. Someone was watching him. He couldn't see who, but he had that uneasy feeling. Sweat was forming on his forehead. He wiped it away with his sleeve and reluctantly pushed himself away from the solid comfort of the wall. He took a few tentative steps guided by the thin wisps of light that illuminated the mist. A long piece of wood landed at his feet. It clattered and came to a stop.

Clive looked around him. There was no one to be seen. Nothing moved.

"Who's there?" he shouted. Away in the distance a steamship whistle sounded three times. Clive stood as still as a statue. "Who's there?" No answer came. He bent down and picked up the piece of wood. It was hip height with a carved burl on one end and a tapering point on the other. "It's a shillelagh," he said in a whisper. A shadow appeared from a crease in the night, walking toward him. "Is this yours?" Clive asked. The man took two steps nearer. Clive took two steps back and stepped into a hole, losing his balance, falling into the mud, his hands slipping as he tried to get up. The man stepped closer, his gait slowing, his face hidden in a drooping hat and scarf.

"Yes. It's mine. Do you know what it is?"

"Yes. Yes, it's a shillelagh. A fighting stick. And a fine one it is too, I might add." Clive's attempt to ingratiate himself was obvious. "You can have it back." The man reached out and took it from Clive's outstretched hand. He twirled it in his hands then stopped and considered it closely holding it under his nose as if smelling a flower.

"Is your name Clive Reagan?" the man asked and Clive nodded. "Then I want you to have it. It's a gift from me and me family."

"Do I know you?" Clive asked, intrigued. The voice was familiar. "You used to know me." The man took the shillelagh and flipped it expertly, catching it by the narrow end with both hands. He raised it high in the air where it hesitated for a frozen moment, before arced back to earth, crushing Clive's knee beneath it. Clive grabbed his leg and howled in pain.

"But you don't know me anymore, you filthy, snitching maggot," the man hissed, stuffing a piece of cloth into Clive's mouth, gagging him. Wide eyed in pain and fear, Clive struggled to speak, spit running down his cheek. His tormentor leaned in closer. "Am I going to kill you?" he asked. He laughed a low, menacing laugh and leaned even closer. Clive's eyes grew wide, his fear enormous. "You'll just have to wait and see now, won't you?" He pulled the cloth from Clive's mouth. Clive sucked in air, whimpering. "Come with me, Clive" the man said, stuffing the cloth back into Clive's mouth.

He grabbed Clive by his collar and dragged the helpless, writhing, piteous figure into the recess between two buildings. He lit a match and held it to Clive's face, illuminating them both. It was the eyes and the menace they held which nailed Clive to the ground.

"How do you know my name?" Clive whimpered, clutching his knee to his chest. "Don't hurt me anymore, please." Tears and spit gushed forth. "I'll give you whatever money I have," he pleaded. "Just please, don't hurt me anymore. I have a wife and child to feed."

Behind the scarf the man laughed. "Give me your money then." Clive reached into his pocket and pulled it inside out. A few copper and silver coins rolled on the ground. "Is that all? That's not near enough, Clive," the man laughed. "Not near enough payment for three years in prison being buggered every single day by the guards." The voice lowered to an animal's snarl. "Not near enough."

Clive looked up at the man standing up over him. As if in a dream, he watched the man lifting the wooden club with both hands, unable to stop the pendulum swing as it descended onto his remaining good knee. Clive's muffled screams had no effect on the man's intentions.

The man leaned down closer to Clive's face. "That was for me little sister." Clive writhed around on the ground alternately clutching at his legs. He rolled over on his stomach and began to crawl away. His torturer followed. "And this is for me mother," and the club crushed his left shoulder. The sound of the bones shattering was as of a fine porcelain cup crashing onto a stone floor.

Clive clawed at the cloth in his mouth, sucking in air, but the cloth was shoved back in and his hand was held to the ground by the man's boot. Clive's vision was blurred by his pain and terror and the apparition looming over him appeared like some biblical visage of doom. Looking up, wide-eyed, the raising of the club and its eventual fall onto his hand was as if it was being watched by someone else. Like mustard seeds in a mortar, the round, carved head of the ancient weapon ground his fingers to shards. Even with the intolerable pain that shot from his hand to his brain, there was a disembodied aspect to it. His eyes hadn't opened when his right shoulder became gristle and bone chips.

"Are you still with me, Clive?" The gag came out of Clive's mouth and he gasped for air. "No. No, Clive. Don't go screaming your head off. You should save your strength. You're going to need it. Either way, no one's going to hear you this late at night down here at the docks."

"Who are you?" Clive managed. Unable to stop it, the man rolled him over. Clive let his head fall into the mud, unable to hold it up. Filthy water seeped into his mouth.

"And this is for me mother."

The club came down between Clive's shoulder blades and he heard rather than felt his spine snap. He was rolled onto his back again, roughly, rain drops falling on his face mixing with his tears stopped when the man leaned over him.

The man pulled down his scarf and struck another match. "Are you still with me, Clive?" Clive's eyes widened with uncontrollable fear upon recognition of his torturer.

"I'm quite certain you'll work it out, Clive, if you haven't already. But you should hurry. I don't know how long you have left." Clive gagged and the cloth was pulled away. "That's right, Clive. You remember me now, don't you?" He stood over Clive holding the club chest high. "But I doubt you'll be able to tell anyone." The club bore down on Clive's face, taking apart his upper jaw and turning his lower jaw into fragments.

"I'll see you in hell, Clive," and the beating went on, but Clive was no longer present.

*   *   *

Detective Killeen was shocked by what he saw. The man he beheld was swathed head to toe in reams of bloody bandages and laying outstretched on a wooden board, he appeared as if crucified. The matron preceded him into the cubicle where she gently touched the shoulder of the woman sitting at the bed-side. She woke with a start, her eyes red and swollen. She was a pathetic figure, small and hunched and shattered.

"There's someone here from the police, Mrs. Reagan," the matron said softly. Slowly she gathered herself enough to focus on the visitor and instantly lunged at him, tears streaming down her face in torrents. Deftly the matron stepped between them.

"It's your fault," the distraught woman screamed. "You told us that we would be safe. That nothing like this would ever happen to him." Her reserves of strength gone she fell into the matron's enfolding arms, sobbing onto her shoulder.

"Now, now, Mrs. Reagan. Calm down. This man is here to help you."

Mrs. Reagan's head shot up and she looked at Killeen with eyes aglow with hatred. "You promised him this would never happen. You're a fuckin' liar, Killeen!" she screamed, spit clouding the air. "A fuckin' liar! That's what you are!"

The matron held her at arm's length, her demeanor stern. "Hush, Mrs. Reagan. You're disturbing the other patients. Calm down will you, please?" Gently, she guided Clive's wife back to her seat by the bed. She shot Killeen a warning look.

Killeen approached the bedside quietly, almost respectfully, almost contritely. What Mrs. Reagan had said was true. He had made those promises, hadn't he? Had assured the Reagan family of their safety from reprisal. Had helped them resettle in a distant part of Dublin. He had lived up to his promises, hadn't he?

As he looked down at the pitiful visage of what used to be a productive, somewhat honest human being, he also had to keep in mind that the condition Clive found himself in presently was in fact a result of decisions he had made years earlier when he'd joined the Fenians.

Clive's breathing was raw and raspy, arhythmical and gurgling like a blocked drain. Each breath sounded final, until the next gurgle of the breath began. Killeen leaned in closer to the stricken man. Quietly, softly, he spoke into the place where Clive's ear should be.

"Clive, can you hear me?" No response came forth, no visible sign of consciousness. Killeen spoke again, this time a little more forcefully. "Did Patrick Shadlow do this, Clive?" Clive's eyes shot open.

"Arrrggghhh! … Arrggghhh!" he cried out.

The matron dashed to his side and shot the detective another of her warning looks. Blood welled up in her patient's throat. She released some of the pressure by removing the gauze but Clive's body shook violently and she had to hold him down while he gurgled and screamed. "I think you've done enough damage here for one evening, detective," the matron said, taking Killeen firmly by the elbow and steering him outside. "I think you should go now."

"Yes, go!" shouted Clive's wife. "Go on back to your nice, safe police barracks, why don't you? You're a miserable excuse for a man, Killeen. And you're evil. Do you know that? And you're a fuckin' liar." Exhausted, she lay her head on the edge of the bed sobbing in complete, utter sorrow.

Killeen backed out of the cubicle, shaken. The last vision he had of Clive Reagan was of him wrapped in a cocoon of bloody bandages fighting for his next breath, or secretly praying for no more.

Chapter 5

"Daniel, will you and Carter come on in here a minute?" Daniel had been at his desk only a moment when Wheeler had arrived. It had been a long night for him. His head pounded the whole night and Rose had suffered another night of colic which had kept him and Kate awake.

Carter entered from the adjoining office, where the maps of the mines were kept. "Come on son, we don't want to keep the boss waiting." Daniel trailed Carter into Wheeler's office. Wheeler took three whiskey glasses from the polished mahogany sideboard and grouped them on the desktop, pouring each a drink from a bottle of bourbon. He spread out the glasses in front of them and taking one for himself he sat back in his leather chair.

Considering them he raised his glass. "Sit down boys, you deserve this and more. That was a hell of a day yesterday, wasn't it?" He drank without waiting for them and placed his glass on the blotting pad in front of him. "Carter, what was the damage to our operation?" Carter finished his whiskey and returned the glass to the desk as did Daniel. Carter took a notebook from his coat pocket and read from it.

"The shafts nearest the Glory Hole took the most damage. One twenty two and one thirty three are completely blocked and unusable." Carter looked up at Wheeler. "Not so bad since they were all pretty much played out and they were going to cross into the Glory Hole vein anyway." Carter returned to his notes. "We lost the locomotive. That's the biggest problem. I'm guessing it will just have to stay where it is." Carter tried to read Wheeler's expression but was unable to, so he continued. "Sections of the tracks need to be diverted and replaced if we're to continue to move ore from the mines to the smelter. That means we have to buy the rights of way or buy the land."

Wheeler steepled his fingers while considering the news. "Well, I guess we're going to have to buy a new locomotive and get those tracks laid down. How long before we're back in business?"

"Depending on getting another locomotive, a month, maybe more."

"That's three million dollars I'll be losing. I don't like that." Wheeler blew softly into his steepled fingers. "I'll work on getting you the train and let you deal with the rest of the mess. In the meantime, we can have our men work over at the Smuggler Mine. Gotta keep them busy, eh?" Wheeler turned his attention on Daniel. "Not drinking, Daniel? Oh, you're not a drinker anymore, are you? Not to worry, it's a good thing. Keeps you out of trouble. What's the situation with the casualties, son?" Wheeler smiled, "Anyone dead?"

Daniel returned his smile, "No, Mister Wheeler. No one died, but we do have several broken legs, arms and hands of course. They're being treated at the hospital and are wondering who will pay for their medicines and care."

Wheeler waved his hand as if whisking the idea away. "Tell them not to worry. I'll take care of their needs and I'll make the Glory Hole foot the bill." Wheeler leaned forward in his chair, placing his hands flat on the desk. "Now, for something more important," Wheeler considered them in turn. The older, wiser, more experienced manager, Carter, and the untested young protégé he was grooming.

Wheeler continued after a pause. "This unfortunate incident has forced me to change my plans. As you know Daniel, I was intending to have Mister Carter here accompany me to Chicago and Washington but obviously, things have changed." Wheeler picked up an official looking document and threw it back on the desk in disgust. "I'm sorry John, but I'm going to insist that you stay in Aspen and take care of things here. What with the disruption in production and the mess over at the Glory Hole, I'm going to need you here. You'll be in charge while I'm gone. Is that OK with you, John?" Carter nodded, showing no emotion.

"So," Wheeler drew down on Daniel, "I'm afraid that I'm going to have to ask you to accompany me to Chicago." Daniel's mind had wandered. What was Wheeler saying? "Now, I know that this places an inconvenient burden on your family, Daniel. But; I need someone trustworthy in Chicago to watch the Queen while I reacquaint myself with some old friends in Washington." Wheeler was looking intently at Daniel. He felt he was expected to say something.

"I hadn't planned on this, Mister Wheeler. My daughter is quite a handful and Kate needs me now," he pleaded. "I'll have to ask her," and as soon as he'd said the words, he knew it was the wrong thing to say. Wheeler obviously had a different relationship with his spouse.

"Do you see a problem there, Mister Carrington?" Wheeler's eyes were steely, the kind that looked at an adversary across a bargaining table and always won.

Daniel tried his best not to cringe but knew that much of his future, both personal and professional hinged on his answer. He swallowed hard. "No, Mister Wheeler. It's a wonderful opportunity, sir."

"Good. Then let's make plans to pack up the Silver Queen and be on our way by Monday, shall we?"

"Next Monday?" Daniel exclaimed, standing. Wheeler remained implacable and Daniel sat back down, wishing that he had better self-control in moments such as this. His face was flushed, he could feel the heat of his embarrassment rising to his brow.

"This trip to Washington is important Daniel," Wheeler stated, "as you both know. The Democrats are gathering political forces to repeal the Sherman Silver Purchase Act and if that happens, the silver industry will cease to exist." Wheeler settled his gaze on Daniel. "Plus, you'll get a chance to meet some powerful folk. So, are you coming with me, Daniel? I need to know."

Daniel was trapped. Either way he risked his wife's disappointment. Wheeler's eyes bored into him; his mouth dried up. He pulled his shoulders back and sat upright and returned Wheeler's gaze. "Can I give you my answer tomorrow, Mister Wheeler?"

Wheeler considered his young protégé. He had liked the boy since they first met. Red Corcoran had praised his bravery and his reliability as testament to his potential worth and in Wheeler's employ he had risen to whatever task was presented to him. A little latitude in this matter might be called for.

"OK, son. I'll give you until tomorrow to give me your answer," he looked from Carter to Daniel and back again. "Carter, I want you to pull Leafy Lane out of the mine and put him to work on whatever it is that Daniel here does. OK?"

"Well, that's it," Wheeler turned his focus back on the papers on his desk. "Oh, Carter. Do you know how to drive a train?"

"Yes. I was an engineer for the railroad before I got into the mining business."

"Good. I may want you to come out east and pick up the new locomotive as soon as I can find one for sale." Carter and Daniel rose to leave. "Oh, I forgot to thank you for the job you both did yesterday. If it wasn't for your quick thinking and that of Leafy Lane, I'm certain we would have a bigger mess on our hands. Thanks again. Now," he waved a hand at them, "I have work to do."

Chapter 6

I t was a hectic scene at the railway station, even more chaotic than usual. The Monday morning train leaving Aspen heading to Glenwood Springs and Denver was regularly scheduled and not usually the subject of such press attention. Mrs. Wheeler was intending to accompany her husband only as far as Denver but looking at the total of her luggage, she could have been mounting an attack on Europe.

Daniel and Kate stood at the edge of the boarding platform grappling with the tension that had recently grown between them. Rose fussed and refused to be held by Daniel, sensing that something disquieting was occurring between her parents. Though the tension between him and Kate had been growing for some time, it had brewed to a boil with Wheeler's decision to have Daniel accompany him and the Silver Queen to Chicago.

The train's whistle sounded.

"There you all are!" Shirley trilled, as she weaved through the crowded platform dragging Red by the hand while No Problem Joe trailed behind. "Here, let me have little Rosie so that you can have a proper farewell." Shirley gave Kate a stern look then smiled for Daniel's benefit. "Come on my sweetheart. Kiss your daddy goodbye, like a good girl." Rosie leaned in, puckered her lips and closed her eyes, mimicking her parents. Daniel took her little face in his and tenderly kissed her chubby cheeks.

"No!" Rosie yelled, pointing her stubby fat finger at her lips. "Here," she said. So, Daniel obediently kissed her on the lips and she squirmed and giggled. "Prickles," she said severely.

Laughing, Shirley took Rose from Kate as a doting grandparent should. She leaned forward and kissed Daniel on the cheek. "Please do be careful. Those big cities are dangerous places. So, I want you to take care." Shirley smiled at him warmly and squeezed his hand. Red shook Daniel's hand.

"Good luck, Daniel," he said, and meant it sincerely.

Joe caught him by the elbow and stuffed an envelope into his coat pocket. "It is always a wise idea to have some emergency money, son." Daniel tried to return it but Joe pushed it back. "No. It's yours. Just in case you need it," Joe said through his wonderful, toothless grin and Daniel shook Joe's outstretched hand warmly.

"Daniel!" Wheeler was calling to him from the train. "Hurry up!" He waved back while holding Kate's hand in his. It was a difficult moment. Things had not been good between them since Rose's birth and the cracks in their relationship were significant enough to be of concern to Shirley. So much so, that Shirley even approached Jerome Wheeler on Daniel's behalf, requesting that Daniel should be excused from this possibly extended trip.

"It would strain the family," she told him after cornering him in his office.

"Look here, Shirley. I know what you're telling me. I'm not blind or deaf."

"But they're young, Jerome. They need a chance." Shirley found herself in an unusual position, pleading for a favor. "He's worked for you night and day for two years now. Can't you take someone else, please?" Wheeler clenched his knuckles on the desk then spread out his long fingers.

"I wish I could, Shirley. I really do. But I need Carter here to run the mines. You've seen what trouble this last cave-in has caused to our town." Jerome was stating the truth. With the locomotive destroyed, not only the mine production but the whole town had been affected.

Having made his case, Jerome softened to Shirley, as he almost always did. She knew way too much about his nocturnal wanderings for him to anger her. "This could be a character-building experience for the lad. Open his eyes a tad." Wheeler spoke in the tone that most always got him his way. "We both want the best for him, don't we?"

"I don't think this lad, as you call him, needs anyone to open his eyes, Jerome. Especially you!" She looked at Jerome intently, matching him, leaning forward as he had done. "I'm worried. I have a feeling that there's something he's hiding from, something he's not told us." Sighing, she leaned back in her chair. "He's uncomfortable talking about his family. Have you noticed? He's full of mysteries, that boy."

"Well, maybe I can solve a few for you, my dear. I have a feeling that we will be spending a goodly amount of time in each other's company during the coming weeks." Jerome stood and Shirley let him take her hand as he guided her toward the door. "I know it's a burden on his family, but he might be taking over this business someday so let's consider it part of his training, shall we? Thanks for coming, Shirley. I'll see you at the station." Wheeler closed the door on Shirley for the first time in their long history.

*   *   *

The train's whistle startled them all. Kate's eyes filled with tears and she held onto Daniel's arm with determination, not wanting him to leave.

"Kate, please. I have to go." Daniel pried Kate's arms off him and bent for his luggage. It was an old valise that Shirley had given him, the same one that Kate had used when she was at school in Chicago. He kissed Kate one last time and climbed aboard the train next to Jerome.

As was his style Jerome stood prominently on the steps of the carriage. Photographers fired off their flash powders as both Jerome and Daniel waved to the crowd.

"Wish us luck!" Jerome entreated the crowd, waving to one and all.

"Good luck and Godspeed," they replied as one voice.

With Wheeler's wife waving from one window and he from another, the train's whistle shrieked once more, the photographers flashed their powder and captured the moment for history as the train huffed and puffed and gradually left the station.

Daniel leaned out of the train's window, waving back at his family falling away behind them. His only company; worry and dread of what might lay ahead of him.

Chapter 7

I t seemed like the sun had barely risen and Harry could already feel sweat running down his back. He slapped the reins on the mule's back to get it to move but it only lifted its hind leg ready to kick if the opportunity presented itself. Harry had no illusions that his mule, as with every one of its four-legged cousins, was out to kill him. With a shrug and a sigh of acceptance he led the mule out from the barn and across the yard. They stopped at the half-empty water trough for both he and the mule to drink their fill or die by noon in the merciless heat.

"Harry Rich, you're the laziest man I've ever known." The disembodied voice came from behind the curtains of the kitchen window. "You've been at it for an hour and you're not even plowing yet? Git a move on." Harry pulled his shoulders back and waved, then turned his eyes heavenward.

"God, I know you're up there. Well, I think I do. But answer me this one question and I promise I'll never ask another one again." Harry poured a hat full of tepid water over his head, tugging at his long hair and beard. "When you made women, what was it you actually had in mind?" Harry took up the reins and goaded the mule out to the green speckled field that might one day be their corn crop. Like all beasts, and man, the crop fought the heat and the elements where only the hardy survived, but only hardly.

"Harry," the harbinger of doom called out to him. Harry stopped at the gate to the field, any pause was welcome in this heat.

"What is it now?" He yelled back as the mule swiveled its ears, craning to hear Harry's latest admonishment.

A stout woman and a small girl appeared on the small porch from the gloom of the house. It was a modest affair for Utah. Three rooms and a kitchen below and a second floor above that held the bedrooms.

"Are you expectin' company?" She pointed off to the east. Harry squinted and shaded his eyes from the sun. Nothing could he see but the swimming air of the desert.

"You're mad, woman! No one comes out here."

"I was mad to marry you, but I'm not blind. There's someone out there and they're heading this way."

Harry respected Bethel's keen eyesight. They all had their charms. "Maybe he's coming to take you away from me," he smiled at the thought. "I wouldn't object," the woman yelled as a young boy and girl ran out of the house chasing each other. They stopped playing and looked off down the dusty road following their mother's gaze.

*   *   *

Patrick's ship slid past Liberty Island in the thin fog of early morning. As Lady Liberty slipped along the length of the boat, he pulled the collar of his coat up higher around his ears and turned his back to the breeze. Leaning over the fantail railing of the ship he wished that his troubles, like the bubbles of froth in the wake, like his past life, would disappear, along with the memories.

"Is this you, Mister Duggan?" The immigration officer asked. Patrick nodded, unsmiling, as the man perused the forged birth certificate, studying both sides intently. "Do you have any family here in the United States, Mister Duggan?" Patrick shook his head. "Got any idea where you're heading to?" Patrick shook his head again. "You can speak, can't you?" Patrick smiled slightly.

"I can speak, sir," Patrick replied with a lisp. Patrick held his hand over his mouth but not before the officer saw the broken teeth. He handed the paper back to Patrick. The officer gentled.

"I wish you good luck, Mister Duggan. It seems as if you've already had your fair share of the other kind." He held out his hand to Patrick. For a moment Patrick failed to grasp the hand, or its meaning. During his years in prison his fear and loathing of men in uniform had tainted his reality. Raising his eyes, he saw compassion in the man. Sincere compassion, and when he shook the man's hand, tears rose. "I genuinely wish you well, son." The man smiled once more. "Next," the officer yelled.

Patrick followed a line of other disembarking immigrants to the boat that would ferry them across the river to the city. The fog had cleared by the time he boarded the little vessel and ahead of them sprawled the rising skyline of the immense city. Patrick was in danger of losing his nerve. After all of the planning that he had been conceiving while on his journey, the reality of finding his family here in this huge city was suddenly overwhelming.

The feeling of insignificance ballooned when he stepped out onto the busy street. Dozens of barrows being pushed by teams of men cluttered the busy street while hawkers, selling all manner of things, harassed and harangued the stunned passengers. Patrick saw the pick- pockets hard at work while the police blindly watched. Taking a chance, he approached a somnolent policeman.

"Where can a man find a place to sleep and a job?" Patrick asked.

The policeman barely opened his eyes.

"With your accent, probably nowhere."

*   *   *

Detective Inspector Killeen sat at his desk brooding, involuntarily recalling what he'd heard and seen in the hospital. Prompted by the certificate of death he repeatedly turned over in his hands, he allowed a surge of anger to roil his blood. In criminal cases such as this, he was rarely embroiled emotionally. He bore no direct responsibility for the death of Clive Reagan so, he wondered, why was it that he felt so burdened by it? Why was it that the pitiful screaming and condemnation of Reagan's widow haunted his dreams and defeated sleep?

"Ivers!" he yelled. "Come in here!" Killeen peered over the top of the sheet of paper, watching the door keenly. "Ivers! Can you hear me?"

"I can hear you."

"Well, come in here."

"I don't feel like it."

Killeen let the papers fall to his desk and resignedly walked out to Constable Ivers' desk. "Do you always have to be so insolent, Ivers?"

"So long as me father is your boss," Ivers replied.

It was true. As a result of the fine body of work that he had assembled over the course of his career, Killeen had been chosen by his superior to personally guide the career of his boss' son. Back from his holiday by a mere week, already Killeen was feeling the need for another. "Alright Ivers, I get your meaning. Now, do you want to do something useful for me?" Ivers continued reading the newspaper. "If it's not too much trouble?" The young man looked up, a smiled on his face. "Something special, is it? Will it be dangerous?" Ivers asked, hopefully.

"Perhaps."

It had been perturbing to Killeen that there had been no proof that Patrick Shadlow was ever in his city in the month since his escape from prison. That was, if you discounted Clive Reagan's reaction when he heard the name. It was not conclusive evidence to be sure, but Killeen's intuition rarely failed him.

As was their practice, the constabulary had pressed their sources for any information but had found none to date. He was perplexed because in his twenty years of service to the force he'd found that secrets flowed faster than the water in the Dublin river in flood, but strangely, there had been a drought of it regarding Patrick Shadlow. Unusual, he thought. It was not the nature of the Irish to keep secrets.

"Out of uniform, you say?" Ivers smiled his widest. "Undercover like?"

"I want you to go to a wake tomorrow."

*　　　　　*　　　　　*

"Damn you mule!" Harry yelled in the animal's ear then he picked up the reins and slapped them on the mule's back. "Go!" he said loudly. The mule remained studiously uninterested.

"You're not sleeping are you, Harry?" Bethel's voice rolled over the ground like summer thunder.

"The mule's dead." Harry returned.

"Kick it. If it doesn't move, I'll come over and kick you for all the good it will do. That feller is still comin' on the road. You sure you ain't expectin' no one?"

Harry had all but forgotten about the distant rider and looked again at the approaching apparition. A lone rider with a horse in tow.

"Send Rebekah out with some water!"

Chapter 8

D aniel's train ride to the World's Fair had become more of an ordeal than a journey of discovery. Jerome had taken an unexplained absence when they arrived in Kansas City and had returned the following morning crowing about a private train car he had won in a poker game. Daniel was relieved that his employer was in good spirits, having observed that the more they traveled east the more pensive and short-tempered Wheeler became.

He stood patiently on the platform furthest from the terminus watching Jerome as he paced back and forth, consulting his gold pocket watch repeatedly. At precisely eleven o'clock the whistle of an approaching train sounded as a locomotive and a string of carriages rolled backward toward them. The boxcar bearing the brightly painted Silver Queen was attached to the caboose of the train and Wheeler watched it like a parent as it reversed along the platform.

The station master approached officiously, trailed by a porter pushing a noisy, iron-wheeled cart loaded with Wheeler's trunks and assorted luggage.

"Your cars are attached, Mister Wheeler. If I could have your signature here, sir?" Jerome took the manifest from the station master and after perusing it quickly signed it and handed it back with a fleeting smile. "I'm sorry Mister Wheeler, but we were not able to find you the guards you asked for." Wheeler made a clicking sound of disappointment and sighed.

"Well, it seems we have a problem, Daniel." Wheeler said, as the man departed. Daniel tilted his head. "I wasn't able to hire any guards."

To Daniel, concern for the security of the Silver Queen was a fantasy. He could see no plausible way that anyone could steal a whole boxcar. "Do you really need the guards, Mister Wheeler?" Wheeler gave him a steely glare.

"There is more to that statue than metals and jewels. It represents the future. What we are protecting here is my vision of Colorado's future, and in that regard, it is priceless." Jerome abruptly turned and walked the length of the station trailing Daniel, headed for the locomotive.

The train's engineers were busy oiling important parts when they approached. "Excuse me!" Wheeler yelled over the hissing steam to one of them. The man turned and Wheeler beckoned him to a quieter place. "Is this a new train?" he asked.

The engineer cupped his hand about his ear. Wheeler repeated his question. The man nodded. "Is it fast?" Wheeler asked.

"Sometimes!" the engineer answered, a twinkle in his eye. "Eighty miles per hour or more going downhill." Wheeler nodded, thanked the engineer and walked back along the platform, deep in thought.

"I want you to guard the Silver Queen," he said to Daniel when they had reached the rear of the train. The brightly painted boxcar containing the Silver Queen sat between Wheeler's private rail car and the caboose of the train. "Grab your things and settle in. Here's the key. I'll make sure you get fed," he said and turned away.

The door creaked as it opened and inside a dull, woody smell permeated the air. Light shone from small windows above the doors, a welcome source of ventilation for the guards.

At each end of the car was a small padded chair and a hammock that hung from the ceiling. A small pot-bellied stove sat in one corner bolted to the floor, with a box of coal beside it and a small table also attached to the floor. A coffee pot and cups sat in another wooden box next to a wooden barrel that Daniel presumed contained water.

Filling the length of the boxcar was the Silver Queen, stacked in various sized crates lashed together and secured to the floor by straps. Daniel went along the stack of crates pulling and tugging, making sure that it was stable and safe. The sheer size and the weight of the statue would give any robber pause to think about stealing something so large and heavy.

Wooh! Wooh! The train's whistle screamed and Daniel was tossed about as the train shunted forward. Steadying himself he stood on the chair and on his toes watched the procession of Kansas City's buildings parade past until there was nothing to see but endless prairie and horizon.

The locomotive gathered speed and bumped along, swaying from side to side. A whoosh of smoke-filled air rushed in as the door swung open.

"Come on over," Wheeler yelled above the wind, and deftly leapt back across the gap between the railcars. Daniel followed and queasily crossed the gap and stepped into Wheeler's newest acquisition.

"I figured you must be hungry so I had the hotel make us a travelling basket. Did you eat last night?" Jerome looked sincerely concerned when Daniel shook his head. "Let's see what they gave us shall we?"

"Aha!" said Jerome. "Pheasant!"

*   *   *

"Here! Have another cheese sandwich," the portly red-faced man said. Drunken Irish hospitality being what it is, Constable Ivers took the proffered slab of cheese and crust of bread, rather than decline the offer and court a fistfight. "What do you say your name is?" the man enquired, wafting his horrible breath lavishly. Ivers swayed, partly in recoil, partly from the whiskey.

"It's Ivers. So's me father tells me." Ivers said jokingly, and immediately recognized his mistake. He could've used any other Irish name, couldn't he? So much for a clever alias. The drunken man laughed and slapped Ivers on the arm.

"That's right. I saw you and yer family at the funeral, didn't I?" Ivers didn't dissuade the man; his misguided familiarity was plausible. "Pity about old Clive, eh?"

Ivers made the appropriate sympathetic noises. "Awful business. Did anyone ever get caught for it?" Ivers asked, quietly. The drunken man focused on him. Moments passed like winters. Ivers held his gaze, unfazed by the danger he was courting. The drunk released his breath in a torrent looking left and right as he exhaled.

"Fenians revenge, is all I'll say." The man stood to leave and Ivers stood with him taking him by the sleeve.

"Was it, Patrick Shadlow like they say?" The man turned on Ivers suddenly alert, curious and dangerous. Ivers had that awful feeling of stepping on a freshly dug grave.

"And who would that be?" The drunk was now decidedly less jovial. Ivers' heart rate jumped. This could be the death of him. "Who told you Patrick Shadlow was involved? He died in prison. At the hands of the English. A true martyr for the Republic. A good man." The man's gaze wandered as did his attention.

"But what about the other Shadlow? His son? The one that escaped from prison?" Ivers knew he was pushing his luck. The drunken man turned slowly and glared at Ivers.

"I'm not sure I enjoy your company anymore Mister Ivers. Or whatever your name is? Good night to ye."

*   *   *

The rider approaching Harry's house was a big man, as was the horse he rode. Even from a mile away he was an ominous figure. Harry removed his hat and wiped the sweat off his brow with his sodden sleeve. He turned as footsteps approached.

"Bethel says you should hide," said Rebekah, Harry's middle wife. She offered him the pitcher of water she carried. Harry drank thirstily as the mule looked on. Harry poured some of the water into his hat and the mule gulped it down gratefully.

"Think it's someone you know, Harry?"

"Cain't think of anyone who would want to come all the way out here for that purpose?" Harry poured more water into his hat and plopped it on his head so that the water ran down over his face into his dark, scraggly beard. He could count his friends on a closed fist so that left only one alternative, and it was not a good one.

"Looks like he's leading a horse." Rebekah's eyesight was keener than Bethel's, being that she was half her age. Noisily, two children ran out to them from the shade of the house. The boy climbed up on the back of the mule while the girl held close to her mother's dress, looking off into the distance.

"Do you know who he is, pa?" the boy asked.

Even from this vast distance Harry sensed who it was, and the realization turned the sweat on his back chill.

"Go on. Git in the house, all of you. Do as I say," he lifted his son down to the ground. "Don't you have chores to do, Jebidiah?" he said, playfully slapping his son on the behind as he ran off, laughing. "Stay indoors until he's gone," he yelled after them.

Harry slapped the mule once more and the animal sluggishly twisted its ears and took several steps forward, sensing that Harry was more interested in the approaching rider than ploughing. The furrow they were digging had veered to the west and was no longer aligned with the previous row, so Harry pointed the plough and the mule back down the line and considered the apparition out there in the wavering distance.

Call it premonition but Harry knew who it was even at this great distance. It had been over three years since he had last seen the man, and then, it had nearly been the death of him. Harry willed away the thought that his misfortunes and the fortune he'd left behind were following him out to this desolate hell of a place. If there was anything that could make this horrible patch of dirt worse, though improbable, it was out there on the dusty road coming his way.

Harry slapped the rear of the mule, sparking it into several more begrudging steps, and tried to ignore the approaching storm. For once in agreement with his mule Harry ceased walking and allowed himself a half-smile. If the approaching rider was hoping to find him living well on the proceeds of the bank robbery, then he was sure to be disappointed. It was obvious that Harry was not living the high life.

"Do you want me to bring you a gun?" Rebekah called from the house.

"Naw. But you might keep one close, just in case."

"Should I make some food?"

"If he's not a relative, I don't want to feed him."

49

The mule tugged at the reins, pulling Harry forward across the dun-colored sand he hoped one day would sprout corn. During these days of constant, monotonous purgatory, he often found himself gazing across the flatness toward the distant mountains above Salt Lake City to the east. They shielded him from the sun till mid-morning and in the evenings, they glowed, iridescent in the orange and crimson desert sunsets. The daily transition from heaven to hell and back was boringly repetitious, but beautiful also. Harry turned full circle taking it all in as if for the first time. He sighed. It would be a fitting place to be buried if that was to be the day's outcome.

*   *   *

The years spent as a guest of Her Majesty's prisons had made Patrick skilled at anticipating trouble, and by using his wits to avoid it, he had survived prison, barely. In New York, he realized immediately that he would need all these skills to survive. Having accepted the steady waves of other European migrants there was fierce competition for jobs and places to live and few of either were easy to find. Apparently, merely being Irish was a condemnation and the contempt lavished on them was obvious and everywhere.

With no money, no job and no food, he suffered for three days. His stomach consuming him, he scrounged through scraps from fruit vendors and in the rat-ridden alleyways behind restaurants, usually collapsing from hunger in doorways before inevitably being chased off by the intolerant police. It was late evening on the fourth day when he awoke, startled by someone tapping him on the shoulder. Starving and afraid, he recoiled from the touch.

"Are you lost, son?" The voice was deep and resonant. Serious, but not at all condemning. Curious.

Exhausted and delirious from hunger, Patrick slowly opened his eyes and left behind the horrid dreams of prison that haunted him every sleeping moment. The man's face was hidden by an odd covering about his head. As Patrick's vision cleared, he saw that it was a friar's cowl and a large wooden cross dangled in front of Patrick's face hanging from the neck of the man standing over him.

"Do you know me?" Patrick croaked.

"No, my son. I don't know you. But you look like you could use a hot meal." The man held out his hand. Patrick took it and he was hoisted to his feet, surprised by the man's strength and then by the friar's height. He was at least a head taller than Patrick. "Follow me," the friar said, beckoning him.

Patrick reluctantly left the shelter of the doorway and followed the friar onto the walled church grounds through a rusty, creaking, metal gate. Within, the gardens were dark and Patrick stumbled on the slippery flagstones of the path.

"Careful there, lad," the friar advised, taking Patrick by the elbow and steadying him as they ascended the stone steps. The friar opened the heavy wooden door with no effort and warm air laden with sweet smells greeted Patrick as they entered the residence. The heavy door opened behind them again and another friar entered. He gave Patrick a quick look over.

"Found another of your flock have you, Father Glynn?" he said in parting as he left the room.

"Don't mind him, my son. Come along with me." Father Glynn led Daniel into an expansive kitchen where three other men sat around a rough wooden table eating silently. They looked up briefly as Patrick entered. "Prepare a plate for another, please, Mrs. O'Sullivan!" A portly woman of grandmotherly age, wearing a bonnet and long white apron, smiled a ruddy smile and hurried to set another plate at the table. "Come on, lad." Father Glynn said. "Let's get you washed and then you will sit down and eat." Father Glynn led him to a bathroom with a toilet, wash basin and bathtub with faucets, both hot and cold.

Patrick turned to the priest in amazement. "Does hot water come from these?" The priest took pity and turned on the faucet, letting hot water flow in the basin. Patrick felt the water and wonder filled his eyes.

"It's hot!" Patrick said, startled. Father Glynn laughed.

"Yes, it is. But let's not waste it." He put a plug in the sink and let it fill then handed Patrick some soap and a clean towel from a closet. "I want you to wash your face and hands and after supper you can have a bath." Noticing Patrick's questioning look he added, "You may stay here the night. Now wash up."

Patrick ate well but, as the priest noticed, said little. He was last to finish and watched the other men clean their dishes, and after thanking both the cook and the priest, they ascended the narrow staircase to the floor above. Daniel watched them go. Father Glynn touched his shoulder. "While you bathe, Mrs. O'Sullivan will bring you something to wear while she washes your clothes." Patrick looked down at his weathered coat and dirty pants, embarrassed. Apart from what he wore, he had nothing.

The Samaritan priest smiled gently and led him to the bathroom. "Mrs. Callahan has drawn the bath for you." Smiling, he handed Patrick a clean white towel. Patrick marveled at its softness. "Bathe quickly, before the water freezes," he laughed. "I will see you tomorrow morning," he said, pausing before leaving. "What did you say your name was?"

"Patrick. Patrick Shadlow." Father Glynn misheard because of Patrick's broken teeth.

"Well, Mister Thadlow. Please place your dirty clothes outside the door and enjoy your night of rest. Sleep well."

Patrick arose from the bath a new man. Mrs. O'Sullivan had placed a sleeping shirt on the chair and when he emerged, she led him up the stairs to a small, warm room.

The little room was like heaven to him. The small lantern shone golden on the coverlet of the bed, a pillow at its end. He touched the bed, it was soft. He felt the pillow, it was warm and soft also. It made him smile. The tiny room and the soft, clean bed, was a small sanctuary that had come unbidden into his life and its occurrence was divine. That night he more than slept; he was carried aloft in pleasant dreams and for the first time in years he floated through the night. Morning was to be a different matter.

After a breakfast of bread and warm milk he and the other three men were shown the door to the street and urged out into the pouring rain by the sweet Mrs. O'Sullivan. Once again, Patrick was reminded that Christian compassion had its limits.

Chapter 9

The boxcar creaked incessantly and chilly drafts raced through it like whistling children but when he started a fire in the small iron stove, the car filled with smoke. Hungry, cold and bored, Daniel folded a blanket around him and dozed curled up in his hammock, swaying with the motion of the train and lulled by the clack, clack, clack of the wheels rolling over the rails. The train had stopped only once during the day and night had fallen along with his hopes of relief and a hot meal, or any meal for that matter. Again, a loud pounding on the door.

He pulled back the iron latch and opened the door. Shielding his eyes from the wind and smoke, across the swaying metal bridge between the cars, Wheeler beckoned him. Securing the door behind him, Daniel leapt across the gap and was pulled inside by Wheeler.

"You must be starving, my boy," Wheeler said jovially as Daniel turned after closing the door. "You know everyone here, don't you?"

Daniel turned and his surprise must have been obvious since Claire Cavendish lifted her hand to her mouth covering a smile.

"This is Senator Cavendish," Wheeler said amiably. Bill Cavendish held out his hand and Daniel took it. He had a strong grip, impressive for a man of his age.

"I remember meeting you, young man. Your name is Daniel Carrington, isn't it?" Daniel nodded, surprised at the senator's memory. It must be an asset for a politician, he thought. "This is my wife, Mrs. Cavendish. I think you've met her before as well." Daniel held out his hand. Claire Cavendish took it, looked up at him and smiled.

"When the senator heard that I had banished you to the boxcar he insisted that you join us for dinner." Daniel smiled his gratitude to Bill Cavendish. "Care for a drink?" Daniel noticed that they were drinking red wine and that the wine in the short-stemmed, crystal wine glasses swayed with the train. Daniel declined.

A waiter struggled through the door of the adjoining carriage, the wind at his back ruffling his hair. He carried a large platter covered with a silver lid and his face showed the effort it took to lower it onto a tray-stand. The instant his task completed he exited.

With admirable efficiency Daniel gathered crockery and cutlery and placed them on the small dining table along with four linen napkins that he placed in front of each person. Wheeler closely watched the process and looked over at Bill Cavendish.

"Good lad, don't you think?" Wheeler said with a raised eyebrow, Bill Cavendish nodded approvingly.

"You do need to look for men with talent these days. The future demands it, Jerome. A strong back isn't enough anymore. Our old ways of doing business are disappearing as fast as the new century is approaching, I'm afraid," Cavendish said, as he and Jerome touched glasses. They failed to see that Claire's eyes followed Daniel as if he were prey. Daniel noticed, and when he dared a look at her he blushed, as if she was seeing him naked.

"Would you open another bottle of wine for us, Daniel?" Daniel saw that Wheeler was pointing to a cabinet low down on the mahogany side board. "Let's eat, shall we? Daniel, would you serve please?" Daniel froze, bottle in hand. They were all looking at him, expectantly. He fumbled with the wine opener and made a mess by pulling at the cork too forcefully, spilling wine over his hands.

"Here, let me help you." Claire said, coming to his rescue. He gladly allowed her to wipe his hands and the bottle before he poured the wine. "I'm not sure what you all want to eat," he said plaintively.

"Let me show you," Claire offered, coming to his rescue a second time. She removed the silver covers from the platters that held artfully arranged portions of meat and fowl on one and a selection of braised vegetables arranged in a circle on the other. Claire looked in the top drawers of the sideboard and found silver serving utensils. Standing beside him, Daniel felt her warmth and when she came closer, he could smell her. His nostrils flared and his heart raced.

"Hold the plates for me?" He did so and she portioned the food gracefully and precisely onto the plates he held. "I like your new clothes," Claire said to him quietly. "You look quite dashing." She was smiling as she placed portions of the various foods onto the plates. "Give these to the gentlemen," she whispered. He did and then picked up the two remaining plates. She looked at him mischievously; his hands shook. "Now, I'll serve you." He could barely hold his hand steady as she placed each delicacy onto his plate. She motioned him closer. "When I sit down, I want you to serve me," she whispered. "Always from the left side," she winked and smiled as she brushed the back of his hand. Daniel once again did as he was told and under watchful eyes, smoothly placed Claire's plate in front of her. He looked up, surprised that they were all smiling at him.

"Please join us, Daniel." Wheeler said, jovially. "You're not a waiter. We're in business together." They were all smiling at him. It was a moment he would remember for decades to come. The sounds of the moving train, the glow of the candles, their flames dancing in rhythm, the glow that came from Claire Cavendish. There was something unearthly in his being welcome amongst men of power and prestige.

During dinner he listened intently and spoke only when spoken to, something he'd heard more than once from his mother. Much of the conversation centered on the upcoming congressional vote regarding the future of silver mining. He soon became aware that Mrs. Cavendish was no shrinking violet when it came to expressing her opinion and holding onto it.

Wheeler held up his arms in supplication "Excuse me, but after such a heated discussion I need some more wine."

"I couldn't agree more," Bill Cavendish said.

*   *   *

Harry knew precisely who it was on the road. He'd had plenty of time to think on it since the man on the horse appeared to be in no hurry to arrive. He also knew what it was that the approaching man wanted. Knew also, that he was in no position to give it to him.

"Do you know who it is?" Bethel barked from the doorway.

"No. But I got a feeling that it ain't good news he's bringing us. Get everyone inside." Harry turned the mule back toward the barn and followed it to the water trough.

The rider was on his property now. Harry could almost make out his eyes. He felt a cold shiver leak down his spine, much like his courage. Should he offer defense or deference to the man who tried to kill him? Twice?

The sands of the desert had hardened over the years and the clop, clop, of the hooves was clearer the closer he came. The sun was high in the sky but the rider cast a big shadow.

"Howdy, Harry," the man removed his hat to wipe his sweaty brow with his sleeve.

"Howdy, Ham."

"Long time, eh?" Hamlett Kincaid replaced his hat on his head.

"Did you miss me?" Harry asked.

"With every bullet I had, unfortunately." Hamlett deigned a brief cruel smile. "You know Doc Holliday died?"

"I heard," Harry said, turning when Bethel appeared on the porch carrying a rifle.

"His tuberculosis finally did him in. He's buried in Glenwood Springs."

"Is that feller gonna kill ya, Harry?" Bethel yelled, perhaps hopefully.

Harry looked up questioningly. Hamlett smiled, reaching into his saddle bag. Harry moved in front of the horse for cover as Bethel levered a bullet into her rifle. But, instead of a weapon Hamlett removed a newspaper, holding it up for Bethel to see before handing it down to Harry.

"Here. Read this." Harry took the newspaper Hamlett handed him.

"It's OK," Harry yelled. "You can go inside now." Harry opened the newspaper. Hamlett nodded toward Bethel but she remained vigilant and unmoved.

"Shit!" Harry yelled when he unrolled the paper and saw the picture on the front page of The Denver Post. "That little bastard is famous."

*   *   *

As Harry railed at the newspaper, the Silver Queen arrived in Chicago to a muted reception. Wheeler and Daniel were met by a small cluster of reporters who had been notified of their arrival. Photographs were taken of Wheeler and the painted boxcar that held the statue and he was briefly interviewed by a young, pale man wearing a droopy hat. Wheeler puffed up for the interview but after scribbling only a few notes on a loose piece of paper the reporter ambled away and disappeared into the bedlam of passengers and luggage.

Wheeler shrugged and looked about the platform. A tall man wearing a bowler hat and a long, black coat approached and held out his business card to Jerome. When Wheeler finished scrutinizing the card the man opened his coat slightly, Jerome nodded and they shook hands. Jerome yelled over the chaos. "Mister Campbell, this is Daniel Carrington. He's my right-hand man." Daniel shook Campbell's hand; it was a firm grip. "He's with the Pinkerton Detective Agency," Wheeler added. "His company is going to help us keep an eye on our girl," Wheeler needlessly indicated the brightly painted railcar. "Stay here with it if you would Daniel, while Mister Campbell and I arrange for someone to spell you."

Daniel was glad that they walked away quickly, his knees were shaking.

∗   ∗   ∗

New York was chilly and wet, and it was mean. Nothing was familiar and nothing was friendly. Everyone was suspicious of everyone else, and everyone was justified. Patrick looked at the heavy, wooden door and loathed it. The shape of the thing, a heart upturned; the opposite of compassion. A nave of false hopes. For the third time, he knocked on the impassive door. He heard footsteps. The door creaked open. But not the same warmth proceeded.

"Oh, it's you, Patrick," Father Glynn said, looking less than pleased at seeing Patrick. "I told you that you couldn't come back here again."

"I couldn't find work, Father. The Lord knows I tried."

"I told you that you can't stay here. Not if you won't confess your sins."

"My sins are too great, father. Not even you could carry them."

"I wouldn't carry them my son. I would relieve you of their burden."

"Will you not help me find my family?"

"You said you had none?"

"Aye, father. Lying is another of me sins."

This hint of confession softened the friar. "Come in, my son." The kindly priest opened wide his door and Patrick gratefully entered. "You look like you could use some hot food."

*   *   *

"Could you spare me and my horses some of your water?"

"Help yourself," Harry said absently, engrossed in the story in the paper.

Hamlett let his horses have their way and looked about as they drank thirstily. "Damned ugly piece of dirt you've got here, Harry. Grow anything but scrub?"

They both looked up as a door slammed and a young girl hurried towards them carrying a metal pitcher and a tin cup. "Want some lemonade, mister?"

"Thank you, young lady." Hamlett smiled his best and removed his hat. The girl frowned, her look concerned.

"What happened to your face mister?"

"Your daddy did this to me."

"Harry ain't my daddy, he's my husband."

"Go on Lucy, get on back in the house," Harry said to her. "Everything's fine here." Lucy turned and hurried back inside the house. Hamlett watched her until she had closed the door.

"She's real pretty. Must be good to be a Mormon, eh Harry?"

"It has its moments, you might say," Harry trailed off.

"Who is that feller?" Bethel barked from the kitchen window.

"No one!" Harry yelled back. He looked up at Hamlett. "That's the other side of the coin," Harry said, quietly.

"He looks like the one what was shootin' at us," Bethel fog- horned across the yard. Hamlett smiled and touched the brim of his wide, black hat. "He come all the way out here to kill ya?" she bellowed. Harry raised an eyebrow and looked hard at Hamlett.

"Well, did ya?"

"I haven't made my decision on that yet, Harry."

"Everything's fine between us, ain't it Ham?"

Hamlett turned in his saddle again, this time he pulled his rifle from the scabbard and pointed it at Harry. Harry shuffled his feet and cast a wary eye on the house.

"I want you to read what they said about your partner in that newspaper. You can read cain't you, Harry?"

"You could tell me what it says. That would save me the trouble and you some time."

"Go on Harry, read it."

Harry held the paper at arm's length, pointing at the photograph on the front page. "Looks like they got hit by lightning," Harry laughed. "It says that they're going to Washington to save the silver industry." Harry looked up at Hamlett, intrigued. "What's that all got to do with me?"

"Tell me, Harry. Haven't you ever wondered what happened to the money you stole? Oh, don't look shocked, Harry. Me and Doc Holliday were partners until the end of his days. And we had an agreement." Hamlett took off his neckerchief and tossed it to Harry.

"When he died," Harry soaked his kerchief in the tepid water and handed it back to Hamlett. "Doc gave me his rightful share of that money. If I could find you." Without taking his eyes off Harry he wiped his dusty face and balding pate. "And I guess I've done that, haven't I?"

"Get rid of him, Harry!" Bethel yelled from behind the curtains. "He says he wants to kill me, Beth." Harry yelled back. "You do want to kill me, don't you?" Hamlett remained impassive. "I did put fire on your face." Hamlett smiled his twisted smile. The burned skin on his right cheek pulled at his lips, twisting it into a grimace. "Go on, Ham. Put me outta my misery. You can see what it's like out here." Hamlett's rifle shifted more in Harry's direction.

"Yes, Harry." Hamlett laughed. "That is something that we need to settle someday soon." Hamlett pulled back the hammer on his rifle, still pointed at Harry's chest. "Do them women have any more rifles in there?" Harry shook his head.

"They cain't be trusted with 'em."

Hamlett laughed loudly. "That's a good one, Harry. As I recollect, the last time I met them ladies of yours, they were shootin' at me and Doc."

"Well, you started it," Harry said, by way of excuse.

"Maybe. Maybe not. But now, Doc is dead, so that makes you and me partners."

Harry kicked at the dirt keeping one eye on the house. "What kind of partnership would that be?"

Hamlett laughed again and the sound made Harry even more uneasy. "The kind where if you come along with me peacefully, I'll consider not killing you today."

Harry gaped. "That's it?"

"That's it Harry. You come with me and find the money and I'll let you live, maybe."

"What? And live out here for the rest of my life? I'd rather you kill me now, Ham. Look around. This is a miserable place. I hate it out here. And them women? Never met a more demanding bunch in my entire life." Harry raised his arms over his head. "Point your rifle at me. Go on!"

"I'm already doing that Harry. What more do you want?"

"No. make a show of it." Hamlett moved his horse closer to Harry, keeping his rifle visible. "He's going to take me away. Don't be sad," Harry yelled.

"What for?" Bethel yelled.

"Don't be sad, I tell you!" Harry yelled.

"We're not sad," Lucy yelled back. Harry looked up at Hamlett.

"How long will you be gone?" Bethel hollered. Hamlett smiled his odd smile and shrugged.

"He's not tellin'. He says he'll shoot me here if I don't go with him."

BOOM!

Harry jumped a foot at the sound and skipped sideways away from the bullet that exploded inches from his right foot.

"See what I mean! Now he's riled up!"

"Mount up, Harry." Hamlett kept his rifle steady on Harry as he walked to Hamlett's spare horse. He was placing his foot into the stirrup when he felt the steel barrel of the rifle against his ear. Harry looked up, confused.

"Not that way Harry. It would probably be best for both of us if you faced backwards while we take our leave of your womenfolk." Harry did as he was ordered and mounted the horse backwards. Hamlett's rifle never wavered. "Think of it as my insurance Harry. In case they want to shoot me in the back."

Harry's family, now numbering seven, three wives and four children, a respectable number for a Mormon family, gathered on the front porch and watched them leave. Only the littlest ones waved. Harry waved back and watched them fade into the distance as he and Hamlett increased the miles between them.

Chapter 10

"It's bedlam out there, Mister Wheeler." And indeed, it was.

The Columbia Exhibition and World's Fair was the largest and grandest event of its kind to date. The World's Fair in Paris was an international sensation and Chicago had set its sights on exceeding it in both its size and excellence. A dozen nations from Asia to Europe had gathered their best technologies to present and demonstrate their technical advances to the rest of the world.

Built atop a reclaimed swamp, this illusory city, uniformly painted a dazzling white, appeared to rise from the sodden earth as if hatched from seed. Stretching for miles the ornate though temporary buildings rose forty feet and sported the newest in facilities including electric lighting along the length of its boulevards, earning it the title of "The Great White Way."

The Colorado Exhibit, which was still under construction, covered several acres. It would house not only the prized Silver Queen, taking pride of place in the center of the hall, but also an extensive array of mining equipment and the most advanced mechanized farming machines.

Electricians and plasterers balanced high overhead on wooden scaffolds, applying finishing touches to the façade of the mâché dome of the building while painters chased them through the scaffolds, covering everything in whitewash. Men yelled orders to each other in a variety of languages and from multiple heights, turning the hall into something resembling a circus more than an organized work force laboring toward a common goal.

"Have you found the men I need?" Wheeler asked. Not the most patient of men, Jerome had been struggling with the reality that he had erred in taking it for granted that there would be men provided for such an important piece of sculpture.

"All I could find was four." Daniel pointed over the heads of the parade of tradesmen where the wagons waited at the door.

"Well if that's the best you can do. You can be their boss. You know how it all fits together." Wheeler nudged Daniel in the ribs playfully and

Daniel turned surprised that Wheeler was smiling. "You're the boss. I just learned that phrase." He leaned closer. "Apparently, it's what they say here." Wheeler was already walking toward the wagons.

As was often the case, Daniel was taken by Wheeler's command of charm. He could turn it on and off like the new electric lights and brighten a room, or a man's life, in an instant. Going from wagon to wagon introducing himself he personally directed the chain of wagons to the center of the hall. Seemingly satisfied, he took out a thick roll of bills and made a show of handing each of the men cash money, to their delight. Jerome hoped his generosity would encourage, if not guarantee, that the men would be helpful.

"Daniel, I want you to inventory the crates. I have contacted Pinkerton's and they're sending someone to guard her at night. I doubt anyone could steal her during the day."

"Where will I be staying, Mister Wheeler?" Wheeler looked at him and wrinkled his brow.

"Oh! I'm sorry, Daniel. I forgot to tell you. I couldn't find you a room. Not to worry. Until I leave for Washington, you can stay in my private car." Wheeler beamed at his solution. "How does that suit you?" Wheeler noted Daniel's reluctance but carried on. "I'll have it brought around to the far end of the fairgrounds."

Daniel dealt with this new plan and tempered his own while Wheeler carried the idea forward. "I will be using my private car on my trip to Washington so while I'm away, you can have my suite at the hotel. How does that sound to you?"

A germ of a plan began to form in Daniel's mind. "That sounds very fair, Mister Wheeler," he said.

Wheeler leaned closer. "See if you can wash up a bit, will you son? You're starting to smell." Wheeler wrinkled his nose. "Well, I'm off to see the politicos that run this town, so don't expect to see me early tomorrow." Wheeler winked slyly. "If you know what I mean?" He laughed and slapped Daniel on the shoulder. "Stay here until the Pinkerton's man arrives," Wheeler commanded, smiling as he departed.

Watching Wheeler march off through the throng there was no doubt that he was a man of importance. Maybe it was the way he walked, or perhaps the swagger in his step. Whatever it was, the milling, mewing crowd parted for him.

Daniel smelled his armpits, Wheeler was correct. Since they'd arrived, he had been the watchman for the statue and had been only able to wash in the cold water in the public restroom at the train station. His personal hygiene had suffered of late. It was dangerous crossing the tracks of the sprawling railyard at night, or in the day for that matter. Several times he'd failed to hear the approach of boxcars coming down the track and had been almost run down.

"Are you Mister Wheeler?" Daniel woke with a start. He'd dozed off laying stretched out on top of the crates. He rubbed his eyes and shook himself awake. "I'm from the Pinkerton's Detective Agency," the baritone voice continued. Daniel's blood ran cold as he considered the very serious eyes of the man in the long black riding coat.

"N, no. N, no," Daniel stammered. "Mister Wheeler left. I'm D, D, Daniel. C, Carrington," he managed to bleat. "I work for Mister Wheeler."

"Pleased to meet you, Mister Carrington. My name is Johnson. No first name." It was the way he stated it, as though he had no need for another name. An object. He made Daniel uneasy. "Here is my card."

Daniel took the business card, and just looking at it made him queasy. "I'll be going then, Mister Johnson," he said, conjuring the courage to be bold. Bold enough not to race out of the building before he was discovered.

Guilt assured him that this man must know that there was a price on his head. Why didn't Johnson just arrest him and get it all over with? Daniel took a deep breath and looked at the man again. Johnson took off his hat, black like his coat, and came closer. Daniel felt as though was about to fall off a cliff. Mister Johnson looked concerned. "Are you alright, Mister Carrington? You look a mite peaked."

It was all Daniel could do to control his panic. Strangely he became aware of the pungent odor arising from his coat, the smell of fear. "I'll be alright, thank you, Mister Johnson." Daniel willed his limp legs to move and walked away without looking back but knowing that Mister Johnson from the Pinkerton's Detective Agency was watching him closely.

*   *   *

The weather had turned miserable and Patrick's prospects followed suit. No one would even look at his face when he applied for employment. Sleeping in doorways, constantly hassled by those even worse off than he, pestered by filthy, muddy minions, young and old, clawing at anything or anyone that could help them survive another miserable day. Shivering in the rain, his lot in prison looked almost attractive.

He might have been the butt of their jokes and their sexual plaything, but at least he was dry. It was in that moment of deep lament that he realized he was back in front of the church. Drawn by the light and the possibility of warmth he pushed open the door and slipped inside.

It could have been the warmth and security it offered. Or, perhaps the smell of incense that lingered in the air? Sight or smell, it brought up from his depths a desperate longing for his family, free from guilt, free from pain? Whatever prompted his conversion in that minute, it was profound and spiritually shaking. Each step he took towards the altar and the flickering candles, the more he could see of the church and of himself as well.

He dared not encroach on the silence and sat in a pew at the rear of the empty church. A door opened and closed with a heavy thud that echoed. Clacking footsteps, leather sandals scraping on the stones came from the left and he watched a bareheaded priest enter and kneel before the altar. Moments later the door opened again and a small procession of similarly garbed monastics entered in procession and in unison knelt on a step, slightly lower. Silence and peace enfolded them, palpable. Patrick felt it, could almost see it, touch it.

"Glory to God, in the highest," the first priest sang. The chorus followed in practiced harmony and in that moment, Patrick felt as if his clothes were suddenly warm and dry and that a ribbon of warmth flowed out from his heart and filled the ends of his being. The chants continued,

65

and he fell into the rapture of their undulations. He lowered his head and knelt down in his pew. Uncalled tears streamed down his cheeks and flooded into his clasped hands. Tears of longing. Tears of lost hope and an overwhelming sadness mingled with the terror of never being able to reunite with his family ever again. It was all too much. The pain that he'd been holding inside, the anger, the hatred of all things English fed by his abuse in prison, flowed out of him as if a great cleansing was being done.

*   *   *

Detective Killeen had had worse days, or so he told himself. One was when his wife deserted him for a wandering man. But he had survived. He had been sound asleep when the knocking on his door woke him. Gathering his dressing gown around him he opened it to find Sergeant Callahan wearing a serious look.

"I think you'd better come with me, sir," the sergeant said. "It's Constable Ivers."

"And what is it about the constable, sergeant?" Killeen was a slow riser.

"He's in Trinity Hospital sir. He's been badly beaten."

It was the same starched, stiff matron waiting for him at the front door of the hospital. "I can't say it's a pleasure to see you again, detective." The matron waited for him to shake the rain from his umbrella and then with a brusque look, turned and led him up the wide stairs. It was a familiar walk for him and she led him into the same intensive care ward where he had last visited Clive Reagan. His senses reacted in a similar fashion to the sight of the row of curtained beds, the soft moaning and the smell of antiseptic.

They'd stopped beside a curtained bed and the matron was preparing to pull the curtain aside. "Will he be alright?" She looked at him curiously.

"I've never thought of you being a considerate man, detective.
Is he family?"

"Not exactly. He is my adjutant. But you didn't answer my question." Killeen was in bare control of his anger. "Will he be alright?"

66

"Sshh, detective," she held a finger to her lips. "We don't want to alarm the other patients, do we?" Killeen took a deep breath and realized again who it was in control here. "Yes, he'll recover, in time," she said softly. "He suffered a severe beating, but the doctor thinks that there was minimal internal damage. He'll be off his feet for a while, but he should be right as rain in a month or so." She pulled apart the curtain and watched the hardened detective wince in reaction to the sight of his constable swathed in bandages, his eyes swollen shut from the bruising around his eyes and cheeks.

"He's resting now, so I'd prefer you didn't disturb him. Rest will be the best treatment for the next few days."

The effect of seeing his underling in such a horrible state turned his stomach and made him queasy and unsteady. Constable Ivers was not his friend, nor his relative, but there was little comfort in that. Killeen felt a wave of pity rise in him. Was this simply another example of how his actions had brought calamity upon another? He was only human. Fallible like most.

"Has he woken?" The matron shook her head sadly. "Will he awake later today?"

"That's something that the doctors cannot say for certain in these circumstances. Some wake quicker than others." The matron allowed the curtain to fall back into place and ushered the detective out of the ward where she offered him a chair across from her at her desk.

"Would you kindly tell me what you know of this matter?"

Killeen had taken out a small, weathered note book. The matron patiently waited until he had found an empty page near the back cover. She observed with a frown that the book was well worn, stuffed with scraps of paper and bound with string. Killeen noticed her disdainful look, shrugged. "I'm not the best at paperwork as you can see. That's what Officer Ivers was supposed to help me with." He smiled, embarrassed at the current misfortune of the man in the bandages who had been doing his bidding.

"All I can tell you, detective, is that he was found on the steps of the hospital around midnight." She consulted two pieces of paper and handed them over to Killeen, who read them thoroughly before passing them back.

"Where are his belongings? Can I see them?" The matron walked to a large closet where bundles wrapped in sheets were neatly stacked. She read the names on several before pulling one from the pile.

"Dublin is a violent city and we get more than our share of derelicts and unfortunates on our doorsteps. They're not all are the results of foul play, but whether or not, they are all treated the same, prince or pauper."

Killeen opened the bundle and inspected the clothing carefully, going through the pockets of the muddy pants and sodden coat meticulously. He was not surprised that there was no money remaining, all indications pointed to a robbery. Then he found something. He was unsurprised. Perhaps he knew it would be there. Inside the top pocket of Ivers' coat, wrinkled and damp from the rain was a neatly folded piece of paper. He removed it carefully and laid it out on the matron's desk under the glow of her lamp. Smoothing it with a ruler he put on his glasses and took in a deep breath.

"Are you alright, detective? You've gone all pale."

*   *   *

The house and all it held was a far-off speck in the distance now. Harry had waved a little and then settled into watching the life he'd led recede into dots on the wavering horizon.

"Are we planning to ride to Colorado?" Harry asked. Hamlett laughed.

"I doubt you'd make it, Harry." Harry's horse came to a stop and he wondered if this was the end of the line for him. Hamlett had given him assurances, but they were far from guarantees. "I'm sure your wives can't shoot us from here. You should probably turn yourself around." Hamlett dismounted as Harry painfully slung his leg over horse's rump and his knees buckled when he hit the ground. Hamlett caught him.

"You're being awful friendly, Hamlett," Harry said, regaining his balance. "If I didn't know you better, I might be fooled into thinking you were a decent man." Harry noticed that Hamlett's pistol was pointed at his stomach. "Then again," Harry said, considering his situation, "I know you better, don't I?" Harry accepted the water canteen that Hamlett handed

68

him and drank thirstily. "You didn't answer my question, Ham. Are we riding all the way to Aspen?"

They'd stopped under a grove of cottonwoods and Hamlett let the horses drink from the small stream that flowed under their shady limbs. The sun had passed its highest point and the shadows of the trees extended to the east. Hamlett sat against the trunk of a cottonwood tree, his pistol trained on Harry.

"Things have changed, Harry. Folks don't ride so much anymore. Trains go everywhere these days." Hamlett opened his eyes a fraction. "How long has it been since you were in Salt Lake City?"

Harry thought deeply, not an easy task given the blazing temperature. "Years I'd guess. We passed through there heading this way, but I've never been back. We grow our own food mostly, and then there is the relay station. They have most of what else we need."

"Then you have a surprise ahead of you, Harry." Hamlett stood and poked Harry with the barrel of his pistol. "Time to get going." Hamlett had Harry turn and tied his hands together behind him then helped him up into the saddle, this time facing forward. "We have an appointment with a train tomorrow and I don't intend to miss it."

Chapter 11

The Chicago Tribune carried the story on the front page and Wheeler wore a look as dark as the ink on the paper.

"What the hell do those politicians think they're doing?" he said, angrily waving a hand full of money in the air. "No one in their right mind is going to trust the government's paper money." Contemptuously he tossed the offending lucre on the table. "If it's not backed up by silver, it has no real value, does it?"

Wheeler paced and smoked and the effect was that of a small train roving the hotel room. Daniel watched, discretely silent as the mood in the room darkened and the emotional temperature rose. "And just what are you and the Republicans doing about it, Bill? I ask you again. What are you and your crony friends doing to keep my business from disappearing from the face of America? We're important to the country, Bill. Can't those dunderheads see that?"

"You had better have another whiskey, Jerome. You're liable to blow a gasket if you keep ranting like this." Senator Bill Cavendish rose and walked stiffly to the small bar recessed inside a mirrored cabinet. He poured more whiskey into Jerome's glass as he refilled his own. "I'm not so sure that it is as bad as you make it out to be, Jerome. I'm certain that the party leaders will counter the threat."

Wheeler stopped pacing and stared at his friend with little affection. "God damn it, Bill. This is my business they're destroying. Neither you nor any of your carpetbagger friends in Congress are going to lose your job over this matter. Me? I've got hundreds of families depending on me, and you and your kind are going to throw them out into the streets. Are you going to face them when they're dismissed after years of hard labor?" A knock on the door broke the tension. "They all trust me, Bill," Jerome was saying as he marched to the door of his suite. "I'm sure it will all turn out well," Bill Cavendish replied, looking to Daniel for support. Daniel smiled back stupidly. Bill Cavendish saw that he had an ally and reached out to touch Daniel's knee in a paternal gesture of camaraderie. "You understand that it's all politics, don't you son? If you don't already believe it, you soon will." Bill Cavendish smiled in a way that made Daniel both believe him and believe that he was basically an honest man. One that could be relied upon. But then again, he was a politician.

"Well if this isn't exactly what we've been waiting for," Wheeler said, brightly. "Come in, Claire, and take my gloomy mood away." Wheeler took her hand and ushered her in. "As you always do. Can I take your coat?"

Claire Cavendish kissed Jerome on his cheek. "You are always such a gentleman, Jerome. Your wife is a lucky woman."

"I'm confident that on some level she might agree with you." Jerome laid her coat across the chair in the entryway. "She may have come to me for love but she stays with me for my money." Wheeler laughed at his own humor without embarrassment. "You remember my assistant, Daniel, don't you?"

"Of course, I do." Claire visibly brightened. "Who can forget such a handsome young man?" Daniel stood as she entered and remained standing, feeling out of place. She radiated beauty and grace and the hand she offered was slender and warm.

"It is nice to see you again, Mrs. Cavendish," Daniel said, pleased that he had controlled his stammer. She held his hand a moment longer than necessary and it took willpower to drag his eyes away from hers. Her smile held him and she spoke volumes with her eyes, something that he'd not ever encountered before. As if she was inside his mind and knew him completely.

"Can I offer you something to drink, Mrs. Cavendish?" Daniel asked.

"I think I'll wait until dinner but thank you, Daniel. You're such a dear."

"Let's head off to dinner then, shall we? You'll be joining us, won't you, young man?" Bill Cavendish bleated as he resurrected himself out of his chair. Daniel hesitated.

"Of course, he'll join us." Claire merrily linked her arm through Daniel's, her husbands in the other. "You'll be our guest if Jerome is too cheap to pay for you." She gave Jerome a teasing smile which he ignored.

Jerome held the door open for them and with Claire between Daniel and her husband and Jerome in tow, they headed off to dinner.

*　　　　*　　　　*

Cadenced footsteps resonated along the corridor of the hospital becoming louder as they neared. Killeen didn't need to look up. Those footfalls were familiar and the closer they came the more he bit his bottom lip. Better he should feel the pain now than what he would have to face in just moments. The footsteps halted. The polished, black leather shoes that had created them stopped in front of him. There was no choice but to raise his head and look his dragon in the face. The dragon turned away from him.

"Matron, I'm Senior Chief Inspector Ivers. Is my son here?" The matron nodded and came around from her desk. Given that it was a hospital the man could've at least lowered his voice considerately, but even the matron looked cowed. "And you, Killeen, I'll see you downstairs." The matron indicated the way and led him off. "Are those my son's belongings?" Killeen nodded. "Leave them." The senior chief inspector pointed his finger at Killeen. "And don't you go anywhere, Killeen."

It was at least an hour, long enough for Killeen to consider the possible outcome of his inquiries. Also, the distinct possibility that he might find himself walking the pavement again.

He turned the piece of paper over in his hands, read it again for the tenth time and refolded it. It was possible that the constable's current condition was simply a random act of violence and robbery; a coincidence perhaps? But Killeen was averse to believe in coincidences. In his experience, coincidences were as rare as virgin births.

He knew it would be dangerous to inquire about Patrick Shadlow. Had Ivers inadvertently given himself away? Once again, the hammer of guilt swung in his direction. Was he to be faulted for throwing the junior officer into a den of conspirators? The Fenians were lower level villains, generally speaking, but still, they also had demonstrated dangerous behavior in the past.

Hushed voices approached from behind the frosted glass door. "I thank you, Matron," Ivers was saying, "for taking such good care of my son. If there's anything I can do to help please get in touch with me immediately." The door opened. "Will you do that?" He smiled, and she smiled, and it all looked so pleasant. Then he turned and walked over to Killeen his countenance a tempest.

"I want to know everything about this matter," he snarled, low like a lioness. "Tomorrow morning." He poked a finger in Killeen's chest, threateningly. "In my office! Nine o'clock." He took two paces, turned back. "And if this happens to be any of your shenanigans, Killeen, you'll be deeper into my bad graces, and that is something you cannot afford. Mark my words."

Killeen watched him walk away, feeling less than enthusiastic about his prospects for sleep. He glanced at the matron for sympathy. It was useless.

"Can I speak to him briefly? Please?" The matron was unmoved, ironclad in her starched white uniform and girded with mass. Killeen was at a loss. "Just a question or two. It would help me find the ones who did this to him. Please, matron?"

She was not a bad woman, just one who had seen too much needless suffering from the criminal underworld whose perpetrators most often went unpunished. "Come on. But I warn you." Killeen was far from comfortable with someone wagging a finger in his face but on this occasion, it was to be tolerated. "If you upset him, I swear, you'll find yourself in the bed next to him and believe me I'll make your life very uncomfortable. Be assured of that." Killeen sheepishly shifted his weight and nodded. "Come on then. But be quiet."

*   *   *

"Wake up, Harry, we're getting off." Harry reluctantly opened his eyes and saw the words Glenwood Springs pass his window as the train pulled into the station. "We're in luck, Harry." Hamlett said softly. "The next train gets us into Aspen after dark and then the first train out in the morning is at 8 o'clock." A smile crossed his face. "With luck, we can get into town, do our business and leave without anyone seeing us."

"What business, Ham?"

"I'll tell you when you need to know. Now, go over and buy us tickets to Aspen and back." Harry took the money.

Comprehending, but confused, Harry went and bought tickets for the next train, but when he turned back, he saw Hamlett in conversation with another man. As he approached, Hamlett shook his head ever so slightly so Harry veered away and headed for the small dining room adjacent to the station. He was drinking a cup of coffee when Hamlett returned, his face flushed.

"Who was that?"

"The one person I shouldn't have met. A friend of Doc's." Hamlett ordered a cup of coffee while Harry waited for some explanation, but none was forthcoming. "When does our train leave?" Harry looked at the clock on the wall.

"We've got an hour."

"You should try to get some shut-eye."

"Why's that?"

"Because we have a long night ahead of us Harry, that's why."

"Wake up, Harry, the train's here." Harry must have dozed off. His neck was stiff and his back sore. He picked up his saddle bag and followed Hamlett into the empty carriage.

"Here, this should do it for us, Harry." Hamlett placed his bag in the rack over the rear seats and indicated where Harry should sit.

"Is this where you tell me why we're going to Aspen?" Harry placed his bag in the overhead rack too. "I thought we were going to Chicago?" The train shunted and Harry toppled into his seat. Hamlett laughed at him.

"Harry, haven't you wondered what happened to all of the money you stole?" Hamlett looked hard at Harry. "You have, haven't you? No? Well, I have. And this is what I think."

Harry was all ears. Of course, he'd wondered about the money. Thirty-seven thousand dollars' worth of wondering about it. Counting it dollar by dollar in his dreams. Very few of the soul crushing hours toiling behind his mule had he not thought about the money? Imagining how wonderful his life could be with all that money. A thousand times he'd wanted to just leave and go find it.

He knew where he had buried it. But was it still there?

Chapter 12

Slowly Patrick became aware of his surroundings. His lungs filled as if he'd been underwater, deeply, hungrily. He realized that he was trembling and as he did, he felt a strong arm enfold his shoulders. The arm around his shoulder drew him to the warmth of another human, and the one who held him instilled a feeling of safety in him. Lifting his head, he saw that he was supported on either side friars. He looked from one to the other and their gentle smiles settled his mind, but not his fears.

"Let me go," he pleaded weakly, his voice a whisper. "I have to go." He stood to leave and they didn't hinder him. Several steps on, he slowed his rush to exit and turned to face them. "Are you angels?"

The priest's laugh echoed in the voluminous church. "No, no." The priest said. "No, we're not angels. But we are here to help you."

"I don't need your help." He needed all the help he could find but it was his pride speaking.

"We heard you, my son. We heard you weeping, from up at the altar." Patrick considered the distance. "We were concerned."

"How long have I been here?" Patrick's empty stomach growled loudly and he grasped it to give it silence. "How long?" he repeated louder.

"A while." The priests shared a look and shrugged. "Dawn should be here in an hour I would guess. Wouldn't you say, Father John?" Father John nodded, he was a much younger man and about Patrick's age. He had a kindly, sweet face and eyes full of caring.

"You've been with me all night?" Patrick asked, incredulously. "And I've been crying the whole time?"

"Yes."

"And you stayed here and didn't throw me out?"

"Yes," Father John said gently.

"Why?" Patrick's voice faltered. He knew the Christian answer by heart. It had been beaten into him since childhood 'Love thy neighbor as you would love me.' The conversion that he had been going through had opened his soul and the love flowed into him. Unfortunately, the strength drained from his legs and the hard, stone floor rushed up to meet him.

*   *   *

The blazing lights and the boisterous crowds of the Fair were now behind them as the horse drawn carriage, compliments of the hotel, clip-clopped down the narrow avenue between the railcars. They were at the distant end of the fairgrounds, where much of the business aspect of the event took place and as such, were now dimly lighted and mostly deserted.

"Here it is, Mister Wheeler," Daniel said.

"Stop please, driver, this is it," Wheeler yelled to the driver. His private train car sat on a small branch that spread out from the main line. Other private cars and their assorted tenders sat in fellowship side by side, but they all appeared deserted.

"I don't much like the neighborhood, Jerome," Claire laughed.

Daniel stepped past her and shook hands with the senator as he alighted.

"Thank you for a lovely dinner, senator," Daniel said.

"Always a pleasure, my boy. And please, call me Bill." Bill was far from sober.

"Thank you for the ride home, Mister Wheeler. You needn't have.
There is a trolley that could have gotten me here."

"Is this where you've been staying, Daniel?" Claire trilled. "It's charming, Jerome, like you." Wheeler was dozing and only nodded, she was looking at Daniel. "I know I've seen it before but I want to go and see the inside again. In case we want to get one for ourselves. Do you mind, Jerome?" Both Jerome and Bill had fallen prey to the peace and quiet and both were nodding off.

Claire climbed over their legs and allowed Daniel to help her down. "We'll just be a moment, driver. Don't run off without me." She laughed and took Daniel's hand as he helped her onto the steps of the train car and climbed up behind her. "You don't mind me coming into your home do you, Daniel?"

77

They stood close on the narrow steps as Daniel fumbled with the lock. Claire placed her hand on his and guided the key into the aperture. There was a moment when they both knew something was about to happen, a realization, an excitement. Together they pushed the door open. Daniel struck a match to the oil lamp by the door. It cast a dim, bare glow across the room.

Claire took his hand and led him back along the narrow hallway. "Is this where you sleep?" She opened the door and took a step inside, breathing deeply not just once, but twice. "Ahhh," she sighed, "man smell."

Even in the dim vague light Daniel could see a transformation taking place. She glowed. She swelled. She reached up for him and held his head in her hands.

"I want you," she snarled and kissed him so passionately he was sure that she had drawn blood from his lip. She was hotter than a fire and she emitted an odor that made Daniel's nostrils flare and for a moment he was someone other than himself. He kissed her back just as hard, pushing his hips against hers and he heard the rising in her loins and the crescendo of her passion. She grasped his hand with eagle talons and pulled it to her, pressing his fingers into her pubis and through the multiple layers until he found her spot and she exploded in his hand.

For just a moment they breathed the same air, inhaled the same passion. The same longing. She pulled away from him straightening her dress.

"Gotta go," she whispered and hurried to the door. Daniel scurried to catch up while he adjusted his clothing, but she was stepping down onto the ground as he reached the door. The driver helped Claire into the carriage and gave Daniel a smile as he resumed his seat. Claire spread the blanket back over her legs and her husband's and smiled a perfect smile as the carriage pulled away.

Daniel looked down at his clothes. He was shocked, his shirt was askew and his tie was crooked. Panic flooded over him until he convinced himself that both Wheeler and Senator Cavendish were asleep and unaware of their antics. He certainly hoped they were.

During the following weeks he spent many wakeful nights fearful of this and also wondering when he would see Claire again.

Claire was similarly involved.

*　　　　　*　　　　　*

Killeen stepped down from the cab and gave the driver a clatter of coins as he alighted. "You'll ask around for me then?"

"I'm useless to you in this matter, detective. They all know I'm your ears." He made a show of counting the coins. "No one will dare talk to me about Patrick Shadlow. I'm sorry about your lad, but they can be a nasty lot."

"If you hear something, anything, give a message to my sergeant, and no one else. His name is Callaghan." He watched the cab set off up the small incline and knew that he was up against a wall of silence. Straightening his bowler, he donned the persona of a superior. It was the only persona he really knew.

His leather heels clicked loudly on the stone floor. Not an unusual sound, but in the spaciousness of the building they sounded like the beat of a kettle drum before an execution. His sergeant gave him a brief half smile but the other officers on duty ignored him purposefully. The stairs seemed longer this morning, their length, their breadth, all familiar but not familiar. Ivers' desk was empty, of course. For a moment Killeen thought favorably of the young officer. But the feeling passed quickly.

He turned away and took the stairs up to the uppermost floor, the inner sanctum of the Dublin Police. He knocked once and opened the door half expecting the tirade to begin immediately. But it didn't. Senior Chief Inspector Ivers stood at the window, his back to the room, quietly considering the spring sunlight filtering into the room.

"Sit down, Killeen, and tell me everything you know."

"I spoke briefly with your son, sir," Killeen began, as he sat.

"Yes, I know. I was with him again this morning."

"It seems that during his investigation into the whereabouts of the escaped terrorist, Patrick Shadlow, it was discovered that he was a policeman and was beaten."

"That's all you know?"

"No, sir. There's more."

"Before you go on detective, let me ask you something." Ivers sat down at his desk facing Killeen, hands clasped in front of him. "Did you personally send my son on this mission?" The chief detective held Killeen's gaze during the awkward silence. Killeen tried hard not to swallow.

"It was on my orders, yes sir. I asked him to attempt to discover the whereabouts of Patrick Shadlow. We had reason to believe that he is still here in Dublin. Settling old scores if you will."

"The Shadlow affair was a couple of years back, wasn't it? I remember that one of them died in prison."

"Yes sir. The father died of natural causes while in prison. An unfortunate occurrence, to be sure."

"What happened to the rest of the family?"

"They sailed to America. It's the younger son, Daniel Shadlow, that we're still looking for. There's a warrant out for him with a sizeable reward for his return to Ireland. New York City is where they disembarked, we believe, and they still may be there for all we know. We have a detective agency called Pinkerton's that has been keeping an eye out for him but they have had little to say, so far."

"What makes you think this Patrick Shadlow was involved in my son's beating?"

"I have reason to believe that it was he who caused the severe beating and subsequent death of a Clive Reagan. It was Mister Reagan who informed on the Shadlows after they blew up the bank." Killeen took a deep breath. "I found this in your son's pocket." Killeen pulled the piece of paper from his inside pocket and handed it across the desk. "It was the only thing on his person when he was brought to the hospital." Killeen watched his superior's face closely. Small twitches appeared around his left eye, but nothing remarkable that would show the tempest that was brewing inside the man. More than a minute passed in weighted silence.

"So, this is personal then?"

"It appears so, sir."

"Then, I think we should take it personally," he stood abruptly, "don't you Killeen?" Surprised by his superior's reaction, Killeen simply nodded. "Get him, Killeen. And get the men who did this."

Killeen rose. "Yes, sir."

"Get as nasty as you have to, Killeen. I want that Patrick Shadlow. And when I do get him, he'll never see daylight again, if I have anything to do with it."

*   *   *

It was very white; all about him were folds of the whitest of white material. He reached out for it but failed, it was beyond reach just as it had been in his dream. Everything was real until one tried to grasp it. Barely visible unreality. He felt a breeze cross his face and heard the rasping of the metal rings on their track. A face appeared, a kindly face, angelic and comforting. It peered into his eyes and smiled.

"Ahhh. So, you're awake at last," the kindly voice said, as she placed a thermometer under Patrick's tongue. His eyes followed her as she checked the bandage around his head, she smiled again. "How do you feel?"

"Where am I?" His voice was raspy and only murmurs escaped.

"You're in a hospital."

"How did I get here?"

"The friars brought you here." Patrick struggled to comprehend. "Let me tell the doctor you're awake. I'm sure he will be glad to hear. You've been unconscious for two days."

The matron knocked on the ward doctor's door and peered around the corner. "Sorry to interrupt, doctor, but the young man is conscious. I thought you would like to know."

"Thank you, matron. Is he lucid?"

"He asked where he was."

"Good news. Thank you, matron, we'll come along and see him then." The doctor returned his attention to the two cowled friars across the desk from him. "It seems you chose a good time for your visit."

The taller and elder of the priests handed back the two sheets of paper that they had been reading.

"May I ask how you know this young man, Father?"

Father Glynn glanced at his fellow friar before answering. "He came to us as they all do. Broken and hungry, needing support in every way. Just another one of the multitudes, I'm sorry to say."

"But this young man?" The doctor cleared his throat to cover his emotions before continuing. He reread the papers in his hand and took a deep breath, letting it out slowly. "But this young boy has suffered such terrible abuse, the likes of which I cannot imagine one human inflicting on another. Do you know where he came from?"

"All I know is his name. Patrick Thadlow."

"Well, we can help him with some of his injuries but some will be permanent I'm afraid." He pointed to several lines on the page. "It's a wonder that he survived." The doctor stood and walked to the door, trailing the friars. "Let us go and see our patient, shall we?"

Patrick's vision was returning when the doctor poked his head inside the cubicle.

"Ahhh," he said, smiling. "You have some visitors." He held the curtain apart and Father Glynn and the younger Father John joined him at his side. The doctor took Patrick's wrist and counted his pulse. Then he looked deeply into Patrick's eyes, pulling the eyelids upwards and turning Patrick's head side to side. "How are you feeling, young man? Besides the headache?"

For Patrick, the question was not a singular one, and the answers to anyone of them would make a rational person sick to their stomach. He probably could have answered the question. Possibly even made a joke about his condition, but he had no doubt that the doctors and nurses had seen his injuries. It was his incontinence that caused him the most discomfort and embarrassment.

Stinging, red-hot tears welled up in him and where words would not flow tears filled the void, running in torrents and drenching the pillow case. But no words came. He opened his eyes and considered the faces of his rescuers. Still no words came. Words were there but they would not come of their own accord. He opened his mouth to express his gratitude but the words would not come.

"Rest, Patrick. It's the best thing for you now. We will come again tomorrow and visit. Please try to eat something." The priests smiled in their practiced kindly manner and departed with the doctor, leaving Patrick with his horrors.

Chapter 13

"Wake up, Harry." Hamlett kicked Harry's feet. He was intrigued how Harry could step onto a train and within minutes of leaving the station fall into a sleep so deep that not even the steam whistle could rouse him. "We're here."

Harry woke slowly and though it was early evening, saw that they were pulling into the Aspen train station. From the crests of Red Mountain and Ajax Mountain, to the familiar sounds of the city, when Harry stepped off that train he was immediately back in his element. He took a deep breath of sooty air and coughed.

"Ahhh," he said standing tall and proud, "there's no place like home."

"Don't get too attached Harry. I plan to be out of here on the morning's train, richer than I am now. Come on." Harry did as he was told and followed Hamlett from the station and up Mill Street into town. Hamlett carried a folded canvas bag wrapped with a leather strap slung over his shoulder.

"Where are we going, Ham?"

"I told you on the train. Weren't you listening?" Hamlett pulled Harry into a dark, smelly alley and pushed him up against the wall holding him by the throat. "I'm not fooling, Harry. We both know that you took the money and stashed it someplace. You're going to take me to it. Now!"

"Is that what the big bag is for? To put all the money in?"

"Either the money, or your miserable body." Hamlett pulled a revolver from inside of his coat and put it against Harry's top lip." Harry smelled gun oil.

"What? Are you going to shoot me here? Someone's bound to hear."

"I don't need a firearm to kill you Harry. And when it happens, I want it to be a surprise."

"But we buried it in my cabin, under the oven. What if someone's there, in the cabin? I gave it to my partner when I left, you know."

"Then I suggest we go and see if they're taking visitors. If not, we can convince them to leave, I imagine." Hamlett waved the pistol under

Harry's nose. "You've got a choice here, Harry. You either find the money, or you stay here permanently. Do you understand me?"

Harry was genuinely frightened by the change in Hamlett. "Alright, Ham. I'll take you there." Harry stopped after a few paces. "On one condition."

"You're not in any position to be making conditions, Harry."

"If you find the money you won't kill me."

Hamlett pondered a moment. "If you find the money, I'll consider it. That's as good as you get today, Harry, and that's because I'm not in a bad mood yet!"

"Well if that's the best you can do." Hamlett jabbed the barrel of his pistol into the small of Harry's back pushing him forward, into the street. Aspen was dark and quiet, quieter than Harry remembered as they made their way to the trail that led to Harry's old cabin.

"You stay here and I'll go see if anyone's home." Harry took two steps on the path and heard Hamlett's footsteps directly behind him and shrugged. The path was no wider than it had been but it was more overgrown than he remembered. They came on the cabin unexpectedly, Harry stopped and looked around him, unsure, confused.

"Where's your cabin Harry?"

"I don't know. It used to be right here." Harry fumbled around in his coat and pulled out a box of matches. Striking the match on the box the match flared and Harry saw the remains of his cabin, burned, charred and in utter ruin. The match died. Harry struck another and ventured into the burned hulk.

"This, is where you hid all that money, Harry?" Harry heard the hammer of the pistol being cocked. "I don't like your chances of surviving the night if that's the case."

"Now, Ham, don't be in such a hurry to kill me, will ya? Let me look around some more." He struck another match and clearly saw that the oven was tipped over and lying on its back. Harry crept closer, got down on his knees and struck another match closer to the ground. He dug into the ground where he knew the hole would have been but felt nothing but gritty charcoal. His mind racing, he pushed the rubble around, digging feverishly in the hope that something had survived, but nothing came of his efforts.

"What are you fellers doing?" Came the familiar voice of Billy Tomb, his uphill neighbor. Harry had only an instant to react. He jumped up and approached Billy, who was holding up a small oil lamp. Harry saw that Hamlett had pulled his kerchief over his face and was standing in the shadows.

"Hi there, Billy. It's Harry. This is, or should I say was, my place." Billy held the lamp up higher and smiled. "Well I'll be damned," he said. "I guess you didn't know your place burned down then?"

"When did it happen?"

"The day you left town. It was the day of the wedding for sure. I came back from work and the firemen were still here. It was all gone Harry. Nothing left of it. Sorry about that." Billy turned slightly watching Hamlett melt into the night.

"Thanks, Billy." Harry shook his hand. "I'll see you around."

"Stickin' around, are you Harry?" Harry ignored the question. His feet were already in flight as he hurried down the path for the last time. Either way, dead or alive, he wouldn't be treading this path again, ever.

Deep in thought Harry jumped when Hamlett grabbed him by the collar and pushed him against a tree. Even in the dim light Harry could see the angry contortions on the man's face. The scar tissue across Hamlett's cheek pulled at his mouth from one side. Harry believed then that it was the last thing he would see before dying.

"Who burned your cabin down, Harry?"

"I was just thinking that it was you and Doc that did it."

"Well, it wasn't." Hamlett eased Harry back onto the ground. "Was the money still there?" Harry pulled Hamlett's hand away from his throat.

"If it was, it is all burned up by the looks of it." Hamlett clutched Harry's throat again and Harry squirmed, trying to twist out of his grasp but to no effect.

"Then it looks as if your time has come, Harry."

"No! Wait! If anyone knows what happened, No Problem Joe would," Harry gushed.

"In that case, you live a little longer, Harry. Let's go see your friend, shall we?" Hamlett nudged Harry along with his pistol. "I don't know if you're a religious man, Harry, but if you are, this would be a good time for you to make peace with your maker. Now get going and take me to your friend."

It was the word friend that hung in the air. Harry had no illusions that Joe considered him far less than a friend. The question was, what could Joe tell them that might save Harry's life?

"I have a feeling that your life span is shrinking, Harry. If we haven't found the money by daybreak, it'll be the last one you'll ever see. I can guarantee that, Harry."

"If anyone knows who took the money, Joe does."

Harry was struggling with finding his cabin burned to the ground. He'd been robbed, and the bitter, angry feeling that he had been violated overwhelmed even his thoughts for self-preservation, momentarily at least.

Careful not be seen in case they were recognized by anyone else, they approached No Problem's stables by crossing the corrals and entering through the side door. It squeaked a little. The stable was empty but for two horses and the lamp hanging above the water barrel was the only source of light.

"It looks like he's in bed, so be quiet," Harry whispered as he eased the door open. Hamlett took out his pistol but Harry pushed it away. "He's an old man, Ham. I doubt there'll be any need for that."

"Old men shoot guns, Harry. Need I remind you of Doc Holliday?" Hamlett nudged Harry forward with his pistol. "To his dying day," Hamlett whispered, "Doc swore he was going to put a bullet in you. He died an unhappy and bitter man because of that, Harry. One way or another, I plan to put things right by dawn."

"Stay here." Harry whispered reaching for the door handle. Turning the handle, he carefully pushed the door open. It creaked and the small wedge of light that shone into the room showed a body turned away facing the wall, covered by a blanket. Cautiously, Harry took a step toward the bed. Joe snored and snuffled but did not stir.

"Joe, are you awake?" Harry said, softly. He reached out to shake Joe's shoulder and heard the distinct click of a pistol being cocked behind him.

"I told them you'd be back one day," Joe said sleepily, rolling onto his back and turning up the flame on the lantern next to his bed. He looked at Harry a moment, appraising his lush beard. "What do you want, Harry?"

"What happened to my cabin?"

"It burned down the day you left town."

"Did Daniel, do it?"

"Leave the boy alone, Harry," Joe snarled. "He had nothing to do with it. He was at the damned altar when the fire got started. You were there, too." Joe was waking up, predictably grumpy. "You must 'a seen the fire as you rode out of town."

"If you can remember, I had more worries trailing behind me than smoke on the horizon," Harry said sarcastically. "Who did it, Joe?" Joe swung his spindly legs out of his bed, reaching for his pants. Harry caught his hand. "This is not a social call, Joe. I need to know who burned my place down and who took the money." Joe stopped and considered Harry. "You've got a hide sneaking into my place in the middle of the night demanding questions be answered." Joe coughed and clutched his chest. "What damned money are you talking about, Harry? That little tin box you kept under the oven? Don't you remember how it was me who set it all up for you back when you first came to town?" Joe considered Harry skeptically, a wry smile creasing his face. "Or do you mean the money you stole from that bank over in Leadville?"

Hamlett burst into the room and grabbed Joe by the collar of his sleeping shirt, lifting him up off the floor. "You know, don't you, old man? And now you're going to tell us what happened to it or I'll tear this place apart and burn it to the ground with you and the horses and Harry inside." Joe looked suitably terrified, but Hamlett wasn't finished. "You will tell us what we want to know, old man, I promise you."

Hamlett hit Joe with the back of his hand, striking him on the cheek. Joe's head snapped to the right. Hamlett hit again and let him fall onto the bed. But as Joe toppled backwards, he hit his head on the edge of a shelf that held his books and fell to the floor with blood spurting from a gash on the side of his head.

Seeing the blood on his hand joe clutched his chest in obvious pain. "Are you trying to kill me, Harry?" He croaked. Abruptly, Joe's countenance took on a surprised look and he fell onto his back, clutching his chest. "Get the doctor, Harry. Please!"

Harry looked from Joe to Hamlett and back. Joe's eyes were screwed shut and he looked to be in extreme pain. "I gotta go get a doctor, Hamlett," Harry begged.

"Not yet. He could be faking it. Let me look around. I want to be sure the money's not here someplace." Hamlett placed his pistol into his belt and tore at the small room lifting everything off the floor, even the bed, looking for a hiding place. Joe, he left alone, lying on the floor, stepping over his tortured body as he went about his demolition.

Harry sat on the floor holding Joe's hand while Hamlett searched the room and the stables. Both the stalls and the loft came under his close inspection. All the while, Joe lay somnolent, shallowly breathing in sporadic bursts. Harry looked up as Hamlett returned sweating and angry. "Well Harry, I don't know if we would have gotten anything more out of him, so I might as well kill you both now."

"NO!" screamed Harry, holding his hands outstretched, looking at the pistol barrel pointed at him. "There's something else. Daniel has a price on him." Hamlett leaned down, his face only an inch from Harry's.

"What kind of a price, Harry? Enough for me to not kill you?"

"Five thousand dollars."

"How do you know this, Harry?"

"I saw the Pinkerton's wanted poster. He had it in his bag. It was him in the poster, I guarantee it."

"Your guarantee is hardly enough, given the circumstances."

"Look here, Ham. We know where Daniel is. He's in Chicago and we know that there is a Pinkerton's Agency in every city in the country, so why don't we go get him and turn him in there in Chicago? You can have half of the money and I'll keep the rest. That's a good deal, I think. Don't you?"

"What about him?" Hamlett pointed his pistol at the unconscious old man lying on the floor at Harry's feet. "He knows we were here." Harry looked down at Joe and felt a surge of pity. Joe had been so important to him throughout the years in Aspen and Harry had survived in no small part because of Joe's help and influence. He wouldn't have become Red's friend if not for Joe.

"Can we at least put him back on his bed?" Harry's compassion was hardly compelling. "He knows nothing, Ham," Harry pressed. "He's unconscious." Harry looked down at Joe. "He's dying, Ham. Can't you see that? If we don't get him a doctor he'll die here on the floor."

Indeed, the cut on Joe's head seemed to be deeper and more serious that either of them had suspected and was oozing blood at a prodigious rate, pooling around his head. "Who would believe him anyway? No one saw us here, except Billy. And he can't be believed by anyone, I promise you."

Harry was pleading in earnest for Joe's life, almost as hard as if he was pleading for his own, which at that moment, he was. Hamlett appeared to be dealing with a difficult problem. His plan was if not unravelling, at least fraying at the edges.

"No," Hamlett said flatly. "Leave him on the floor. That way it will look like he fell getting out of bed. Come on, let's get out of here."

Harry held up his hand. "Shouldn't we stay here until the train leaves in the morning?"

"Harry," Hamlett smiled his gruesome twisted smile, "that's the best idea you've had so far."

Relieved that the threat of his imminent murder had passed, Harry relaxed. Joe was unconscious and unaware of the danger that had temporarily passed over them both. For the time being, anyway.

Hamlett looked down at Joe. "I imagine someone will come and find him tomorrow. Do something useful Harry, tidy the place up so it looks like this was an accident."

"What're you going to do?"

"I'm glad you asked, Harry. I'm going to keep an eye on you.
That's what I plan on doing."

In the gloom of the room Harry carefully went about making Joe's place look in order. It was a futile effort. With a sigh, he sat on the edge of Joe's narrow bed and looked down on Joe with sincere compassion. While Hamlett sat on the chair with his back to the door, Harry lay back on Joe's bed and let his head fall on Joe's pillow. The pillow was dirty and the stuffing uncomfortable but Harry drifted off. Joe drifted off, also.

*   *   *

Daniel was taunted nightly by the various apparitions of Claire Cavendish, entering his dreams in a myriad of ways and forms. She had touched him and her touch had set him on fire and not since his first vision of Kate had he felt this way. Parts of his being and his body were controlled by his longing for her. He'd never felt this thirst of passion before and if he had, it was a mere reflection of the craving he had now.

It was little wonder that Claire had drawn him in deeply and filled her senses with their sexual fragrance. Living in such a confined space with minimal bathing opportunities no doubt a normal person would have recoiled from the smell. But not Mrs. Cavendish, she drank it in like a thirsty camel.

Most evenings he would sit down to write to Kate and sometimes would even get a page or two written before falling asleep. There was little to add to these letters in recent days.

He almost jumped out of his skin when he heard the knock on his door and he had regained no color when the door opened and Claire Cavendish burst in. He was half out of his chair when she attacked him. She pushed him back down and tore at his shirt, kissing his chest as if she was quenching a fire. He tried to put his arms around her but she pushed his arms away and thrust her head down into his lap.

Daniel grasped her head between his hands and tried to pry her head from his crotch. She grappled with his belt with practiced ease and within seconds his erect penis was inside her mouth, his back arched and he couldn't help but grip her hair and pull it viciously. She moaned, but he persisted and finally in a moment of fiery passion he burst forth. Smiling and laughing, Claire let the liquid fill her mouth and gloss her face with the juices of his passion.

"Gotta go," she said huskily, and raced for the door. "The cabby won't wait more than five minutes." She hesitated and came back to the still shaking Daniel. "I want more of you," she kissed him lightly on the lips and he tasted his essence. She took the edge of his shirt and wiped her mouth, laughing. "I'm a messy eater, aren't I?" and then she was gone. Accompanied by the clatter of the horses' hooves she disappeared into the night.

*   *   *

"What do you have for me Killeen? You've been on this for a week." Senior Chief Inspector Ivers asked.

"It hasn't been quite that long, sir." Killeen hurried to reply.

"It's been plenty long enough, Killeen. Tell me what you know and don't go into details of how you know it. I haven't felt well lately and your details won't help my appetite, I'm sure."

"We found the men responsible for your son's condition." Killeen consulted his small note. "One of them has, with some inducement, come forward with what I believe is the most probable scenario. Your son was beaten to send a message to the police. To me personally, in this case. To stop pursuing Patrick Shadlow."

"Did your new friend say where this prince of the people might be now?"

"My guess is he's probably in America by now. Apparently, he sailed on a ship heading for New York, over one week past." Like sparring boxers, Killeen watched his senior officer digest this information. Their eyes locked on each other's. Seconds dripped slowly, like a leaking faucet.

"What do you suggest we do to get him back here?"

"I think I know a man who might be willing to go to America and find him and bring him back." The senior chief inspector raised his eyebrows.

"Is he a man to be trusted?"

"Aye, sir. He was one of our own and he has a grudge to settle in this case."

"Well, if he can spare the time and is willing to go off on this wild adventure, then you have my permission. The department will provide him with whatever he needs." Killeen stood to leave. "One thing, Detective Killeen," the senior officer removed his eye glasses somberly, "this matter should stay absolutely between us, do you understand?"

Killeen nodded. "Absolute secrecy, sir. I understand."

"You're a good man, Killeen. I can see a glowing future ahead of you after this matter is concluded. Good luck."

Walking down the wide flight of stairs to his office he paused at the injured younger Ivers' empty desk and considered his problem. Looking over the balustrade down onto the floor below he caught the eye of his old friend Sergeant Callahan and beckoned him to come up to his office.

"Do please close the door, sergeant and take a seat." Killeen took his seat opposite and came directly to the point. "This Shadlow case has taken a nasty turn sergeant, and I'm afraid that I have become more deeply involved." The sergeant nodded. "Do you remember when the Fenians blew up the Bank of Dublin?" The sergeant nodded. "What was the name of the officer who was injured in the explosion. Do you remember him?"

"I do. It was James Lynch. I see him down at the pub, on Friday night usually. Why?"

"I need to talk to him. Would you ask him to come in for a chat?" Sergeant Callahan nodded. "As soon as you can please, if you wouldn't mind. It's quite important. Thank you, sergeant."

The sergeant left and Detective Killeen gathered on his desk all the paperwork connected to the Shadlows and their deeds. He had no idea how far he might have to cast his net, but he did know who it was he wanted to catch.

Chapter 14

"Daniel, are you here?" Daniel was awakened by the baritone voice of Jerome Wheeler and by the harsh tone. Surprised by Wheeler's sudden appearance, Daniel grabbed his pants and stuck his head out of the door to his miniature bedroom. The sun had barely risen and the fog still lay low on the marshy fair grounds.

"How soon can you get packed and have this pig sty fumigated?" Wheeler yelled, not at all pleased. Daniel emerged pulling on his boots and tucking his shirt into his pants. "Looks like you had a hard night, son." Wheeler said, softening and removing Daniel's socks from one of the carved chairs before sitting down. "I'm off to Washington tomorrow and this train car is coming with me. If those dumb-ass politicians up in Washington think that I'm going to sit idly by and lose my business while they're picking fleas out of each other's asses, they have another thing coming."

Wheeler watched absently as Daniel went about the small space, tidying. Daniel saw Claire's underpants under Wheeler's chair. His heart raced as he scooped them up and crammed them into the side pocket of his jacket. Wheeler saw what he did.

"Ahhh," he said. "Well, I'm not surprised," Wheeler chuckled, standing up. "Clean this place and have it ready by morning." He gave Daniel a sly smile. "You can have my suite at the hotel while I'm away, as I said. Perhaps you'll enjoy the change of scenery." Wheeler walked the three paces to the door, he turned. "You've been writing to your wife, haven't you?"

"Yes, Mister Wheeler. I wrote her a letter last night," Daniel lied. "Good boy." Wheeler stepped down to the ground and climbed into the waiting cab. "Come tonight and have dinner at the hotel. Come at seven o'clock, the senator goes to bed early these days."

Daniel waved him off and hastened to clean the mess he and Claire had made. He reasoned that Wheeler would be gone for a week at least. Was that enough time to travel to New York, find his family and return with them before Wheeler did? It was a long shot, the odds were not good, and its success would depend on many things working in his favor, but it might be possible.

*　　　　*　　　　*

There was a soft knock on his door and Detective Killeen looked up to see his sergeant standing at his doorway with another man.

"Ah, this must be Constable Lynch?"

Sergeant Callahan stepped aside and allowed Lynch to enter. He was not an old man, nor young. Probably Killeen's age, but he moved with an old man's measured steps and used a walking cane.

"Please sit, constable. Can I get you some tea?"

"No, thank you, sir, but it's kind of you to offer. And since I've retired, I'm no longer a constable. It's just Jimmy Lynch these days, sir."

"How have things been for you since the accident Mister Lynch, "The doctors are good and the nurses, well, they're all fair of face."

"But, how is your life these days, is what I was really asking?"

Michael Lynch took a deep breath and then another. Killeen sensed the inner turmoil and waited until the man across from him had regained his composure. The burned skin around his left eye and cheek had pulled the skin drum tight, twisting one side of his mouth into a permanent wicked smile. Jimmy Lynch took out a stained handkerchief and blew his nose noisily.

"Sorry about that, detective. Sometimes it all gets to me."

"I'm sure it does. Take your time."

"It was all going so well until the explosion," Lynch began. "My wife and I had a little one, and we were so happy. Now look at me. I'm half the man I once was, with no job and no prospects for one. The wife left with the baby, of course. They're gone up to Belfast to be near her kin. Doubt I'll ever see them again." Lynch let out a long sigh but braved a smile of sorts. "Without my pension, I'd be out on the streets."

"Well Mister Lynch, it's about your prospects that I wish to talk to you." Killeen saw the glimmer of hope rise in the man's eyes. "Do you have any obligations that would stop you from travelling? Perhaps, for a month or more?" Lynch straightened his back, keenly interested.

"Not since me wife left, there's no problem there, sir. Where was it you were thinking of sending me?"

"Have you ever wanted to visit America?" Lynch smiled. "Why?"

"I would like you to find Patrick Shadlow and bring him back to Ireland."

Lynch's smile widened, just as Killeen knew it would.

*   *   *

"Drink the broth slowly, Patrick. It's hot," said the soothing voice of Father John. He had taken an interest in Patrick's recovery and come to pay him a visit at least once a day for the past week. "Would you like to try to feed yourself today?" The priest took Patrick's hand and gently folded his fingers around the spoon and guided his trembling hand to Patrick's mouth. "That's wonderful. I can see you'll be better in no time at all."

Patrick allowed the warmth of the broth and the loving peace to renew him. His muddled mind was slowly clearing. The pleasure of tasting food again was surprising and he drained the bowl. "More, please?"

The young priest brightened and returned quickly with more broth and a slice of bread. "Perhaps later this afternoon you might let me to read to you? Would you like that?" Patrick nodded, handing back his bowl. Father John smiled, pleased that Patrick had eaten. It was a good sign. Now it was the other wounds Patrick carried in his heart that needed his care.

*   *   *

The young stable boy rounded the corner, running through the gate, up the steps to Shirley's house and almost crashed through the door. Luckily, Red had seen him coming and opened the door when he arrived, out of breath.

"What is it young feller? Is the barn burning?" Red asked. The boy buckled over as he spoke.

"No! Mister Corcoran," he panted, "it's worse. You gotta come quick. No Problem's laying on the floor, all bloody."

"Go!" he yelled. Without even grabbing his hat or coat, he chased after the boy running as fast as he could manage through the busy streets.

"Have you called out for a doctor?" Red asked as they ran.

"No, sir. I just came right over to your house. He's your best friend, isn't he?"

"Yes, yes. You did the right thing." They were racing past the Paragon when Red spotted Sheriff Hunter who saw them coming and noticed their alarm. "Sheriff ... get the doctor ... come over to No Problem's stables ... I think we're going to need him ... urgently ... tell him to hurry ... we'll see you there."

The stables were deathly quiet when they arrived. The horses silently solemn. Following the boy, Red found Joe unconscious, laying where Harry and Hamlett had left him, on the floor. A pool of blood had congealed by his head.

At first Red thought he was dead, but Joe drew a short, raspy breath and wheezed it out again. Red gently picked him up off the floor and carefully placed him on the bed. After inspecting Joe's wound, he placed his handkerchief against it and then began to notice things that didn't seem right.

Joe's bed was rumpled as if he had slept in it, but Joe was wearing his pants. Also, there was no blood on the pillow and the pillow itself looked as if it had born a head that had shed dark hair. That alone was odd. No Problem hadn't seen a dark hair nor hair of any color on his head in over twenty years. Yet there were long, dark hairs on the pillow. Whose were they, if they weren't Joe's?

Something else troubled him. The place was untidy, very unlike Joe. Also, his trunk which held his old army uniform, medals and memories was partially open and looked like it had been searched. On closer inspection, he saw that everything in Joe's room had been moved. Who had been here and done this, he wondered?

He was kneeling beside the bed holding Joe's boney hand when the doctor arrived with Sheriff Hunter. Red left the small room while the doctor examined Joe. The sheriff joined him.

"Have you sent for an ambulance?"

"It's on its way," Sheriff Hunter replied. "How long ago did you find him, Red?"

"It was the stable boy who found him, so I guess about a half hour ago?"

The doctor called them back inside, his expression puzzled.

"This must have happened last night." The doctor pointed to the pool of blood, rust brown where it had hardened. Red saw what it was the doctor was pointing out to him. A clear print of a large man's boot was outlined in the spread of the pooled blood. The sheriff saw it too and gave Red a raised eyebrow.

"Excuse me, doctor. Did you step in this spot?" The doctor shook his head. "Maybe it was the stable boy?" Red passed a look to the sheriff.

"That's a big boot, Red."

The clanging bell of the approaching ambulance and the arrival of the nurses gave them all a chance to consider the situation.

"I wonder who would do this?" the doctor said.

The sheriff and Red exchanged questioning glances. "You don't think this was an accident, doctor?"

"Joe's face was swollen and bruised. I doubt very much that he did it to himself." He looked at Red, sincerity abounding. "I'm sorry about your friend. I assure you we'll do everything we can for him."

With a wave of his hand the doctor closed the doors to the ambulance and the driver whistled to his team to go.

"How's about we go back inside and have a look around, Red?

I'm not easy with this being an accident either."

"Let's do that."

Chapter 15

T he train was roaring through the night heading toward Washington, D.C. Daniel was deep in thought. Things had changed.

"I'm sorry about the change in plans, son." Wheeler sat in one of the ornate chairs, his feet pointing at the small, unlit fireplace. Wheeler sucked on his port dipped cigar, rambling on as Daniel dozed. "Here! Have some more port wine?" Wheeler handed the carved crystal decanter across the small divide. "I know you were looking forward to a few nights in the hotel, doing whatever it is you do at night." Wheeler threw a sideways glance in Daniel's direction. "But this is a big-time political battle brewing in Washington and I need you there with me. You understand, don't you?"

"Yes. I understand, Mister Wheeler. I'll do whatever I can to help." Daniel burped smoke. "You can trust me, Mister Wheeler."

His plan had been to wait till Wheeler left for Washington and use the time he was absent from Chicago to go to New York, find his family and return before Wheeler did. It took two days and two nights on the train to get to New York and two days for the return. It would give him two days to find his family within the week that Wheeler had told him that he would be in Washington. With any degree of good luck, Wheeler would never know he was gone. It was a simple plan, and could simply go wrong at almost every turn.

Armed only with the address to where he had sent his letters, it was useless to ponder what he might do once he arrived in New York. He had only the vague memory of it. What he did remember was that it was immense and dangerous.

Nor did he have any way of knowing what conditions he would find his sister and mother living in. Having been forced to entrust them to a man he didn't know, in a dangerous city they did not know, he was just hoping and praying that he would find them alive.

*　　　　　*　　　　　*

"Get up, Harry. It's time to catch the train." It was the singular thing that Hamlett had said to him in two days of travelling. Barely a grunt or a grumble had come from Hamlett, but Harry was constantly aware that his pistol was most always pointed at him.

Harry had even made the effort and tried to befriend him, knowing full well that his life might someday depend on it. But, Hamlett was not a talkative man in the best of times and he was constantly watchful of Harry making it a long, sleepless train ride. Little wonder that they arrived in Chicago tired and irritable.

"Where can we find a cheap place to stay?" Hamlett asked a cabbie.

"How cheap?" he replied. They had few choices and Harry had none, since Hamlett had all the money.

"Show us what you got," Hamlett instructed the man while pushing Harry into the cab. Neither mentioned the mass of traffic or the impressive height of the buildings. Their mutual distrust laid waste to that type of conversation.

*   *   *

In a scene reminiscent of one similar only a few years prior, Killeen stood on the same fog-shrouded dock watching a boat loaded with Irish families departing their native shores, bound for America. He and James Lynch stood together nervously shuffling their feet, their breath clouding the air. Steam rose from the ship's funnel, filtering the yellow light from the same gas lamps. The ship's whistle blasted the night with three short blasts.

"All ashore that's going ashore," a ship's officer announced through a megaphone. "All passengers aboard now, please."

"Well Sergeant Lynch, James, I sincerely believe you've earned your promotion and I wish you the best of luck on your quest."

"Thank you, sir. I'll do my best." They shook hands and Lynch picked up his suitcase. "You can count on that."

"I have no doubt of it." They walked together a few paces toward the gangway where other embarking passengers lined up to board the ship. "You do have the name of the detective who will be meeting you? And the hotel you are to stay at?" Lynch nodded as they walked. "You will have money available through the Bank of England in New York and they can forward it wherever you need. If there are any problems, cable me immediately." A crew member took the luggage from Lynch and inviting him to follow, headed up the gangway to the ship.

"Don't worry about me, sir. I'll get Mister Patrick Shadlow and I'll bring him back."

"You do understand that there is a reward offered for his apprehension, don't you?" Killeen saw the surprise on Lynch's face. "There's also a reward for his brother, Daniel Shadlow."

"Would I be entitled to any of that?" Lynch eyed Killeen.

"That would depend on who apprehends them. But? I should think that you'd be entitled to a share of it, if you were successful." They nodded to each other one last time and Killeen watched him walk up the steep ramp. Oddly, he noticed that Lynch's limp was suddenly less pronounced.

Killeen watched the ship pull out into the tidal current and continued watching until both it and Lynch had disappeared into the dank mist. He lingered on the dock after the other well-wishers had left, questioning whether it should've been he who was sailing on that departing ship. He peered into the dark water, hoping for answers. None came. The water lapping at the dock pylons was oil-slick and murky, as uninviting as the journey across the ocean to America, as uninviting as the dangers that would lie ahead for James Lynch.

Pulling his hat further down onto his head, he stuffed his hands into the pockets of his coat and headed back to the waiting cab. He'd done what he could. He'd notified the American diplomatic authorities that Patrick Shadlow might be amongst their population and to watch out for him. He had also cabled the Pinkerton Detective Agency, informing them of the reward offered by the English government for Patrick Shadlow's return in addition to that offered for his brother, Daniel. Killeen was confident that doubling the reward would spur their investigators into action. He felt confident he'd done all he could.

Killeen's knowledge of the United States was sparse and filled with Indians with bows and arrows and cowboys who shot people on a whim or when robbing banks. Perhaps sending a partially impaired, disfigured man out into the new frontier was not as good an idea as it had seemed at first. Though, James Lynch did have the necessary motivation for the job.

Senior Chief Inspector Ivers had declined to meet with Sergeant Lynch. His participation was to be unofficial, though it was Ivers' intervention and active involvement in the matter, on behalf of his son, that made it possible. The escape of Patrick Shadlow from prison and its embellishment in the newspapers had become like a thistle in the government's bed. They wanted the Shadlows back in jail even more than Killeen and Ivers did.

*   *   *

Gentle hands caressed the places that others had scarred. The lotion, cool where once there had been burning coals, tender where there had been scaldings and beatings. From the base of his neck to the backs of his heels the skin had been tortured and the muscles there surrendered their defenses reluctantly. Still he tried. Winces, there were many. Tears? More than a few.

"Can you tell me where all of this happened to you, Patrick? It might help to talk about it, you know?" Father John was doing his best, in God's name, to right some of the terrible cruelty that had been inflicted on this young man. Patrick was not much older than he and he felt protective of him.

"I can't tell you."

Father John was familiar with reticence and knew that a soul released its sins begrudgingly. "Are you Catholic?" he asked. He had seen Patrick make the sign of the cross as he stood to leave the church, but he needed to know.

"I don't believe in God anymore. No good God would have allowed this to happen to me. And to others." Patrick closed his eyes.

Father John patiently waited. Patrick rolled onto his back, facing the priest.

"Your wounds are healing nicely," Father John said, moving to the chair next to the bed. "I'm hoping that we can heal your spiritual wounds also." Father John took Patrick's hand in his, looking into his eyes. "Is it too much for you to let me help?"

Patrick understood what needed to be done. Where there had been pain and no promise, Patrick saw a door open. He smiled at the priest. Slowly he enfolded his hand into the priest's and saw the realization that they had been looking for the same thing. Patrick took the priest's hand and guided it under the sheet to his penis. "There are wounds here too," he said.

The priest showed no shock, he smiled and gently squeezed. There came the sound of footsteps and the priest stood up hurriedly. When no one entered, he relaxed and smiled benignly at Patrick, looking down on him.

"It is my job to heal and I am willing to heal you in every way. Just tell me your confession." Smiling, the priest touched Patrick's hand. "You know it will be a sacred trust."

"Let me think about it, Father."

Father John leaned in and kissed Patrick on the forehead. "Peace, be with you, Patrick," he said before leaving.

Patrick was at peace. Though it was only a small islet of tranquility in a raging sea of troubles, he found sanctuary there for a while and slept an untroubled sleep. His first in years.

*   *   *

"How is Joe?" Shirley asked as soon as Red entered.

"He's comfortable but he hasn't regained consciousness yet." Red walked to Shirley and taking her in his arms swept her up into the air. "But he's a tough old coot, so I wouldn't worry too much about him. It's your husband you've been neglecting these past few days."

Content in every way, Shirley looked down into Red's grey blue eyes and kissed him on the lips. "You're just like a child, you know? The moment you're not the center of attention you make a fuss," Shirley said, laughing. "Now, put me down and let me get your dinner. Let me down, I tell you!"

"Not until you kiss me again. You don't want me going to one of them whorehouses I heard about?" He lowered Shirley to the floor but kept his arms around her. "I did my part now you do yours, or I'm not letting go." Shirley kissed him long and hard.

"There, that should see you for a couple of hours," she said, smiling and straightened her dress. "You're getting pretty frisky there, Mister Corcoran. You gettin' spring fever, are you?" Red reached for her but she deftly slipped away. "Maisie! Will you help me here?" Shirley laughed loudly as Maisie came from the kitchen.

"You want I should throw a bucket of water over him Mrs. Shirley?" Maisie had to dodge quickly as Shirley escaped Red and bolted for the kitchen.

"I don't know what to do with him. He's dormant as a mushroom for months and then, now he's all about chasing me. Explain that, Maisie?"

Shirley ventured back into the living room through another door but Red was waiting for her. "Stop it, I say! Red! Behave yourself!" Shirley giggled, out of breath. "I mean it. Behave yourself." Red reached out for her again. "Red! Stop it. Or I'll get angry," she laughed, as Red made another grab for her dress which she brushed off. "You men are just like children," she said wiping the back of her hand across her brow. "Now go wash your hands and sit for dinner."

"You know you're the only person I take orders from, don't you?" Shirley smiled and pushed him toward the kitchen.

"Yeah? Me, and every other woman in the world. I was wrong about you men. You're even worse than children. Now go on. Kate's coming over for dinner."

They heard a knock on the door and Kate entered, carrying her daughter on her hip. "Hi, Mom," she called.

"Oh, good. You're here. How're my girls?" Shirley kissed Kate on the cheek and led the way into the dining room. "Maisie has made us a nice dinner, so sit and talk to me. How's Daniel? Have you had any more letters from him this week?"

"Yes, I have. How is Joe doing?"

"Hi, Kate." Red said as he entered. "Oh, he's about the same. The doctors said it could go on for a while. He's not a young man anymore either." Red sat while Shirley played with her grand-daughter on the couch.

"Come on, Red. Don't get pessimistic. He's going to be fit as a fiddle soon."

"Maisie, the food smells wonderful." Maisie smiled brightly, hurrying about setting dishes of hot food around the table. "Have you heard from Daniel lately, Kate?" Red asked. Kate nodded.

"I got a letter yesterday."

"Has he said anything about Jerome's plans?" Shirley asked.

"He says that Jerome is going to Washington and while he's there he's staying in Jerome's suite at his hotel. He's happy about that. Living in Jerome's railcar has been difficult, he says."

"When does Jerome head to Washington?" Red asked.

"From what he said in the letter, Senator Cavendish and his wife are planning a big political dinner in Washington early next week so I think he's going there soon."

"Wouldn't it be wonderful if we all went out to Chicago and visited Daniel while Jerome is away?" Shirley said, excitedly. "What a surprise for him." She put her hands to her cheeks and beamed at her idea. "Oh, Red? You've never been to Chicago, have you? We can see that foot specialist while we're there, Kate. What do you say?" Red chewed slowly, giving himself time to ponder the situation before answering.

"I think we should wait until Joe is back on his feet. For me, the World's Fair can wait." Red's words hung in the air.

"You're right, Red. I wasn't thinking of Joe." Shirley toyed with her food. "But it is an excellent idea, don't you think?"

"Did you know that Harry Rich was in town?" Red said, casually.

"When?" Kate and Shirley asked simultaneously, both looking at Red intently.

"The sheriff had his suspicions and asked around. Billy Tomb told him Harry and another feller, a big man, were digging around what's left of his old cabin the night before Joe was found." Red paused and considered the information that he was about to share. "Something else odd was that the doctor said that Joe had been beaten about the face as well as having a gash on his temple. Something else too, the sheriff and I both saw that there was a large boot print in Joe's blood that none of us put there."

The silence was palpable as Shirley and Kate digested the shocking news. They looked to each other for answers but none were forthcoming.

Chapter 16

Washington was not how Daniel had imagined it. It was neither like New York nor was it like Chicago. Other cities appeared to grow randomly; Washington was the result of intentional design.

His principle job, among more menial ones, was to deliver Jerome to meetings and to get him there on time. Also, whenever the senator's secretary was not present, Daniel was charged with taking the notes from these meetings which he kept in a leather valise Wheeler had purchased specifically for that purpose.

He had resigned himself to being stuck in Washington with Mister Wheeler and therefore he would be unable to implement his plan to find his family. In the evenings he ate in his room while Wheeler was out with the Cavendishes doing important things with important people. He enjoyed his evenings and the unfamiliar luxury of ordering whatever food he desired, which would be delivered to him on a wheeled cart. After dinner he would sit at his desk and organize the important papers that had been acquired during the day. More often than he wanted, during these times, thoughts of Claire precluded thoughts of Kate.

While sorting the papers one night, he noticed that he had gathered up some incidental papers belonging to the Democratic Party, written on the Party's official stationery. One document sent a shudder through him and after reading it twice, he knew he had to give it to Wheeler. He also needed a drink.

*　　　　　*　　　　　*

James Lynch also needed a drink. After a week of seasickness any sane man would want one when his feet hit dry land. Again, he wondered why sailors went to sea at all but knew why they were so often drunk on shore. He stomped his feet on the concrete dock to reassure himself that it was as solid as he remembered dry ground to be. The crossing had been a rough one, even in the estimation of the hardened crew. What a relief it had been for all aboard when their ship entered the calm waters of New York Harbor.

Joining the queue of disembarking passengers, he successfully navigated a barrier of questions asked by official persons and was unceremoniously deposited at a landing dock by ferry boat. Trailing the jumble of passengers, he passed a jubilant crowd awaiting the arrival of family or friends. Some held signs bearing names written on them and he saw a tall man in a long black coat holding one bearing his name. Normally he would have acknowledged the man, but his instincts cautioned him. Avoiding eye contact, he continued along with the throng then hid behind some crates, far enough away to observe the man.

After the ferries finished unloading the last of the passengers the man he was watching was joined by a policeman. They spoke briefly and walked away in different directions. The man in the black coat tossed the sign on heap of rubbish and walked toward Lynch, heading for the exit. Lynch stepped forward as he passed.

"Are you with the Pinkerton Detective Company?" Lynch asked emerging from the shadows. The man slowed.

"Are you Lynch?" The man replied. They locked eyes, each gauging the other. "I thought you had a limp?"

"I thought you worked for Pinkerton's."

The man laughed. "What made you think I don't? The name's Rafferty." He handed Lynch a business card. Slightly worn, Lynch noticed.

"Can I keep this?" Lynch asked. Rafferty took back the card, reluctantly.

"Sorry. It's is my last one," he replied. Lynch nodded. Without asking, Rafferty picked up Lynch's suitcase. "Come on," he said merrily, "let's get you to your hotel. Where are you staying?" The man hailed a passing cab and they climbed aboard.

"The Chichester Hotel," Lynch told the driver.

"Is this your first time in New York, Mister Lynch?"

"Yes, it is, Mister Rafferty. It is my first time in America."

"Driver, could you take me by the Bank of England on the way to the hotel?" Rafferty entertained Lynch as they drove along streets bustling with people, energy and money. When they arrived at the hotel, he took his suitcase and removed the walking cane strapped to it. "Have you heard anything regarding the whereabouts of Patrick Shadlow, Mister Rafferty?"

Rafferty smiled weakly. "Not much." Lynch noted that no sign of disappointment crossed Rafferty's face. "But we do have some leads," he said, brightening. "We'll get onto them tomorrow and go chase that Shadlow feller down, eh?"

"Yes, I suppose we will. I'll see you tomorrow morning then, Mister Rafferty." Lynch turned and using his cane to lean on, walked up the stone steps and into the hotel. The large, wood and frosted glass doors opened onto a spacious foyer dotted with tired furniture, potted ferns and sleepy guests.

"Which way to the toilet, please?" The thin, young man behind the desk pointed to his left. Lynch thanked him and carrying his bag walked towards the men's room but continued around the perimeter of the room until he found a window overlooking the street.

From behind the curtains he watched the cab he had arrived in driving away, but it had no passenger. Lynch was not a detective but he'd been around crime and criminals for long enough to have developed a second sense about them.

The young clerk at the desk handed him his key and carried his suitcase for him to his room. Tired from his trip, he fumbled with his wallet to give the young fellow a token of his appreciation.

"May I ask you a question, young man?" He asked the boy. "Do you work here often?"

"Yes, sir. Six days a week."

"How much do you make in a week?"

"I make twenty dollars on a good week, sir. That is, with tips of course."

Lynch took out a ten-dollar note and held it up for the boy to see, receiving the expected response. "I have a few questions for you.

Do you mind?" The boy nodded. "Firstly, I want you to keep my whereabouts private. Can you help me with that?" The boy nodded and smiled as Lynch handed him the money.

"Secondly, is there another way out of this hotel that doesn't go through the foyer?" The young man was most helpful.

After the young man had left, Lynch laid his case on the bed and took a long hot bath but didn't unpack. Refreshed and hungry, he dressed and left the hotel by a side door that opened into the alley.

Taking his bearings, he walked away from the hotel until he found a busy restaurant, drawn in by the sounds of familiar smells and accents. When he finished his meal, he motioned to the bartender for the bill.

"Where is the worst Irish bar in New York?" he asked. The bartender laughed.

"That's easy. That would be Finbarr's, down in the Bowery. But why in God's name would you want to go there? Are you tired of living?"

Lynch laughed along with the man. "No, that's not the case. It's not my death I'm seeking. I'm looking for a friend and that's the type of place I would likely find him." The bartender handed Lynch his change. "Thanks," Lynch said, and left with a plan.

Lynch hailed a cab and told the driver to take him to Finbarr's but the driver declined unless Lynch paid him the fare first. Heeding the warning he'd just received from the bartender; he hoped his first night in New York would not be his last.

*   *   *

The door to his room opened softly and closed quickly, silhouetting his visitor. Near darkness enveloped him again but for a sliver of light coming from under the door. Patrick was not surprised to hear the rustle of garments and the feel of Father John's flesh against his as he slid into the bed beside him.

Nothing physical happened between them the first night. Father John was wrestling with his feelings for men and Patrick hung on the edge of a cliff trying not to panic as his prison memories threatened to overwhelm him. The trepidation they shared had abated by the time Father John left the bed and donned his robe.

The following night was different in every way. There were needs that they both were victim to. Father John needed to be shown what to do for him to satisfy his fantasies and unspoken desires, and Patrick was just the one to do it. In that first night of passion their roles became their needs. It was necessary, and only natural that one would want to dominate the other.

"If you will tell me what it is that I can do for you, Patrick, I promise I'll do it. I know you're troubled. Perhaps I can help, if you'll let me?" Patrick allowed the priest to kiss him again and he kissed him back. "But there are things about me I cannot tell you," Patrick confided. "It would be dangerous." Patrick pushed the priests head down onto him. Father John looked up, smiling.

"Not if I heard it in your confession," he placed the tip of Patrick's penis in his mouth, savoring a forbidden fruit, "then I could never tell anyone." He gently sucked and Patrick hardened. "It is a sacred vow. Your confessed sins are my obligation to hold secret unto my death."

"If I do confess to you?" He pulled the priests' hungry mouth away from him and turned his face up, looking into his eyes, the madness rising. "You will promise to help me. On your honor, and in the name of Jesus."

There was a palpable heat in the air. Both parties were about to commit to a dangerous path. Father John was going to be a committed homosexual and Patrick was going to be a blackmailer.

"I believe I killed a man, Father," Patrick began and continued with his confession. Patrick abused the priest that night, partly for ignoring his vows of chastity, and for all the times in prison when he was the sexual victim. He reveled in the change of roles. It felt good to be a predator. By the time he left, Father John was no longer a virgin, and he had also committed to secretly help Patrick find a family named Carrington.

*   *   *

"I don't like Chicago, Ham," Harry said, as they trudged through the mud. "They should have called this the Great White Swamp." Hamlett grabbed the back of Harry's coat, saving him from being run down by a horse drawn wagon slithering through the mud toward them.

Nothing makes a city look drearier than rain and fog, and it had rained continuously since their arrival. On each prior attempt to visit the

World's Fair grounds they had been driven back by rain and wind howling in from over the lake. On this day, the rain had withdrawn temporarily.

Hamlett had purchased a guide book and had gained a thorough knowledge of the fairgrounds. Careful not to be seen by Daniel or Wheeler, they scouted the expanse of Colorado State Exhibition building. In the center of the pavilion, the Silver Queen stood towering above the other exhibits.

A tall man in a long coat carrying a clip board stood near the statue. "Howdy," Harry said, in his most pleasant tone. The one he had used to woo women, back in the day. The tall man nodded to him. "Can you tell me anything about this statue?"

"No. I'm just here to watch it," the tall man said, "until the feller who is supposed to be watching it comes back from Washington." Harry and Hamlett exchanged glances.

"When will that be?"

"Don't know that."

"Do you like your job?" Harry asked. The man looked down his nose at him.

"I'm a professional detective. I work for Pinkerton's. Minding a statue is not my idea of an effective use of my talents. If you know what I mean?"

"We could mind it for you," Harry said.

"Well, I guess we could use one of you." The man looked Harry over twice and then pointed at Hamlett. "Do you want the job?" Hamlett nodded, resisting the urge to smile. "You got it. Here, write down your name and come back here at ten o'clock tomorrow." The man watched Hamlett print his name on the paper on the clipboard, then he held out his hand and Hamlett shook it.

"Is there a Pinkerton's Agency office in Chicago?" Harry asked, casually.

"There's an office in every city worthy of calling itself one."

Harry smiled and for once so did Hamlett.

Chapter 17

WASHINGTON, D.C.

"Will you be ready in the morning by seven o'clock, Daniel?"

"Yes, sir. And I'll have a cab ready to take us to the Capitol Building at eight. It will be waiting at the door of the hotel."

"You're a good man, Daniel. I don't know if I could've done this without you." Wheeler hesitated before opening the door to his room. "I'm going to have a bath and a massage. Perhaps that will put me in a better mood for tonight's festivities." Jerome winked.

Daniel smiled. Wheeler's euphemisms for sex were becoming more familiar to him. Wheeler might be an older man, Daniel assumed as old as fifty years, but he had the stamina of a spring colt.

Outside the wind was blowing steadily. Pulling his collar up around his ears and his hat down, he turned into the wind and walked briskly to the train station to investigate departure times to New York City.

Since their arrival in Washington he had not seen Claire Cavendish or the senator though their names were often in the newspaper. For over a week, Wheeler and the Cavendishes had been the focus of a whirlwind of parties and receptions and tonight was to be the grandest of them all. A lavish affair for the political leaders in hope of tipping the vote in their favor to keep the Sherman Act, tabled for a Senate vote the following day.

When it came time to leave for the gala, he considered his reflection in the wardrobe mirror and smiled at his appearance. He'd heard it said that clothes maketh the man, but until this moment he'd not appreciated its meaning. In his new formal attire, Wheeler had insisted, he looked quite different. More like a man of means, perhaps?

Daniel's transition from adolescence to manhood had passed by him almost unnoticed. His face was fuller and facial hair was now a daily issue and now he better understood why men grew beards.

When Wheeler saw him, he broke into a wide smile. "My, my, don't you look splendid. I doubt that Claire Cavendish will be able to keep her hands off you tonight," he said, with a smile and a devious wink.

At Shirley's house, the dinner conversation was sparse and somber. Shirley and Red ate silently while Kate and Maisie fed the baby. They had taken turns sitting with No Problem Joe in hospital. He'd been there for three days with no noticeable improvement. The doctors had consulted with them on Joe's condition and had shared their grave concerns for his recovery. With head injuries of his type, they said, and considering his advanced age, there was no definitive course of treatment, other than to let nature run its course.

All heads turned they heard a sharp rapping on the front door. Standing on the porch was the Catholic priest who had also been at Joe's bedside.

"Oh, it's you, Father Francis. Please come in." Kate ushered the priest into the dining room. Usually a man of calm demeanor, he was now pale and noticeably uncomfortable, wringing his hands as he spoke.

"Good evening, Mrs. Corcoran, Red. I'm sorry to interrupt your supper, but I think you should come to the hospital immediately. It's Joe Bolon of course. He wants to see you both. I have my buggy outside if you can come now." Red and Shirley leapt from their chairs.

"Does this mean he's getting better?" Shirley asked anxiously, donning her coat and hat.

"I can't tell you that, I'm afraid. He's very weak, as you know."

They were met at the hospital door by Doctor Wallace, the head medical practitioner, and together they walked down the hallway talking quietly as he led them to Joe's room.

"Unfortunately, that's about all we can tell you about Mister Bolon's prospects, now." The doctor shrugged. "But, if I was religious," he glanced at the priest, "I'd be praying for him. He could fail tonight, or he could last another ten years." Again, he looked at the priest and smiled.

"Only God knows, eh, Father?" He smiled to Shirley and Red in turn. "Be of good cheer. I have found it has always been strong medicine." Red and Shirley shook hands with the doctor before he left them.

"I'll let you two go in privately." The priest said with compassion. "Joe told me that he wanted to talk to you before letting me hear his confession. He was quite firm on that."

Red and Shirley entered the room, but after several minutes Shirley reappeared and sat next to the priest on the wooden bench in the corridor. She said nothing and the priest respected her silence. Smiling weakly, she reached out and took the priest's hand and together they prayed for Joe's recovery.

Fifteen minutes passed before Red joined them. He was stoic as ever and Shirley embraced him, drawing strength from him. "He wants to see you now Father." Red drew a deep breath. "He's ready." The priest smiled a sympathetic smile. "Thank you for coming to get us." Shirley said, sincerely. The priest disappeared into Joe's room, closing the door softly.

Shirley took Red's hand in hers and looked up at him. "Joe's a good man, Red. You should be proud to know him." Shirley was shocked when Red laughed.

"After what he just told me, I'm not completely sure about that. Come on. Let's walk home. It's a nice night for a walk."

"Did Joe mention Harry?"

"Yes. I think it was Harry who did this."

*   *   *

Ostensibly a team, Lynch kept his new-found partner Rafferty at arm's length. Routinely, at the end of each day's investigations, Rafferty would leave him at the front door of the Chichester Hotel and would watch him enter. Lynch, for his part, would wait until he was certain that Rafferty had left then exit the Chichester and walk two blocks to where he actually slept.

For the past four nights, he'd gone back down into the Bowery, visiting saloons and bars, playing the role of a newly arrived Irishman. His facial disfigurement was a big advantage here, where obscurity was cultivated. At most places he was cordially invited into the drunken groups, not just out of sympathy but also because Lynch was using his budget to buy liquid friendships. With the Irish, it worked every time.

He'd found the bar he was looking for on the fourth night. It was in an alley and down a flight of stairs. Not a typical drinking establishment but more of a social club of sorts. Initially, faces had turned in his direction when he arrived and there was a noticeable drop in the level of conversation until he'd ordered a whiskey and sat by himself offending no one. They were a suspicious lot, to be sure, and that was exactly what he'd been looking for, suspicious people, the Fenians.

Lynch was patiently sipping his second whiskey when a youngish man, perhaps in his late twenties, came and sat down beside him. Lynch waited until the man's curiosity found voice and he turned to face him.

"Yer new 'ere. Ain't ya?" he said, in a challenging tone.

"A recent arrival, yes," Lynch replied, and pulled his face into a half smile.

"Where you come from?" the man's tone changed little. "Dublin. And you?"

"We're all Irish, here. Some are Dubliners. Do you know anyone?" He found it difficult looking directly at Lynch and Lynch knew he had an advantage.

"I heard that there were some Fenians in this neighborhood."

"Where did you hear that?" The unpleasant tone had returned.

"A cabbie. An Irishman. A Republican to be sure." Lynch paused for effect. "He brought me here." Lynch watched his new friend make eye contact with a pair of burly men standing at the bar. He saw their raised eyebrows also.

"What happened to your face?"

Lynch laughed. He touched it gently and his smile disappeared.

"Explosion," he said, watching the reaction.

"How?" the man was insistent. Lynch was ready.

"Bank of England, in Dublin, a couple of years back. Fenians business."

"You say you blew up the bank in Dublin?" the man looked incredulous and stood slowly. "What's your name?"

"Lynch."

"Wait here," the man said, then joined the two men at the bar.

Patrick was now well enough to eat with the clerics at their communal table. They were cordial, but distant, leaving no doubt that his relationship with Father John was not condoned. Patrick was unconcerned. After what he had endured in prison, he considered he had been to hell already.

"You'll be leaving us tomorrow, Patrick," said Father Andrew, the principle monk. "It seems that Father John has made some arrangements for you. That is correct, isn't it Father John?"

Patrick saw Father John tense. He cleared his throat.

"Yes, Father Andrew. I've made arrangements with a local family." Father John looked up and met the gaze of the other monks around the table.

"And how do you know these people Father John? We're not throwing Patrick back into the fire, are we?"

"Not at all." John sent a quick look in Patrick's direction. "They're a local family and members of our parish. Their name is Doyle."

This was the first Patrick had heard of this plan. All heads turned his way. "I'll always be grateful," Patrick said, truthfully, "and I'll always be thankful for your kindness and generosity." Patrick looked at each of the faces and lingered on the fallen face of Father John. "I'll never forget any of you."

That night as they lay in bed holding each other, there was a bitter sweetness in the tears Father John spilled on their pillow. Tender kisses filled the night and rose like a flooded river the nearer it came for them to part as lovers.

When the time came, nearer to dawn than was safe, Father John lingered sitting on the bed. He reached into the sleeve of his robe and took out an envelope and folded it into Patrick's hand holding it tightly. Wiping away his tears he rushed off, closing the door quickly behind him. When the sun had risen and daylight had filled his small room Patrick opened the envelope. Inside there was some money, not a large amount but enough to feed him for a week, and a letter which Patrick folded without reading.

He would look for a place to discard it, unread of course. No, he thought again. It might be of value in the future.

*   *   *

"That's more than enough for me, Mister Rafferty. I've had my fill of bad beer and Irishmen to last me a month." Lynch needed to know if Rafferty was having him followed.

If Rafferty did indeed work for the Pinkerton Detective Agency, then he would know about the reward offered. If he was not an employee of the agency and knew of the reward, then that was another matter entirely. Rafferty had kept him busy every day in his failed investigation and so Lynch had not as yet visited with the Pinkerton Company. That needed to be corrected.

"I'll see you tomorrow?" Rafferty said in parting. Lynch nodded. Again, he went into the Chichester Hotel and stood beside the window watching to make sure that Rafferty had left. When he had gone, Lynch visited with the young man behind the desk, leaving him with a note to give to Rafferty if he came looking for him in the morning. The young man nodded and gratefully took the money Lynch handed him.

Lynch changed into the same clothes he had been wearing every night he'd gone out on his forays but this night he tucked his pistol into his belt. Straightening up he looked at himself in the mirror and saw nothing out of the ordinary.

Once again, he had to pay a cab driver in advance to take him down to the Bowery. The driver was solemn and wary which suited Lynch. Comforted by the feel of the pistol in his pocket he tried to relax and ignore the screams of the city all about him. Tonight could be telling, and it was possible someone might die. He raised his eyes skyward and prayed that it wouldn't be him.

His initiation into the secretive realm of the Irish underworld was imminent, as was his possible demise. He looked at the stairs that led down into the dungeon-like bar. The worn stone steps glistened in the remnants of the rain storms that had peppered the day. He took a deep breath and steeled himself.

Pushing the door open with his good shoulder he heard the din of conversation diminish as he entered. Resting his cane against the table he looked at no one but the bartender, ordered a whiskey and waited. As he expected, he was approached by the fellow he'd met the first evening. The man nodded and sat next to Lynch, sipping his beer.

"Are you enjoying New York, Mister Lynch?" he asked, not looking in Lynch's direction. Lynch followed his gaze. The same two men at the bar were watching him.

"I am."

"Would you be here with a purpose?"

"Perhaps. Perhaps not." Lynch said, smiling back.

"Would it have anything to do with the Bank in Dublin, then?"

"Perhaps."

"Did you know Paddy Shadlow?"

Lynch touched his face with a half-smile. "We were close once. That's all I'll say."

"Did you know that his family's here in New York?"

"Is that so?" Lynch replied. The men at the bar were casually not watching but Lynch suspected that both men were following the conversation closely.

"I've even heard that there might be a reunion of the family."

"That would be nice for them."

"You're not interested?" the man asked, his tone suddenly friendly. Lynch sat in silence until the man sitting next to him could stand it no more. "You did hear me, didn't you?" Bitterness had returned to his voice. Lynch nodded, keeping one eye on the men at the bar.

"Perhaps." He considered his new friend and spoke slowly so the men at the bar could understand. "That news could be dangerous, if you know what I mean? I hear that there is still a price on their heads." Lynch turned slightly to see the reaction, the corners of the man's mouth turned up ever so slightly, he knew its meaning.

"Did you know a Clive Reagan?" the man asked, observed by his comrades. Lynch was prepared.

"Do you have a knife on you?" Lynch asked. The man drew aside his coat and showed Lynch that he did. "If I saw that despicable traitor walk into this bar, I'd ask to borrow it."

"So, he's not a friend," the man looked keenly into Lynch's eyes. "Ah." Lynch reeled him in. "We once were. Close we were too, until he turned the Shadlows in to the police. Then we were all done for."

"How is it that you weren't caught, then?"

"I went north to Dublin and changed me name."

"What was it back then?" the man was now involved in Lynch's story and hanging on every word.

"Reagan, I'm sorry to say." The man looked shocked and confused. "Aye," Lynch had been considering his next move carefully. It was the quickest way to find the Shadlows, but also the most dangerous. His ruse could be undone at almost any time, since the robbery he had professed to being involved in was now legend among the Irish ex- patriots. "Regrettably," Lynch paused theatrically for effect, "Clive Reagan is me brother."

"You mean, he was your brother." The man said, ending the conversation.

Chapter 18

No Problem's Stables were dark and crypt silent. The stable boy had forgotten to light the lamp so Red set about finding matches and when lit, the lamp threw weak shadows about the barn. The few horses stabled there shuffled and sniffed the air, curious.

After Joe was taken to the hospital Red along with the sheriff had returned to Joe's stable. Sharing their suspicions, they took a careful inventory of the scene, noting amongst other things the boot print on the floor which appeared to have been made before the blood had congealed. Now, after hearing what Joe had told him of the events of that night, things were slightly clearer. Clearer perhaps for him, but if he was correct, more dangerous for Daniel.

Carrying the lamp with him Red stood at the door to the small room where Joe slept. Considering what Joe had told him about the events of the night he was attacked, it was shocking to think that Harry would just leave Joe there on the floor to die.

Red had no illusions about Harry Rich. They had plenty of history and had been friends, of sorts. But, though that was all in the past, Red knew the man and knew that Harry was not a callous person. He was many other things, all true. But doing something such as this? It was not in his nature. Or was it? Red felt that there was something deeper at the root of his behavior, and that led him to wonder who the other man with Harry was. And, why were they there? Possibly Joe knew but he didn't say. Red had his suspicions though, and they involved Daniel deeply.

Joe's room seemed like a tiny tomb. He was no longer a presence here. Neither in this place, nor in this world. So much gone forever. Red sighed sadly, remembering the countless nights they had talked and laughed until the whiskey bottle was empty and reminisced on the many secrets and stories that would die along with Joe. He felt Joe's loss deeply, comparable only to the loss of his wife and infant son.

Wiping the tears from his cheek he blew his nose on his clean handkerchief. He would miss Joe. Gradually a new emotion rose in him like a deep breath exhaled. Joe's death made him angry. And what if Harry was the cause?

Following Joe's instructions, Red did as Joe had requested and using a small knife tore open Joe's pillow and felt around in the lumpy stuffing. He was wondering how Joe could suffer such a horrible lumpy thing on which to rest his head when he felt two hard objects, balled tightly, tied with string. His hands trembled as he opened them. Each package contained a tightly folded dun colored envelope. One was Joe's will; it said so on the envelope. The other, a heavier envelope, was addressed to Daniel.

*   *   *

"It's nice of you to take me in like this, Mister Doyle," Patrick said, sincerely. "I'm very grateful."

"Well it's the least we can do." Jimmy Doyle took Patrick's small bag containing some thread bare clothing given to him by the friars. "Them priests speak highly of you, and Gemma trusts them. She's a devout Catholic. Got it from her mother, not me," he sniggered. Patrick smiled sympathetically. "She works in a bar down in the Bowery. Low life place. But, she's payin' the rent. More than her brother does, to be sure. He's a good boy. Just a mite lazy." Jimmy Doyle led Patrick up the steps of the four-story tenement. The interior of the building was noisy, crowded and full of smells. The walls were cracked and peeling, the stairs, rickety in places. "Best you not hold onto the railing too much," Jimmy Doyle advised, stopping on the stairs to make his point. "It's liable to give way."

"I'm thankful for the advice, Mister Doyle."

"Call me Jimmy. Everyone does. Here we are," he said, out of breath, opening the door onto a cramped, two-room apartment.

"You can sleep on that cot over there." He pointed to an army cot with a blanket on top. "Sorry that I don't have a pillow fer ya," he held his hands wide. "We're not that kind of hotel, you see," laughing at the expression on Patrick's face. "Come on lad, settle yourself in. I've some soup I can heat up fer ya."

"No. No, thank you all the same Jimmy. I dinna wish to be any trouble." Patrick noticed how his accent had reappeared. The door opened and a beefy fellow entered removing a blood-stained apron. He was a surly sort and eyed Patrick suspiciously.

"Ah, and this is my son, Brendan. Brendan, this is? What did you say your name was?" There came an uncomfortable silence as Patrick hurriedly reviewed the implications of his answer.

"Patrick Carrington," he said boldly and held out his hand.

Brendan gave his hand a fleeting shake.

"Got any food, dud?" he asked, walking into the small kitchen.

"Yes, you do," he said, helping himself to the soup.

"Save some for our guest, Brendan. He's on the mend from pneumonia."

"Another one of them friar's pets, is he?" Brendan inhaled his soup. Finished, he strode to the door and turned back to Patrick. "What did you say your name was again?"

"Patrick, Patrick Carrington."

"Alright then." He closed the door behind him and as he did, they heard heated words coming from the outside on the stairs. The door burst open and a winsome girl barely out of her teens walked in flushed and wild-looking. She had red hair of the kind that shone as if spun silver ran through it, hanging in twisted curls to her shoulders framing her freckled face.

"Arhhh! That son of yours. Are you sure you're the father, dud?" she hugged him, kissing him on the cheek and then noticed Patrick. Releasing her father, she held out her hand to Patrick beaming him a smile. "And you must be our boarder? I'm Gemma," she said.

"I'm Patrick," he mumbled. They looked at each other for a moment and in that look volumes were spoken. Patrick felt himself break out in a sweat, her smile affected him so.

"Are you going to faint?" she asked, pulling up a chair for him. "I know you've been sick. Father John told me you had pneumonia." Patrick looked up at her vacantly, he couldn't think of anything to say.

"There you go again, Gemma. You gone and struck another man dumb," Jimmy laughed. "Let me make us all a cup of tea," Jimmy said, smiling as he went into the kitchen and fiddled with the kettle.

Gemma sat across from Patrick holding his gaze. He was unable to look away. They didn't speak. Didn't need to. Like two old friends just happy to be with each other again.

"Here's your tea, Patrick. I didn't have milk so I hope you like it black." Jimmy gave Gemma a wink, smiling devilishly. "I already told him we're not that kind of hotel," he said, laughing and slapped Patrick on the shoulder. "Good to have you here, son. Make him feel at home, Gemma."

Gemma smiled at her father. "I'll do my best to make him feel at home, dud."

Jimmy Doyle wrestled with his coat. "I'm off down to the corner shop. Wouldn't have a few coins to help me along, would you?" Gemma pursed her lips, reached into her pocket and counted out some coins.

"Here!" she said handing her father the coins. "Don't drink it all. Remember to bring back some eggs and milk." She said to the closing door.

"Well that's the last we'll see of him for a while." Gemma moved her chair closer to Patrick's.

"Why don't you tell me about yourself, Patrick Thadlow?"

*   *   *

The office of the Pinkerton's Detective Agency was in the center of the city, in one of the tall building that rose up out of the ground, like sunflowers. Lynch hoped that Rafferty had been thrown off by the note the young man at the hotel had given him stating that Lynch was ill and indisposed. He needed to establish the credentials of the man who was wasting his time and leading him around the city by the nose.

As he had done many times, he stood to the side of the door after entering, making a show of fumbling for something in his coat pocket and dropping his cane. A young woman in her twenties, hearing the clatter of the walking stick on the stone floor, hurried to pick up his cane, concern on her pretty face.

"Can I help you, sir? You look like you've lost something."

Lynch gave her his least frightening smile knowing the reaction it would have. Pulling out his Irish Police badge, he handed it to her as he searched his pockets again.

"Oh, I see you're from the Irish Police, sir." Lynch looked up and held out his hand for the badge which she handed back with a smile.

He smiled at her again. "I had the name here of a fellow I wanted to look up while I was in your fair city. I had his card here somewhere."

"Come and sit here. Perhaps I can help you find your friend."

"Oh, he's not my friend really. A friend of a friend, you might say." Lynch sat in the offered chair, taking in his surroundings. "This is quite a business you have here."

"Yes, sir. We have detectives in every city in the United States. There are a lot of dishonest people out there, so business is good." She laughed a splendid laugh. "Now, how can I help you find your friend? What is his name?"

"P. Rafferty. I'm not sure of his first name."

"Let me see what I can do." She stood and walked to a long bank of filing cabinets searching until she found what she wanted. Lynch watched her, she was tall and slender, much different from Irish girls. She spoke with a man at another desk and pointed toward Lynch. The man looked hard at Lynch and stone-faced, accompanied her back to her desk. "Good morning, sir. My name is Griffin. Would you follow me, please? I may be able to help you."

Lynch followed the man into a small, wood-paneled office with electric lighting and a desk neatly stacked with file folders and wanted posters. "Please sit down." Lynch did and waited for the man to speak again. "Who are you, and what is your interest in Peter Rafferty?"

Lynch handed over his badge and his official papers. The man studied them and handed them back. "Mister Lynch. Or should I say Sergeant Lynch. The man you are asking about was once employed by our company. He was one of our best detectives but, unfortunately, he is no longer with us."

"Was he fired?" Lynch asked and was surprised by the length of time it took for the man to respond. When he did speak, his voice trembled.

"No. He wasn't fired." The man took a deep breath before speaking again. "He was my friend, and he was murdered. The man you are associating with is impersonating Peter Rafferty and I'd stay as far away from this man as possible if I were you, Sergeant Lynch."

Chapter 19

The restaurant's plush dining room was crowded with the typical representatives of the overindulged segment of Washington society. In rarified seclusion, they boisterously toasted each other's power and flaunted their wealth far from the eyes of the voters. Insensitive, inept and inbred is how Daniel saw these political clowns cavorting in their circus. Except for the lack of powdered wigs, the American system of democracy differed little from the centuries' long, unjustified entrenchment of the rich in England and Ireland.

The mood at Daniel's table was somber. The Congressional voting had not gone well for the silver industry and the political decisions being made affected the livelihood of thousands of men and their families dependent on them. Should the vote in the Senate be upheld, the result would mean a major redistribution of populations forcing tens of thousands of desperate, unskilled men and women to traipse about the western states looking for work. It was a dire situation and the grave implications weighed on all of them.

Wheeler had been polite but subdued through dinner, allowing Claire Cavendish to carry the burden of the conversation.

"Is there any chance that there might be a second vote, Bill?"

Bill Cavendish shook his head. "I'm sorry, Jerome, but we simply don't have the numbers." Bill looked at his friend sympathetically. "And, I doubt the president is going to veto the bill." The Senator patted Jerome's hand to garner Jerome's complete attention. "I'm sad to say, my old friend, the great silver boom is over. But, looking on the brighter side, I assure you there will be more mineral booms in the future." He held Jerome's hand until Jerome relented and smiled. "That's better. I say we have another bottle of wine," he signaled the waiter. "If we're going to be depressed, we should be drunk too."

Jerome held up his hand. "No thanks, Bill. I've made up my mind. Daniel, I want you to go back to Chicago tomorrow and pack up the Silver Queen. If they're going to try to put me out of business, they should think again. I won't go down without a fight." Jerome signaled for the check. "I'm sorry to break up this lovely, maudlin evening, but I want to be clear-headed in the morning. I have work to do."

The waiter came with the check and Wheeler handed him a large denomination note and waved him off with a smile. "Thank you, waiter. We had a lovely dinner." He leaned across to Daniel. "Always be grateful. Especially when times are bad. Remember that."

"We can't let you go off like this, Jerome." Bill tapped Claire on the wrist. "Let's share a cab. We can enjoy the sights together."

The night was chilly and the atmosphere in the cab even more severe. Wheeler hunkered down in his coat with his collar about his ears deep in thought, while Bill and Claire all but disappeared under the blanket they shared. Bill quickly nodded off, leaving Claire and Daniel to share glances full of unspoken desire.

When they arrived at their hotel the footman opened the cab door and Wheeler and Daniel stepped down.

"When will you be leaving Washington, Jerome?" Claire asked. "I'm not sure yet, but soon. I have some things to do and I plan on staying in Washington until I get them done. It could take a day or two." Wheeler smiled at Bill Cavendish. "It depends on how many old favors I can call upon."

"What about Daniel? Are you sending him back to Chicago tomorrow?" Claire asked. Jerome looked at Daniel and then at Claire.

"Yes, and the sooner he gets there, the better," Wheeler said, seriously. "Come on young feller, we've a busy day ahead of us tomorrow." He took Daniel by the shoulders and turned him away from the dangerous, longing looks Claire and he were sharing. "Wish me luck." Wheeler said over his shoulder as he waved them off and steered Daniel up the hotel steps.

"Good luck, Jerome," they said in unison. Claire added. "We'll see you again before you leave, I hope?"

The cab clicked off and Claire cast a last look back at Daniel. "Who is Jerome hoping to meet tomorrow that's so important?" she asked her husband.

"The President."

"I really don't like Chicago. Have I told you that before, Ham?" Harry whined, looking out of the grubby window at the pedestrians dashing about in the rain. They were drinking in a dilapidated bar near the train station frequented by other vagabond workers from the Fair. "It's alright for you. You're inside out of the rain." Harry watched the scene outside, "I've never seen so much rain. And, I'm out in it all day long. Have I ever told you ...?"

"Shut up, Harry. You're monotonous."

"You don't even know what that word means."

"Shut up, Harry! If that little shit friend of yours doesn't show up soon you'll be a permanent piece of the landscape. In the mud, if you know what I mean." Hamlett gulped his beer. "You've earned some money. You should be happy. You can eat now." Hamlett laughed, loudly. Harry's job as a roustabout at the fairgrounds paid minimum but at least he didn't have to beg money from Hamlett anymore.

Harry pulled at his beard, "I think I'll go and get a shave and a haircut with all my new-found wealth." Hamlett considered him closely and shook his head.

"Not a good idea, Harry. Better you look like a grubby Mormon." Hamlett smiled his twisted smile. Hamlett picked up a discarded newspaper. "It says here that Congress has repealed the Sherman Act." He looked at Harry curiously. "That should put Leadville out of business I suppose?"

"A lot of towns are going to become ghost towns when silver mining ends." Harry looked out at the rain again. "Aspen will die, I imagine. Like all the rest."

"What about that big silver statue? They'll want to take it back to Colorado, I bet?"

"Maybe that'll get Daniel back here soon." Harry brightened. "We can tie him up and take him downtown to the Pinkerton's office, get our reward and be on our way. How's that for a plan?"

"I have no idea how you lived so long, Harry. I mean it."

"Do you have a better plan?"

Hamlett grinned. "What we should do is break his bones until he tells us what he did with your money." Hamlett considered Harry closely. "Do you have a problem with that?"

Harry blanched. He didn't like pain. Neither his, nor anyone else's. Never had. Hamlett watched him closely as Harry's need for survival dueled with the fate of the unwitting Daniel. Harry swallowed hard and took a gulp of his beer, steeling himself for his betrayal.

"Not if it stops you from killing me." Harry was clear on the outcome should his plan fail. "You're the boss." Harry said, with a smile.

"Don't you forget that, Harry." Hamlett leaned closer. "He'll tell us all he knows, I assure you."

Harry sipped his beer, now tainted with remorse.

Hamlett smiled his twisted smile. "We only have to wait for him to come back to Chicago."

*   *   *

"Mister Rafferty?" They were walking in the middle of the street side by side. It was quicker and easier than battling the morass of street vendors clogging the sidewalks. "What do you know of a group named the Fenians? Ever heard of them?"

"No," Rafferty replied. "Should I have?" Rafferty looked sideways at Lynch but kept walking.

"Mister Rafferty, if you had been diligent in your investigations, you should have heard that the Shadlows are members of the Fenians." Lynch looked sidelong at Rafferty. "They're terrorists, intent on ending the English occupation of Ireland. I would have thought it quite a good lead to follow." Lynch paused. "But then, I'm not part of a nationwide detective company, am I?"

Rafferty was trouble, Lynch knew it now. Possibly more than just trouble, he might also be a murderer. What Lynch had discovered from his new friends in the Bowery was what he already suspected. That

Patrick Shadlow was either on his way to New York, or already in the city.

His communication with Killeen was via the Bank of England and through them he had sent a letter detailing his progress and what he had discovered. That was two days ago, before his suspicions about Rafferty were confirmed. No reply would come for at least two weeks so until then he had to make his own way, for better or worse.

"Come on with me, I want to show you something," Lynch said, noting that Rafferty was increasingly nervous the deeper they went into the Bowery. Lynch was delighted. They stopped at the entrance of Finbarr's. Rafferty hesitated.

"Something wrong, Mister Rafferty?" Rafferty stood at the top of the steps, deliberating. Lynch watched him closely.

"Why bring me here, Mister Lynch? There's nothing to be learned in a cesspool like this."

"Aye, that's most likely. But I've heard one might find some of the Fenians here, and I am a curious man." Rafferty looked up and down the alley before following Lynch down into the bar. Lynch pulled open the door for Rafferty, smiling at him. "Where I come from in Ireland, whiskey and beer set tongues wagging. Where better to find out information about Mister Shadlow, eh?" Lynch held the door open knowing that the first person to enter would garner the most attention and Lynch wanted the bartender to get a clear look at Rafferty. "After you, Mister Rafferty."

It was as Lynch had expected it would be, dark and quiet. It became even quieter when Rafferty entered. Pretending to drop his cane, Lynch bent down, giving everyone at the bar a good look at Rafferty.

"Why don't we sit over there, Mister Rafferty?" Lynch pointed to the least dark booth against the wall. "I'll go and get us drinks." Lynch limped to the bar and spoke to the bartender making sure that he was not overheard.

"Could you do me a favor?"

"Besides pouring your beer?"

"Aye. Can you find out who the man sitting with me is?" Lynch passed a ten-dollar note across the bar.

"I don't have change for that!"

"Sshh." Lynch signaled the bartender closer. "Take it. It's for the widahs and orphans," Lynch winked at the bartender, "of the war." Lynch pushed the bill under the bartender's hand, turning to walk away. "I'll be back later."

Chapter 20

Daniel was becoming increasingly nervous, constantly glancing up at the overhead clock. Wheeler had insisted on accompanying him to his train which was due to depart for Chicago, eight o'clock. They stood together awkwardly on the platform crowded with other travelers and families saying their farewells. He would've preferred to have been there alone, better to make his escape. Blessedly, the train's whistle blew promptly and the conductor hurried the stragglers aboard.

"There you are, my boy. Off you go. Make sure that you pack the Queen up in the exact same crates that it came in, eh? Make sure you count them too. I don't want any to go missing." Wheeler extended his hand to Daniel and they shook hands.

"Yes, Mister Wheeler. I'll do the best I can."

"I'm sure you will. I'm counting on you, son." Wheeler said as watched Daniel boarded the train carrying his one suitcase.

"Good luck with the president." Daniel yelled, as the conductor read his ticket and directed him to his seat. The whistle blew again and the train chugged into motion. Daniel made a point of waving to Wheeler as the train drew away from the station hoping that Wheeler would turn and walk away immediately. He did just that.

When Daniel saw Wheeler turn to leave, he grabbed his suitcase and dashed to the rear door of the carriage. The train was picking up speed and was almost at a horse's gallop. He opened the door and was about to leap when he felt a hand on his shoulder.

"Whady'a think yo' doin'? Yo' gonna kill yo'self," the conductor said, alarmed. Daniel shook him off.

"I forgot something," he said, throwing his suitcase off the train. They had cleared the platform and were travelling over the rough broken rocks of the rail bed passing in a blur. He made his decision and with only one look back, leapt from the train and rolled out of the way of the grinding wheels. When he stood, he looked at the departing train and the conductor scratching his head.

"Lordy, I hope that woman is worth it," the conductor mumbled and went on about his business.

Luckily, few people saw him scramble back onto the platform and of those few, nobody gave him a second look. Hurrying to the closest toilet he appraised his appearance. His coat had a tear on the left elbow and another on the knee of his pants, but other than a scrape on his knee he was disheveled but unharmed. Finding an empty stall, he quickly he changed his clothes and discarded the torn coat and trousers as he rushed for the ticket counter.

"I would like a ticket on the next train to New York please." The man on the other side of the grill looked up at the clock.

"Train leaves in twenty minutes," he said. "When does it get to New York?"

"Tomorrow morning, at eleven o'clock."

It was a great risk he was taking and the magnitude of it rose in his mind as did the danger. Eventually the train's whistle screamed and it slowly pulled away from the station, taking Daniel on the most important journey of his life: to reunite with his mother and sister. But first, he had to find them.

*   *   *

The sign above the door of O'Malley's Pub read, Sein Fein.

"This is where I work," Gemma said, opening the door. Noting Patrick's hesitation, she smiled at him. "I'm not a prostitute, if that's what you're t'inkin'."

Gemma laughed and led him into the bar, crowded even though it was barely noon. It was a rough place judging from the clientele, with a wide window facing the street and a row of stools along the length of the bar.

"I like that." Patrick pointed to a sign above the bar. It read,

Bad Food. Bad Service.
No Expectations. No Hope.
Irish welcomed.

"Sein Fein is an invitation to anyone wanting a Republican Ireland," Gemma said unnecessarily, leading him along the length of the bar. "It's a Republican bar as you might have guessed. If anyone has news from Erin, this would be the place you'd hear it first. Come, meet my brother."

Brendan sat at the bar, beer in hand, drinking with heavyset brogue speaking friends, coalmen judging by their smudged faces and blackened clothing.

"Bren," she tapped him on the shoulder. "This is Patrick. Did you meet him?" Brendan gave Patrick a quick look and turned back to his drink. "Yeah, I did." Brendan sniggered. "He's another of them strays you bring home from the church." He turned and gave Patrick a hard look. "I even doubt he's an Irishman with the name Carrington."

Gemma looked at Patrick curiously, "I thought yer name was Thadlow?" Brendan turned to face Patrick, suddenly very interested.

"That's not the name he told me," Brendan said. Gemma was suddenly suspicious.

Alarmed by the trap he had set for himself, Patrick abruptly turned and headed for the door.

"Wait," Gemma said, following after him. She caught him out on the sidewalk and slowed him down. "Where do you think you're going, Patrick? You don't know where you are and you have no place to stay. Please, stop walking away from me."

Patrick's panic ebbed and he slowed, allowing Gemma to catch up to him. Drained by his poor health he leaned against a wall; his panic having sapped his strength. Gemma stood close but apart, looking concerned and worried. Patrick braved a smile.

"I'm sorry, Gemma. I had to get out of there."

"I don't like being lied to," she said, fiercely. A minute passed like a season. Patrick kept his eyes on the ground, his dulled wits striking him mute. When he finally faced her, she was looking at him not with condemnation, but with curiosity. "Who are you, really?"

Patrick shook his head. Gemma shook her head also and with a sigh turned and walked away, confused and frustrated by his silence.

"Gemma, don't go!" he called after her. But Gemma didn't look back. "Please," he said loudly. "I have no one else to turn to. I need a friend." Gemma stopped walking and turned back to face him, her face filled with doubts. She'd liked Patrick from the very start. For what reason, she had no answer, but the feeling was there. She couldn't help but feel for him. His tears melted her heart. His shoulders slumped as if bearing the weight of his life's burdens. He looked so lost, so very, very lost.

"I'll think about it," she said, softening. "But only after you tell me what's going on with you." She tapped her forefinger on the tip of his nose. "The truth! You promise?" He nodded, tiredly.

"Can we go someplace quiet?" Gemma looked unconvinced, but she relented.

"Let's go to the park. It's not far. You can tell me everything there."

*   *   *

The bartender gave him a fierce look when Lynch sat down. Several hard men also shot him menacing glares meant to give warning in an unmistakable manner.

"You've got some balls coming back, I'll say that fer ye," the bartender said. "You're not popular here, I'd say."

Lynch smiled. "I doubt you'd be wrong."

"Them men that was here? They wanted to kill you both," the bartender said. "Not that I was inclined to stop them." The bartender smiled.

"I want to thank you for not letting that happen." Lynch laughed, as did the bartender. "Did you give the money to the widahs and children's fund?" Lynch asked. The bartender smiled and patted his pocket. Lynch ordered a beer and sipped as the bartender went about serving the other customers. When he found a chance, he ambled over to Lynch, conspicuously wiping down the surface of the bar.

"Where did you meet that feller?" the bartender asked quietly.

"He said he was working for the Pinkerton's Detective Agency. Do you know of it?"

"That'll be the day," the bartender laughed. "If that's the case, I'm glad that you brought him in here," the bartender angled his head. "Might have saved your life."

"How's that?"

"Since you mentioned that business in Dublin, we've done some checking up on you, Mister Reagan. It seems that either you, or someone with your name, turned spigot to the cops and that's why the Shadlows were caught. What do you think about that, Mister Reagan?"

As carefully as he had prepared for this inquisition, Lynch still felt the crawling in his gut as he conjured the lie that would either see him in the gutter bleeding or lead him to his quarry.

"What I think," Lynch said, wrinkling the creases of the scar tissue around his mouth into a grotesque mask of pain. "Is that me brother, Clive, should rot in hell for the trouble he caused that brave, patriotic family. He had no right." Lynch said, vehemently pounding his fist on the bar top gathering looks. "And had no balls, giving them up to the police like he did." Lynch took out a kerchief and dabbed away his crocodile tears. "All I want now is to find them and apologize. As God is my witness, I was not the one that gave them up to the police."

From behind his kerchief Lynch watched the bartender closely. He had spent a career watching liars lie and he knew that the difficulty in lying was to do it convincingly. He wiped away another imaginary tear. With the disfigurement of his features, this small gesture almost always engendered sympathy. After a minute of repeatedly cleaning the same glass the bartender walked away and spoke with a group of men at the far end of the bar. They occasionally cast sidelong looks his way as he sipped his beer.

After a while, the bartender returned, wiping more dirty glasses with an equally dirty cloth. Like contenders in a boxing match, he and Lynch considered each other. Several times the bartender glanced at the men at the far end of the bar. A standoff.

"What would you say," the bartender said in a quietly, conspiratorial way. "What if I told you that your friend," he lowered his voice to a whisper and mimed the name of Patrick Shadlow, "might be, and I repeat, might be, here in New York?"

"Does Daniel write to Kate often, Shirley?" Josephine Wheeler asked across a round, polished table covered with poker chips. "How is he getting along in Chicago? He must be lonely."

Sitting around the large polished walnut dining table, a half dozen middle-aged, socially prominent women were enjoying their weekly poker game at the Wheelers' home on Francis Street. The Wheelers' owned the finest and tallest home in Aspen where, on a weekly basis, Mrs. Wheeler served a small luncheon buffet of delicate sandwiches, sherry, whiskey, cigars, poker and gossip.

Shirley was central to these little get-togethers. She, being the most prominent brothel keeper in the town, knew the town's dirty secrets which very often involved the husbands of the women present. That Shirley would be integral to these social poker games was a paradox. Women of their social status in larger cities would most probably not understand. But in a small booming city such as Aspen, knowing the thread of lies woven by the tycoons of the town was the fabric which held not only their marriages together, but the town also. And Shirley was the glue.

Though these little get-togethers were well known and invitations highly desired, Mrs. Wheeler would never admit publicly to these soirees. These little get-togethers were important to the town's social fabric. It was where she and her friends kept track of their husbands' dalliances. Through Shirley of course.

Sometimes, the gossip Shirley shared was painful to hear. Particularly for Josephine. Hearing how much time her husband spent at Shirley's brothels was difficult. But, all things considered, she deemed it manageable. Josephine Wheeler knew well of her husband's appetites, and when she could take him no more, she was happy to foist his appendage on some other woman. She just wanted to know who. Publicly she was devoid of jealousy, publicly the epitome of quiet sophistication. In other words, she hated Shirley.

"Does he write to her regularly?"

"Yes. Why do you ask?" Shirley considered Josephine Wheeler over her cards.

"Oh, I was wondering if he'd mentioned Senator Cavendish, or his wife."

"Yes, he's mentioned them. They're friends of Jerome's. Why do you ask?"

Mrs. Wheeler placed a card on the table and was dealt another. "Well, I hear that Claire Cavendish had set her eyes on your young Daniel." She looked at each of the ladies in turn, her intent undisguised. "I hear she's quite renowned for playing around with all of the young, handsome men in Washington."

Shirley could tell by her tone that Josephine Wheeler had something more to tell. "Are you saying that she has made advances on Daniel?" The air in the room stilled. The other women all looked up from their cards.

Josephine Wheeler knew she had a winning hand, and not just her cards. For these past years she had been in tow of Shirley Dore. Or whatever her real name was? Shirley was included in these gatherings only because she was the dispenser of the sordid gossip concerning their husbands and Mrs. Wheeler delighted that this time the tables had turned. "I'm not saying that she did, and I'm not saying that she didn't,"

Mrs. Wheeler paused to savor the moment. "I'm only saying that the woman's reputation has many tongues wagging in Washington." She looked around the table and lastly at Shirley. "If I was her husband, Senator Bill Cavendish, that is," she added for effect, arranging her cards, "I would've divorced her just on her reputation alone." Mrs. Wheeler brayed her horse laugh which no one else joined.

"Are you saying that Daniel is one of her lovers?" The effect was instantaneous. Every woman at the table saw the meaning and knew the intent of this conversation. There was no love lost between these two women, everyone knew it. Two champion boxers facing each other in the ring.

Mrs. Wheeler placed another card on the table accompanied by a stack of chips. "All I'm saying, is," she smiled, wanly, "that a young man as handsome and charming as young Daniel would be in danger of infidelity if he was ever left alone with that woman. From what I hear. That's all I'm saying." She put more chips on the table. "I raise you, Shirley," Mrs. Wheeler said triumphantly, increasing her wager. The other ladies, out of this game, sat mute.

"I'll see your bet," Shirley said, pushing a stack of chips into the center of the table. "And I doubt Kate has anything to worry about regarding Mrs. Cavendish. I'm sure Daniel will manage." Mrs. Wheeler lay down her cards and Shirley tossed hers on the table, having lost the hand. "Plus," Shirley said, as a parting salvo, "Your husband is there to take care of him. Isn't he?" Shirley scooped her remaining chips into her bag and stood to leave. "Well ladies, I must get back to work. I have a business to run. Thank you for a lovely afternoon."

Josephine Wheeler had knowingly planted a seed in Shirley's mind, and it was growing at an alarming rate.

Chapter 21

There was no sleeping on the train. It was noisy, drafty, cold, and rocked from side to side endlessly. There were moments that Daniel thought favorably of the luxury of lying in the swinging hammock in the Silver Queen car. It was equally noisy and drafty, but at least he could sleep.

Weary and disheveled, he arrived in New York's Central Station physically exhausted. Hawkers and barkers hawked and barked their wares both inside the building and outside in the street where the noisy traffic made that of Chicago seem comparatively peaceful.

After washing his face in the station's restroom and then storing his suitcase at the baggage claim he ordered breakfast in a café and gathered his wits. The task of finding his family in this chaotic metropolis was daunting, but refreshed by the coffee and sandwich he collected his thoughts.

Presuming that he could find them his plan was to hurry them to Chicago with him. What he was going to do with his family when they reached Chicago, he had no real idea and prayed inspiration would come to him before their arrival. He also hoped that Wheeler would never know he was absent. Guessing that Wheeler would have to wait several days to see the president before returning to Chicago, in his estimation, he had three days at most.

Taking the envelope with his family's last address he approached a cab. The driver was scratching his horse's nose speaking to it softly.

"Excuse me, sir. Do you know where this address is?" Daniel asked.

The driver read the address and looked at Daniel with misgivings.

"I do. It's down in Five Points."

"Can you take me there?" Perusing Daniel's mismatched pants and coat he gave Daniel a quizzical look.

"I vill. But … you vill give me ze money first," he said.

"Why do I have to give you the money first?"

"It's a bad area. Not safe for a man like me. Lots of gangs. Irish."

He spat on the ground emphasizing his point and continued stroking the neck and cheeks of his old horse. "And, how do I know a youngster like you," again looking Daniel up and down, "can pay me?" The cabbie smiled slyly, spreading his hands palms up. He shrugged.

"How much?" Daniel pulled out several bills from his wallet.

The cabbie smiled and quick as an adder, snatched the money from Daniel's hand. "Just about zis much," he said, smiling widely. "Come. Sit up vis me. You are new here. Zho," Jakob patted his horse's flank as he stepped into the driver's seat. "I give you a tour, for free."

Daniel climbed up next to the driver, appreciating the view from above the pedestrians. "I used to drive a wagon," he said. Jakob gave him a quick look.

"Vhere? In Ireland?" he laughed.

"No. In Colorado. Over mountain passes." The cabbie looked at him side-long. "In the winter." Daniel noticed the change in the cabbie's expression, it was in his eyes.

"You zeem young to be vandering about ze country. Vhy is it you come to New York? Are you hiding from zumzing?"

"No," Daniel forced a laugh, "I'm trying to find my family," he said, and received another sidelong look from the driver. It was several minutes before Daniel spoke again. "I haven't seen them in more than two years."

Jakob was a good man with an eye for the good in all men. He turned and looked at Daniel and when he saw the tears running down his cheek, he felt compassion for him. "My name is Jakob. Vhat is you name?"

"Daniel Carrington. It's good to meet you, Mister Jakob."

"Just call me Jakob," he laughed. "My last name you could not pronounce."

They rode shoulder to shoulder, rocking with the motion of the cab, traversing the trolley tracks, dodging the dozens of beer and coal delivery wagons clogging the streets. Daniel craned his neck to see the tops of the rising city buildings while Jakob answered his questions by the score.

The further into the city they rode, the darker the neighborhoods became. The people on the streets in these areas looked unwelcoming and wary. Daniel recognized their glowering glances and stares. They reminded him of the people in Leadville.

The streets were filthy. Stinking piles of rotting garbage as high as a man's head littered the sidewalks making them all but impassable and forcing pedestrians to walk in the street, clogging the roads even more. Colorful ribbons of washed clothes hung across narrower streets, draped over strands of rope, or the wires that carried electricity.

"Zee vhat I mean?" Jakob said, pointing to a man beating a woman with a heavy stick. "Don't pay it too much attention. Zhis is a place vhere a man eizher owns a whore, or is vun." A fistfight spilled out in the muddy street involving several scruffy men violently attacking each other, leaving one lying face down a pool of blood around his head mingling with the mud. "Just be grateful zhat it's not you, laying zhere in zhe mud." Jakob spoke quietly, touching his forefinger to his prominent nose.

Everywhere he looked crowds of people filled the narrow streets to overflowing. Masses of people of all shades went about their business moving in and out and around the shadows of the dilapidated tenement buildings, festooned with drying laundry. Deeper into the bowels of the city they went. Deeper and darker became the city.

"How is it zhat you haven't zeen your family for two years?"

Daniel considered his answer carefully. "I had to leave them here in New York."

"Vell zey should be happy to zee you zen," Jakob was probing.

"Yes?"

Jakob continued to observe Daniel as he maneuvered his cab through the congestion of beggars and grubby children playing in the street. "Zhis is the address vhat you gave me. Zhat building." Jakob pointed at a building whose cracked bricks and tilting fire escapes made it look more of a deadly challenge to descend than to risk burning in the fire. Jakob sensed Daniel's trepidation.

"I tell you vhat, Daniel." Jakob placed his hand on Daniel's arm to focus his attention. "I vill go around zhe block and come back here. If you find your family, come and tell me." He pulled on Daniel's sleeve to maintain his attention. "If you don't find zem, I take you back to the train station, OK?" Jakob smiled widely. "I doubt you would make it very far dressed like you are."

Daniel climbed down, uncomfortable in his surroundings, uncomfortable in his clothing and fearing the worst. Jakob recognized the fear and smiled at Daniel. "Go on. Go find zem. I'll come back here zoon. Come and tell me vhat happens, eh?" Jakob smiled and reached out his hand to Daniel. "Good luck, Daniel." They shook hands and Daniel was reminded of the way Red Corcoran shook hands, powerful and sincere. "By ze vay, Daniel is a gut name," he laughed, as he drove away.

As with a ship departing, stranding him on a lonely island, Daniel watched Jakob drive away. Coming out of his trance he was inundated by the noise of the city. The run-down tenements were the warrens of the damned that housed the teeming poor of New York. About him children played, eyeing him strangely, almost savagely. This was a foreign land to him.

Both sides of the narrow street were lined with similar buildings, leaning on each other, seemingly over-burdened by the humanity they harbored. For the fiftieth time, he reread the address on the envelope and walked up the steps and into a hell he'd never known existed. Like the structures about him, he felt oddly tilted as he pushed into the innards of the building.

In the entry way, he saw a series of empty cavities in the wall which had at one time been mailboxes and Daniel realized why no mail was received here. The crying of infants, mixed with yelling and screaming in languages Daniel had never heard before, increased in volume as Daniel climbed the stairs. Pungent smells of cooking and decay filtered through his nostrils and even the air in the building, stagnant and still, seemed clogged with them.

Standing outside of the door numbered 3C, his heart beat a tattoo in his chest. As he lifted his hand to knock a loud voice came from behind the door. He hesitated, listening. Suddenly the door burst open, and a large scruffy man in his thirties stood in the doorway looking down at Daniel menacingly.

"Whaddy'u want?" the man growled. Daniel withered under the man's malevolent gaze. He swallowed hard and forced a smile.

"I'm looking for Mister Hogan." Daniel's voice quavered. The man looked at him silently. "Mister John Hogan?" Daniel continued. "Does he live here?"

"Why are you looking fer him?"

Daniel showed him the envelope. "Is this his address?"

"Hey, Hogan! There's another bill collector here to see you." Laughing, he stepped past Daniel onto the stairs as John Hogan came swaying towards him. Daniel recognized him immediately, though he noted with alarm that John Hogan was not in good health and his face was ashen. But when he recognized Daniel his countenance brightened and twenty years fell off him magically.

"Oh my God! Daniel, you've come back!" Hogan exclaimed, hugging Daniel like he'd never been hugged before. This old man of diminutive size hugged like a goliath. When he finally let go of Daniel, tears were streaming down his cheeks. "Oh, your mother and sister are going to be so happy." He turned and led Daniel into a small living room. "Myra, Megan, come here. You have a visitor." Hogan giggled like a schoolgirl and held Daniel's hand tightly.

This was the moment Daniel had been dreaming of. The moment when he could again hold his mother and tell her of his undying love for her and his sister. This was the end of his quest, what he's been living and fighting for.

Megan was first into the room. "Daniel!" Megan screamed, rushing into his arms and throwing herself about him. Over her shoulder he saw his mother enter and he broke away.

"Oh, thank you God," his mother said, as Daniel scooped her up in his arms and showered her with kisses.

"So, this is the missing brother then?" A gruff voice said from the doorway. They all turned. Hogan cleared his throat noisily.

"Gill this is Daniel," Hogan said.

"Ah!" Gill intoned as if having finally solved a puzzle. Daniel felt the hair on the back of his neck prickle. He forced a smile and extended his hand. "Ah!" Gill said again taking Daniel's hand.

"Daniel Carrington, is it?" Gill asked. Daniel nodded. "Good," he said, and with a devilish grin turned and left, his heavy tread resounding on the stairs as he descended.

"Who's he?" Daniel asked, looking from Megan to Hogan.

"Oh, never mind him. He's Megan's friend," Hogan looked at Daniel weakly. "He pays some of the rent too." Hogan looked down at the floor then brightened. "This is a cause for celebration. You are all a family once again. Aren't you happy, Myra?"

But Myra was unable to answer. Her face was buried so deep into Daniel's chest that they were breathing as one, reunited at last.

"Sit down lad and tell us everything that's happened to you. I'm sure we'd all love to hear it, wouldn't we?" Daniel remained standing, his face a mix of emotions, his cheeks wet with tears.

"Mister Hogan, I'm sorry but I'm afraid we leave for Chicago as soon as we can." Both Megan and Myra looked stunned by this news but Daniel smiled to reassure them before he continued. "Mister Hogan, I cannot possibly tell you how much I owe to you for taking care of my family for all this time. And I know you haven't been receiving the money sent to you." Taking an envelope from his wallet he pressed it into John Hogan's hands. "Here, it's the money I owe you. Here, take it. I insist." Hogan reluctantly took it and held onto Daniel's hand, smiling broadly at him.

"You're a good son, Daniel Shadlow." Tears welled up in his eyes, "I knew you were."

"Can you all be packed by sunset?" Megan nodded, smiling, her arms about her mother. "Good! Let me go tell the cab driver. He's waiting for me." Daniel smiled reassuringly. "I'll be back," he said and raced back down the stairs.

Out in the street Jakob was nowhere in sight. Anxious minutes passed and Daniel was ready to panic when he saw the cab turning the corner. Striding quickly toward it he stepped on board before Jakob had stopped. Jakob noted the change in him.

"Ah. So, you found zhem? I can zee it on your face." Daniel smiled and nodded. "But, alzo I zink you are in zum trouble. Yes?" Jakob watched Daniel's smile disappear. "Let me ask you," Jakob leaned closer. "Did you meet a big man dressed in a green coat?" Daniel nodded. "Vell, I vaited a few moments. Not zhat I'm spying on you. But, I zee zhis big man, rush from zis building and run zhat vay." Jakob maneuvered his cab into the street. "Vell," he said with a grin, "I'm a curious man. All ve Jews are, and ve have developed a nose for trouble. Usually our own trouble," he smiled, "but it's a good zhing." Daniel was attempting to step out but Jakob stopped him. "Sit a moment, I have zumzing to tell you," he said.

"What is it?" Daniel asked, as they approached the corner.

"Zhat big man, he went in that saloon zhere," Jakob indicated a bar they were passing, "and when I vent past it, he was pointing back at vhere you vent. I zought to myself zhat vas strange. Vhat do you zhink Daniel? Are you in trouble?" Daniel remained silent, looking everywhere but at Jakob. Jakob nodded and smiled. "I zought zo."

The sign over the bar read O'Malleys Pub, and through the window Daniel saw Gill in animated conversation with several tough- looking men. Panic rose in him. What if, in finding his mother, what if Gill was planning to turn him in for the reward? He turned to look at Jakob and the fear on his face must have been alarming.

"Daniel," Jakob said, slapping the reins on the horse's back. "I zhink you should leave this place kvickly. I zink you are in great trouble and I get a bad feeling from zhat man." Jakob navigated the cab to the far end of the block. "Go back now and get your family," he pushed Daniel out of the cab. "I vill meet you here in vun hour."

Taking out his wallet Daniel withdrew a twenty dollar note and offered it to Jakob. Jakob laughed and tore the bill in half, handing one half back to Daniel. "You got a lot to learn my young friend." He held up his half of the bill and touched it to Daniel's half. "Zis is to make sure that you can trust me," he laughed and winked. "I zink you are in great need of a friend. Now, get your family." He shooed Daniel away, smiling.

"I zee you back here in vun hour. Now go!"

Daniel turned and bolted but as he did, he saw Gill and another man rush from the bar. He hid behind a fruit barrow as they rushed past him and alarmed, he watched as they hurriedly climbed into Jakob's cab. Jakob gave Daniel and smile and a shrug then touched his forefinger to his nose before clicking the horses off at a trot.

Needing to know more, Daniel took a deep breath and casually entered O'Malley's, sat down at the bar and ordered a beer. Even before the beer arrived, he'd overheard enough to know that Gill was no friend of his family.

He hurried back to Hogan's apartment, arriving flushed and out of breath. "John, we have to leave here as soon as we can." They all looked at him frightened. Holding his mother's hand, he spoke quickly and quietly. "Pack what you need, but please do it quickly."

"Why the rush, son?" Hogan asked. "You've only just arrived. Is something wrong?"

Controlling his fears over what he had observed and heard, he took a deep breath before continuing. "John, I can't tell you the reason, but we need to be ready to leave in an hour." Daniel saw that his mother was quavering. He took her in his arms and he held her to him, tightly. "Don't you worry mum, I'm not letting either of you go again." He gathered Megan into his embrace. "I promise you." He smiled reassuringly. "Now go pack."

After his mother and sister had left the room, Daniel motioned Hogan out onto the stairs and quietly told him of what he had seen and what he was planning to do.

"I want you to come with us, John."

Hogan smiled. "I'll be alright, Daniel. I know them. They'll not hurt me." He patted Daniel on the back. "Now go and wait for your cabbie. I doubt you'll ever see him again though."

"I think I will, John," Daniel held up the twenty-dollar bill torn in half. Hogan smiled.

"You're a smart lad, Daniel Shadlow," Hogan said, laughing.

*   *   *

A cool breeze chilled them as they walked through the park. Patrick was deep in thought weighing the possible outcomes of his confiding in Gemma Doyle. Father John was a friend to them both and he had given no cause for suspicion, but Patrick was rightfully suspicious of everyone. Gemma was already torn by her feelings for Patrick. He was someone out of the ordinary, someone who was more deeply wounded than she and had need of her. They found a quiet spot, a deserted bench by a small pond fed by a leaky creek. Gemma sat close and shoulders touching, felt him trembling. She heard him take a deep breath, letting it out in a long, sad sigh. When she looked at him again, his eyes were filled with pain.

"Carrington is not my real name, Gemma. It's Shadlow." Patrick watched her reaction. She held her breath. "I'm on the run from the police." He breathed deeply before continuing, "And I'm looking for my family. Their name is Carrington now."

"How can I help?" she asked, sincerely.

"Do you know where I can find some Irishmen called the Fenians?"

Gemma looked at him, silently. Seconds ticked by. They sat looking at each other, each holding back truths and secrets. Gemma took Patrick's hand in hers. Ducks flapped in the pond. Patrick turned away to watch them.

"I envy birds," he said softly. "They can spread their wings and fly away when there's trouble."

"Then you'll have to explain to me why it is that so many of them end up on our dinner tables?" She laughed and squeezed his hand, making him smile. It was the first smile that she had seen on his face and it delighted her. Cracked, chipped teeth, disfigured face, it mattered little when he smiled at her.

"Come," she said, pulling him to his feet. "I think I know where you might find your Fenians."

"Where are we going?"

"Down to the Bowery," she said merrily. "A place called O'Malley's. Nowhere else outside of Ireland will you meet a worse lot of men. It's another place where my brother goes to drink." Patrick looked concerned. She smiled at him. "Someone there will know about your Fenians, if anyone does." Patrick smiled at her and she stepped closer. "Come on. You can trust me."

Lighter of spirit, Patrick walked hand in hand with Gemma, through the verdant lanes of Central Park, joining the strolling lovers and the throngs of well-dressed women pushing babies. Sooner than he would have liked, they merged into the city with its traffic, noise, dirty air and danger. Like a lamb, she led him down into the depths of the teeming city, and willingly he went with her, hand in hand. Like a lamb to its slaughter, she led him.

Chapter 22

Sergeant Lynch no longer had any desire to keep Rafferty's company. He didn't know who Rafferty really was, but he did know what he was. He was a criminal and possibly a murderer. Another concern was his feeling that the Pinkertons considered the Shadlow case of low priority and as a result had very little helpful information. As far as he could tell, except for the mysterious Mister Rafferty, he was on his own.

Lynch was already waiting outside of Finbarr's when the bartender opened the front door. "You're an early drinker," he said, as Lynch followed him into the empty bar. Certain they were alone, Lynch fanned ten one-dollar bills across the bar. The bartender smiled at Lynch's reflection in the mirror. "Have you ever heard of the Fenians?" Lynch asked.

The man turned to face him. "Maybe," he said, reaching for the money.

"What do you know of the Shadlows?" Lynch asked, watching the man closely. The bartender smiled and though the bar was empty as a church on Monday, he looked both ways before answering.

"I heard that one of them is in the city looking for his family.
They live over in Five Points I heard."

"Is that so?" Lynch mulled.

"That's what I heard," the bartender obviously enjoyed sharing secrets. "And, I also heard that the youngest one is in the city too.

"What about that fellow I was with?"

"Don't know his name, but I hear word he's a bounty hunter."

"Where might I find the Shadlows?"

"Ask at O'Malley's."

Lynch took a ten-dollar bill from his wallet but did not hand it over. The bartender looked both ways and leaned closer. "I hear that there is someone spying on the mother and sister." The bartender smiled a knowing smile. "I imagine there'd be more than a few down there who'd happily turn their mother over to the police for handful of silver."

"O'Malley's, you said?" Lynch stood to leave.

"Aye. But what about that money you've got in yer hand?"

"Ah." Lynch put the ten-dollar note into his pocket and smiled. "First, let me see if your information is correct." Lynch said as he departed.

The bartender glowered at his back but pocketed the bills Lynch had left on the bar and smiled. He'd made more money off his first customer than he made in half a week.

*   *   *

Daniel stood on the corner frantically putting on a casual air. Doubt pulled at him. Doubt after doubt after doubt. Would Jakob come back? Would he bring that man, Gill, back with him? How long would it take? What if someone recognized him? On and on it went. He decided to buy some fruit but only had large bills, and that drew attention in this decidedly poor neighborhood. Overwhelmed, the vendor piled mounds of vegetables into a large sack and when Daniel tried to give the food away, he succeeded only in making a bigger scene.

"Hey zere, big shpender." Daniel turned, relieved at seeing Jakob. "Put it all in here. I take it as a tip." Gratefully Daniel climbed into the cab. "You must be in zum big shit. Zem fellers went right to the Pinkerton Detective place." Daniel looked alarmed. "Not to vorry. I told all zhe ozher cabbies zhat zhey refused to pay me. I zink zhey'll be a vhile getting back here." Daniel looked confused. "Go on. Go get your family." Jakob held up his half of the torn bill. "Zhis is not going to keep me here forever. I vill go around zee block zen come back. You be here. Understand? Go!"

Daniel raced up the stairs but stopped at the doorway and entered slowly not wanting to disturb the tender scene. They were such a pitiful group. Something a Dutch master painter might try to capture on canvas. A scene he would always remember.

"There, there Myra," Hogan was saying, sitting with her on a threadbare couch, his arms around her holding her tenderly, gently smoothing her hair. Daniel saw that Hogan smiled at his mother in a most loving and tender way.

"You've been so kind to us John," she said, raising her head to look at him. "I don't know how we can ever repay your kindness."

It had been such a long time since Daniel had seen his mother that his memories of her and reality collided. She was smaller and thinner than he remembered, her eyes had become cloudy and grey. A shudder of love unspoken rose through him sending a spiral of shivers up his spine. He swallowed hard and squared his shoulders.

"Daniel," he felt a tug on his sleeve. "Will we be coming back here?" Megan asked. Daniel took her in his arms and looking at Hogan included him in his response.

"I doubt it very much," he said. "Mister Hogan, I really wish you would change your mind. I have enough money for us all to start a new life in Colorado."

Hogan smiled and stood. Helping Myra to her feet he took her and Megan in his arms and hugged them fiercely. Tears flooded his eyes and he shook his head to shake them off. He took their hands in his.

Hogan looked at Myra with the depth of sadness that the Irish had mastered. "I'm afraid I'm too old to be starting out anew." Volumes of unfulfilled love, unspoken, unexpressed. Hogan took Myra in his arms and kissed her on the lips. "Ah," he said, to answer Myra's surprised look. "I've been wanting to do that since I met you, Myra Shadlow," he said, smiling broadly, bravely. Myra smiled back at him, loving the man who loved her. "Now let's get you all to safety," Hogan said, brushing off the gloom.

Leading the way, Daniel carried the two small suitcases that Megan had packed as they walked slowly down the stairs. The children still played and the world barely noticed them leaving, and for that Daniel was grateful.

Outside in the street the messy chaos of life clattered past them as they gathered in a small clutch, hiding their faces. Minutes passed with Daniel anxiously looking up and down the street for Jakob. Then he saw him.

"Here's Jakob," he announced to his small brood. "John, we're going to have to go now. Unless you'll come with us."

Hogan shook his head and bravely walked with Myra to the cab as it stopped for them. Daniel helped Megan into the cab and then helped Hogan assist his mother. "Jakob this is my mother and sister."

"It's a pleasure to meet you. Have I met all of your family now, Daniel?"

No," Daniel said. "This is John Hogan. He's a very special part of our family." Hogan reached up and shook Jakob's hand.

"You don't have a brozer, do you?" Jakob asked, looking at Daniel.

Daniel and Hogan looked at each other. "Why do you ask?" Jakob shrugged his shoulders.

"Zumzhing I heard from zhose men I took to Pinkerton's."

"But that's not possible," Daniel said, equally amazed and confused. Hogan patted him on the back and leaned in closer.

"I'll find out whether it's true or not," Hogan said quietly to Daniel. "If it is, where should I send him?"

Daniel hurriedly took out more money from his thinning wallet. "Here's some money for him to get a train ticket to Colorado." He leaned closer. "Tell him to come to Aspen," he whispered into Hogan's ear. "We'll be there." Pushing the money into Hogan's pocket he felt a profound surge of love for the man a who had saved his family from starvation and worse. He hugged him again so hard and sincerely, that Hogan laughed and pushed him away.

"Off you all go," Hogan said bravely, holding onto Myra's hand until the cab pulled away. "Have a safe trip and a happy life to all of you," he yelled as they departed and continued waving until he was lost from sight. When Daniel turned back his mother was crying. Megan and Daniel sat on either side of her and wrapped their arms around her, comforting her.

"Vhere are ve going, Daniel?" Jakob asked.

Daniel sat back and considered the rumor that his brother may also be here in the city. It was unbelievable news, wonderful if it was true. But what if it was not? Time was still his greatest enemy. How much time did he have to return to Chicago before Wheeler discovered his absence?

"Take us to Central Station, please." Jakob turned, smiling.

"I zink zat's a very good idea. Zumtimes, running from trouble is the visest zhing to do." He laughed out loud. "Zat's vat has kept me alive. Mazel tov!"

Draped in their worries they drove through the streets of the teeming city. Myra slowly regained her composure. Daniel could only imagine how attached she must have become to John Hogan and wondered if Hogan had told Myra or Megan of Paddy's death.

Jakob stopped the cab outside the train station. "I vill vait here for you."

Daniel walked briskly into the station to the ticket window. "When is the next train to Chicago, please?" The man behind the grate looked at his timetable.

"Eight tomorrow morning."

"Shit!" Daniel said, causing the man to look at him harshly. "Isn't there one leaving earlier?" The man shook his head.

"There are. But they're all full. You've heard of The World Fair, haven't you?" Daniel nodded. "That's why the trains to Chicago are all full."

"I'll take three tickets please," he said, handing the man much of his remaining money. The man issued the tickets which Daniel read and then put into his inside pocket of his coat. "Eight o'clock?" The bored man nodded. "Thank you," he said and dashed back through the terminal to the cab.

"Where can we get a cheap place to stay for the night, Jakob?" Jakob thought awhile. "How much money do you have?"

Chapter 23

Gemma led Patrick from the park, down into the lower part of the city, past places he would never want to ever see again. The further they ventured, the worse became the condition of the muddy streets and of those who sloshed about in them. They were harassed by several groups of feral youths who leered at Gemma and made obscene gestures, but from his experiences in prison Patrick knew they were of little real threat. Abruptly, Gemma stopped and braced her arm firmly across Patrick's chest. They were emerging from a fetid alleyway, in the shadow of a building and across the busy street he saw the entrance to O'Malley's. Gemma was suddenly nervous.

"Let me go in alone. If I don't come out right away, don't be worried." She looked up into Patrick's eyes with a twinkle in hers. "I'm sure someone in there will be willing to buy a lass a drink." Gemma winked and smiled at Patrick and kissed him on the cheek before dashing off through the traffic.

She entered O'Malleys and Patrick leaned back against the wall and watched the door. A man exiting the bar caught his eye. Once a tall man but now bent by infirmity, the man limped and used a walking stick. It was what he did that caught Patrick's attention. Oddly, he furtively looked up and down the avenue both ways, twice, before turning left and hurrying off, glancing back over his shoulder several times as if avoiding someone.

Patrick's curiosity was besting him and he was considering leaving the safety of the wall when Gemma rushed out of O'Malley's, crossing the street at a run.

"Come with me," she demanded, grabbing his hand. Patrick was hesitant. She was insistent. "There's talk of a man named Hogan and he's hiding your family." She pulled at him to follow her. "Come on," she said, "I've got the address where they are."

"How do you know this, Gemma?" Patrick hurried along after her. They turned the corner onto the Avenue and Patrick stopped walking. Gemma came back to him.

"What's wrong? Don't you want to see you family again?"

"What happened, Gemma?" Patrick watched her closely. "In O'Malley's? What happened?" When she looked at him again the shine had gone from her eyes.

"Are you not trustin' me now?" she screamed at him angrily. Shocked, Patrick stepped closer to her, wishing that she would not be so loud. He reached for her. She pulled away from him. Patrick looked around, only two people were paying them any attention but they soon went about the business of ignoring them.

Without warning, Patrick pulled Gemma to him and enveloped her in a passionate embrace. Over Gemma's shoulder Patrick had seen the old man with the cane turn and walk back towards them searching the addresses on the buildings. Through half-closed eyes, he watched the man walk past them and again noted the limp and the burns on his face. Both were odd, and strangely familiar too. He tried to detach himself from Gemma, but she was having none of it.

"God almighty, but you're a good kisser. Come here! I want some more of that," she said with a smile. "And here I was, thinking that you were one of John's lover boys." Enthusiastically, Gemma threw her arms around Patrick's neck, but he pulled away, looking for the old man, but he had vanished.

"Come on Gemma, quickly," he said, pulling her along with him. "Why?" Gemma asked, pulling her hand back, confused by his change.

"Come with me." Patrick took hold of her hand again and hurried her across the street. Following ten paces behind the man with the limp, Patrick pointed at him. "Have you ever seen that man before?" Gemma shook her head and continued to let herself be dragged along, following the man with the limp. He was looking at the buildings, reading the numbers over their doors. Abruptly, he stopped and entered one of them. "Gemma, please tell me that that is not the same building that we're looking for?" Patrick pointed to the building. Gemma nodded; her expression quizzical. "I get a feeling he's trouble," he said, and felt Gemma affectionately squeeze his hand. He did his best to smile. "Now tell me," he said calmly, quietly. "What did you hear in O'Malley's?"

"Just what I told you, I heard," she said, troubled by the tremors in his hands and the look on his face, a dangerous look, furtive. "I heard they were with a man named Hogan. And that," she pointed at the building across the street "is his address." Patrick wondered how she found this information and was about to voice the question. "They talked about a reward, too," she continued, her voice tapering off. Patrick didn't hear the last part, though in hindsight he should have. It might have saved he and his family a world of trouble.

Taking Gemma's hand, he led her across the avenue. But, as they approached the building, a man in a long coat and hat suddenly emerged and ran down the avenue away from them. "I have a feeling that we're not the first ones to come visiting today."

There came a flurry of activity around the stoop of the building. Amid shouts from the interior of the building, the man with the burned face appeared and pushed his way through the small crowd gathered in the doorway. For a second, no more, he looked directly at Patrick. It was a fleeting glance, almost not a glance at all, but there was recognition. The man pointedly took a second look before he hurried off down the avenue.

"Do you know him, Patrick?"

"No." Patrick lied. But he did know him. It was the eyes. In a flash of memory from the past he recognized the policeman who had testified against him in court. Even with the scars twisting the skin on his face Patrick knew exactly who he was and why he was here. He was absolutely, deadly sure of it.

Now Patrick noticed something different about him as he watched him hurry away. He was now walking with no noticeable limp with his cane hidden under his long coat. Something was wrong, Patrick's senses told him.

"Come on. We have to find this man, Hogan," Patrick said, taking her hand as he ascended the steps.

Inside the building there was an ominous quiet. Soft crying came from somewhere on the floors above. "Does Mister Hogan live here?" he asked a girl of around ten years. She silently pointed up the stairs. Panic rose in Patrick's chest as they hurried up the stairs. The weeping became louder. The half-dozen people they passed on the stairs looked at them fearfully, wary, hostile.

On the third floor they found three people crowded around the open door to an apartment, peering in. Patrick and Gemma entered slowly and found a middle-aged woman tending to an older man, lying on the floor, blood pooling on the floor beneath him.

"What? Are there more of ya now?" she screamed. "Are you here to finish him off, are you?" Patrick put out his hands defensively.

"No, no, I'm looking for someone."

Gemma rushed to the injured man's side and helped hold the towel to his wounds. Patrick knelt at his side and took one of his hands in his.

"I'm looking for my mother and sister. Myra and Megan Carrington, I'm Patrick, her son." Suddenly Hogan's eyes opened and he clutched Patrick's arm, pulling him down closer to his face.

"Patrick Shadlow?" Hogan whispered. Patrick nodded. Hogan managed a smile, his eyes fluttered. Patrick looked at Gemma but Hogan pulled him back closer. "Daniel was here. He took them away."

"Where?" Patrick said, shocked. Though reeling from the surprise, Patrick remained calm and patient as Hogan drifted, then awakened. His eyes became bright and aware. He squeezed Patrick's arm harder, pulling him closer.

"Aspen, Colorado," he whispered into Patrick's ear. "Tell no one."

"Who did this?" Patrick asked.

"Dangerous man," Hogan labored a breath. "Looking for you … and your brother. … For the reward. … Be very careful. …Trust no one."

Patrick looked at the woman holding Hogan's head. She was a kindly woman with a sympathetic face, haggard and harried by her circumstances.

"What can I do for you?" he asked Hogan.

"Find them. … Keep them safe," Hogan was losing his grip on life and on Patrick's hand. "But be careful." Hogan's thinning voice trailed away.

Patrick inspected the wounds and found them severe, worse for a man of Hogan's age. There was little chance of survival. Whoever did this to John Hogan had showed little mercy.

Out on the landing two children peered inside the apartment curiously. They turned at the sound of fast approaching footsteps. Patrick looked over the balustrade and saw two men running up the stairs, already on the second-floor landing.

"Can I use your fire escape, please?" he said quietly to the elder of the two children. She nodded and they followed her into the nearest apartment where she pointed to the partly open window that led onto the fire escape.

Quickly, they climbed out onto the rickety, iron stairs and hurried as fast as they could down to the alley. Once on the street they ran in the opposite direction of O'Malley's and didn't stop until they had put a half mile between them and the men in Hogan's apartment.

*   *   *

"Come in Leafy, you don't have to knock," Shirley said, then saw that Leafy was out of breath. "What's wrong?" Leafy held onto the doorjamb, breathing deeply.

"Is Red here?" Leafy gasped.

"Yes, he is. Red!" Shirley called, leading Leafy inside. Red appeared from the kitchen and knew from the look on Leafy's face that something was not right.

"Has there been another collapse?" Red demanded.

"Oh, Lord, I hope nobody has gotten hurt," Shirley gasped.

"No, no. It's something different." Leafy took a deep breath. "Daniel's gone missing."

Shirley grabbed Leafy by the forearm and turned him to face her.

"What do you mean, missing?" she demanded. Red took a step closer.

"Wheeler sent a telegram to John Carter saying that Daniel did not return from Washington as he was supposed to. He said that Carter should come to Chicago to ship the Silver Queen back from the exhibition. Carter told me that I had control of all the production shifts." Leafy looked from Shirley to Red. "Only temporarily, he said."

"When is Carter going to Chicago?"

"He's already left, on the six o'clock train." Leafy said.

The door opened and Kate entered carrying her baby on her hip.

"Hi, everyone. Why the gloomy faces?"

"Kate, I think you had better come in here and sit down," Shirley led her to the settee and took the baby from her.

"What's wrong?"

"Kate, now I don't want you to be alarmed but Daniel has gone missing."

"What do you mean missing?" Kate said jumping to her feet.

"That's the same thing I asked. Why don't you sit back down? I don't know what all this means but I think I know how to get to the bottom of it." Shirley looked at Red. "I think I'll pay a visit to Mrs. Jerome Wheeler."

"Do you want me to come with you?" Kate asked.

"No, I don't think that's wise. Let me handle this. She may be more forthcoming without any witnesses."

"I'll drive you over," Red offered.

In the buggy, Red took the reins but before they drove off and with Kate watching from the window, Shirley placed a hand on Red's arm forcing him to look directly at her. "Red, I'm only letting you drive me if you promise not to come in." She waved to Kate. "Now smile and wave so Kate doesn't think there's anything to worry about."

Red did as he was told, as he always did, and waved at Kate as they drove away. "Does she have anything to worry about?"

"I guess we'll find out soon enough," Shirley said with a sigh. "But, there's nothing like going to the horse's mouth to get the truth, I say." Shirley smiled at Red. "My problem is, I've been talking to the wrong end of the horse for years. It's time I changed that."

Chapter 24

"There is a letter for you, Michael. I put it on your desk."

"Thank you, sergeant," Killeen said, heading for the stairs.

"It's from America."

At the top of the stairs he stopped at the desk of his recently returned adjutant.

"It's good to see you back at work, Constable Ivers. How are you feeling?"

Ivers ignored him, his face still bruised, his broken arm bound in a white plaster cast. Killeen disappeared into his office and Ivers went back to rearranging the papers on his desk. The tension between Killeen and his constable had descended to a barely tolerable level of disdain, and for the constable, pure dislike.

Killeen picked up the letter. It was addressed to him in a strong, legible hand with notations from the Bank of England's officers in New York. Slitting the envelope, he took out the single page and read what his man Lynch had discovered. It was brief.

Detective Killeen,

I have been in America for one week and have made some progress. Pinkerton detectives are unreliable, uninterested and unprofessional to this date. No sign of P. Shadlow. I have been gaining knowledge in small pieces. New York is very expensive can you send me more money?

I will write weekly to keep you informed.

Sincerely, J. Lynch.

With Lynch's letter in hand Killeen walked up the stairs to the chief inspector's office and knocked politely on the door jamb before entering. Ivers waved him in and invited him to sit.

"What have you heard from your man in America?" he looked up at Killeen. "I have to tell you that the Exchequer's office is none too pleased with this matter." Killeen handed the letter across the desk to his superior who read it quickly. "I see this was posted two weeks ago."

Killeen nodded in the affirmative. "What have you heard about this Patrick Shadlow?"

Killeen drew a deep breath as he took back Lynch's letter. "Since the incident where your son was injured, we've heard not even a whisper. I'm taking that to mean that he has fled to America." A long pause in the conversation followed while the men considered the problem and each other.

"I rather doubt that I can get much more money for your man Lynch. But I will try," Senior Chief Inspector Ivers said. "It's the least I can do." Killeen took this as a sign and stood to leave. "When can we expect to hear from your man Lynch again?"

"He said here that he would write weekly. I'll keep you informed, sir."

"Do that," he said, as Killeen reached the door, "and Killeen?

Don't spread this around." Killeen nodded and closed the door behind him.

Walking back down the stone steps to his office he motioned Sergeant Callahan to come up to his office and when he arrived, he closed the door.

"What is it, Michael?" the sergeant asked.

"Do you think Jimmy Lynch can be trusted? Fully?

*   *   *

The streets were merely muddy, rutted tracks in the poorer sections of the city. Dirty, scruffy children chased a small dog and Lynch wondered if it was from playfulness that they chased it or from hunger, since neither the dog nor the children looked as if they had eaten in weeks.

Cautious and on alert for Rafferty, he'd found his way to O'Malley's. It was early afternoon and the traffic on the street was at its peak. Dodging horses and wagons and looking both ways to ensure he was not being followed, he pushed open the door to the bar and entered. Lynch was used to being looked at and not being seen. His disfigurement was such that people mostly recoiled and then looked away out of respect, or something else. It was as though he was invisible and he had become adept at using it. As today, when he entered O'Malley's, everybody looked at him, but no one saw him.

He sat at the bar, ordered a beer and tuned his ears. The bartender paid him no heed and went back to his friends who were involved in a heated discussion. Separately, but nearby, was another group of men mostly laughing along with a woman who was the center of their attention.

With the skill of a seasoned actor, using his cane for show, he moved to a stool next to one of the men talking at the bar. The man turned to face him, none too pleased, but when he saw Lynch's face, he smiled weakly and went back to his conversation. It took less than two minutes for Lynch to find out what he'd hoped for. The men spoke in Celtic brogue in the false faith that they were speaking privately. They were incorrect.

There came a flurry of movement and Lynch saw one of the group of men talking with the young, red-haired woman who had just joined them. He paid them little attention until one of the men she was talking to made a lunge for her and grabbed her by the arm. Having heard all he needed, Lynch saw this moment as an opportunity to leave and headed for the door, but not before he saw the young woman being kissed by the man who had assaulted her.

Out in the street Lynch took his bearings and after looking either direction set off at a brisk pace to find the address he'd overheard. Just a number and a name, but it was the most information and the best clue he'd had so far. Eventually finding the building he was looking for he entered and asked a young girl for the apartment of Mister Hogan. The girl silently pointed up the stairs and held up three fingers. Lynch patted the girl on the head as he stepped onto the stairs.

Suddenly, there came a commotion from above and a man in a long coat came running down the stairs. Lynch hid under the staircase and watched Rafferty race out the front door of the building and dash across the avenue. Then, there came a wailing from above.

Lynch climbed the stairs as quickly as he could until he came to the open door of an apartment from where the crying came. On the floor lay a man with his head bashed and bleeding. A woman of older years knelt next to him crying and staunching the flowing blood.

"Is that Mister Hogan?" he asked. She nodded, sobbing.

"Why? Why, do you want to kill him?" the woman screamed at Lynch. "He's a good man," she wailed. Lynch had seen enough. He smiled at the woman.

"It was not me madam, I assure you." he said, as he left her. "I'll go and get some help," he called back, with no intention of doing so.

Out in the street Lynch looked both directions. He was obviously getting close to his quarry. His problem was that Rafferty may have beaten him to it. A thought occurred to him. Perhaps following Rafferty was his best chance after all. As he turned, he thought he recognized the man kissing the girl from the bar. He looked again, but they had disappeared.

Chapter 25

Red was almost frightened. He'd never seen Shirley so angry. When she emerged from the Wheeler mansion her face was flushed, her hair was a mess and she was carrying her hat in her hand, leaving Red to wonder if she and Mrs. Wheeler had come to blows. A wise man, Red held his peace while Shirley fumed all the way, until he stopped the buggy a block from their house.

"Why are you stopping here?" Shirley snapped at him. Red placed his hand on Shirley's arm tenderly.

"I can see you're upset." Red said calmly, pausing until Shirley looked at him and saw the deep concern in his eyes. "Do you want to tell me what Mrs. Wheeler said to you?"

Shirley sighed and looked far off to the peaks of the mountains, wishing that she could be up there with the blue sky and the wind, free of the deepening storm clouds in her heart.

"I'm worried about Daniel, Red. I think he's in more trouble than we realize. After what No Problem told us, I haven't had a night when I haven't worried about him." Shirley placed her hand over Red's. "And after what I just learned from that woman, I'm even more concerned."

"Why so?"

"Well, it seems that there is a woman who has set her sights on our Daniel and that concerns me very much."

"Do you know who it is?"

"Yes, I do."

"What can we do, Shirley? We don't know where he is."

"Not now, but when I get my hands on Jerome Wheeler's neck I will."

"How do you plan to do that without going to Chicago yourself?"

"That's my plan, Red."

"What are you going to tell Kate?"

"I don't know yet."

"We have to tell her something."

"Do you think she knows Daniel robbed the bank?"

Shirley shook her head and laughed. "You didn't even know for sure until Joe told you."

"But you did?" Red asked honestly. Shirley smiled and patted his hand.

"The moment Harry took off his shirt in the courtroom, I knew."

Red considered Shirley with the adoring eyes of a devoted husband. "I'll never know you completely, will I?" Shirley kissed the back of his hand, feeling the weathered, rough skin and loving its feel on her lips. She looked up into his eyes and Red saw the veil close behind them. "That's all in the past, Red. Our problem now is Daniel's safety. If Harry is hunting him for some reward and he followed him to Chicago, then we need to help him." Shirley held her hands to her face cooling her cheeks. "And now that he's gone missing, we can't be sure that Harry hasn't already found him." She took Red's hands in hers, "I think we should leave as soon as possible."

"Alright, but what about Kate? What are you going to tell her? More importantly, how much are you going to tell her?"

"I'll think about that. Now let's get home. We have some packing to do."

Kate was waiting for them when they returned. Sitting at the same window where she had once sat and watched Daniel pining for her from under the tree across the street. She bounced her daughter on her hip but when the buggy pulled up and she saw the expression on her mother's face she knew something akin to a storm was arriving. As indeed it was.

"Maisie, would you please make us some tea," Shirley asked as she entered, taking off her shawl. "I think we're going to need it," she said to Kate. Noticing the worried look, she came and held Kate and her baby and embraced them.

"You look awful, mom," Kate stated, truthfully. "Have you been brawling with Mrs. Wheeler?" she said, making them all smile.

Shirley looked at her reflection in the hall mirror and adjusted her hair and skirt. "Let's just say that I had a good round and we fought to a draw and leave it at that, shall we?" Shirley smiled at them both and took Kate's hand, walking with her to the dining table. "Kate, I want you to sit a moment with me."

"Is it something to do with Daniel? Is he hurt?" Kate said, worry darkening her sweet face.

"I'm certain that he's perfectly alright, so don't worry yourself about that." Shirley braced herself against the weight of the lies she was telling. "But I was thinking," Shirley trailed off, hoping that it was in the telling that the lie became reality, "that Red and I should go and visit with him in Chicago."

"Not without me," Kate said, defiantly.

Maisie entered with a tea service on a platter and placed it on the table. She gave Shirley a raised eyebrow before returning to the kitchen.

"Don't even think about leaving me here, mother. Rose could stay with Rachelle. It won't be for long, will it?"

But how long was it going to take? They had no idea. All they knew was that Harry and another man, a big man by Joe's description, were trying to kidnap Daniel for some reward. Offered by whom, they had no idea. And for what crime? Joe didn't say. The Pinkerton's Detective Agency was the only company they knew of in that business and if they were seeking Daniel then that was serious business. Unfortunately, the more they discovered, the more confusing the situation with Daniel became.

But considering that Daniel had now gone missing, if Harry wasn't the cause of his disappearance, then they had solved one problem but were facing another. Was it Harry or the Pinkertons, or even Claire Cavendish, at the root of this situation?

Shirley made up her mind and set a course. With the paucity of information available to them the only logical path was to go to Chicago and find the boy and then sort it all out, Harry be damned. But should Harry have been involved in Joe's death, or Daniel's disappearance, he would be better off dead than alive when Shirley found him.

Chapter 26

J akob steered his cab this way and that, weaving through the bustling thoroughfares that traversed the city while Daniel watched over his mother and Megan, nervous and vigilant.

"Where are you taking us, Jakob?" Daniel asked. "Be patient, ve're almost zere."

Ten minutes later they stopped outside the smallest of a row of buildings, all with shop fronts, crowded with stalls and vendors clamoring for business. A multitude of bearded men wearing black hats and long, black coats and dark-eyed women hurried about conversing in languages and gestures distinctly foreign to Daniel. Jakob stepped down from his seat as two young men approached the cab. They eyed Daniel impassively. Jakob turned to Myra and smiled proudly.

"Zhese are my sons. Zis vun is Joshua, he's zhe smart vun." The younger man lifted his black hat. He had a mischievous smile. Daniel noted the dark curls that hung in front of his ears though the rest of his hair was cut short. "And zhis is ze not so smart vun. But he is good- looking, yes? Zhis is Shlomo," Jakob said with a flourish, obviously doting on his oldest son. Shlomo took off his tall, black hat, nodding to Daniel and his family, unsmiling, cautious. "And zhese people," Jakob announced proudly, spreading his arms wide, encompassing Daniel's family. "Zhese are my new friends," he said with an impish smile.

Jakob was a truly generous man. Daniel saw it in his smile and he felt it emanate from him. Something about him was both foreign and familiar and Daniel felt strangely reassured and calmed by the feeling. He courteously offered his hand for Myra and Megan to take which they accepted, smiling at his charming, gentlemanly manners. Perhaps it was the danger that they all faced, but a bond of kinship of sorts had grown between them.

"Come vis me. You vill be safe here. Come!" He pointed to his youngest son. "Joshua. Take the cab and make me some money, eh?" His son leapt into the driver's seat and quickly disappeared into the traffic.

Jakob took Myra's hand and he led them down a flight of stone steps leading to a small door.

"Zhis is a place vhere Jews like me come to sing and dance. Like in our old counties. Zhere are Jews from all over Europe here. Come, it is a place to be happy while you are my guests. Come into my life, please."

Jakob opened the door onto a large basement room filled with chattering people of all ages. "Zhese are my friends!" Jakob said loudly and was met with a chorus of greetings.

Children ran about the room and played noisily while men sat at wooden tables playing chess or debating loudly. The smell of cabbage cooking and of unknown spices, the clatter of pots and the clamor of loud conversations assaulted their senses. Off to the side, in a darkened corner at the rear of the room, a violinist played a rousing melody for two men who danced arm in arm.

Daniel was confused about exactly who Jakob was referring to as family. Apparently, it made no difference. Chairs suddenly were offered and a table was cleared for them and set with a pitcher of clean water and glasses. They could only nod and smile as dozens of Jakob's friends came to their table to introduce themselves. He looked at his mother expecting her to be intimidated but she seemed to be enjoying the calamitous scene revolving around her.

They were joined by two women of his mother's age who sat on either side of her and held her hands. She looked from one to the other smiling with a genuine look of peace as they sought to make her comfortable. She smiled brightly when another woman brought them hot tea in delicately decorated porcelain cups.

Jakob stood off to one side deeply involved in conversation with two men also wearing beards and long coats. Occasionally looking their way, the men nodded and then left together after shaking hands with Jakob. Intrigued, Daniel watched them, noticing that they put on very large fur hats before leaving.

"This is my wife, Esther, and this is my sister, I always forget her name. Oh, yes. It's Safina," he chided playfully. Jakob took Daniel aside.

"I have sent zumvone to zee if you are in any danger. If you are, I vill try to help you. I have zum experience viz danger and it doesn't frighten me."

He laughed and translated for his wife in their own language.

Jakob's wife said something to him and he laughed. "My wife says that I should be frightened. She says zhat I'm not zo young anymore." Laughing, Jakob kissed his wife on her cheek and held her at arm's length, smiling at her adoringly.

Three children, two girls and a young boy, placed bowls of soup in front of them and a beautiful, young dark-haired girl shyly put a plate of bread in front of Myra, smiling at her in the most angelic way. Daniel could see that his mother was touched by the welcoming from those around her. After living on the edge of starvation and at her wits' end for worry about her own children, this was more than just a welcome relief, it was relief embodied.

Jakob grabbed the young girl by her waist, making her giggle, "And zis is my daughter, Sarah." Jakob beamed with pride.

"Now, Daniel. If you vill give me zhe ozher half of zhe bill," Jakob looked intently at Daniel, "zo we can all be friends, eh?" Jakob laughed and Daniel found the missing half of the twenty-dollar bill and handed it to Jakob, receiving a hearty slap on his back. Laughing loudly Jakob left the table and went to a cabinet and pulled down a bottle of clear liquid from a shelf full of them.

Jakob returned to the table and Sarah placed four glasses on the table which Jakob filled. Daniel lifted his and smelled the liquor which assaulted his nose.

"Come on, vhat's wrong viz you? It's for good luck. Drink!" he demanded. They did as he did and all began coughing, all except Jakob who burst out laughing and poured more liquor into their glasses.

"What is that?" Daniel demanded.

"Raki!" Jakob said proudly. "It's vone of our little businesses. Pretty smooth, don't you zhink?"

"I'd hate to think what bad Raki tastes like," Daniel said, smiling.

Jakob burst out laughing.

"Good Raki tastes like zhis," he held up his glass to the dim electric light. Small shafts of colors emanated from the liquid. Jakob drank and slapped Daniel on the back. "Bad Raki," he said, proudly, "tastes like zis too!" Laughing loudly at his own humor he leaned over and gently slapped his daughter's behind.

Jakob became suddenly distracted by something over Daniel's shoulder and excused himself. Daniel watched him walk across the room to join his sons in an animated conversation. About them children ran and laughed, elderly women in black dresses wearing scarves patted them, or chided them as they dashed in and out of the room or darted amongst the tables.

"Daniel, do you know what's going on?" Myra asked. It was obvious that Megan was equally concerned.

"Everything is going to be alright, mum. Trust me," he lied, and choked as his throat swelled shut with the doubt and the danger that still lay ahead of them. Steeling his emotions, he forced himself to look directly into their eyes, pouring his false confidence into them. He felt a touch on his shoulder. It was Jakob and he looked very serious.

"Come vis me, Daniel. I zhink we should discuss vhat I have heard in private." Jakob smiled for Myra and Megan. "Everyzing vill be OK, ladies. Please excuse us," Jakob said politely, lifting his chin in a signal his wife understood. She immediately engaged Myra and Megan in distracting conversation as Jakob led Daniel into a small alcove where his sons waited.

"Daniel, I believe you are in very bad trouble, yes?"

Daniel averted his eyes and studied the floor. Raising his eyes to meet Jakob's caring gaze he briefly looked over at his mother. Jakob sensed the difficulty he was having and reached out his hand and placed his over Daniel's.

"Before you answer, let me tell you vhat my sons have discovered." Jakob nodded to his sons. "I'm sorry to tell you zhat zhe man your family was staying wiz has been killed. Murdered." Jakob watched Daniel's expression closely. Shock and sadness clouded his face. "Vas he a friend of yours?"

Daniel held out his glass and Jakob filled it and watched Daniel drink it quickly. "John Hogan," Daniel found that his throat had closed tighter than a priest's purse and he gagged on his words. Jakob patted Daniel's shoulder, giving him time to continue. "John Hogan," Daniel began again, "has been keeping my family safe for the past two years and I owe him everything. We're alive because of him." Tears filled Daniel's eyes and rolled down his cheeks. "What happened to him? Who killed him?"

Jakob spread his hands wide. "Zhat I cannot tell you. But the reason, I can tell." Daniel dried his eyes and waited. "You have a price on your head, Daniel, and the Irish gangs are looking to collect on you." Daniel took a deep breath and steeled himself for the confession he had to make and his mind roiled at the dilemma he was being forced to navigate. If Jakob admitted knowing that there was a price on his head, would Jakob not also be tempted to turn Daniel into the authorities? What could Jakob and his family gain by not doing so?

"My father and brother blew up a bank in Dublin. That's where we came from. It was stupid thing to do but they were involved in a revolution against the English." Daniel looked at Jakob and found no obvious threat, so he continued. "The blast killed a policeman, and my father and brother got caught before they could get away," Daniel lied smoothly.

"Vhy are zhey looking for you? Were you a robber too?"

"No, no!" Daniel said emphatically. "I was trying to warn them."

"So, vhy they are still looking for you?" Jakob rocked back on his chair. Daniel shrugged in the same way that Jakob had done making Jakob smile. His smiled waned. "And your fazzer and brozzer? They are still in jail?"

"My father died in prison. My brother? I don't know." He looked up and was surprised and confused by Jakob's smile.

"Vhaz is your brozzer's name?" Daniel frowned at the question.

Why would Jakob want to know that?

"His name is Patrick" Daniel said softly. "It was my father's name too."

"Zo, I vas correct it seems." Jakob looked from one son to the other and Daniel followed his gaze. The younger one nodded. Jakob returned his attention back to Daniel. "Vat vould you say if I told you zhat your brozzer is not in prison anymore." Daniel's shock made Jakob smile. "Ahh! And vat if I told you zhat zhere are people looking for him here in New York. Vhat would you say to zhat, Daniel Shadlow?"

*   *   *

Patrick sat nervously in a pew at the rear of the church waiting his turn to enter the confessional booth. His decision made; he was now coming to grips with the possibility of eternal consequences. Contemptuous of the coded teachings of the Catholic Church he held no less contempt for its servants. Still he was bothered by the possibility that, if they were right, he would be damned.

It was a Wednesday evening and the priests, as Patrick knew, held confessions from four o'clock in the afternoon until six o'clock. Intending to be the last penitent, he waited until the elderly woman who had been ahead of him had walked to the front of the church to kneel and pray her penance. Steeling himself, he opened the door to the confessional and began his confession which came readily to him despite the intervening years of negligence in its practice.

"Bless me Father, for I have sinned," he said to the thin black veil that separated the penitent from the confessor. Immediately the veil was swept back and Father John's smiling face filled the small window between them.

"Patrick," he exclaimed in a hushed tone, "where have you been? I've been so worried about you." The young priest's words were heartfelt and it pained Patrick that he was about to take his virginity a second time, though in a very different manner. "Are you here to make your confession?" Father John's tone was jubilant, destined to be crushed.

"No, Father. I'm here to commit another sin."

"How can that be, my son?" Father John replied, raising his cloak of sanctity about him.

"I need money, John," Patrick said. "I need one hundred dollars."

"That's a lot of money, Patrick."

"I need to get to Colorado." It was to Patrick as if a devil had walked over his grave. He had a feeling of impending disaster and instantly regretted that he had told the priest of his intentions. A premonition possibly. "I know you have money here, John." Patrick waited, but no reply came from the young priest. "If you don't give me the money," Patrick paused once again, this time for effect. "I'll go to the head of your order and say that you raped me. I have your letter."

"He won't believe you," John replied through clenched teeth.

"I'll describe what your penis looks like, John. He'll have no qualms then, will he?"

"Why are you doing this, Patrick? I took you in." Father John's voice broke, and tears filled in the blanks in the conversation. "I saved you. How could you betray me?"

"John, I needed you. Just as you needed me. Now go and get the money. I know where you keep the donations."

Father John was in very deep trouble. "Can I give you the money tomorrow? It would be safer for me."

"Tomorrow morning. First Mass is at six o'clock." Patrick's tone was hard. "I'll be waiting by the front door." Patrick rose and exited the small cubicle.

"But, but…" Father John's voice trailed off. Overwhelmed by this consequence of his sinfulness he sat alone in the confessional like a convict in solitary confinement, privately confessing his very sincere prayers of repentance.

Chapter 27

I n the brief time that Lynch had been in New York he'd molded to its ways. His experience and instincts, honed over a career, served him equally well in this city as they did in his own. Cities were places where word of easy money, legally gotten or ill, sped through the criminal communities like fleas on rats. And he was certain Rafferty knew this also. Now he had to find him.

After neatly folding the last of his things and placing them in his suitcase he sat on the end of the bed and cleaned his revolver with a hotel towel. Doing something familiar like cleaning his pistol calmed him while he considered his next course of action.

By pursuing a trail of rumors, he had found the Fenians and come very close to finding the Shadlows, so it was likely that Rafferty would follow the same trail. But, since the incident yesterday, the situation had changed and had become considerably more dangerous.

Absently, Lynch cocked and fired the unloaded pistol three times as was his habit. Satisfied it was in working order he inserted six cartridges into the cylinder. Being right-handed he pushed the pistol inside his belt on his left side, the side on which he used his cane, then he buttoned his coat and appraised himself in the mirror while he considered his problem.

One thing he knew for certain was that he had come close to his quarry. The Shadlows had fled, but where? Were they alone? If not, who were they with? Patrick possibly, he thought. He had more than a month's head start so it was conceivable that with the help of the Fenians, Patrick could already have found his family. But, if he had not yet found them, then what had happened to them? Lynch had a sudden thought. Was Patrick Shadlow aware that he was being hunted?

Lynch considered what he would do in the same circumstances, concluding that the most logical decision would be to either hide or run. Admittedly, New York was a huge city but Five Points was a small, lawless part of the city where Irish gangs operated openly and in total impunity of authority. If one wanted anything, from sex to information, this was where one came. The gangs there knew everything about everybody.

There would be no safe place for them to hide in this part of the city, so they had to run. But run where?

Following his intuition and pieces of information Lynch discovered Finbarr's, which turned out to be a stroke of good fortune. It was the belly of the underworld. Loud and arrogant, both in their speech and swagger, the Irish gangs were an open book to Lynch and inevitably he had found out what he wanted to know. It very likely would have been the same with Rafferty. By spreading money around in exchange for information he could have achieved a similar result.

That he had seen Rafferty fleeing Hogan's apartment without being seen himself was an advantage. Now, if he could find Rafferty before Rafferty found the Shadlows, lives might be saved since he now knew with absolute certainty that Rafferty would kill for the reward money.

He dashed off a quick letter to Detective Killeen over breakfast and took it to the Bank of England office on his way to Central Station. It was early morning and the bank had just opened and the manager to whom he gave the letter was condescending but promised to place his letter in the international mail bag.

Working on the premise that someone had warned the Shadlows they were in danger, Lynch reasoned that the chances of them being found by Rafferty increased daily. For their safety they would need to leave the city quickly, which meant by train, and Rafferty would also know that. Finding Rafferty before he found the Shadlows was his best bet. Then, if successful at the very least, he could watch him and wait.

Central Station was clogged with morning travelers when Lynch arrived. Preparing for a considerable wait he deposited his bag at the baggage claim. After familiarizing himself with the vast train station he studied the schedules of the departing trains and their assigned platforms, all the while watching for Rafferty.

After checking out of his hotel he caught a cab to Central Station. With a large cup of coffee and a newspaper, he positioned himself on a bench on the mezzanine where from behind his open newspaper he could watch the broad expanse of the station and the entrances to the platforms.

It was nearing eight o'clock when he noticed him. Begrudgingly, Lynch gave him credit for his tactic, standing off to the side of the main area, scrutinizing everyone purchasing train tickets. He gave him low marks for leaning against a pillar with no luggage, his head on a swivel. One hunter watching another. The thought made him smile.

*   *   *

It was the singing and the dancing that eventually made Daniel tired enough to sleep. His introduction into the Jewish community had left him leg-weary and hungover when he awoke. His mother and sister had been coaxed by Esther to accompany her to a small alcove in the basement so that they could have some rest before their journey and Jakob had reassured them all that they would be safe.

"Vhat are your intentions, Daniel?" Jakob asked, his concern obvious and sincere. Daniel debated telling him the truth and decided that Jakob was a man of honor, who deserved his honesty. Sitting together at a small table, alone in the same room where they earlier had been dancing and singing, Daniel felt the worse for the evening's wear. "You know zhat you can't stay in zhis city." Daniel nodded, reawakening his headache. "Vhy is it zhat zhe English vant you back zo bad?"

"I think they want me for political reasons," Daniel said, surprised at the clarity with which he saw the situation. "The English are angry and afraid of the Irish," Daniel squared his shoulders, "and they think I'm a revolutionary, but I'm not."

Jakob leaned forward and placed his hand on Daniel's shoulder. "I zhink I know how you feel. Remember all zhe people you met last night? Zhey are all running away from zumpzing too." Jakob held his hand to his head stilling the pounding slightly. "And me? Vell, every von of us is escaping zome zort of oppression. Zhat's vhy ve came to America, to escape oppression." He spread his hands wide. "Zhis is vhy ve come here." Jakob patted Patrick's shoulder. "And," he held up a finger, "a boy should not be punished for the sins of his fazzer. Zo, where are you going with your little band of gypsies, eh?"

"There is a train leaving at eight o'clock for Chicago," Daniel said quietly. "I have a job there. At the World's Fair." Jakob's eyes widened and he smiled broadly.

"Zhat must be vonderful. Ah, how I vould like to zee it," he said wistfully. "But foist zhings foist. Go and get your family. Ve go straight to zhe train station, OK?" Jakob took Daniel's hand and shook it heartily. "I vill go and get the cab."

*   *   *

Patrick and Gemma had stayed the night with friends of hers, sleeping under a blanket on the floor. There had been no physical contact between them and Patrick had barely slept, welcoming the coming of the first light. Rousing Gemma gently, he whispered in her ear.

"I have to go." She'd looked at him strangely.

"Can I come with you?" Gemma's loving look softened his heart and steeled him for what lay ahead.

"No," he replied. "It's something I have to do alone." Gemma looked crestfallen; Patrick quailed. "Alright, you can come." Now, standing in front of the church arm in arm, Patrick hesitated.

"What's wrong?" Gemma asked.

Patrick clenched his jaw tightly. "I'm going to rob the church."

"Don't you think you'll go to hell for that?" She laughed. Patrick didn't.

"Stay out here," he demanded.

The congregation at the early morning mass was sparse. Elderly parishioners, mostly women, sat or knelt with discomfort on ancient bones following the incantations and intoning the necessary responses. Patrick took the back pew off to the side, in the angled shadow of a carved stone column. When the mass had ended and the parishioners were filing out, Father John nodded to Patrick as he bid the last of his flock farewell. For the sake of the other priests who might be curious, Father John knelt in prayer in the pew next to Patrick. Several minutes passed. Father John occasionally lifted his eyes and when they were alone, he pulled an envelope from the sleeve of his tunic and placed it on the wooden pew. He said nothing. Patrick slid the envelope containing the money into his coat pocket.

"Thank you, John," Patrick said sincerely, and reached out his hand for him to shake, but John pulled away from him.

"Unless you wish for me to hear your confession, I want nothing more to do with you."

A smile crept onto Patrick's face but the sadness in Father John's eyes swept it away. There was true and utter sadness there. As if the fire that burns brightly in the soul of every man and woman, the undeniable thing that keeps us breathing even when we don't want to, had died, extinguished by a downpour of self-loathing.

They both looked up as Gemma sat down beside them. "I'd like to make my confession to you, Father," she asked. The sound of her voice lingered in the air, hanging, reverberating. With a sigh, Father John placed his hand on Patrick's shoulder lightly in a simple parting gesture and disappeared into the confessional.

"I won't be long, Patrick. Wait for me?" Gemma smiled and followed the priest, leaving Patrick alone in the gathering light to search his heart for answers to questions he dared not ask.

Chapter 28

"Is anyvone vatching?" Jakob asked his son, Shlomo.
"Yes, papa. I saw a man watching the ticket counter." Jakob looked at Daniel and raised an eyebrow. "He's wearing a long coat and a black hat."

"What can we do?" Daniel asked quietly, not wanting to alarm his mother. "How are we going to get on board without being seen?"

Jakob looked at Daniel, his eyes twinkling. "Zo," he said, a thin smile growing across his face. "How vould you like to be Jewish, eh?" Daniel looked surprised. "Shlomo," Jakob ordered. "Give me your coat and hat! Take zhe cab to zhe back of zhe line. Tell the police you are picking up your mozzer, eh? Give me that blanket. Joshua, come vis us." Jakob and Joshua then led them into the cavernous hall carefully avoiding the ticket area.

"Vait here," Jakob said to Myra and Megan as he placed his long black coat over Daniel's shoulders and gave them a smile. "Ve vill be right back." Leading Daniel and Joshua into the men's lavatory he herded them into a stall at the far end. Closing the door, he pulled out a small knife from his belt.

Daniel retreated as far into the corner as was possible. Jakob laughed. "It's not for you, Daniel." Jakob turned to his son. "Give me your hat." Joshua reluctantly took off his hat. Quick as a flash, Jakob grasped one of Joshua's curls and cut it off at the hairline.

"Papa! What are you doing?" Joshua asked, and was rewarded by quickly losing his other curl.

"You have lost your dreidels. Happy Bar Mitzvah!" Jakob smiled broadly. "Congratulations, you are a man now," he said, shook his son's hand then hugged him. "Now give me your coat."

"Put Joshua's coat on." Jakob placed Joshua's black hat on Daniel's head and tucked the dark curls of Joshua's hair over the ears and under the hat. Satisfied with his arrangement, he nodded and opened the door to the stall.

No one paid them any attention as they stood in front of the mirror. Jakob looked at their reflection and smiled broadly. "Zhere!" he said, proudly. "Now, you are Jewish." He laughed again and placed his hand on Daniel's shoulder looking at their reflection. "Maybe, not yet a Jew. But you're getting to look like one and zhat vill be good enough for zhe time being." He slapped Daniel on the back and grinned. "Now let us go and catch zhat train."

It was not possible to traverse the station without passing through the main terminal where they knew someone watching for them. "Myra, pull down your scarf and Megan, put this blanket around you," Jakob advised them. "Now, we all look like Jews."

Mixing amongst the crowds, Joshua indicated the man watching everyone buying tickets. Jakob nodded. "He's not so good as the good vuns," Jakob whispered to Daniel after they had passed. "Even my mozzer could zee him, eh?" In their long, black coats and distinctive black hats, they did indeed look like a family of refugees. But perhaps, it was not disguise enough.

Risking a glance over his shoulder Daniel was alarmed to see the man intently watching them and more so when the man tucked his newspaper under his arm and began to follow them. Fortunately, their platform was crowded with passengers boarding trains on both sides. Jakob glanced behind them as they approached a train conductor inspecting the couplings of the carriages with a coal-smudged engineer.

"Excuse me, sir," Jakob took off his hat in deference to the uniform. "Where might ve find our seats?" Jakob asked, showing him Daniel's tickets. The conductor looked at them and failed to muster a smile. With a look akin to hatred he pointed to the carriage ahead of them. "That one," he said brusquely, and went about his business. When they had gone a few yards, Jakob pointed to the train on the adjacent track.

"He was hostile towards us. Why?" Daniel asked.

"Ve are strangers to zhem. It is not so free here for people like us. As you are finding out." He gathered them together and inclined his head behind them. "Zhat man is still vatching us so I suggest zhat you get onto zhe ozher train. If he is following you, he must buy a ticket for zhat train. Zhen, you can change trains. Yes?"

Jakob saw Joshua approaching and held up his hand for him to wait. The man following them failed to see the signal, busy blending in among the departing passengers as obvious as a tree in a desert. "Come. Take your bags Daniel, go get onto zhat train over zhere."

They did as they were told and pretended to say farewell to Jakob on the platform. Theatrically they were up to the job because no sooner than Jakob had waved goodbye and turned for the exit than the man who had been following them abruptly turned and raced off back into the terminal. Jakob gave Daniel a signal and watched him quickly lead his family across the platform and board the train heading for Chicago.

The train's whistle screamed and the conductor walked along the platform encouraging passengers aboard. Jakob waved and Daniel waved back but Jakob was distracted by the sudden reappearance of the man who'd been following them hurrying down the platform and preparing to board the other train. If he found that Daniel's party was not on board, he would discover the ruse.

"Start a fight vis zhat man, Joshua," Jakob said, pointing to the man hurrying towards them.

"Why?"

"Because, I told you so! You're a man now, so start an argument."

"What about?" Joshua asked, confused.

"What do Jews always argue about?" Jakob yelled as if to a simpleton. "Money, of course! Go on! You're a man now, act like von. Go get into a fight."

As Joshua verbally accosted Rafferty, Jakob smiled proudly and discreetly blew them a kiss, then turned back to join his son in compounding Rafferty's confusion and problems.

Their argument was drawing a crowd, as Jakob had hoped. When Daniel's train began to pull away from the station, he breathed a sigh of relief and eased himself and Joshua away from the confrontation, profusely apologizing for the mistake to a bewildered Rafferty.

They felt the train push forward and Daniel took off his hat and waved back to Jakob from the train window. He owed so much to his new friend and he wondered if he would ever see him again to thank him for saving him and his family. Another whoosh of steam and the train moved forward a little. Then a little more, and a little more, and in rhythm with the bursts of steam from the locomotive they pulled away from the station. Daniel sat down and breathed a sigh of relief, smiling at his mother sitting across from him, Megan's arm around her shoulder.

As he watched the departing train, Jakob saw a disfigured man carrying a cane hurry along the platform and nimbly jump aboard. Then, two young people raced past and leapt aboard the last carriage, just as Daniel stuck his head out of a window and waved back to them.

"Good luck, my young friend," Jakob said sincerely, waving one last time.

In his seat Daniel closed his eyes reliving an earlier time when he had left from a similar platform on a journey that had now brought him full circle. He looked at his mother and sister with all the love he had. His problem now was explaining his family to Kate, Shirley, Red and Jerome Wheeler. But it was not his only problem.

*   *   *

Sergeant Lynch had noticed the small clutch of Jewish people walking through the terminal and paid them little attention. They blended in with masses of other travelers hurrying this way and that, toting mounds of luggage, heading to or from their trains. Boredom was Lynch's principle enemy. He caught the yawn midway and was holding his hand up to cover his mouth when he saw Rafferty fold his newspaper and step away from the wall he'd been supporting.

Lynch matched Rafferty's pace and descended the wide staircase to the lower level, keeping him in sight. Rafferty's attention was fixed on someone ahead, but in the confusion, Lynch was unable to identify who it was he was following. Rafferty turned onto platform fourteen but stopped and hid behind a post, intently observing someone. Abruptly, he turned and ran from the platform heading for the terminal. Confident that Rafferty had seen his quarry, Lynch waited and watched. Signs overhead indicated that the two departing trains were heading in opposite directions. The one on his left was northbound for Boston, the train on the right was headed west for Chicago.

Lynch's attention was drawn to the Jewish family he had barely noticed before, hurrying across the platform from the northbound train to the one bound for Chicago. Lynch thought it curious. More so when he saw Rafferty race back onto the platform heading for the train to Boston only to be accosted by a young, angry man loudly accusing Rafferty of theft.

Lynch heard the whistle blow and the Chicago-bound train began to move. An older Jewish man waved to someone on the train and Lynch saw a head appear and return the wave. The young face at the window now had no hat and neither did he have curls over his ears and he thought he recognized him. Lynch's predatory instincts rang in him like a church bell. He raced for the departing train and managed to leap onto one of the last carriages. Looking back at the station and he saw a worried look on the old Jewish man's face. He felt confident that Patrick Shadlow was on this train.

*   *   *

Patrick and Gemma had walked around the station twice and had noticed Rafferty. He looked out of place, overly observant. "I don't like the look of that man," Patrick said to Gemma. All of a sudden, Rafferty left his position and walked off briskly.

"Two tickets to Chicago please," Patrick asked. The agent stamped the tickets.

"Platform fourteen, sir," the agent said. "You'd better hurry. The train leaves in five minutes." Patrick and Gemma hurried through the terminal but Patrick pulled Gemma aside at the entrance to the platform.

"Why did we stop? The train's about to leave," Gemma begged. But Patrick pulled her back beside him, pointing at Lynch standing behind a column, discreetly watching those boarding the trains.

"That's the man I saw leaving John Hogan's place," he said, indicating Lynch. Gemma looked.

"Are you sure?" she asked. Patrick nodded.

"I think he's the one who did in that man Hogan. Look, he's watching someone. See how he's looking over the top of his newspaper?"

As they watched Lynch, a man ran past them onto the platform as the train's whistle blew. They both recognized him. The watcher from the terminal. Lynch also saw him approaching and carefully avoided being seen. He was running for the northbound train but then they saw him accosted by a young man dressed in black making a scene. Seeing the man occupied, Lynch chased after the departing train and climbed aboard.

"Quick, we have to catch that train!" Patrick said, dragging Gemma her behind him.

"Why this one? We can catch the next one," she complained.

"No!" he snapped at her. "I don't know why, but we need to get on this one. Come on!"

What Jakob saw was a scar-faced man rushing past him, running for the departing train. He was followed by a young couple running for the same train but they waited for the last carriage before they too, leapt aboard.

"I'm sorry, sir. Come on Joshua, I zhink you were mistaken. Ve are very zorry," Jakob said, leaving Rafferty loudly complaining to an uninterested station porter.

Jakob cast one look back over his shoulder and smiled when he saw that Rafferty did indeed board the train headed for Boston. "Vell, ve have done our best, eh? Let's hope zhat more troubles didn't get on zhat train vis zhem. But, I zhink zhey did. Come, Joshua. Let's get Shlomo and go eat."

Chapter 29

Shirley and Red sat together holding hands, their shoulders touching, their tired bodies rolling as one with the train as it swayed. Kate dozed in the seat across from them, her head resting on the soft-sided bag she had brought. The motion of the train was as a sleeping draft to Red and Kate. They woke, looked out of the window at the passing scenery and then dozed off again. Shirley found sleep impossible and was more than a little envious.

Dawn was casting thin, pale light above the endless horizon. The pastures and fields were a blur and the passage of the train and time itself passed like the past. Shirley stroked Red's hand and looked at her brood with love and wonder. Her daughter, beautiful and strong, married and with a growing family. Her husband Red, snoring on her shoulder, was a man of courage and strength. She had made some very bad decisions in her life, but everything seemed to have turned out well.

The train slowed, approaching a water station. There was nothing as far as the eye could see but for the windmill drawing water up to the elevated water tank that quenched the thirst of the smoking, hissing locomotive. Red stirred and stretched.

"Where are we?" he asked, sleepily.

"About three hours out from Kansas City," Shirley answered softly, not wanting to awaken Kate. Red stood, stretched and walked the length of the carriage shaking off the cramped muscles before sitting back down again. He placed his arm around Shirley's shoulder and she leaned her head onto his shoulder.

"Have you thought of what you're going to tell Kate?"

"I've thought about it, yes. Do I know how much to tell her?" Shirley pulled Red's hand to her breast and looked deeply onto his eyes. "I'm not sure about that. I'd like to wait until we get to Chicago and find out where Daniel is … but I don't think that's fair to Kate. She is his wife."

Filled with water the train began its forward motion with a jolt, waking Kate who looked around as if confused and rubbed her eyes as she stretched.

"Where are we?"

"We'll be in Kansas City by lunchtime, if that's what you mean,"

Red laughed, making Kate smile.

"You two look very serious. Is something wrong?" Kate yawned. She looked from one to the other and sensed that her mother was having difficulty expressing whatever it was on her mind. Kate sensed that it involved Daniel. Her mother had been tight-lipped ever since No Problem Joe died, and since boarding the train yesterday morning Shirley had been as closed as a coffin. "Are you going to tell me?"

Shirley looked at Red for reassurance and reached out for Kate to take her hand. "We have something to tell you about Daniel and I don't want you to get upset." Shirley took a deep breath before carrying on. "Daniel has a secret." Shirley watched Kate, measuring her reaction.

"Is he a murderer? If he is, don't you think you should've told me?" Shirley squeezed Kate's hand forcefully before she pulled it back.

"No! No, he's not a murderer. Well I don't think he is, do you Red?" Red laughed, shaking his head.

"What is it then?"

"Remember when I told that Harry Rich was in Aspen recently?"

"Well, it appears," Red continued, "that Harry and another man came looking for Daniel."

"Why?" Kate sounded skeptical.

"Kate, my darling," Shirley took a deep breath, "according to Joe, Daniel is wanted by the English police and there is a reward for his capture. That's why Harry wanted Daniel," Shirley lied, watching Kate closely. "So, when I heard from Leafy that Daniel had disappeared, I thought…." Shirley trailed off. The sound of the wheels clattering over the tracks suddenly seemed exceptionally loud.

Shirley tried to elaborate but Kate held up her hand and looked out of the train window. She felt Red give her a little hug of encouragement and looked up at him. He was in love with her and she couldn't be happier having him by her side during this trying time.

"You're not telling me everything are you?" Kate said forcefully. "I know you, mother. You two are keeping something from me. I know it. What are you hiding?" Kate pulled her knees up to her chin and looked at Shirley defiantly. Red excused himself, giving Shirley and Kate privacy. Whether or not he showed it, Red was very concerned about Daniel's safety, considering what had happened to Joe. Harry was once Red's friend, but thinking back on it, perhaps he never was? He was a liar and a cheat and a bank robber, all of which was true. Still, Red doubted strongly that Harry was the one who killed Joe. More likely it was the large man Joe said was with him. Why Harry had returned to Aspen had little to do with the reward on Daniel's head. Red suspected it had more to do with the bank robbery in Leadville.

*   *   *

Harry felt a hand grip his shoulder and looked up.

"Are you done losing?" Hamlett took the cards out of Harry's hand and threw them on the table. "We need to talk." Hamlett said, motioning Harry to the stools at the bar. "If you didn't gamble all your money away Harry you could've bought a train ticket home, couldn't you?" Harry signaled the bartender for two whiskeys and drank his drink before he looked at Hamlett.

"That was a winning hand, I want you to know."

Hamlett laughed loudly. "You couldn't even deal yourself a winning hand if you were the only one at the table, Harry. You're the unluckiest gambler Doc Holliday ever met. He told me that himself. Among other things," Hamlett said, jabbing Harry in the ribs, laughing.

"Doc didn't really say that about me, did he?"

Hamlett watched Harry wither. "Do you know a feller named John Carter?"

Harry looked up, surprised. "Why?"

"He's here in Chicago. Came in yesterday, ordering people around like he owned the place. I haven't seen your little friend so I guess he's still with Wheeler in Washington." Hamlett drank his whiskey. "Funny thing though, he wants the Silver Queen broken down and packed up. He's hired a crew of men to do it."

"Are they doing it now?"

"Started after lunch."

"That means the little shit is coming back here soon," Harry said, smiling. "We could tell the Pinkertons when he's here in Chicago."

Hamlett allowed Harry to enjoy his moment. There was much more money at stake than just the reward money on Daniel's head and Harry was going to help find it willing or not!

"Who is this John Carter?" Harry pointed to his empty glass and Hamlett signaled to bartender for another round.

"He's Wheeler's right-hand man. He runs the mines and he's Wheeler's enforcer. You might want to tangle with him but I assure you I don't." Harry drank his whiskey. "Ahhh. That was good. How about another, Ham?"

"Is he friends with whatever his name is?"

"Daniel? I couldn't tell you that. As far as I know Carter was more interested in poking Wheeler's fat daughter."

"If we kidnap their Daniel, would he come after us?"

Harry considered the question carefully, signaling the bartender to refill his glass. "Is that what you're planning to do? Kidnap him?"

"Let's see what happens tomorrow."

Chapter 30

Their train was pulling into Cincinnati, Ohio. Night had fallen and the approaching lights of the city had been their entertainment for most of an hour as they came nearer. Exhausted by their sudden departure from New York they had shared little conversation during the trip and Pennsylvania had passed under them with little comment. Myra had slept most of the way, her head on her son's shoulder and holding his hand tightly. Occasionally, she would stir and look up into his eyes with a look of pure delight and love. He in turn would smother her in hugs of reassurance. It was important to him that she know that he was there to protect them. It was his job, now and forever.

After the disembarking passengers had departed, they gathered their things together on their seats and covered them with one of the blue and white striped blankets that Jakob had given them. While the ladies refreshed themselves, Daniel studied the map showing the rail lines reaching from the East Coast to the West. Making sense of the maze of broad and narrow lines on the map proved to be challenging but by his calculation they should arrive in Chicago late the following day.

Myra returned a new woman. Her hair brushed and holding onto Megan's arm, she smiled brightly when she linked his arm in hers. "I look such a horror," she said weakly.

"You look lovely, mum," Daniel said sincerely, and holding hands they entered the train station restaurant as happy a family as Lynch had ever seen.

Sergeant Lynch had to admit to a twinge of jealousy as he watched them enter the restaurant. There was no doubt about the love they shared.

The young man and young woman with their arms around the older woman. He watched them seated at a table in the far corner of the café before taking a place at the counter where he ordered steak and fried potatoes fighting the urge to watch them.

While he drank his coffee, he dealt with the dilemma that the further he was removed from New York the more difficult it would be to gain the help of the local authorities. As far as he could tell, the Pinkerton Detective Agency was independent of the official authorities and if not aloof from them, were at the very least not well respected by them.

Looking about him, he seriously wondered if he could enlist anyone to help him return a fugitive to a foreign country. If some crimes knew no borders, then he wondered whether his jurisdiction stretched across an ocean, and half-way across a continent? Where did crimes end and refuge begin?

The steam rising from his coffee reminded him of how, in comparable manner, his authority was evaporating. Perhaps the long arm of the law did have limits. If so, Lynch suspected that he was close to reaching that limit. The train's whistle startled him.

*   *   *

Patrick and Gemma had seated themselves at the furthest end of the rear carriage. When the conductor came asking for their tickets, he had taken Patrick's money without a question. Since then they had sat opposite each other with Gemma facing forward to warn Patrick should the man with the disfigured face come into their carriage.

"Go and see what he's doing," Patrick said to Gemma, when the train had come to a halt. He knew who the man was. Not his name, that he couldn't remember, but he knew that he was the policeman who had been injured when their bomb had exploded. None of them, meaning neither he nor his father, nor Clive, or anyone else involved had intended to harm anyone. It was the stony, cold edifice of the institution that they had wanted to disfigure.

Patrick did feel some remorse for the injuries that had been inflicted on Lynch. In the countless hours of introspection during his incarceration he'd acknowledged the foolishness of his and his father's actions for which they had paid a heavy price. What he could not justify was the pain they had inflicted on his mother.

As a result of their actions, his mother, his sister and younger brother had been cast like flotsam onto the sea, forced to face their future alone and betrayed. Patrick's frequent bouts of guilt were at times overwhelming, and when they came at night, they shook his soul, leaving his pillow drenched with his tears. Yet now, his redemption was possible, if he could find his mother and ask her forgiveness.

It was possible that the man they were following might lead him to his family. But it was dangerous. Why was this man at John Hogan's place and why did he beat John Hogan lifeless? The man's actions at the train station were suspicious. He appeared to be both following someone and eluding someone. Who was it that he was following? Who was he eluding?

The carriage was empty of passengers so Gemma was unconcerned when she called for Patrick to join her at the window to the adjoining car. "He's watching someone," she said.

From the window, Lynch was discretely watching something or someone on the platform. Abruptly, he stood, descended to the platform and walked into the station restaurant.

"Should we follow him?" Gemma asked. Patrick considered the danger that the man would recognize him. But who was he was following? Patrick had to know.

"I can't go in there, but you can," he said.

Gemma hesitated a moment. "What should I do?"

"Order some food and watch him. Have some coffee and order some food. I want to know who he's watching."

Chapter 31

Daniel's problems were his constant companions. Throughout the journey he'd been tormented by the thought of having to face Wheeler and explain his disappearance. His options were limited. One being, he could tell the truth, the result of which was that he had managed to reunite with his family. This was a laudable action, possibly. And possibly, Jerome Wheeler, being a reasonable man, would place his hand on his shoulder paternally and congratulate him for his courage and initiative, maybe.

But what he would tell his new family was a far more complicated problem. He'd have much explaining to do when he introduced his mother and sister to Kate and Shirley and there was no way to avoid the recriminations that would arise from his lack of honesty. Whichever way he explained the sudden appearance of his family he was going to be seen as a liar, and that troubled him immensely. Avoidance was one matter, deception was another.

He didn't dwell long on alternative options, mostly because they all led to more questions and more lies, or confessions. One other possibility, risky at best and with poor chances of success, was that he could hide his family until they reached Denver and resettle them there secretly. If it was this option he chose, he would have to be extremely careful and become a very convincing liar, but it was an option.

As his mother returned from the lavatory, Daniel saw that she was accompanied by a tallish, stooped man steadying her against the rolling of the train car. Daniel watched them closely; Megan slept.

"Thank you, Mister Lynch. You are most kind," Myra said, holding onto his hand to steady herself.

"It is my pleasure," he said, smiling at her. Daniel then noticed the taut skin stretched across the man's left cheek. His first reaction was to look away but something about the man was unnervingly familiar.

"Mister Lynch was most kind, Daniel. I almost fell coming out of the loo." Daniel could not miss the smile that passed between them. "Are you going to Chicago, Mister Lynch?" Daniel asked.

Lynch hesitated a moment as if deciding and suddenly Daniel recognized him. That night in Dublin when he had hit the policeman about the head with a brick, the one who then was blown heavenward by the explosion. Daniel was convinced he was seeing a ghost. But it was him, and they both knew it.

"Yes, I am," Lynch replied.

"Now we have someone else to talk with on the journey, Daniel. Won't that be nice?" Daniel looked less than thrilled as his mother carried on. "You're Irish, aren't you Mister Lynch?"

Lynch nodded. "Aye, that I am."

"W, w, where from?" Daniel asked, nervously.

Lynch was on guard as much as Daniel. His origins could trip him up.

"I'm from Belfast," he said convincingly, smiling at Myra.

"An Ulsterman, are you?" Came the sleepy question from Megan.

He'd not realized she'd been listening.

"I'm not a Royalist if that's what concerns you." Lynch smiled his contorted smile at both women.

"Mister Lynch, this is my daughter Megan, and my son Daniel."

Lynch leaned forward and shook hands with Megan, she returned his smile. Daniel also shook Lynch's hand, briefly holding eye contact, as scared as he'd ever been.

"I'm pleased to meet you," Lynch said cordially, "and I hope we have another chance to speak. It will be a long and lonely journey if I don't have that opportunity." With a parting smile Lynch turned and wove his way back along the train car, disappearing into the carriage behind them. Daniel watched him until he had closed the carriage door and shut out the rushing wind.

"He's a nice man don't you think?" Myra said. "Even if he is an Ulsterman," she smiled at both of her children and wrapped the blanket around her shoulders.

*   *   *

"Wake up, Patrick," Gemma's voice was insistent and her shaking wasn't helping in the least.

"What is it? Are we there yet?"

"No, we're somewhere in Pennsylvania."

"Why did you wake me?"

"I've been watching that man in the next cabin and I saw him talking to some Jewish people. I thought you should know." Suddenly Patrick was wide awake, rubbing his stubbly chin, forcing his eyes open.

"Say that again."

"Say 'please?'"

"Alright. Please, say again what you just said."

Gemma laid her head on his shoulder. "I said, I saw that burned man watching someone from the passageway between the train cars and then I saw him waiting there for a long time and then he went in and helped an old lady back to her seat. She's sitting with a girl and a man in a black hat." Gemma felt the stiffening of Patrick's muscles and the tension rising in him.

"Then?"

"He talked with them. I had to hurry back when I saw him coming my way. I don't know if he saw me watching him. I hope not."

"So, he's back in his seat in the next carriage?" Gemma was facing forward. She suddenly moved over to Patrick's seat and then forcefully pulled Patrick's head to her open lips. Not unwillingly, Patrick succumbed to Gemma's embrace but he did see Lynch give Gemma a long look as he passed headed for the toilet and again when he returned to his carriage.

"Who is that man, Patrick?" Gemma panted. She'd liked Patrick from the beginning and her feelings toward him had grown. She was not blind. He was a flawed man, but she had known many of those. A man of deep and dangerous secrets which he would not share, but she'd known many of those as well. That he was dangerous and possibly violent, well, she'd been attracted to those types of men her whole life, hadn't she?

Gemma took his hand and pushed it into her blouse, watching his reaction to the softness and warmth of her breast, caressing the taut skin that stretched across her chest when she breathed in deeply, as she was doing. The passenger across the aisle from them appeared asleep, his head resting on a folded jacket against the window. She wrapped the blanket about them more tightly and lifted her skirt up to her hips and guided Patrick's hand into the garden between her legs.

With her guidance his fingers pressed gently on her special spot and combined with the rocking of the train over the uneven tracks, she flooded with pleasure in a way she had never felt before. The bumps, the constant swaying of the carriage, the sound of the wheels rolling along the rails and her moistness that invited Patrick inside. Was it possible without being noticed?

Gemma fondled Patrick to full erection, enjoying the feeling of power over him as he gazed into her eyes, his expression masked by his need. She turned and settled against his hips. With only a slight adjustment he slipped into her and he heard her soft, deep moan as he pushed himself deeper.

It was not a hurried affair. Patrick was young and healthy and was well proportioned. Gemma reached behind her and clutched his hip as he moved about her pleasure spots. Time and time again she was forced to bury her face in the blanket, climaxing, returning to him each time with a smile of love and wonderment.

"Do you like me, Patrick?" she whispered.

"Do you think you could sneak past that man and see if it really is my brother in the other rail car. If it is him, could you pass him a note?"

The spell was broken. She felt him withdraw, both emotionally and physically. It wasn't sad she told herself, rearranging the blanket, her back to him. She hoped that the stranger across the aisle was still asleep. He wasn't. He never was. He was smiling.

"Do you think that man would recognize me?" Gemma asked.

"We have to take a chance. If he's a bounty hunter, I have to warn my brother." Patrick took a piece of the timetable and wrote in pencil along the margin. "Here give this to him. If it's Daniel he'll recognize this. Don't let my mother see. Can you do that?" He folded the page and handed it to her. "You're in no danger, Gemma, I assure you of that."

Gemma took the paper and placed into the front of her blouse. "Trust me, Gemma," he said kissing her on the cheek.

Limp lamplight shone faintly on the dozing passengers. Gemma placed a shawl over her head and nervously edged her way down the carriage. She didn't see but rather felt the man as she passed him, asleep, his face turned to the window. Relieved, she opened the door to the next carriage, closing it quickly behind her.

The wind was chill and the smoke from the steam engine gathered and swirled in the eddies between the carriages. She braved a quick look through the small window before opening the door and several passengers registered the disturbance to their sleep. She made as if to use the toilet, noting that Daniel was indeed awake and was watching her.

Catching Daniel's attention wasn't difficult. She pointed her finger at him and beckoned him. He looked at her, tilting his head, confused. Losing patience, she withdrew the folded paper from her blouse and pointed at him. Suddenly, the toilet door opened and she clutched the paper to her chest as a large man emerged. Smiling drunkenly, he gave Gemma a leering glance as he swayed back to his seat, looking back as often as was safe.

Gemma opened the door peeking into the now empty toilet. Daniel was still watching her so she motioned him with her finger to join her, again.

Daniel pointed to himself. Gemma sighed and shrugged at the stupidity of the modern man. She placed one hand on her hip and pointed directly at him curling her forefinger as she did so. No reaction was forthcoming from Daniel. "Ahhh," she inwardly sighed in understanding, she pointed at her breasts. He understood, maybe.

She stood in the small passageway with her back to the door and waited. Any normal man would be racing across the seats to get a free piece of ass on a train, she thought to herself. That kind of thing was a new rage she had heard in New York. Gemma could barely imagine the contortions a couple would have to assume to manage sex in a water closet on the back of a bucking bull.

Daniel knocked and Gemma opened the door. "Did you want to see me?" he asked, confused. Gemma pulled him into the lavatory and closed the door. He reached out to kiss her.

"Stop it!" Gemma said, harshly. "That's not what I want." Daniel recoiled, shocked. "I want to ask you something." She watched him closely. "Are you Jewish?" Daniel looked at her oddly, smiled and shook his head. "Are you Daniel Shadlow then?" The affect was immediate and Daniel turned for the door, difficult given the small confines. He grabbed the door handle but she placed her hand on his holding it tightly, stopping him from opening the door.

This was too much of a coincidence. "No, I'm not!" He said loudly and pulled open the door, but she pushed it closed and kissed him passionately. Stunned, Daniel surrendered like a Frenchman and submitted to her hushing and calming kisses. He pushed for more but she pulled away and took his face in her hands looking deeply into his eyes.

"Well, if you were ...? I would tell you that your brother Patrick is on this train." Again, the effect was immediate. Again, Daniel reached for the door handle. She kissed him more, returning him to her confidence. "If you don't believe me, you must at least read this," she implored. "Patrick wrote it to you just now. He said not to tell your mother that he is on the train and to watch out for the man with the twisted face. He's a bounty hunter." Daniel looked at her skeptically, a pall of silence filled their closeness.

Knock! Knock! Someone knocked on the door of the lavatory.

"Just a minute," Gemma called out.

"Who are you?" Daniel asked, his back against the door.

Gemma looked at him sweetly, seeing the similarities in their souls, seeing the vast chasms of difference too. "I'm his friend," she said, and a sad smile passed over her face. Knuckles rapped on the door. "Go now. You are all in danger. Go!"

Daniel swiftly exited, smiling stupidly at the man waiting his turn and returned to his seat clutching the note. Gemma then exited, but the surprised man paid her little heed as he pushed past her.

Entering the adjoining carriage she closed the door quickly so not to disturb those sleeping or the man watching. Carefully and quietly she moved down the carriage but when she came to the seat previously occupied by the mysterious man, the seat was empty. Her heart skipped.

Fighting the urge to panic she slowly walked the remaining dozen paces to the end of the car and opened the door closing it quickly behind her. On the platform between the carriages she stood in the smoky wind, risking quick glances back into the train car. After a while the man emerged, but from a different seat. One near enough to the door for him to have watched her and Daniel.

She lingered at the small window too long. Their eyes met and even at night she knew he recognized her.

Patrick's anxious expression awaited her. "Did it go well?"

"It went well." She smiled falsely and placed his hand on her breast.

Chapter 32

Sergeant Lynch was quite pleased with himself. He had his quarry in his sights and was certain of his identification. Like Daniel, he vividly remembered the night of the explosion and unconsciously touched his tortured face, as he did reflexively whenever that memory crossed his mind. The pain in his face was constant, especially when he smiled, which was a rare thing. It was a tolerable affliction and the scarred skin was a shield of sorts masking not only his true feelings but his intent as well. An advantage in his current endeavor, but generally not so.

While the train rolled through the blankness of the night, he contemplated the letter he would write to Killeen asking what he was to do after he had arrested Daniel Shadlow. It concerned him that the longer he remained on this train the further he removed himself from the niceties of his profession and the power of his jurisdiction. He was after all, heading out into the wild-west.

He felt some small satisfaction in the knowledge that the young man in the next carriage was indeed the one he saw at the bank robbery. Though now dressed in Jewish rags he still had the look Lynch would always remember as clearly as when he had surprised the lad in the alley on that dreaded night. The fury in his eyes as he swung the brick time and again was imprinted on Lynch's mind's eye.

Perhaps it was the blackness of the night rolling past his window, but more likely his exhaustion that caused his deepening melancholy. Considering in his reflection he admitted to himself that he had been unsurprised when his wife had deserted him. He knew in his heart that it was because of his injuries that she had run away. The honest mirror reminded him every time he looked in the cursed thing to shave the left side of his face where the skin was damaged.

He caught his reflection in the train's window. With his left side hidden he didn't see much of a difference from when he was a younger man, simply older. His right side was his real face he told himself as he drifted off into a fitful doze. Memories of happier times spent with his wife and even lovers before her floated across the curtain of his mind.

Perhaps there was something ahead of him that would help erase the pain. Perhaps he was secretly hoping for a new life.

*   *   *

"Did you have sex with her?" Megan whispered into Daniel's ear. He'd thought nothing of her coming over to rest her head against his shoulder. Now he turned to face her, surprised at her boldness and observation. "It didn't take long," she said, looking up at him, laughing at his discomfort.

"Sshh!" he said holding his finger to his lips. "No!" he whispered emphatically, "I did not have sex with her." He shot her a terse look. "But, if you promise not to tell mum, I'll tell you a secret," he whispered, watching her reaction closely. Megan's newfound mental and social skills were both a surprise and perplexing to him. Deciding to tell Megan what he knew, felt as if he was stepping up to the edge of a cliff. Tension pulled at his stomach. The train rolled on.

"I promise," Megan said, nodding.

"Come with me," he said, motioning her to be silent so as not to wake their mother. When they reached the rear of the car, Daniel knocked on the lavatory door and when no one responded he pushed Megan in and closed the door behind them.

In the close quarters Daniel noticed for the first time how much Megan had grown. She was but an inch shorter than he was and it surprised him.

"You've grown so tall, Megan," he said and she blushed.

"I'm a woman now, Daniel. Not a little girl anymore. New York made me grow up."

"I can see that," Daniel replied. Megan had filled out and her breasts pushed against the material of her dress. Daniel blushed when she caught him looking at her chest.

"What's your big secret?"

"What if I told you that Patrick is on this train?"

"How do you know this?" she asked, her voice calm.

Daniel paused and smiled at his sister. Her reaction was not what he'd anticipated. Not at all like the slow-witted girl he'd left two years ago. It forced him reconsider his little sister again and this time he looked deeply into her, smiling.

"Why are you looking at me that way?" Megan asked, smiling also.

He could never find the words to tell her what it meant to him that she was not as feeble-minded as they had all suspected. Perhaps she might have been once, but not now. Now, she was someone to be reckoned with.

"That woman came to warn me that Mister Lynch is not what he seems." He waited for Megan to respond, but she didn't. "I don't know much more than that. But if he's a bounty hunter we have to get away from him."

"How do you know Patrick is really on the train and that she's not another bounty hunter?" Daniel pulled out the page of timetable that Patrick had written his message on and showed it to Megan.

"I recognize Patrick's writing," he said. "He always wrote my name wrong, remember? Look here," he pointed to the very first word and indeed it was misspelled. "Daneil ", it read. "He always spelled my name wrong to make me angry. I know it's him."

"What are we going to do?"

"I have a plan, but I have to talk with him first. I want you to go back there and find the woman you saw me with. Tell her that I'll meet Patrick in the men's lavatory at the next station. Tell him to wait until the train is about to leave. Can you do that?"

"What about Mister Lynch?"

"I doubt he's awake, but just ignore him." Megan frowned. "I don't know how it is that Patrick is out of prison, and I don't know how he found us, but if people are looking for him, we should be very careful." In Daniel's mind's eye he could see Megan squealing in excitement at seeing her older brother. "Try to stay calm."

"I'll be careful." She pushed past him and opened the door and before he could say more, she'd opened the door to the adjoining carriage and disappeared into the rushing wind.

Chapter 33

D aniel fretted until Megan reappeared, swaying with the roll of the carriage. Her head covered by her scarf her expression was a mystery as she sat down next to him. Silently they watched their mother sleeping for a minute or more. Daniel could feel the trembling in his sister's arm.

"Was it him?" he whispered. Moments passed then he saw her smile appear and then tears.

"Yes," she whispered. "But he's not the same," she added, to Daniel's dismay. She held her hand to her face and wiped away her tears with the back of her hand. "He'll meet you at the next station. But he says to be careful that Mister Lynch doesn't follow you." Megan smiled and squeezed Daniel's arm. "Mister Lynch is a bad man, isn't he?"

Daniel placed his arm around Megan and held her until she dozed. Dawn was near breaking and he needed a plan.

*   *   *

Patrick woke with a start. Light streamed in through the window. Panic brought him upright in his seat. Gemma was gone. They train were slowing and farms and buildings were passing in orderly fashion as the train entered the outskirts of Cincinnati. He relaxed when Gemma appeared returning from the toilet, or from the car ahead.

"Is she really your sister?" Gemma looked at him closely seeking a resemblance. "She doesn't look like you?"

"I don't look like me anymore. I doubt my mother will even recognize me," he laughed, half believing himself.

"I think we're coming into Cincinnati," she said as she sat. Patrick nodded. "Are you going to try to see your brother here?"

Patrick nodded again.

"What if that man follows you."

Patrick had thought of several options not short of violence. He had no reason to hate the man who had killed John Hogan. It was not a personal matter. That the murderer was a threat to his family, that made it personal.

"If he tries to follow Daniel into the men's room, I want you to distract him. Do you think you can do that?"

Gemma laughed. "I've spent many hours studying your lot. If I can't capture a man's attention then I think I've wasted my teenage years."

With a look that spoke the words he was unable to speak, he leaned into her and kissed her in a way he'd never done before. A longing of the heart to find a home. It was a kiss that enveloped Gemma and she felt his love.

The train jolted to a stop amid the clatter of grinding metal and hissing steam. "Stay here and watch." Gemma said, easing herself from his embrace. "I'll buy us some food. We should be here for half an hour, so that man should be back on the train by then."

"If he isn't back on board, we might have a problem."

"I'll take care of everything, don't worry." She winked as she left and Patrick watched her walk around the knots of passengers and disappear into the station proper.

*   *   *

Daniel and Megan assisted their mother down onto the platform and together they walked to the restrooms. Daniel pulled his blue striped shawl around his shoulders while he scanned the train windows hoping to see his brother. When he didn't, he stepped into the men's facilities. It was a simple affair, a long row of enclosed toilets with a urinal along the opposite wall. Nearer the door three washbasins were being used by weary travelers.

In the station restaurant, they took a booth and Daniel saw Lynch enter and glance around the room. Lynch smiled when he saw them and gave them a wave as he took an empty stool at the counter. Daniel nervously played with his cutlery and wondered if the plain metal knife would be of any use. Megan had already secreted one in her pocket.

Excusing himself Daniel went outside to study the large map of the rail system on the wall of the station. On one of the printed timetables, he drew a rough map of the route they would be taking to Chicago and located a place where there might be an opportunity to lose Mr. Lynch. At a town called South Bend.

The train's whistle blew and Daniel hurried his mother and sister onto the train, noting that Lynch was in no hurry to board and seemed to be loitering near the toilets.

"All aboard!" The conductor shouted and Daniel was relieved to see Lynch head for the train. Daniel climbed off the side of the train hidden from the platform and ran to the rear of the train, emerging from between the carriages.

The restroom was empty and deathly quiet when he entered but for the puffing of the train as it began to pull away from the station.

"Patrick," he called. Immediately a door opened and a man he did not recognize emerged and made a direct path toward him. Daniel was suddenly afraid. He had anticipated the immense joy of seeing his brother again but this was something unplanned. As the man came closer Daniel's panic grew. Suddenly Daniel was taken bodily by the man and hugged in a manner that shocked him. He froze.

"Daniel, it's me, Patrick," he said, softly. Daniel peered into the stranger's face and it took more than a breath for him to realize that it was, indeed, Patrick. "Don't be alarmed. I may not be as pretty as I once was, but I'm still the same brother you left in Ireland."

Daniel would always remember this moment when as long-lost brothers they met again. Filled with a surge of love for his brother, he held on tightly, ignoring the increasing tempo of the train's departure.

"There's a cop on the train looking for you," Daniel said seriously. "I think he's the cop that got blown up when you blew up the bank."

"Yes, I know. I remember him from the trial." Patrick said, unsmiling. "He's dangerous and he's probably after you, too."

"Me?" Daniel said, shocked.

"I had no idea that the English would care so much about you," he laughed. "Me on the other hand, I'm a wanted man, an escaped convict."

"Quick, we don't want to miss the train." Daniel led the way out of the toilets and they chased the departing train. "I've got a plan to get rid of him," Daniel yelled as they ran.

"What is it?"

They both grabbed onto the railing of one of the last cars and safely aboard they took a moment to inspect each other. "You're looking older, Daniel," Patrick said, smiling.

"You too."

"How is mum?" Patrick asked. Daniel smiled at his brother. "She's tired but Megan is strong."

"What's your plan?"

"There's a place called South Bend. It's three hours outside of Chicago. Trains go north or south from there. We have to make Lynch think that we are changing trains and going north, not south. I don't know how we're going to do it yet."

"I'm sure Gemma will find a way. She's crafty."

"Is she your wife?" Daniel asked.

"No. And I have to ask, are you Jewish now?"

"No!" Daniel laughed. "Not yet, but one never knows about the future." Daniel took Patrick's hand and held onto it tightly. "We'll meet in South Bend in the restroom. We'll have to be clever and lucky if we're going to make him change trains."

Daniel made his way back along the carriages and noticed that Lynch looked surprised that he appeared from the rear of the train. When he rejoined his family, his mother wore a worried look which passed into a weary smile when he sat beside her and held her hand. They had ten hours before their next adventure. In a place called South Bend.

Chapter 34

"You look so worried, Kate." Shirley tried her best to sound cheerful. "You shouldn't be. I'm sure he'll be in Chicago when we get there." She smiled and patted Kate on her knee. Truthfully, she and Red were both very worried and the little that they knew was far from comforting. Daniel had disappeared. It was so unlike him, and that in itself was cause for alarm.

Shirley leaned into Red for support and comfort and being the stalwart partner that he was, he pulled her close and kissed the top of her head. Red was deeply concerned, though he kept his fears to himself. The boy, or should he say the young man, had shown nothing but reliability until now.

Kate was also a worry for Shirley. Her manner had become more abrasive since Daniel had left for Chicago. When Red or Shirley asked about him, Kate was vague and dismissive. Red had supposed that it was her way of dealing with the worry and being annoyed with him for not being with her and the baby. It was natural.

And then there was what Joe had told him regarding Harry's visit. Red was convinced that Harry was somehow connected to Joe's death. It seemed that Harry was the cause of the problem once again. With little to proceed on, he set about putting what facts they knew into some semblance of a theory. A daunting task, full of suppositions.

Billy Tomb, Harry's neighbor, swore to Sheriff Hunter that he had seen Harry and another man at Harry's burned-out cabin. Being that he was the only witness, Billy's statement was taken as the hallucinations of a drunk, which Billy most definitely had become. But Red was undeterred and when pressed about that night, Billy reaffirmed what he had said, also agreeing with them that he would make a bad witness should he have to testify in a courtroom. Red agreed with Billy but he also believed him.

*　　　　　　*　　　　　　*

"What's wrong, Daniel?" Myra had watched him sharing whispered conversations with Megan when they thought she was sleeping. Perhaps it was the fresh air or Daniel near again but she felt as if after a long sleep, she was waking up to life once again. The hypnotic melody of the rails and the swaying of the carriage had lulled her into long, deep sleeps, deeper by far than usual. Besides her aching neck, she now felt refreshed in a way she'd not felt in many a year. More than just physically replenished; emotionally too.

"You two are up to something." Myra's look was serious. "I can always tell." Daniel and Megan exchanged glances, surprised by their mother's alertness. They both looked at their mother curiously, noting the sparkle that had returned to her eyes and the slight turn up on her mouth when she smiled. "What's the trouble? Why are two you so restless?"

Daniel faked a smile. "I'm nervous about what I'm going to tell Mister Wheeler when we get to Chicago. I might not even have a job now."

"Ah, Daniel, you worry too much," she said, smiling at him. "You always did."

Daniel decided then that all mothers naturally knew how to turn the screws on their children. So much for the misconception that men ruled the world, he thought. Nestled against his mother, his breathing slowed and his eyelids became leaden.

He awoke with a start. Something was wrong. It was written over both their faces. "What's happened?" he asked, looking around for danger. None seemed to be apparent. He looked back inquisitively. Megan was red-faced and his mother wore as stern a look as he could ever remember.

"Is it true?" she demanded of him.

"Is w-w-what t-t-true?" he stuttered, as a child caught in a lie.

"What Megan told me."

Daniel looked at Megan and knew his sister had betrayed his trust. She returned his look sheepishly then considered her hands the way she used to do when she was nervous or uncomfortable.

Daniel recognized the look. "Is Patrick truly on board this train?" Daniel nodded and watched the wave of emotion wash over his mother's face. "Megan says he's with a woman." Daniel nodded again. "How did he find us?" Daniel shrugged. "Tell me the truth, Daniel." Her eyes held him. "Are we in danger?"

It was a question he'd been grappling with also. Lynch was onto him, he knew that. But, whether it was for financial gain or revenge, he couldn't tell. What he did know was that they had to get as far away from him as quickly as possible.

Whatever his real intent, Daniel was certain that Lynch would only make matters worse when it came time to make his family known to Wheeler and Kate.

"I know who Mister Lynch is, mum," he said softly, so as not to alarm her. "He said he's an Ulsterman, but he's not."

"How do you know?"

"There was a policeman that got injured in dud's stupid plan. Do you remember?" Myra nodded. "Well, Mister Lynch was that policeman."

"How do you know this?"

"I hit him on the head with a brick that night and Patrick saw him at his trial. He was still in bandages then but Patrick recognized him."

"Why's he here?" she asked, her anxiety growing. Daniel shrugged and glanced at Megan.

"What do we do now?" Myra whispered, her hand shading her mouth. "He doesn't seem to be in any hurry to do anything to us. He actually seems quite pleasant," she trailed off, looking out the window.

Daniel took out the train timetable and leaned closer so that they could speak in whispers. "There is a place coming soon where two trains leave in different directions at the same time. Our train is one of them. It's the only place where this happens between here and Chicago. If we can make Mister Lynch think that we are changing trains and get him to take the train heading north we should be able to get away from him. That train doesn't stop again for four hours so that would give us a head start on him."

Myra and Megan exchanged glances. Neither was smiling.

"I think I have an idea how we're going to do it." Searching through his pockets he found the stub of one of their tickets and after writing on it passed it to Megan.

"As soon as the train stops, I want you to hurry back there and give this to Patrick, then come back." He pushed the note into Megan's hands.

"What are you planning, Daniel?"

"Hopefully, some magic."

＊　　　　＊　　　　＊

"Heard anymore from your sergeant?" Killeen's superior was descending the stairs from his tower of power.

Deep in thought, Killeen looked up, startled, almost dropping the papers he'd been studying. "Err, not as such, sir," he said, contritely. "What've you heard then?"

"Nothing. Yesterday I sent him a cable requesting an update."

"Well, keep me informed and tell me as soon as you hear from the man."

Killeen watched his superior stride down the staircase, as much like a Caesar as had any man since the departure of the Romans. It was true that he'd not heard from Lynch in over a week and that caused him some concern. Returning his attention to the statement he was holding, he questioned whether or not he should share this additional information with his superior. That Sergeant Lynch had withdrawn the total sum of his allotted funds and had then disappeared.

＊　　　　＊　　　　＊

Sergeant Lynch was barely awake. Numbed by the relentless clatter of steel wheels rolling over the rails he had repeatedly woken to find his chin resting on his chest, startling himself awake each time. So near to his quarry, yet so far.

With his ability to detain Patrick Shadlow diminishing the further he travelled, he decided he should make his arrest in Chicago, with the assistance of the Pinkertons if possible. Consulting the timetable, he saw that the first town where he could notify them of his intentions was at the next stop, in South Bend. It was his optimistic and probably unrealistic hope, that in alerting them to the Shadlows arrival they would lend their support.

What little he knew of these Americans, arresting a foreigner on their soil was a specious act and could unleash sentiment against him and what he represented. Those who had emigrated from Ireland were familiar to him but they had changed noticeably during their absence. Those who were once downtrodden had found a haven, and their confidence and hope in this new country were the direct result.

As for himself? What new possibilities might present themselves to him in this broad, new land? His facial disfigurement seemed less of a blight to him here. As if he were walking among sympathetic people, similarly suffering. He felt more acceptable here.

Not for the last time did he search his reflection in the train window, looking to see evidence that he had changed. But his distorted face remained inscrutable. Still, he imagined that he was more like those around him. Less an outcast.

*   *   *

Thoughts of a similar kind occupied Patrick's mind. Rolling over the rails, Gemma's head resting on his shoulder, he'd had time to consider once again both his actions and the consequences of those actions. His prison experiences had tainted his view of society as being civilized. No society should allow a person to be treated as he and his father had been brutalized.

His attack on Clive had satisfied his thirst for revenge, but it had not satisfied him. Was it wrong to do what he did? He shuddered at the memory and deliberately turned away from it and the weight it laid on his conscience. He breathed deeply of the American air and considered his feelings for Gemma, questioning why she should be in his life. Perhaps there were good people in this world.

Outside, the landscape was brightening and the horizon clearing, as was his mind. Both his world and his future were illuminated by the same dawning light. In this new land, he could be free once again. He could create a new future. Raise a family. Become someone his mother could be proud of, if he could escape being returned to England bound in chains.

Chapter 35

The train's whistle screamed, announcing their arrival at South Bend. Time for Daniel to put his plan into action. After the train entered the station they sat patiently watching the departing passengers gather their belongings and prepare to exit the train, typically followed by a brief period when the carriage was relatively empty. He nodded to Megan and together they helped Myra to her feet. She smiled at each of her children, winked at Daniel, and so their ruse began.

Initially, he'd been angry with Megan for telling their mother the truth about Patrick and the danger they faced. That was until he recognized the joy and excitement on her face when she asked about Patrick. Then she became more as he remembered her. Alive once again, alert and involved in the plan that Daniel proposed.

When Harry Rich proclaimed that, "The secret in cheating is successful distraction." Daniel was far from convinced, given Harry's dismal record at gambling. But, with few other options available he was compelled to give it a try.

While exiting their carriage, Myra made a point of waving to Sergeant Lynch before they headed into the station. Lynch waved back, noticing nothing out of the usual. He was also familiar with the routine and was in no hurry to enter the station, or the restaurant where the food would be just as awful as it had been in every stop along the way. The mere thought of a big bowl of hot Irish stew and soda bread at his local public house in Dublin brought him near to tears.

But, unable to ignore his hunger, he stepped down from the train stiffly. Deciding to stretch his legs and to ease his back pain, he walked along the platform, mingling with passengers boarding his train heading to Chicago and the passengers going north boarding the train on the adjacent platform. Nothing appeared out of the ordinary.

Megan was watching him closely, so when Lynch turned his back she hurried into the ladies' restroom and found Gemma waiting. Quickly she told her of Daniel's plan and after Gemma left to share the news with

Patrick, she scrutinized the facilities. In the restaurant she nodded to Daniel and taking her mother's hand accompanied her to the ladies' restroom. While Myra washed her face and hands, Megan checked the stalls and opened the door of the furthest one.

"Stay in here until I come back for you," she whispered. Myra nodded. "Wish us luck. I'll be back for you." Megan closed the door to the stall, ignoring the looks given her by two of the women also using the facilities.

At the restroom entrance, concealed by a privacy wall, she watched and waited for Lynch to enter the restaurant. He did as she had hoped but paused when he saw Daniel at the ticket counter appearing to purchase tickets. Predictably, he hurried into the restaurant. Seizing her chance, Megan dashed back to the train.

Failing to see the Shadlows in the restaurant, Lynch exited and was surprised to see Daniel now standing on the platform nearest the train that was heading north. Lynch was suddenly confused. Daniel saw him, smiled and waved. Lynch waved back. Daniel was still wearing his ridiculous Jewish disguise, fooling no one, looking about anxiously. Lynch was now beyond curious and becoming alarmed.

To his left, Myra and Megan emerged from the bathroom arm in arm, making a tender tableau. A mother, head covered in a shawl, leaning on her daughter's arm, one supporting the other. Unexpectedly they walked quickly not back toward the train they arrived on, but towards the train facing the opposite direction.

Lynch watched intently as they joined Daniel and showed their tickets to the conductor and carrying their few possessions, boarded the train heading north. Lynch had assumed that it would be a typical stop where he would have half an hour to eat and get his telegram off to Chicago before his train departed again. Now, suddenly, he was in danger of losing his quarry. Worse still, their train's whistle blew and the conductor was announcing, "All aboard."

Alarmed, Lynch raced back to his train and grabbed his coat, discretely tucking his pistol into his belt. After checking the compartment where the Shadlows had been and neither seeing them nor their luggage, he ran as fast as he could manage for the north bound train.

The hissing of the steam engine was rising in tempo and the train had begun to move, daring him to catch it. Struggling, he ran alongside the carriages until he saw Daniel's hat and the blue and white shawl through the train window. Now certain they were on the train, he grasped a handrail and leapt aboard.

Inside, the train carriage was crowded but he saw Daniel's family pushing forward through the crowd toward the forward carriage. Following at a distance Lynch smiled, pleased with himself that he had not fallen for their ruse. But his smile vanished when he opened the door and peered into the next carriage. They were nowhere to be seen. Now in a panic he barged through the carriage, roughly pushing people out of the way, searching for them. They were not there. They had disappeared. Where had they gone?

The train was gaining speed as he raced back to the space between the carriages and looked back behind the train. The light was not good but he spotted them. Curiously, the mother was sprinting like a teenager as they dashed across the train tracks. Lynch fleetingly considered jumping, but the train was moving too quickly and he prudently judged leaping from the train as an invitation to break a lot of his bones.

Gripping the iron railing tightly, he stood on the tiny, bucking platform between the swaying train cars and helplessly watched the red lamp on the rear of the south- bound train fade into the distance. He was heading north. Headed where? He had no idea, and no ticket.

Fuming that he had been outsmarted, he placed his bag in the rack above a vacant seat and sat down heavily, breathing hard. He noted the man across from him looking concerned.

"Are you alright?" the man asked.

"Where is this train headed?" Lynch replied, testily.

"Detroit," the man answered, watching with interest when Lynch pulled out his train schedule and studied it. "Are you running from someone?" The man asked.

Lynch smiled and saw the man recoil.

*   *   *

Daniel was unfamiliar with things about him going smoothly. His journey to Aspen, when he thought about it, was the smoothest part of his life's journey to date. Since arriving in Aspen he'd been hopping from one potential catastrophe to another, from one slippery rock to another, never able to stop for fear of falling into more trouble most often because of Harry. But something extraordinary had happened with their plan to misdirect Mister Lynch. It had all worked out perfectly.

Racing back to the platform, he, Megan and Gemma, still wearing the shawl over her head, laughed for joy watching the train bearing Lynch and the dangers he posed heading away from them.

Megan hurried into the restroom and emerged holding her mother's hand. Patrick was waiting outside for her when she appeared. Myra said nothing. Could not find words. She looked up into his tortured eyes, seeing the hurt there. Seeing the change in him. The pain and anger resident. She looked at him closely, looked at him as his mother and her eyes filled with tears as she stroked his cheek. He was no longer the boy she had known; it was written clear on his face.

"I'm so sorry, Patrick," she said, sincerely. "Your father..."

Patrick gathered her to him, enveloped her in his loving embrace.

"I know mum, and he paid the price, so let's leave him in peace."

"I love you, Patrick," she blurted out and kissed him hard and held him more tightly to her.

"We're all together now, mum. Things will be better from now on."

Myra managed a smile for him. "Yes, I think they will."

"Did he fall for it?" Patrick asked Daniel.

"Hook, line and sinker." Daniel yelled joyfully, and took his brother in his arms, enfolding Megan and Myra in his embrace. Such a feeling of love and togetherness none of them had felt since leaving Ireland. It was a fleeting glimpse of heaven on Earth, being surrounded and embraced by those loved and longed for. Gemma silently stood apart, uninvited into the celebration. The train's whistle screamed.

"Go get aboard quickly and we'll get some food," Daniel said, taking Patrick by the elbow. "Do you have any money, Patrick?"

Patrick laughed. "You know I've been in prison, don't you?"

Happy to be together again they hurriedly bought sandwiches and apples, paying with the last of Daniel's money. Still laughing as in days gone by, they raced for the departing train and barely caught the rear carriage.

"What a good job you did of impersonating my mother, Gemma." Daniel smiled at her and she brightened.

"It was exciting." Gemma said, happily. "I've done some things in my time, but that was the best one so far. Will there be others?" she asked, hopefully. Then she saw a gloom come over Daniel's face. "Did I say something wrong?" she asked.

"No, Gemma. Nothing to concern yourself about." Daniel's thoughts were focused on what he could expect when they arrived in Chicago. When he opened his eyes, they were all watching him intently.

He smiled back bravely, dreading the fast approaching, inevitable event.

Chapter 36

"Next stop! Chicago, Illinois." The conductor strolled through the cars making the announcement, waking Daniel. "End of the line, folks. Chicago, Illinois." The train conductor smiled at Daniel's little brood.

The Shadlows departed the train with a twinge of regret. The train was where the Shadlows had become a family again. For them all, it had become more than a conveyance; it had also given them security and a semblance of safety. That is, if you disregarded the appearance of Mister Lynch.

For Patrick and Gemma, it had also been a special place. Where they had spent dozens of hours nestled in each other's arms. It had given them both time to think. Patrick had fought his vengeful demons while Gemma battled the temptations that had dragged her down the paths she had taken. Both had silently wrestled with their failures and their sins, and though neither had discussed the subject, both dreamed of a new future with or without the other.

The Chicago Grand Terminal was massive. Constructed for the opening of the World's Fair, it was sprawling. Stout Doric colonnades supporting a high ceiling were enhanced by electric lighting fixtures and tall, colored glass windows. Designed to appeal to the imagination, the entrances faced all four directions, inviting passengers and visitors into an exciting modern city with an outward looking view on a future glowing with possibilities.

Daniel had conjured a rough plan of action. He intended to find a hotel for his family, acquire some more money and then secretly dispatch them to Denver. Should Wheeler not be in Chicago yet, his plan was to borrow the money Wheeler had left for emergencies in the safe at the hotel. His imagination reeled at the potential pitfalls in his plan. Should Wheeler have returned before him, Daniel was hopeful of convincing him that he needed to borrow the money to pay off gambling debts.

Studying the scheduled departures for Denver, Daniel considered his options. He was under no illusion that Lynch would have exited the train at the very first opportunity. Nor, that he would be hurrying as fast as possible south to Chicago on the first available train. Daniel had seen the look in his eyes. Despite his gentle remarks to Myra and Megan, he saw the anger resident in the man. So much pain and need for revenge that merely the thought of him made Daniel tremble.

The traffic was chaotic and frustrating, more so to Daniel than the cab driver. But the brief respite gave him a chance to think. Time to gather his courage because with so much at stake it was likely that he was going to have to lie, and lie often. There was nothing to be gained from telling the truth now. It would only lead to more questions, more difficult ones to answer.

The cab halted in front of the hotel and Daniel leapt out, handing the driver his last half dollar coin. "Please, can you wait for me?"

"I'll wait five minutes," the driver said, and Daniel dashed into the hotel lobby, leaving his family in the cab.

"Can I have a withdrawal note, please," he asked the uniformed man at the reception desk.

Quickly filling out the request for fifty dollars, he handed the note over and received a look of disdain in return. Little wonder, he thought, since he'd been wearing the same clothes for almost a week.

"I'm sorry sir," the man smirked, "but that account has been closed." Shaken, Daniel took the key to his room and darted for the stairs, not hearing what the man said as he left. He should have taken the time to listen.

At the door to his room, he inserted the key and was turning it when he heard voices coming from the other side of the closed door. Cautiously, he put his ear to the door. Heavy footsteps were approaching. Panic overcame him, and he turned and raced for the stairs, leaving his key in the lock. He had reached the first step of the stairs when he heard the door open.

"Who was at the door, Red?" Shirley asked. Red listened to the departing footsteps on the stairs and retrieved the key left in the door. He turned back to Shirley, his face a blank expression. "Red, who was it?"

"I think it was Daniel," he said, perplexed, holding up the key. "Where is he?" Kate asked, hurrying for the door.

"Get your coats!" Red ordered. "He went down the stairs."

Bumping into startled hotel guests as he ran, Daniel was almost at the front door. Looking back one last time to see if he was being followed, he ran headlong into a large man entering the hotel, knocking the man off his feet. Embarrassed, Daniel reached out his hand to help him.

"I'm so sorry, sir. Here 1-1 -1,. Let me help you up," Daniel stammered.

The man indignantly righted his tall hat and glared up at Daniel, flushed face and angry. Daniel was horrified. Panic assaulted him. He darted for the door, leaving a stunned, embarrassed and bewildered Jerome Wheeler sitting on the lobby floor. Immediately, Red's strong arms helped him to his feet and Shirley's slender hands brushed off his coat restoring to him some dignity.

"What happened, Jerome?" Red and Shirley asked together.

"I was knocked to the ground," Jerome said in amazement, "by Daniel. Did you see him?"

"No, we didn't," Shirley answered. "Red said he ran off."

"Well, don't waste your time here, go find him," Wheeler demanded.

"Did a young man get into a cab just now?" Red asked the doorman.

"Yes, sir. That's the cab going around the corner, there," he said, as another cab stopped in front of them. Artfully, the doorman opened the cab door and Red, Shirley and Kate climbed inside.

"Follow that cab that just went around the corner please, driver." Red called out. The driver nodded and slapped his horses into action. Red sat between Shirley and Kate, uncomfortable, troubled by so many questions demanding answers.

"Why would he run away?" Kate asked, justifiably confused.

"I don't know, Kate." Red replied.

"Did it have anything to do with that woman?" Kate asked. Red and Shirley looked at each other shocked.

"What woman?" They said in unison.

"Oh, don't say you didn't know. I knew about Claire Cavendish even before Mrs. Wheeler told you." Kate was staring at Shirley defiantly. "Abigail told me. Oh, don't look so surprised, mother. You have your spies and I have mine."

Neither Shirley nor Red spoke as they digested this news. Kate wondered if they were breathing. That Shirley was surprised that Kate knew of Claire Cavendish was not surprising. That she had ignored the possibility of it happening was.

"It's just a rumor, Kate," Shirley tried to explain. "I wouldn't put any stock in it. Rumors are just hot air. Isn't that right, Red?"

"I'm sure Daniel will explain everything," Red trailed off, concentrating on the cab they were following.

"Driver, don't let them see that we're followin' them, OK?" Red pushed a five-dollar bill into the driver's hand and hoped that the ending of this journey would not be a bad one.

"Where are we going, Daniel?" Patrick asked, concerned as they all were. Daniel tapped the driver on the shoulder. "Could you find us a hotel in the city?"

"Not for under a hundred dollars a night," he replied. Daniel studied the traffic ahead of them for a while, considering his options, which were fewer than few.

"Can you drive us through the Columbia Exposition?"

The driver looked at him curiously. "You can't get in without a pass." Daniel found his credentials and passed them up to the driver. "I'm with the Colorado Exhibit," he said.

"If you say so, son," the driver said. Daniel was smiling as he sat.

"What are you so suddenly happy about?" Myra asked.

"Have you ever been to a World's Fair?"

It was a journey through valleys of light draped like stars falling from the sky in cascades. Hundreds of thousands of glowing electric bulbs festooned the sparkling white structures from spire to grass in strings of blisteringly bright light. As if traveling into the future, they rode down the wide Boulevard of the Americas surrounded by throngs of equally bewondered people.

All around them the excitement of the crowd was palpable and infectious. Meagan and Gemma at times couldn't be restrained and jumped from the slowly moving cab to peer into some exhibition hall or other, returning festooned with ribbons. Myra was speechless, watching the parade of smiling people agog with the spectacle of innovation and progress.

A wave of pride was swelling in Daniel's heart. Unrecognized at first. Simply a feeling of well-being. Smiling at his mother, he looked about him with altered vision. The responsibility he'd been carrying on his shoulders became lighter, and if only momentarily, his fears left him. He felt as if he'd stepped back from the front lines of a battle. Even if it was delusion, it was a welcome respite.

Having seen it all before, Daniel was less affected by the novelty, but it awoke feelings that he was on the cusp of many possible futures. All about him were throngs of humanity, crowds of people all clamoring for a better world unfettered by the bondage of their past. In this seething, happy crowd, Daniel saw the future of America and he wondered how many folks like he and his family had come to America just a few steps ahead of retribution from the law.

Watching Patrick, Daniel could almost feel the potential that came from families joining together for the sake of prosperity. Patrick noticed him watching him and smiled back. It was as if in that smile that Daniel saw not only the past that was haunting them but the dangers that they were facing. Suddenly, once again, Daniel was afraid. What did he fear? He ran through the list in his mind. Wheeler, Kate, Lynch, the list went on.

Bravely, he clasped his mother's hand more tightly and steeled himself for whatever might lay ahead. He smiled at his mother for her sake and retreated into the warmth and comfort of having her close, savoring their time together should he be forced to send them off to Denver ahead of himself.

"We're at the end of the fairgrounds. Where to now, mister?"

Daniel stood and gave the man directions. They had entered a different part of the fairgrounds, dimly lit and dangerous. A dark place where surly men stood in groups warming their hands over open fires. They watched suspiciously as the cab passed them by, not one of them offering a smile. Daniel experienced another glimpse of a future so rapidly approaching, and it was unsettling. That not everyone could reap the riches of the future, was a revelation that startled him. What would happen to those left behind in the new and exciting world?

It occurred to him that he had been seduced not by a woman, though that was true, but by the wealth and power of the advantaged. In this young country, one truly could make a better life, but not everyone would.

"Down there," Daniel said, praying that Wheeler had left his train car where it had been previously. Yes. There it was. "Down there please, driver." Wheeler's carriage sat at the end of a row of railcars ready to be attached to locomotives.

"Will you wait for me please, driver? I won't be long." Daniel climbed the steps and entered the carriage, lighting the oil lamps along the walls. Soon the car was lit and he helped his mother and sister up into the lavish, small compartment.

"My, oh my!" Myra gushed, surprised and delighted at the comfortable, inviting space. "Will you look at this?" she said, entering and looking about, smiling all the while. "I could live here."

*   *   *

"Sorry sir, you can't go in without an official pass," the guard said to Red. Untying her coat and releasing it from her shoulders, Shirley leaned forward exposing her cleavage and smiled at the official.

"Sir, my son is in that cab just up there, and I think he's heading for some mischief. Couldn't you help us follow him? I would be most grateful." Shirley's eyes and her ample bosom had its desirous effect.

"What was that you were saying, miss?"

"I said that," Shirley felt Red slip money between her fingers. "This is for you," she said. Forcing his eyes from Shirley's bosom he pocketed the money, smiled at her, doffed his hat and waved them through.

Kate, the prude in the family, tut-tutted. "Shouldn't you be putting those things away for the night, mother?" she said, draping her mother's shawl about her shoulders and closing the gap. "And why are you laughing, Red? You can't be proud of her, can you?"

Red laughed out loud. "You have NO idea how proud of her I am, young Kate." Kate flashed Red a disdainful smile for trade. "I suggest you enjoy the spectacle while I keep an eye on Daniel's cab." Red called out to a vendor pointing to the mysterious pink, gossamer wisps of confection he was hawking. "Whatever that is, I think we all should try some. What do you call this?"

The man handed over three of the brightly colored items spun around wooden sticks. "Cotton candy," he yelled, taking Red's money.

"This is like heaven on a stick," Shirley exclaimed at her first taste. Their merry mood faded as they reached the end of the Illuminated grounds and drove into the darker reaches of the Fair. Passing the sprawling warehouses and crossing rail tracks they rattled onwards in pursuit until they came to a halt between one of the many rows of darkened box cars like coffins on wheels.

"I think they've stopped, sir." The driver spoke softly, aware that something clandestine was in the making. All three stood and searched the shadows. "They're down there, off to the left," he added.

"Why are they here?" Kate asked. The question on all their minds.

"I don't know," Shirley said. "But I intend to find out. Come with me, Kate."

"I'd think I'd better come too," Red said to Shirley's back, winking to the driver. "You'll wait for us?" The driver nodded touching his finger to his nose. Red nodded and laughed.

They approached as quietly as was possible, treading carefully over the rough, rocky ground. Daniel's cab driver was surprised when they appeared out of the darkness next to him. Red put his finger to his lips.

"How many people went in there?" Red asked the cabbie, pointing to the dimly lit railcar.

"Two men and three women," he replied. Red and Shirley exchanged looks. Red put his finger to his lips and the driver nodded.

It was obvious where Daniel had gone. The lone source of illumination for hundreds of yards came from the train car in front of them. Figures moved about silhouetted against the curtains. Two figures moved together, a man and a woman. They entered an embrace and when they did, Kate began marching toward the rail car so quickly Shirley couldn't hold her back.

"I'd better go with her," Shirley said. "You should stay here, Red." Red nodded. "This is woman business and it could get ugly." Red smiled knowingly.

*   *   *

Lynch was not to be undone. He'd silently fumed while his train headed north. His traveling neighbor knew to keep his distance and did so admirably, but kept one eye on him the whole journey. For the latter part of the trip, Lynch plotted. Not only did he plot, he gathered resolve and was more than ever committed to finishing his mission.

He would not arrive at the next station until one o'clock in the morning and would have to wait there until he could catch the next train heading south to Chicago. It was unlikely that the telegraph office would be open at that hour so the earliest he could notify the Pinkerton Agency in Chicago would be sometime the following day.

What was in doubt, given his past dealings with the Pinkertons, was whether they would place any importance on his request to detain the Shadlows at the train station. They would be arriving a full day before him, so it was probably an unreasonable request since the Pinkertons job was to assist him in the capture of the Shadlows, not kidnap them. Although, as he drifted off into a cramped uncomfortable doze, he did savor the improbable possibility.

*   *   *

Kate and Shirley inched closer to the darkened rail car. The closer they approached the more disturbing the actions of the silhouettes became. Kate was shocked to see the figure of another woman join the two silhouettes in their embrace, so close that they formed one body. It was cause enough.

Breaking free of Shirley's grasp, she hurried to the steps and lifting her skirt high she climbed up to the platform outside of the train's door and prepared herself for the confrontation with her husband. Was she more angry than disappointed? Or was she more embarrassed than hurt? Her hand on the door knob she paused, marshalling her tempest before barging in.

With Shirley at her heels she pursed her lips and snapped open the door. Whatever it was she thought she would see when she opened the door, was a falsity and paled in comparison.

His back turned to Kate, Daniel was holding two women closely, intimately, she thought. He turned quickly when the door opened and his mouth fell agape. Kate briefly noticed that one of the women was older but also that Daniel had a firm grip on the younger one.

"Kate!" Daniel said, his face registering all the shock one man's countenance could display. "What are you doing here?"

Not one prone to anger, or so she thought, Kate stepped forward and pulled Daniel away from the woman he was holding and slapped him so hard across his face that his head swiveled. Pushing him aside, Kate raised her hand to strike Megan.

"Stop it, Kate," he yelled, grasping her wrist. Shirley came from behind her and held Kate's arms to her side. "What are you doing?"

Kate and Shirley both looked around the dimly lit space noticing the other couple standing across the room, looking alarmed. Kate pointed her long finger at Daniel so near his face that Daniel could see the lacquer on her nails.

"I caught you with a whore, Daniel," she yelled. "After what I've heard about you, I'm not surprised either."

"Kate, I have no idea what you're talking about," Daniel pleaded. "I know what you're thinking, but this is my sister, Megan. And this is my mother."

The room shrank about her, it wobbled and floated before her eyes. Kate was stunned, overwhelmed with indecision, then embarrassment. What on earth had she done?

"Mum, Megan, this is my wife, Kate." Silence enveloped them, so profound that one could've heard dandruff drop. "And this is Kate's mother, Shirley," he continued.

As if they were all cast in wax, nobody moved. The tension and mystery coalesced in the dim light on nervous faces, the sounds of hearts beating. All heads turned towards the door when they heard a sound come from outside. Then they all felt a bump against the train car.

Chapter 37

"Why are you all here, Kate?"

"We were worried about you, Daniel," Shirley said defensively. "You, here in Chicago, all alone. We thought we might cheer you up, that's all. And then, when we heard that you had gone missing, we became concerned. Kate especially. That's true, isn't it, Kate?"

"Who told you I was missing?" Daniel asked.

All heads turned when they again heard a noise come from outside and something bumped up against the rail car.

"We heard it from Jerome, of course." Shirley hoped she would be believed and watched Daniel closely. She was shocked at how much he had aged in just a month. He looked exhausted. It showed in the deep circles under his blood-shot eyes, as if he had aged a decade since she'd seen him last.

Silence like a cloak covered them all. Daniel gripped Kate's hand tightly considering the possible outcomes of his deceits. Like a man given his choice of which gate to enter hell, he stood frozen by fear and indecision. The noise outside came again.

Watching the figures entwined in silhouette, Red was mostly amused by the situation. Being a man, and knowing many men, he was not so surprised that young Daniel was misbehaving with another woman. His surprise was that Daniel had an appetite for more than one woman at a time. To his left somebody moved, a shadow amongst the shadows.

Suddenly alert, Red retreated further into the darkness cast by the freight car. Down on one knee, his old shooting stance, he removed his hat and risked a peek under the train car. The shadow had disappeared. The distance was not great, but the lighting was far from helpful. Red waited. Something out there shifted, moving toward Wheeler's train car. Red watched. Silently, the outline of a man of medium build came into view as the light from the rail car briefly illuminated him.

Keeping a close eye on the man, Red inched around the protruding metal couplings and side stepped along the length of the rail car. Carefully shifting his weight from one foot to the other, wincing at sound of each gravelly step, Red crept up on the man who seemed focused on listening to the conversations inside the carriage. He was two steps behind him when the man stepped up onto the carriage and put his ear to the door. Deftly, Red reached up and grabbed the man by the ankles and pulled his feet out from under him, dragging him down the iron steps and onto the ground.

Red was on top of him instantly and ripped his hat off. His right hand clenched ready to punch, Red suddenly stopped, stunned.

"Well, well, well. And just what are you doing here, Harry?" Red said, letting loose of Harry's throat. Harry lowered the arm covering his face.

"Oh, hi there, Red," Harry said, as if nothing was out of the ordinary.

"Don't you go being all friendly now, Harry." Red lifted Harry up by the collar of his coat and pushed him roughly against the side of the train car. "Just what are you up to?"

"Honest Red, I was only curious."

"Curious, Harry? I've never known you to be like that. Though I will say that you are a curious man." Harry smiled at Red, but Red held a tight grip on him. "What are you doing here? Does it have anything to do with your visit to No Problem Joe?"

"It wasn't meant to be like that, Red," Harry quailed. "Joe was my friend." Red lifted Harry up so that his feet dangled an inch above the ground and kept his face close to Harry's.

"Who killed him, Harry? Was it you?"

"No. No. No, Red, I promise you. It wasn't me."

"Who was it then? Tell me, Harry."

"Hamlett Kincaid. From Leadville. You remember him. The sheriff's son."

Red was so shocked and surprised by Harry's answer that he loosened his grip and Harry spluttered as his feet touched the ground. Still holding onto him by the collar of his coat, Red considered Harry anew. Looking long into Harry's eyes, at the man who once was his friend, whom he had saved from certain disaster more than once, his sense of disappointment saddened him deeply. In the past, Red had always kept a distance between himself and Harry's troubles, or at least he had tried to. Now, at this moment, Red regretted knowing him at all.

Suddenly, Harry tried to break away, but Red had a hold on his coat and foiled his escape. Neither fooled nor pleased, Red pushed Harry back up against the train and roughly patted his pockets searching for a weapon.

"I ain't carryin' a gun, Red," Harry said, lifting his hands in supplication. "Hamlett? Now, he's got one and he's not afraid to use it either."

"This ain't the Wild West, Harry. People don't carry guns in Chicago."

"Hamlett does. He threatened to kill me with it if I didn't help him."

"Help him to do what, exactly?"

"You're not goin' to like this, Red." Harry was shrinking in both bravado and size. Red considered the situation as he listened to Harry's story.

"Come with me, Harry. You've got some explaining to do."

Red had no inkling of what he would find when he opened the door to the train car and found it full of people in various emotional states. Shirley stood with her arm around Kate's shoulder. Daniel had his arms about two women, while off to the side another couple stood holding hands, nervously looking at the intruders. No one spoke, tears were in the offing. Still no one spoke.

Harry squirmed to face Red, looking perplexed. "Guess who I found outside."

Shirley, Kate and Daniel all looked at Harry in various shades of disbelief and anger.

"What are you doing here, Harry?" Shirley said, unamused.

Red gave Shirley a warning look. "I think we should talk about that privately." Shirley nodded. "Now," Red said, forcing a smile, "who are all these people you have here, Daniel?" Shirley could not have been prouder of Red at that moment.

"Red, this is Daniel's mother, Myra," Shirley said, introducing them, "and this is the rest of his family. This is Megan." Kate reached over and took Megan's hand in hers, a small but telling gesture. "And this is Daniel's brother Patrick, and his friend, Gemma."

Red nodded to each in turn but did not let loose of Harry's collar. "Pleased to meet you all. Daniel, you are a man of many surprises," he said, laughing. "And this here is our old friend, Harry Rich."

Harry smiled and politely shook hands with everyone but Daniel.

"What about me, Harry? Aren't you going to shake hands with me?" Daniel's tone was not what Harry expected.

Reluctantly, Harry shook Daniel's hand briefly, unsmiling.

"What is this place?" Harry asked.

"It's Wheeler's private train car. He won it in a card game." Daniel allowed them all to appreciate their fine surroundings. "I was hoping my family could stay here until I can get them onto a train for Colorado."

"I'm guessing that Jerome has no idea about this?" Shirley asked.

Daniel nodded.

"Here's what I suggest we do," Red said with his usual authority. "I suggest we have a talk with Jerome and see if we can't straighten this mess out." Red laughed. "I'm interested to see his reaction." He placed his hand on Daniel's shoulder. "I can tell you one thing, son. He's far from happy with you deserting your job like you did."

"I didn't think he would be back so soon, Red."

"I don't think that's the issue," Red added.

"What are we going to do with Harry?" Shirley asked, stepping closer. Harry withdrew behind Red for protection but Red still had a good grip on Harry's collar. "You haven't told us exactly why you're here in Chicago, Harry. And don't try to tell us that you came here for the World's Fair." Under Shirley's barrage Harry retreated further into Red's shadow. Silence reigned. Red looked at Shirley, who looked at Kate.

Daniel's pallor and expression were corpse-like. Kate smiled at him, hoping for a smile in return, but none came. An uncomfortable minute passed while Harry fidgeted and Red tightened his grip. Daniel released Kate's hand and took his mother's and sister's in his. Patrick joined them, placing his arm around his mother's shoulder gathering her to him.

"Patrick, do you think you will be alright staying here tonight?" Patrick nodded. "OK. Then I'll go and see Mister Wheeler," Daniel said, "and try to explain." He sighed deeply, his shoulders fell and it tore at Kate's and Shirley's hearts to see him so defeated. Mistakenly they thought that he was only worried about his job. Little did they know that they were all about to be drawn into Daniel's nightmare. "We have no more money," Daniel simpered, plaintively.

Shirley reached into her bag and from a silk purse took some bills and smiling, placed them into Myra's hand. Myra tried to resist the gift but Shirley would have none of it.

"Myra, please take this." Shirley said seriously though smiling. "It's not as if I don't have more," she laughed. "Anyway, we are all family now." Tears ran down Myra's cheeks and to Shirley it was more than payment in full. It was what Shirley had always done, even when she was a lowly prostitute in Leadville, she shared whatever she had with those in true need. Myra cried and Shirley held her tenderly.

"Alright, Daniel," Red said, uncomfortable with all of the emotions flowing. "Why don't you, Kate and Shirley go back to the hotel in your cab and I'll follow in the other one." Red released Harry's collar but kept him corralled with his big arm around his shoulders. "That way Harry and I can have a talk, privately."

Daniel forced a smile for the sake of his family. "I'll come back for you tomorrow. There is a bedroom down there and these couches are comfortable to sleep on."

Patrick nodded. "We'll be fine, Daniel. Good luck."

"I'll come back for you tomorrow," Daniel said with a smile as he left them.

Chapter 38

When they entered the hotel, they were unsurprised that Jerome B. Wheeler was waiting for them looking far from pleased. As they approached, Wheeler pulled out his gold pocket watch and made a show of winding it and without ceremony he turned and led them into the almost deserted dining room. Waiters were busily clearing tables and resetting them for breakfast, purposely ignoring the arrival of unwanted customers.

Wheeler chose a table against the wall and Shirley smiled as she allowed him to pull out her chair for her, pleased that Daniel did likewise for Kate. Wheeler sat and cleared his throat noisily.

"Well, Daniel," Wheeler's pause was leaden. "I have to say that I am disappointed in you, though I'm sure there is some explanation." Daniel remained silent knowing that when he did begin telling the story of his mysterious disappearance it would open the door to a multitude of ensuing questions each, or all, of which would invite more questions, with possibly damning results.

"I'm sorry Mister Wheeler, I," Daniel began.

Abruptly Wheeler turned in his chair to face Harry. "Why in God's name are you here, Harry?" Wheeler bellowed at Harry, ignoring Daniel. "I thought you'd gone off to Utah with your brood and your tail between your legs. What on Earth could bring you to Chicago?"

"Him." Harry pointed at Daniel. "There's a reward out for him." All looked from Daniel to Harry and back to Daniel. "Yes, him! Daniel Shadlow." Daniel cringed as all eyes turned towards him.

"Is that true, Daniel?" Shirley asked. Daniel nodded and squeezed Kate's hand. "We thought your name was Carrington."

"Yes, it's true. My real name is Daniel Shadlow." Feeling Kate's hand withdraw from his, he looked at her with such sadness, so lost.

"And you, Harry, thought you'd turn your old partner in for some reward money?" Red said, in disgust. "Is that what you thought?"

"No! It wasn't like that!" Harry pleaded, contrite under the waterfall of condemnation. "I promised Daniel I wouldn't tell on him. Didn't I?" Daniel looked away.

"If that's what you promised him, then why are you here, Harry?" Wheeler asked pointedly. "I doubt that you're here for the World's Fair."

Harry swallowed hard, considering his reply. Red was becoming increasingly impatient. He knew some or most of Harry's story, having forced it out of him on the ride to the hotel. It was time for Harry to come clean. Indeed, it was.

"You were in Aspen recently, weren't you, Harry?" Harry looked about the table, searching for a friendly face. None appeared. "Go on, Harry, tell us the truth. You're among friends, remember?" Red's deep voice became even lower as his anger with Harry simmered. "Tell us the real reason you were in Aspen, Harry." Harry remained mute. "If you just wanted to kidnap Daniel for the reward, why hurt Joe? He must've told you that Daniel was gone?" Red let the silence build for the same reason that a scaffold was erected in the sight of a condemned man. "You must've been disappointed not to find him there. Is that why you beat him?"

Red's words fell on the table like a cloudburst. All eyes were fixed on Harry, the effect on him visible to all. He diminished in size before their eyes. Daniel looked at Harry in wide-eyed disbelief.

"No, Red!" Harry protested. "It wasn't like that. Joe's my friend." Harry looked around at the silent faces around the table. "He's alright, isn't he?" Nothing was said. "He was alright when we left him. You've got to believe me, Red." Still not a word was uttered, his jury in deliberation. Harry could feel the temperature around him falling, like his prospects. "It was Hamlett that hit him. I would never do him harm, Red. You know that. You have to believe me."

If it is true that a dying man sees his life pass in review, Harry had a similar experience looking at Daniel and the secrets they shared. How much the tables had turned. How his life had decayed, how his dreams of riches had died? Tried by a jury of peers and damned by his actions, Harry had fewer friends now, by the number four, leaving him with none. He could read the condemnation in their eyes.

"I'm sorry," was his singular defense. Typical, horrid. But so Harry.

A confessional silence enveloped the table. Clouds of doubt and recrimination gathered. An impending tempest. Harry hung his head in shame. Not since he'd faced down Doc Holliday, on the day he met Daniel, had he felt so outnumbered.

"Is Joe dead?" Daniel asked, looking around the table from one face to another, not wanting to hear the answer, already knowing in his heart that Joe was no more. One by one they nodded to him, each relaying the sadness they all felt at Joe's loss.

Daniel leapt out of his seat and rushed at Harry, grabbing him by the throat, squeezing his neck so hard that Harry's face turned bright puce and foam formed at the edges of his mouth.

"Stop it, Daniel!" Red yelled, wrenching Daniel's fingers from Harry's throat. "Listen to me," he said loudly. Daniel relaxed his grip, but only slightly. "Daniel, I don't think it was Harry that killed Joe." Red spoke in a calm, even voice, watching Daniel closely, letting the fury subside. Curiously, no one else but Red had come to Harry's assistance. "Now, sit down Daniel and let's see if we can't make sense out of all of this."

A moment of peace agreed upon, they settled back into their seats. All but Daniel, who stood behind Harry thrusting imaginary daggers into his back. A pall of sadness blanketed the table. Kate took Daniel's hand and guided him back to his seat. He fell into his chair, his eyes beading with tears.

"What's all this about a reward for you?" Jerome asked Daniel. "I think we should start there." Wheeler's affection for Daniel was evident, his voice soft but serious. "Is there truth in what Harry says? Is there a reward for your capture?" Daniel nodded. "By whom?" Wheeler trailed off.

"Pinkerton's Detective Agency," Harry stated proudly. "Five thousand dollars. For bank robbery."

"What?" came in unison from all.

"What bank robbery? Where?" Wheeler asked loudly, forgetting about the waiters milling about, suddenly very interested. Jerome looked intently at Daniel. "Is he telling the truth, Daniel?" Daniel's eyes fell to his lap and Harry beamed, as if pardoned. Wheeler shook his head in disbelief.

"What? Another bank?" he thought to himself, shaking his head, inwardly smiling.

Jerome had always suspected that Harry and Daniel were guilty of robbing the bank in Leadville. Though it had never been discussed, Red had been there when Shady Lane showed them the broken runner from Joe's old sled. He had found it on the Leadville side of Independence Pass and it was a crucial piece of evidence that potentially tied them to the robbery. Now, to his astonishment, it appeared that Daniel had been involved in another bank robbery. The boy was full of surprises. Jerome resisted the urge to smile at Red, who appeared just as shocked.

"It was back in Ireland," Daniel was saying. Red, Shirley, Kate and Wheeler again exchanged glances. "My father tried to blow up the Bank of England. He died in prison, but my brother escaped. He's with us now."

"So, there would be twice the reward then?" Harry murmured, not quite to himself. Harry's head snapped forward from the slap Red delivered to the back of his head, knocking his hat off.

"That's enough out of you, Harry," Red said sternly. "You're already in deep shit here. Don't get in deeper."

"I guess the Pinkertons think they can deport you back to Ireland?" Wheeler said, thoughtfully. "But they can't send you back if they can't find you." Wheeler paused before asking his next question, fearing the answer. "Is Harry the only one on your trail?" Wheeler watched Daniel's face closely and what he detected there was unsettling. "That you know of, I mean," he added. Whether the others noticed he couldn't be certain, but what he saw was fear in Daniel's eyes. "Of course not," Wheeler answered for him.

"Who was with you in Aspen, Harry?" Red interjected. "Hamlett Kincaid," Harry said, shamefully. "The sheriff of Leadville's son." Looks of horror and shock darted about the table like bats.

"Why him? Red said he tried to kill you," Shirley said, shocked.

Red already knew the answer. He and Harry had discussed many things during the cab ride to the hotel and being somewhat forceful with Harry, he now knew almost everything. Almost.

"How did this happen, Harry?" Wheeler asked, and Harry told of being taken at gunpoint by Hamlett and how much he missed his family.

Shirley and Kate exchanged knowing, doubting looks. How Hamlett had forced him to go to Aspen hoping to find Daniel, for the reward, he lied. More glances darted about the table.

"So, all you were looking for in Aspen was Daniel?" Wheeler asked. "Just for the reward?" Harry swallowed hard. Daniel knew the look. A lie was coming.

"Yes," Harry nodded.

"And nothing more?" Wheeler added, raising an eyebrow.

"How did you find Daniel?" Red asked.

"Your photographs were in the newspaper with the Silver Queen. Ham thought we could grab him and take him to the Pinkerton's office in Denver, get the reward and I could skedaddle back home to be with my family again. I really miss them." Harry conjured his most pitiful countenance. "He threatened to shoot me if I didn't help him."

"But how did you find Daniel at Jerome's train car?" Red pressed. "Hamlett's working as a guard for the Silver Queen. He saw what was going on and figured that Daniel would come back there."

Wheeler and Red exchanged more looks, as did Shirley and Kate. Silence crept about the table stalking the truth, like a cat hunting a mouse. Wheeler decided to let Harry stew and turned his attention back on Daniel, nervously playing with the cutlery on the table.

"Where have you been for the past week?" Wheeler asked, sitting back on his chair, watching Daniel intently.

"I went to New York to find my family."

"And did you find them?" Wheeler asked, curious regarding the smile that came from Shirley. Less so from Kate, he noticed.

"Yes, he did, Jerome," Shirley interjected happily, hoping to elevate the somber mood, "and they are such nice folk. Aren't they Kate? Red?" Smiles of various duration came and went.

"Where are they now?" Wheeler asked and Daniel explained that they had only arrived that evening and that he had put them in Jerome's train car until they could find either a train to Colorado or a hotel. Wheeler listened without interrupting.

"I'm sorry for letting you down, Mister Wheeler. I didn't want you or anyone to know what I was doing. I was hoping that I could get back to Chicago before you and then you would never have known." Daniel's contrition was clearly written across his face and even Kate relented and took his hand in hers.

"Can I have a word with you, Jerome," Red said, standing.

Wheeler nodded.

"Why don't you all go into the bar." Wheeler said. "We'll join you there shortly. Not you, Harry. You stay right where you are. I still need a word with you."

Shirley led Daniel and Kate to a small table by an open fireplace. The waiter came and they ordered tea. Silence steeped until the tea was poured, Shirley presiding.

"Are you happy to see us here, Daniel?" Shirley opened the conversation with something safe. Daniel brightened as a drowning man would after seeing rescue on the horizon.

"Of course, I am," he said, reaching for Kate's hand.

"You know we were all worried about you, don't you?" Shirley inclined her head to Kate. Daniel bit his lips. "Why didn't you tell us about your family, Daniel? Why lie to us? We're your family too, aren't we?"

Daniel took a deep breath and exhaled slowly. This was the moment he had been dreading since he married Kate, knowing all the time that the longer he waited the worse it would be. That each day living this lie was another cup of guilt poured into the overflowing barrel of remorse in which he was drowning. Each breath he took before his confession was one of the last he would take before he told all. Almost.

He started at the beginning and was honest in the retelling of the bank robbery in Ireland and their escape from the police there and their escape to America. Shirley and Kate sat transfixed by the story and Shirley felt a wave of sadness overwhelm her, empathy for the tragedy that had befallen Daniel's mother. As the story progressed Kate softened, squeezing Daniel's hand in support when he faltered.

"The rest of the story you know. I left my mother and sister in the hands of Mister Hogan in New York and I've been sending them money all the while." Daniel paused and looked around the table. "That is, until the letters were returned to me. I worried that they were in trouble." Daniel raised his eyes to meet Kate's. "I guess I should have told you, Kate. But I didn't want you to know about my past. I was embarrassed."

Kate leaned over and wiped away Daniel's tears. When he looked up she leaned into him and draping her arms around his shoulders she kissed him on the lips tenderly.

"I'm glad you found your family," Kate said.

"How did you find them so quickly, Daniel," Shirley asked. "New York is a big city."

Daniel pulled his chair closer to Kate's and held her hand in both of his. He told of his Jewish friend and savior and of finding his family while eluding the men looking for him for the reward. He failed to notice how Shirley's expression changed, worry wrinkled her brow. Daniel had used the plural.

"Do you know who it is looking for you?" Shirley watched Daniel's expression closely.

Again, Daniel breathed deeply. Another point of decision as to how much to tell. "Yes. There is a man from Dublin, an ex-policeman."

"How do you know?"

Another deep sigh, another long pause. "He followed us onto the train from New York. I don't know how he found us. Patrick recognized him as the policeman who was injured in the bombing. We didn't know at the time, but I became suspicious when he tried to make friends with my mother. Later, Patrick told me that his name was Lynch and that he had testified at Patrick's trial."

"How did your brother escape from prison?" Kate asked.

"I don't know. But I'm certain that the Fenians had something to do with it. My father and brother were saints for their cause to free Ireland."

"Do you think they're looking for you, or your brother?" Daniel shrugged. Shirley's experience with the law was that it had a long arm and a longer memory. Daniel shrugged. "Where is this man Lynch now? Do you know?" Daniel's smile surprised her.

"We tricked him into taking the wrong train at South Bend." Daniel reached into his coat and retrieved a train schedule. "He got on a train heading to Detroit, here," he said, pointing on the map with a smile. Shirley smiled back, impressed by Daniel's courage and resourcefulness.

"If he's followed you so far as to cross an ocean, and across this country," Wheeler added, "I doubt he's the type to give up easily." Shirley blanched, almost sick to her stomach. "Plus, there's that reward money." Through the years she had known many bounty hunters and none were good men. They were a breed apart from the rest. Now she was very worried.

"Let's continue this tomorrow, when we're rested." Shirley said, surmising they had enough to think about for one evening, "I know I'm exhausted. Daniel, why don't you go freshen up in your room, take a hot bath and let Kate and I sort out the sleeping arrangements." Daniel still held on tightly to Kate's hand, barely smiling. "Go on. Your family is safe tonight and we'll fix things in the morning." Shirley came around and kissed Daniel on the cheek, urging him toward the stairs. When he had gone a small way off, Shirley took Kate's hand.

"Did you know any of this, Kate?" Kate shook her head. Shirley pursed her lips signaling to Kate the severity of the situation. "I think that husband of yours is in a lot of trouble. Let me go talk with Red and Jerome and see what we can do." Kate looked down at the floor, silently fuming from the gossip she had heard. Shirley pulled her back. "Listen to me, Kate. I want you to go upstairs and take care of your husband. He needs you now. Look at me, Kate! Being a wife is not all sweet and simple. There are times when you have to smile and give yourself to him. No matter what you think you know."

Kate shook off her dark thoughts and pulled her shoulders back.

"That's better, now smile for him. You two have been working hard and long on your family. Go on up and make it a larger one. I think you both need it." Kate smiled at her mother's frankness. "Even if you don't make a baby tonight, the practice is fun." Shirley said, smiling for her daughter. Shirley had no complaints with Red in that department. She was a lucky woman and he was a lucky man.

"Go now. Be his lover tonight. Let me take care of things here." Shirley turned Kate towards the stairs and gave her a gentle pat on her behind. "Go on, go take a hot bath with him. See what happens." Shirley smiled watching Kate climb the stairs.

Chapter 39

"What's the real reason you're here in Chicago, Harry?" Shirley was staring at Harry in a far from friendly manner. "Tell me truthfully." She had come to sit next to Harry, one table away from where Red and Wheeler were in deep discussion, their faces in profile.

"I told you everything, Shirley. Honest injun', I did."

"I know you, Harry. There's something you're not telling me."

"Does Kate know about you and me?" Harry smiled. Shirley resisted the urge to slap him. "You know Ham will kill me if he doesn't get the money."

"For Daniel's reward, you mean?"

"That, or the other money," Harry trailed off.

"What are you getting at Harry?" Shirley said, stiff-backed, drawing attention from Red. She beamed him a smile and he went back to his conversation with Wheeler.

"The robbery in Leadville, of course," Harry said reaching for her hand which she pulled away, flinching. "I know you know we did it, Shirley. You knew when you saw me take off my shirt in the courtroom."

Shirley closed her eyes briefly. She had secretly hoped that she was wrong back then. Apparently, she was not. She'd never been the slightest bit nervous dealing with Harry in the past. But now she saw him differently. Harry was truly dangerous.

"The money from the robbery," Harry was saying. "That's the money Hamlett really wants and I'm a dead man if I don't give it to him."

Shirley was looking at him, skeptically. "Look. I know where it was. I buried it under the oven in my cabin." Harry kept his eyes on Shirley. "But I didn't even know the cabin burned down until I came back with Hamlett. You gotta help me, Shirley. I need to know where the money went. Who took it? Daniel?" The blood had drained from Shirley's face. She darted a look at Red and forced a smile. "You just won't let go of that boy, will you, Harry?"

Harry smiled. "Not until I get my hands on the money we stole." Shirley felt the skin on her neck crawl and she shivered. "It's him or me, Shirley."

Without warning, Shirley stood and swung her fist at Harry's head. But years of experience with being slapped by irate women had sharpened his reflexes and he caught her hand an inch from his face.

"What's going on over there?" Wheeler said loudly, as he and Red both stood. Shirley smiled, regaining her composure.

"Just me and Harry talking. Nothing out of the usual," she said. Sitting back down she considered Harry anew. "What do you expect us to do about that, Harry? It's your problem."

"Is it?" said sly Harry.

Shirley wondered how Red would react if he heard their conversation, doubtful he would respond well. Harry had gotten himself into this mess and now he wanted everyone to come to his rescue. It was so typical of Harry. So damned typical.

"Why did Hamlett find you, Harry?" Shirley asked. Harry looked away, then back at Shirley.

"Doc knew it was us who robbed the bank when he saw the hair on my back." Harry tried his best at playing the victim, failing as usual. "He demanded half of the money for not giving us up to the judge. The sheriff was crazy angry. Do you remember?" Shirley had to smile, considering her past life spent with the sheriff as his mistress and him the father of her daughter, Rachelle.

"You still haven't explained why you and he are partner."

"Doc told him everything before he died and gave Hamlett the share of the money I promised him for getting us off. My money. That's why he came after me in Utah. He wanted what I promised Doc."

"Where is he now?" Shirley asked.

"Hamlett? He's probably at the saloon waiting for me. We share a room at a flop-house over by the fairgrounds. He snores like a train."

"What are you going to tell him? About tonight."

"Yes. What are you going to tell him, Harry?" Wheeler interjected over Harry's shoulder, sitting down in the chair next to him as he and Red joined them. Harry swallowed hard, visibly, noisily. He looked down at his shaking hands.

"If I tell Hamlett that Daniel's here in Chicago, he'll want to grab him. There's a Pinkerton's office downtown. He's already been there." Heads bobbed knowingly. "But, if he finds out that I didn't tell him, he'll kill me." Harry's bravado evaporated. "He wants the money we stole." Red shot Wheeler a look. "My money," Harry groaned. "And Daniel's, of course," he added. And there it was.

Wheeler raised an eyebrow at Shirley. Looking around the table she wondered who else knew about the stolen money. She feared for Daniel and bit her lip. All eyes were on her. Even the wandering waiters seemed to hush. Why was she suddenly the one to shoulder this burden? It was all Harry's fault, wasn't it?

"Did you force Daniel to rob the bank, Harry?" Shirley kept her eyes fixed on Harry's.

"We had a bet and he lost," Harry said with a sly smile. "He had no choice."

Shirley had already guessed as much.

"Alright, Harry," Red said sternly, "tell them what you told me."

And so, Harry retold the story, Shirley keeping him focused.

"Well here's what I suggest, Harry," Wheeler said, after some reflection. "I suggest that you go back and tell Hamlett nothing about tonight. Do you think you can do that?" Harry nodded glumly. "You did say that he's working for me guarding the Silver Queen, didn't you?" Harry nodded. "Well, that's something in our favor. Go home, Harry. Skedaddle, and we'll see if we can't keep you out of the graveyard one more time."

Harry quailed out of the room. After he'd left, Wheeler led them to the foyer and stood with them by the front door of the hotel.

"I'm guessing that the youngsters are taking Daniel's room tonight?" Shirley nodded. "Well, since the hotel is full, I'll let you two have my room, then."

"What about you, Jerome? Where will you sleep?" Shirley asked, concerned. Wheeler smiled.

"Don't go worrying yourself about me, Shirley. I know this town. I'm certain I'll find some place to rest my weary head." He winked at Red mischievously. "Until tomorrow then?" he said, climbing into a cab.

"Do you think Jerome would mind if we ordered a bottle of wine and had a bath while we think about what we should do?"

"You were thinking champagne, weren't you?"

Shirley smiled at him in the way that always caused Red to stir. He stirred all night at every smile Shirley gave him.

*   *   *

Kate slipped into the room while Daniel was running his bath. From the reflection in the mirror she could see into the small, misty room. Daniel sat on the commode, his head in his hands, buried into a towel. She could hear that he was crying.

Respecting his privacy and his emotions while dealing with her own, she stepped out of his vision as she disrobed. Was it true that he had been with another woman? Abigail's mother's gossip was generally seeded in the truth and usually to be relied upon. But, should she condemn Daniel before asking him if what she had heard was true? What was her part in this? Could she have been a better wife to him?

While he splashed about in the tub, she took off her dress and petticoat and down to her underwear she appraised herself in the long mirror. Turning this way and that, she let down her hair and unbuttoned her camisole, standing topless in the low light of the room. Shadows played over her as she contemplated the longer pull of her breasts and the protrusion of her dark nipples. Running her hands through her hair and elongating the length of her waist she ran her hands over her breasts and over her hips as she had seen some of her mother's girls do. A splash came from the bathroom.

Daniel was half out of the bath when she pushed open the door. He froze and she stepped to him placing her hands on his wet chest. She noted how deeply his eyes were sunken and how his heart pounded under her palm. Something had changed in there, in his heart. She kissed him gently. He slowly relaxed his lips and joined her. His soft, soapy hands slipped over her breast causing her to gasp. He kissed her harder and slid his hands under the material and squeezed her soft buttocks, she gasped again. She pushed him away.

"Get back into the tub," she suggested, and with a smile he wisely did as he was told. "Don't sit down, yet." Large enough for two persons to bathe at the same time she stepped into the tub and stood behind him. "Turn around." Soaping her hands, she gently washed his back from his nape to his firm, manly bottom. Down his legs she ran her hands. Up to his hips and between his legs.

"Turn around," she demanded and he complied. He moaned at her touch, her hands gently caressing him. When he could no longer stand it, he pulled her up by her hair and held her a little away from him. His eyes roamed over her and she shivered. Her underpants were soaked and clung to her body, filmy, silkily.

"Turn around," Daniel whispered in her ear and she complied, savoring his warm touch, caressing her breasts so that they became taut once again, just as they used to every time in response to his touch. It was time for marital bliss.

Chapter 40

"Where've you been?" Hamlett snarled. "Some of your pals over there have been askin' for ya'." Hamlett tilted his head to where several roughnecks from the Fair played cards. Harry looked lustily at them and their pleasures and nodded to them. "You talk too much, Harry." Harry considered Hamlett, hurt by his rebuke.

"Why do you say that, Ham?"

"For one, that fellow over there." Hamlett pointed his finger at a burly man. "He asked me if we'd found the man we were lookin' for. How do you suppose that happened, eh?" Hamlett punched his finger into Harry's chest.

Harry recoiled. "They all work at the fairgrounds, Ham. They wanted to know why I came here all the way from Colorado, that's all." Hamlett shook his head in disgust. "I was just bein' friendly, Ham," Harry trailed off.

"Have you heard anything?" Harry shook his head and sipped his beer. Hamlett finished his drink in one swallow. "Keep watch, Harry. I think they're getting ready to pull out. I've seen Wheeler so your young partner must be close by, I'd say."

Torn between bad choices, Harry was tempted to confess all to Hamlett. He recognized that the secret he held was dangerous, but he kept silent in the hope that Wheeler would come up with a plan. Hamlett watched him ruminating.

"Is there something you want to tell me, Harry?" Harry shook his head. "Then you had better get back out there and see if he's here. Off you go, Harry." Hamlett pushed Harry in the back, pushed him out of the bar and into the awful night. He wanted Harry to be tired, continuously tired. It was how he kept Harry on his leash. Not enough food, not enough sleep, constantly under threat of death, it all worked. Harry was his. Body and soul.

Harry didn't go directly back to his hotel. He walked and fretted all night, finally returning to his lumpy bed in the wee hours serenaded by

Hamlett's snoring. When he crawled under the thin blankets and scratchy sheets, sleep battled him. What with the grumbling in his stomach and the din of the waking city he was caught in a tumbler of doubt and fear. One question kept returning. If it wasn't Daniel who set fire to his cabin, who else could it have been?

He ruled out Hamlett. Judging by his reaction he seemed equally surprised at the sight of the burned out remains of the cabin. Someone had been poking around the cabin while they had been in jail and according to Red, Leafy had discovered two men searching it. So, Harry concluded, someone must have been waiting for the right time to dig up the floor in his cabin looking for the money and Daniel's wedding would have been exactly right. But who could it have been?

Harry saw the dawn break. Hamlett dressed and disappeared. The chilly wind fluttered the dingy curtains and drafts darted about the small room. Strangely it felt like a prison cell and he shrank back under his covers at the prospect of remaining in Hamlett's clutches. He dozed thinking an odd thought; that his life on the dry, lake bed farm in Utah wasn't so bad after all.

*   *   *

Stiff, sore, cramped, unwashed, unkempt, lame and in a bad mood, Sergeant Lynch gratefully took the hand of the sympathetic porter as he alighted from the train in Chicago. Stopping after a few paces, breathing the fug of the station, he wished immediately to be home in Ireland where the air was clean and so moist you could swallow it.

Abruptly the world around him teetered and he swayed. The station swirled about him. He reached out his right hand and found the security of the iron pillars, dropping his cane he held on with shaking hands. Slowly it passed, his vision cleared and his stomach growled. How long had it been since he had eaten? Too long, his stomach replied. Mustering his strength to reach down for his cane, a gentleman entered his vision and retrieved it for him.

"Thank you very much, sir. I'm grateful to ya," Lynch said, sincerely. He took several deep breaths and felt much better for it. Smiling again he considered the man. The man smiled back at him.

"Would you be Mister Lynch?" he asked. It was difficult to hear over the noise of the locomotives. "Of the Dublin Police?" Lynch nodded, relief writ large on his face. The man held out his hand. "My name is Coleman. I'm with the Pinkerton Company." Lynch took his hand and tightened his grip more than was necessary. Finally some help, he thought.

"Thank you for coming."

"Do you need a hand?" Coleman asked, solicitously. Lynch shook his head but leaned heavily on his cane.

Under his narrow-brimmed black hat, Coleman wore his dark hair cropped short and a black coat, shorter than most but with a slight flare at the hips. Others, wearing more traditional longer coats, were mostly forgettable in their similarity. Mister Coleman, Lynch decided, was out of the ordinary. It was only when he was climbing into the cab that Lynch understood how much so. Coleman wore a revolver in a holster on his hip.

"You look like you could use some food. When did you last eat?"

"Last night, I think," Lynch replied, after a moment of thought.

"In some wretched place. Smelled of cow shit." Lynch noted that Coleman was guiding him toward the station restaurant and tugged on Coleman's sleeve. "Please, Mister Coleman, could we eat elsewhere? I've seen enough of these kinds of places." Coleman laughed heartily. He liked this oddly disfigured man. He was refreshingly honest.

"Do you like steak and whiskey, Mister Lynch?" Coleman asked, and was gifted to see the gleam of a thousand stars light up behind Lynch's eyes.

"Oh, yes, please," Lynch said, beaming as Coleman hailed a passing cab.

*   *   *

Knock. Knock. Knock. Shirley tapped softly on the door. "Come on you two, it's time to get up." Daniel opened the door. "Good morning," she

249

said brightly, hiding her anxiety. "My, but don't you look like a new person." She smiled at him warmly and kissed him on the cheek as he ushered her in.

"Kate is still getting dressed."

"Hurry on, Kate, we don't want to keep Jerome too long."

"Where's Red?"

"He's waiting downstairs. He wanted to speak with Jerome privately." Daniel's woes clouded his face. Shirley touched his arm reassuringly. "Oh, don't you go worrying. I'm sure everything will turn out well." Kate emerged from the bathroom brushing her long brown hair. "Oh my, Kate. You look lovely," Shirley gushed. Kate shook her hair, smiling at her reflection. "I guess you took my advice for once." Shirley said with a laugh.

Daniel reached for the door but Shirley stopped him. "Daniel, before we go down, I want you to tell Kate everything." His heart sank.

"What do you mean, everything?"

Chapter 41

Sergeant Lynch felt good about the world as he made his way through the traffic, following Coleman's directions, confident that Coleman was a man he could trust. The previous evening, they had eaten dinner in a dark, unremarkable bar that Coleman guaranteed served the best steaks in the city and the man was indeed truthful on that subject.

According to Coleman, the telegram from Lynch asking to be met at the train station and alerting the Pinkertons to the Shadlows' arrival was sitting on his desk when he arrived for work. Nothing out of the ordinary, he said. Coleman even showed Lynch the telegram to validate his meeting, should there be doubt.

Lynch found the cafe Coleman had suggested and sat at the counter drinking coffee and watching the passing parade of Chicago. Picking up a newspaper left on the counter he scanned the front-page story regarding the overturn of some piece of legislature pertaining to the silver industry. It failed to keep his attention but he did note the photograph of a large silver statue, named the Silver Queen, which was being removed from the Colorado Exhibition Hall in some symbolic protest.

At ten o'clock Lynch arrived at the Pinkerton Detective Agency office and was greeted by an unsmiling Coleman who quickly ushered him from the office and led him out onto the busy street. It was only after they had gone several blocks that Coleman realized that Lynch, relying on his cane, was struggling to keep pace.

"I'm sorry, Mister Lynch," he said apologetically, "I didn't realize I was rushing you." Coleman cast a look around the spacious park that traced the city lake front and found a bench to sit on. He pulled up his collar and turned his face to the weak sunlight and breathed deeply. A silent minute passed. The gulls wheeled and cawed.

"Is it always this windy in Chicago?" Lynch asked, after a shiver traced down his spine. Coleman laughed.

"That was exactly my impression when I first arrived here. Not at all like Philadelphia." For several minutes they watched the whitecaps on the lake and the activity on the ships unloading at the pier. "I needed a change of scenery," he said.

"I like the architecture here," Lynch said. "I like the wide avenues. We don't have them in Dublin," he trailed off, remembering Dublin's narrow pathways and byways which had grown into thoroughfares over the passing centuries. "Your cities in America seem to be laid out with care." Lynch looked behind him at the phalanx of tall buildings facing the lake. "It's all very modern."

"And it is all moving faster and faster these days, Mister Lynch. It's a race to the future, they say." Coleman sighed. "When I was a boy, it took six months to cross this country. These days it can be done in a week." Coleman spread his arms wide, encompassing the breadth of the country. "From sea to shining sea, in seven days. Less from Chicago."

Lynch nodded. "I don't wish to be impatient, Mister Coleman, but have you any news of Patrick Shadlow?"

Coleman turned to face him. "Before I answer that, I have a few questions for you, Mister Lynch." Coleman's face wore a thin veneer of a smile. "May I ask what exactly your jurisdiction is in this case?" Lynch removed the warrant along with his credentials and handed them to Coleman.

"My superiors in Dublin gave me the task of arresting Patrick Shadlow and returning him to England to complete his prison term."

"It says here that he was arrested for bank robbery?"

"That's correct. I was there at the time," Lynch said, watching Coleman's reaction. "I owe my disfigurement to Patrick Shadlow, you see." He turned his attention back on the lake. Seagulls noisily begged at their feet. "I would never have thought that gulls would be so far from the sea."

"Our lakes are as big as oceans, Mister Lynch, or should I say, Sergeant Lynch?"

"Mister is best I think, under the circumstances."

"What is it that you want Pinkerton's to do for you here in Chicago?"

"My government has given me a commission to apprehend Patrick Shadlow and your government has given its permission for me to do so. They in turn have requested help from the Pinkerton Detective Agency, and as you can see," Lynch pointed to the reward contract Coleman held, "they are offering five thousand dollars reward for his capture."

"Won't the police do that for you?" Coleman received a shake of the head.

"Not their business, they say. Although I'm getting the feeling that the police here are dodgy." Lynch gave Coleman a wry smile.

"You observe many things, Mister Lynch," Coleman agreed, laughing. "This is a substantial reward. All manner of men would be interested in claiming it." Coleman pursed his lips and drew his coat closer about him, deep in thought. "About this reward?" he said after a while. "Is it to be paid to Pinkerton's or to you, Mister Lynch?" Lynch considered both the question and the purpose.

"I am led to believe that it is given to whoever can deliver Patrick Shadlow to the British Embassy in New York."

"So, you wouldn't take a part of the reward then?" Coleman watched Lynch carefully.

"I don't have any right to it. Not here on American soil anyway." Lynch spoke carefully and slowly so that his meaning was not misinterpreted.

Lynch was having doubts about Coleman. After his experience with Rafferty and the Pinkerton's organization, he was very skeptical. "Whether you, personally, would be entitled to a share of the reward would be a matter between you and your company, I should think." Lynch studied Coleman while he let the information sink in. "So, tell me, Mister Coleman, what is it that you've found out?"

"There was a murder in New York several days ago that drew some attention to someone named Shadlow, or Carrington." Lynch nodded, intrigued at how rapidly this information had come into the hands of the Pinkertons. Having travelled so far with such little sleep, the days and nights had melded into one long arduous river of discomfort. He had to think hard to put it into a time frame. Suddenly he realized that Coleman was talking and he had not been listening.

"I'm sorry, Mister Coleman, I must've missed what you were saying." Lynch looked at Coleman apologetically.

"Not a problem. I know how it is traveling on the trains. Impossible to sleep." Lynch nodded in agreement. "What I was saying is, I was wondering if you contacted the Pinkerton's office in New York while you were there?" Lynch nodded. "Then that could explain it," Coleman trailed off.

"Explain what?" Lynch asked.

"Do you know a man named Rafferty?"

*   *   *

Kate, Shirley and Daniel sat at the table drinking coffee in silence. Shirley the brave-hearted one, Kate the wounded one, and Daniel the condemned one. Kate had listened to Daniel's story silently, as much in confusion as in surprise at his story. She never once reached out for his hand but twice took her mother's.

"So, in truth, those people we met last night at the train really are your family?" Kate asked him, pointedly. Daniel nodded wearily.

"Let's go downstairs and have breakfast." Shirley said, enthusiastically. "I don't know about you two, but I'm hungry this morning." She smiled and patted Kate on the behind as she opened the door and ushered them out. "Now, let's put on our brave faces and see what the men have decided. Come on, cheer up both of you," she said, leading them to the stairs. "Let's go eat."

Red was waiting for Wheeler when his cab arrived. Looking the worse for the night on the town, Wheeler managed a grimace that could have passed for a smile.

"I do love this town," he said to Red. "What a wonderful night I had. Red, I wish you could've joined me," he said, playfully. "They have some women here that I swear have fallen down from heaven. Honest living, breathing angels, I tell you." Red climbed the stairs with Wheeler listening to his descriptions of the women of the night.

"Have you thought about what we should do with the boy?" Red asked.

"I think Harry is a more pressing matter, don't you?"

"I agree. We have to keep Harry away from Daniel," Red said seriously. They were walking through the hotel lobby heading for the restaurant. Wheeler slowed.

"Do you know the saying, 'Keep your friends close, but keep your enemies closer?" Red nodded. "That's what I'm thinking we should do." Red nodded again. "I'll see what I can arrange. In the meantime, we should get Daniel's family out of Chicago quickly. Especially if there's someone looking for them. The sooner they're out of the city, the better for everyone. And I really do not want anyone following them back to Aspen."

"Do you think Pinkertons are still interested in arresting Daniel? I mean, it's been years."

"I'm not sure," Wheeler answered honestly. "I'm thinking that their powers to detain a foreign citizen are somewhat limited." Wheeler saw Shirley waving and noted the lack of smiles from Kate and Daniel. "It doesn't look all that good from here, Red. We might have some fence mending to do with the youngsters." Wheeler caught Red by the sleeve. "Do you think Harry told Shirley the truth about Leadville?"

Red paused. "I hope not."

"What about Harry? Can we trust him not to tell his partner that Daniel is here?" Wheeler raised an eyebrow.

Red shook his head sadly. "No. Not unless Harry's found religion."

"Let me see what I can do." Wheeler said, encouragingly. They had walked only a few paces when Wheeler stopped Red again. "Do you think this Hamlett fellow would actually kill Harry?" Red paused.

"I have not one doubt, Jerome. He's a nasty piece of work and he's tried to kill Harry once already. I was there, if you remember?" Wheeler took Red's reply seriously.

*   *   *

"I got asked to guard that big silver statue all the way back to Colorado," Hamlett said. Half-drunk, Harry looked at him briefly and went back to his beer. "You're coming too." Hamlett barked. Harry ignored him. "If you don't want to go, I can always shoot you here?" Hamlett laughed, enjoying his own humor. "You'd just be another dead drunk, Harry." Hamlett sat beside Harry preventing his escape.

"Why are you doing this, Ham?" Harry whined. "I thought we were friends?" Hamlett laughed at him.

"Friends? Look at me, Harry!" Hamlett grabbed Harry's shoulder forcing Harry to look at Hamlett's burned face. "You're mad, Harry. Do you know that? Why would I ever want you as a friend? Every time I look into the mirror, I see how much I hate you, Harry. And if you don't find me either the money you stole, or the reward for this little piece of shit, you'll be mine to do with as I please." Hamlett stood to leave, "Do you understand me?" Harry barely raised his eyes. "I say we grab him here and turn him in tomorrow!"

Harry lifted his head wearily. It was almost dawn. He'd barely had a moment's sleep, battling the devil's dilemma between being killed by Hamlett or having to face a prison sentence for Joe's death. He covered his head with his pillow since neither choice ended well for him.

Still, he wondered why, after all these years, his friends had turned on him. It was the look that Shirley gave him that pained him the most. That damning look he'd seen before. What right did she have to be so high and mighty? She was a prostitute, wasn't she? And Daniel, he was no better than Shirley in his condemnation. Nor was Red, for that matter. All of them. All jurors and Wheeler the judge.

But then there was the missing money from the robbery. Who had stolen it from him? Shirley vouched that Daniel wasn't involved. He was at the wedding the whole time, she said. One thing he was sure of: whoever took the money must've burned the cabin down to cover the robbery. It made sense. He tossed these facts and fears about in his head while hiding under his pillow. He had never felt so desolate. He tried to cry, but was incapable, of course.

Suddenly, in a moment of insight, he realized who had stolen his money. He sat up, smiling with relief, joy and happiness. It was so clear, he wondered why it had taken him so long to figure it out. Now, he just had to get back to Aspen before Daniel and in the meantime, avoid being murdered by Hamlett.

Chapter 42

"Am I fired, Mister Wheeler?" Daniel stood two steps below Wheeler, their difference in status amplified. Jerome stepped down to Daniel and considered him. There was so much about this young man that he admired. Talent, resourcefulness, obvious bravery. Wheeler could see it all, right here in his open, honest face. Honest if you didn't know of his bank robbing exploits.

"Come with me," Wheeler said. "I think we need to have a talk." Wheeler led Daniel to a vacant setee. They sat silently for several minutes. "I talked with Harry last night, Daniel. He told us everything."

Wheeler watched Daniel closely. A soul laid bare. Saw the wind leave his sails, saw his compass spin.

Daniel had never felt so naked under any man's eye, not even his father's. Why couldn't Wheeler simply fire him and set him free? There was nothing left of him. The tensions had exhausted him, the burdens he'd carried had whittled him down to a nub. The lies, stacked on top of lies, had in themselves built a wall that was increasing the distance him from his friends, and from Kate.

"How much did Harry tell you?"

"He said that you two robbed the bank in Leadville." Wheeler smiled, "He's not much on details, that Harry, is he?"

"Did he tell you where he hid the money?"

"No. He only said that they couldn't find it, though he still believes that Joe knew who stole it. Harry's friend hit Joe when he wouldn't tell them."

"Who's Harry's friend?" Daniel immediately asked.

"That deputy feller from Leadville. Hamlett Kincaid, the sheriff's son." Daniel closed his eyes and slowly shook his head. Wheeler understood the young man's dilemma. Moments passed before Wheeler spoke again. "Bring your family for lunch. I may have some news by then." He reached into his pocket, withdrew some money and folding the bills handed them to Daniel with a smile. "I'm sure you could use some money," Wheeler said, patting Daniel on the shoulder in a kindly way as he left.

"What were you talking to Jerome about, Daniel?" Shirley asked. Kate was equally curious.

"He invited my family for lunch. That's all," he lied.

"Well, why don't you go and fetch them?" Shirley took his hand. "I would wager a bet that your mother would give the devil her soul for a nice hot bath. They can use our, your room." Shirley smiled at him, felt him relax. "Go on now." Shirley was pleased that he gave her a smile, a faint smile, but a smile all the same.

Daniel didn't move and his reluctance to leave Kate under these circumstances tore Shirley's heart. She took Daniel's hand and then Kate's, pressing them together. "Come on, you two. This too shall pass, I promise you." Shirley came close to Kate, whispering into her ear. "Go on. Kiss him, Kate. Make him come back to you, my darling daughter." And so, she did.

*   *   *

Sergeant Lynch was neither surprised nor alarmed by Coleman's recounting of the charges against Rafferty. According to Coleman, the agency had quite a folder of allegations against him. If Rafferty was wanted by the Pinkertons, and also by the police for questioning regarding the death of John Hogan, there could be a mutually beneficial partnership in the making.

Coleman confided that he had started out in law enforcement as a bounty hunter. It was a short-lived career, he said. Having taken only two men into custody, been shot at twice and wounded once, he felt that the odds of surviving were not in his favor. His current employment with Pinkerton's was more clerical and therefore less dangerous. Mostly related to keeping abreast of information regarding the outlaws they were hired to apprehend.

Regarding Lynch's task and the Pinkerton's involvement, he was less than confident that an arrest warrant issued in Ireland would garner a much public support. Much of the population, including many in law enforcement, would be unsympathetic. Americans were proud that their country was a land of fresh starts, a country where any man could begin a new life, with a clean slate.

All this added to Lynch's feeling of urgency. Though his quarry could already be aboard a train heading west, his policeman's intuition told him that this was not the case. After all, it had been a long journey for the old woman and she would need to rest. He felt confident that when they did resume their journey, he would see them at the train station and be able to apprehend them there.

Familiarizing himself with the oversized map of the network of principle rail lines, he failed to see any direct route west. There was none. Shifting his attention to the departure board he studied the schedules of trains departing westward and though many were unfamiliar destinations, he saw that most trains heading to the West Coast went through Kansas City. All he knew, without doubt, was that they were on the run and they were heading west.

After writing down the departure times of the trains headed west, he walked about the station identifying the quickest routes between platforms. Satisfied that he knew where the appropriate platforms were, he bought a large mug of coffee and positioned himself at a table on the mezzanine where he could observe the ticket counter and watched.

*   *   *

For a moment Shirley had the impression that she was back at the Paragon. Noisily surrounded by women in various stages of undress, she felt almost as if she were back in her brothel in Aspen. She laughed as did Kate when Myra and Megan emerged from the bathroom swaddled in clean white towels, giddy and giggling with unabashed joy to be clean and scrubbed.

Shirley took it upon herself to help Myra look and feel more fashionable and though they were not of the same shape or size Shirley had found something suitable for her to wear. Also, pressed by her mother,

Kate had found dresses for both Megan and Gemma and did her very best to make the two young women socially presentable.

To all, Myra's transformation was miraculous. Once upon a time she had been a tall, athletic, tawny, red-haired maiden, but she had suffered from the weight of sadness and the burden of responsibility had diminished her stature. Now, she stood tall once again, her shoulders straight and broad as she pirouetted in front of the long mirror. Shirley, smiling, linked her arm through Myra's.

"You look like a new woman."

"Indeed, I feel like it too." Myra considered their reflection in the mirror and laughed. "I can't thank you enough, Shirley," she said. "We have so much to talk about. Daniel and Kate. How they met ..." Shirley squeezed Myra's arm lifted her finger to her lips.

"Indeed, we do," Shirley said intimately, inwardly balking at what could be told and what would stay secret.

Daniel knocked twice and entered with Patrick. For a long moment, no one spoke and an awkward silence descended on them. To Shirley, the moment was poignantly memorable and she wished Red was there to see it. She could feel the love in the room so palpably that she felt tears well up. It was Daniel who put it all into perspective.

"It's been so long since we were all together like this," Daniel said, smiling broadly. "We're a family once again," he said, gathering up his mother and sister in his arms extending them wider for Patrick to join them. Joy burst forth like a storm of laughter raining tears.

Suddenly Gemma headed for the door. "Gemma, come back," Patrick called. "Where are you going?" Before he could stop her she'd closed the door on him. Distressed and confused, Patrick rushed out catching Gemma in the hall. "Where were you going?"

She pulled away giving him a stern look. "I'm happy for you, Patrick. I really am." He reached for her again but she eluded him. "One big happy family, you said. But not to me." He reached for her again but she eluded him. Several passing hotel guests gave them a harsh look. Patrick took Gemma's hand in both of his. She turned away from him but he gently turned her face back to him. Tears welled in her eyes. She blinked and one tear escaped tracing a silver streak down her cheek.

"Gemma," he said, softly and drew her to him. "You're a part of my family, too." She looked up at him and brushed away a tear with the back of her hand.

"Why would you say that, Patrick? I'm no good. You hardly know me!" she bawled and fell into his arms, a flood of tears falling on his shoulder. The door opened. Shirley gave Patrick a quizzical look.

"Everything alright?" she asked. Patrick nodded. Shirley opened the door wider. "Come on everyone, let's go eat," Shirley said, directing her newly acquired family into the hallway and down the stairs to the dining room.

*   *   *

The sky was gray and the storm marching in from over the lake hurled raindrops at him like bullets. In a rotten mood, Harry moped around the fairgrounds avoiding work as diligently as most other men begged for it. Sulking his way along the main avenue toward the Colorado Exhibit he considered his dilemma.

On the one hand, his prospects for a long life had never looked worse, being that he was a missive to a sadistic bully who held him in contempt, and hostage. Clearly the sword Hamlett held over Harry's head was Doc Holliday's admission to Hamlett that he had misled the jury and that Harry was indeed guilty of the robbery. But it was not his only concern.

In addition, and although it was a debatable point, Harry had been complicit in the death of No Problem Joe, and that was a very serious matter. Reality was dawning on him that if either of these charges were proven, he would go to prison and of that he was certain. But he had a plan. It was quite simple really, as were all of Harry's plans. Convinced that he now knew who had taken his money and where it might be hidden, all he had to do was keep Daniel out of Hamlett's grasp. Unknowingly, Daniel was the key to the puzzle.

The Colorado Exhibition Hall was still abuzz with visitors gawking at the modern mining equipment. Even before he reached the center of the hall he could see that the Silver Queen's position of prominence and honor was vacant. Strangely and oddly vacant. Where she had previously stood towering over the crowds, now there was just an empty space. It made the hall seem hollow. Someone tapped him on the shoulder and he jumped.

"Ham!" Harry said in surprise, as if Hamlett had been privy to his mental meanderings. "The statue is gone," he bumbled.

"The last wagon left an hour ago." Hamlett smiled his twisted smile. "Do you want to see where they took it?" Harry had no choice. Hamlett took him by the arm and pushed him out of the hall and into a street. "Come on, Harry, we don't have all day."

A mile later, into the shunting area they walked between the rows of empty boxcars until they came to a junction where many rail lines joined.

"Here it is." Hamlett said. Harry looked up at the gaily painted train box car. "Come inside," Hamlett said, swinging a chain on which hung a large brass key.

Harry trailed him up the metal steps and followed him into the railcar, illuminated only by small barred windows near the ceiling. It was close in the cramped space, barely enough room for one man to pass another. Filling the train car, stacked to the rafters, were wooden crates that held nearly six tons of silver and gold. Harry began to sweat.

The proximity to so much wealth brought on Harry's fever. His eyes glazed and he felt sweat run down from his armpits down to his wrists. He reached out his hand to steady himself but.

"Come here, Harry," Hamlett commanded and led him along the narrow corridor to the rear of the train car. "This is where we sleep. Nice cozy quarters. All the better to keep my eye on you." Hamlett laughed loudly and slapped Harry on the shoulder. Harry eyed the two hammocks and the small iron stove and the bucket for waste. Hamlett removed the pistol from his belt and placed it on the small table attached to the wall and sat in one of the wooded chairs looking at Harry.

"Here's what I'm thinking." Hamlett smiled. Harry shuddered. "If your little friend Daniel is coming back to Colorado too, I say we grab him on the way." Harry looked at Hamlett quizzically.

"We just grab him?" Harry questioned, doubtfully.

"That's right, Harry. We'll turn him in for the money." Harry felt the rush of a reprieve but it was not to be. "And then I kill you." Hamlett laughed loudly, enjoying his own humor. "I know it's only five thousand dollars for the little shit," he trailed off. "It's less than the money from the robbery. But, the way I see it, you'll never find that money, or who took it. So, the five thousand I get from Pinkerton's and the pleasure of killing you will keep me happy for a spell. I think it's a clever idea, don't you, Harry?"

Chapter 43

Jerome Wheeler entered the hotel's dining room looking splendid. Handing his coat and tall hat to the hat-checker and with a nod to the maître's, he ploughed through the crowded room, grandly waving greetings to friends and associates.

"Good afternoon, everybody," he said, with a smile to each of his guests. "You must be Daniel's mother, Myra," Jerome effused, bending from the waist and kissing her hand in the continental manner. Myra blushed, swooning at Jerome, whom she felt was the most handsome man she had ever seen. "I can see the resemblance to Daniel in your radiant smile," he said, prompting Myra to blush more. "And this is your family?" Daniel introduced them as Jerome circumnavigated the table smiling and shaking hands.

"Do you have you any news, Jerome?" Shirley asked, putting to voice the question that was on the mind of all assembled. No one spoke.

Wheeler took a sip of water. "Good and bad, I'm afraid. But it will keep until after we eat," Wheeler said jovially. "Let's enjoy our lunch, shall we? But first," Wheeler raised a finger. "Daniel, would you mind exchanging seats with me? I'd like to sit by your beautiful mother, if it pleases her?" Myra's blush, under her lightly freckled skin, turned her cheeks bright crimson.

With the seating arrangements completed, they ordered lunch and Jerome insisted that they have wine. The meal was sumptuous, beyond anything that the Shadlows had experienced before and they relished every morsel and crumb that was presented. The lunch passed pleasantly as Myra and Jerome chatted with Shirley and Red and Kate and Daniel mended their differences. Patrick held Megan's hand and occasionally Gemma's.

Finished with their meals, the men stood while the ladies retired. Jerome maintained his smile until the ladies had gone sufficiently far away, then he glared at Daniel and Patrick and his mood darkened.

"Sit down," he commanded. Red sat also, noting that Jerome's transition from bon-homme to captain in chief was instantaneous and dramatic. Daniel was unsurprised; he had been expecting the worst. Wheeler sat silently, looking from Daniel to Patrick and back for a full minute until Red could stand the suspense no more.

"What did you find out, Jerome?" Red asked. Wheeler took in a deep breath and exhaled pensively before he answered, signaling to Daniel the worst of the worst.

"When I was over at the Pinkerton's office earlier to settle my bill with them for their services I had an opportunity to ask a few questions of someone I know there." Jerome paused and no one interrupted. "According to the information I received, there is someone out there searching for you, Patrick." Wheeler took in a deep breath before continuing. "And I believe he's looking for you too, Daniel." Wheeler watched them closely, gauging their reactions. "It's most likely the man who followed you from New York. The one you tricked into catching the wrong train. But it also might not be him. I don't know? My friend at Pinkerton's was not very clear on that point. What I do know is this: The Pinkerton Detective Agency, of whom I am a very good client, has assured me that they will take no active part in your capture." He watched their smiles suddenly appear. "Not so fast." Their smiles disappeared just as quickly. "Unless," he continued, dampening their joy. "Unless, someone with a legal warrant brings you into their office, in person. They don't have the resources to chase every criminal, they say. So, that's the good news."

"And the bad news?" Red insisted.

"There is still a reward outstanding for your capture, Daniel. And for your brother too. Whoever it is looking for you knows that, and he is here in Chicago." Wheeler took another long breath. "And, he is very determined, it seems." Their waiter refilled their coffee cups. "Then, there is this business with Harry Rich. He wants you too, Daniel. And not just for the reward for your capture. You know what I mean, don't you?" Wheeler lifted an eyebrow and under his gaze, Daniel swallowed hard. Patrick cast him a worried look.

"What do you suggest, Jerome?" Red leaned forward. Wheeler considered the answer, looking from Daniel to Patrick.

"I think we should split up." He placed his coffee cup on the table. "Daniel, you should stay with me. And Red, I think you, Shirley and Kate should go with Daniel's family to Kansas City on a different train. I know they'll be disappointed but it's for the best." Daniel gave Patrick a shrug. "If there is more than one person following you, we might deal with them more effectively if we meet them separately." Wheeler leaned back and watched the reactions. Red looked worried.

"Ah, just in time. Here come the ladies now." Wheeler stood, holding Myra's chair for her. Red, Daniel and Patrick did the same. "Shirley, can I see you and Red for a moment?" Wheeler inclined his head toward the foyer.

Daniel watched them leave, his brow deeply furrowed. Kate looked concerned. "Is anything wrong?" Daniel forced a reassuring smile and took her hand in his.

"Everything will be alright, trust me." He kissed her on the cheek and stood. "I'll be back in a minute."

Wheeler sat with Red and Shirley on a brocade sofa, their heads together. "Here's my question, Shirley," Wheeler began. "Do you think Harry will tell that deputy feller that Daniel is here in Chicago?" Shirley looked at Red and nodded.

"Of course he will, Jerome. Harry can't keep a secret," Shirley said, unsmiling. "You should know that by now."

"That's what Red and I thought too," Wheeler agreed. "So, in that case, Daniel will be the bait. That should be enough incentive for them to travel together with the Silver Queen back to Colorado. If that's not enough then I'll make the offer financially irresistible. Whether or not it can be proven, I want that Hamlett Kincaid to stand trial for Joe's death. I believe we owe it to him."

"What about Washington? Don't you have to go back there?"

Wheeler shook his head. "Not if I can help it, Red. Those folks can't be trusted. At least Harry is predictable," he laughed, spotting Daniel approaching them. "I'll go make the travel arrangements while you and Shirley take Daniel's family out shopping. I'll take the boy along with me and make certain that this Hamlett fellow sees him. That OK with you, Red?" Wheeler nodded his head in the direction of Daniel's approach.

"It's as good an idea as any I could come up with," Red replied, looking at Shirley. "We could all use some distraction, don't you think, Shirley?" Red elbowed Shirley gently, making her smile.

"Oh, there you are, Daniel," Shirley said. "We were just saying that Red and I should take your family out sightseeing and shopping since Jerome needs you." She bussed Jerome and Daniel on their respective cheeks and blew off in a whirlwind, carrying Red in her wake.

"I want to have a word with you before we leave, Daniel. Sit down." A minute passed. Wheeler smiled and waved to someone. Daniel began to perspire. "I'll be honest with you, Daniel. The fact that you are still my employee stands on weak timber presently." Wheeler allowed his words to sink in. "You're a bank robber. Several times over if I believe everything I hear," Wheeler trailed off. "Now, I find out that there is a reward being offered for your return to England or Ireland or someplace. The only thing I see going for you now is that you're married to Kate." Wheeler let the implications set in. "That's about it, son. You're in a mess of trouble as I see it."

Wheeler watched Daniel closely, intrigued to be observing a young man maturing before his eyes. The air between them, gravitas laden. Wheeler leaned forward so that their knees touched. "It's time you made a decision." Wheeler's expression was granite cold. "If you want my help, you must promise me that there will be no more lies between us. You must be truthful with me from here on. Do you get my meaning?" Daniel nodded. "On your word of honor?"

"Yes, Mister Wheeler. On my honor."

Wheeler stood as did Daniel hoping that the worst was past. Wheeler took Daniel by the elbow and facing him, he smiled a sly smile. "Do you know what happened to the money?"

Daniel felt the blood drain from his face. "No." He swallowed hard.

"Am I to believe that neither you nor Harry know who took it?"

Wheeler's eyes were sparkling as they drilled into him.

"I have no idea who took it, Mister Wheeler. If anybody did steal it, that is. I know where it was, but with the fire and the collapsing roof it might have burned," Daniel lied. Wheeler continued to hold his gaze.

"What about Harry? Could he be lying? Maybe he spent the money?" Daniel shrugged. Wheeler smiled. "Come with me, son. If we're going to elude one of your enemies and fool another, we have some work to do." Suddenly he stopped. "Do you know what? I think I might enjoy playing poker with Harry again. He always was a terrible gambler." Wheeler laughed loudly, as the door was opened for them.

A sudden flash of light caused them both to cover their eyes. Two reporters appeared at their sides barraging Wheeler with questions about the future of the silver industry. Deft at handling these sorts of situations, Wheeler held up his hand and calmed the clamor. Then, taking their questions in turn he skillfully announced that the industry would survive and that those employed in the silver mining industry would always have a job. After a picture was taken of him standing alone on the steps of the hotel the photographer positioned Daniel on a lower step and quickly took a picture of them together.

Chapter 44

J erome B. Wheeler, the public face of the American silver industry, was scowling at the newspaper when everyone arrived. Having successfully cajoled the hotel manager into manifesting a non-existent room, the Shadlows arrived at breakfast in a merry mood, rested and outfitted in new clothes. Composing himself for his guests Wheeler greeted them all warmly, profusely complimenting Myra on her fashionable attire.

Wheeler passed the newspaper to Red and Shirley, who looked at him in shock. Then he gave it to Daniel and Kate, who both looked up at Wheeler in alarm when they saw Daniel's picture on the front page.

"Are you all packed?" Wheeler asked Shirley. "Kate and I were up past midnight packing."

Wheeler took a deep breath, exhaling slowly, shaking his head. "I think it best I get you all out of Chicago as quickly as possible so I have tickets for you on a train leaving for Kansas City at noon." Myra looked dismayed. Wheeler smiled for her. "Don't worry Myra. Daniel and I will meet you there tomorrow. I'm guessing that you should be there several hours before us."

"Why Kansas City? Wouldn't it be best to go back to Aspen?"

Shirley asked. Wheeler pointed at the newspaper in Myra's hands.

"No matter how dim-witted the person interested in your capture is, all he has to do is read the paper to know we live in Aspen. The last thing I want is for him to follow us there."

Wheeler looked around the table at the expectant faces. No fear showed. He noted that rather than surprise or fear, the Shadlow family held similar expressions in response to this news. Acceptance was the word that came to mind.

Wheeler pulled him aside. "Listen Red, I'm sorry about the picture in the paper. I wasn't thinking," Wheeler trailed off.

"What's done is done, Jerome. But, we'll have to be careful from now on."

"I'm wondering if our man might already be watching at the train station. Do you know what he looks like?"

"Daniel says he's about my size and has scars on his face."

"Do you think you'll all be safe until I get to Kansas City?" Wheeler asked.

Red laughed out loud. "We'll be fine, Jerome. If anything happens, I'll set the women loose on him." Red laughed again. "They'd tear him apart like lions. I'm the one you should worry about."

"Shirley, I've given Red the train tickets and Daniel and I will see you at the station. In the meantime, we have some business to attend to." Myra was holding onto Daniel's hand tightly. He kissed her on the cheek and smiled at her.

"I'll see you all later at the train, I promise," Daniel said, climbing aboard Wheeler's cab. Waving back as they departed, several silent minutes passed before Daniel turned to face Wheeler. "Where are we going, Mister Wheeler?"

"We're going to make Harry Rich an offer he can't resist."

Wheeler was counting on Harry being Harry. If he was still an eminently corruptible coward, and there was no reason to think otherwise, then his co-operation could be bought. It was Wheeler's experience that when a man was faced with a choice between friendship and betrayal, it was money, or its mere possibility, that won out every time.

He had decided to risk the Silver Queen.

*   *   *

Harry was disgruntled. It being a word that sprung to his hungry mind and having no idea what a "gruntle" was, he chewed on it. Dragged around by Hamlett, being fed occasionally and only whenever Hamlett was hungry, Harry lamented his lot. He had lost the last of his money playing poker and was now even more at the beck and whim of his dangerous partner.

They were sitting on the iron steps of the Silver Queen's boxcar when a small steam engine backed up to them. An engineer walked back to the connection and turned the crank handle until it locked onto their car. "If you two are comin', you'd better hang on," he said, as he climbed back onto the engine and the train began to move.

"Where are we going?" Hamlett ignored him.

Wheeler and Daniel accompanied by another man were waiting on the platform when the train bearing the Silver Queen pulled abreast of them. A serious looking man in a long black coat stood behind Daniel and his presence spoke volumes, if one was to notice. Harry noticed and saw that Hamlett did also, feeling for the heft of the pistol in his coat pocket.

Wheeler was confident that neither Harry nor his partner would threaten Daniel in such a public place, but he was glad that he had brought along support all the same. Wheeler nodded to the man in the black coat and he approached Harry and Hamlett before the train had come to a stop.

"These are for you," he said handing Hamlett two sheets of printed paper. "Read these over and both of you sign them." He handed Hamlett a pencil. "Are you Harry Rich?" Harry nodded. "Mister Wheeler wants to talk to you."

Harry took several steps toward Jerome and Daniel, but he paused briefly to glance back at Hamlett and recognizing that look, was glad that the man in the black coat stood between them. Harry swallowed hard, his mind close to buckling with thoughts of salvation. When Harry looked at Wheeler's and Daniel's faces, he honestly felt that his fortunes had turned. That finally his luck had changed. He smiled. Here were his friends. He was safe. He was wrong, as usual.

Sergeant Lynch had so much to complain about; but didn't. He was no longer the kind of man he was in his younger days. In no uncertain terms, his wife had taught him this quiet acceptance, if nothing else. He groaned as he stood to stretch his arms and legs, looking down at the wrought iron seat he'd been sitting on and wondering if it was a reproduction of some medieval torture apparatus. Rubbing his behind, he could feel the imprint of the chair on his buttocks. Rubbing them felt good. The ladies at the next table laughed good-naturedly and he smiled back.

Refreshed by only a smidgen, Lynch reread his timetable noting that he would want to pay close attention to the next departing trains headed west. From his perch up on the mezzanine, he was able to watch the passengers pass through the stone arches to the platforms and remain unobserved.

He'd now watched more than a dozen trains depart westward and his attention was flagging. But suddenly, after watching thousands of people anonymously traipse through his field of vision, he caught a glimpse of someone he thought he recognized. Hurrying down to the main terminal floor he followed the man discreetly, hidden by the intervening crowds. Abruptly, his target turned onto a platform where the train was headed to San Francisco.

Following at a distance, he watched the man stand with two others intently watching a train reversing into the station. It was when the tall man turned and walked toward the train that Lynch positively identified him. It was Coleman, the Pinkerton's man. Not only that, but he was with the men whose picture he recognized from the newspaper. Lynch almost jumped for joy. It was Daniel Shadlow. He took out his newspaper and compared the picture in the paper to the man on the platform. They were one and the same; it was Jerome B. Wheeler.

Lynch watched Coleman walk to the gaily painted train car and speak with two men there. A scruffy-looking bearded man walked back with him and joined the other two in what looked like a stand-off. Coleman, looking back at the train often, appeared to guard them. After a short conversation the bearded man returned to the train and Coleman, accompanying the other two men, turned and walked back along the platform towards him.

Hiding behind a stack of luggage Lynch watched them pass him and exit the platform. He also observed the men on the train and was surprised when the larger man took the scruffy man by the neck and roughly pushed him inside the train car.

Ignoring the men on the train he hurried back to the platform entrance and observed Coleman and the men talking together. After speaking for several minutes, they shook hands and went in different directions, but not before he saw Coleman hand Wheeler a weighty package. Lynch now faced a major decision.

Coleman was disappearing into the throng. Whose side was Coleman on? What was in the package he passed to Wheeler? Who were the men on the train? He had little time to make up his mind, both of his quarries were slipping away. Coleman headed for the station entrance and the other two turned and walked in the opposite direction. He decided to follow his principle targets and did his best to keep them in sight but lost them in the swirling crowd. Fearing that he had lost them for good, Lynch searched the long row of platforms twice before remembering that there was a train due to leave for Kansas City. Consulting his timetable and the large clock on the wall he raced for the platform.

There they were; he recognized Wheeler's tall hat. Approaching them carefully, he saw that they were saying farewell to someone on the train and it took no skill for him to deduce to whom they were talking. Lynch jumped a foot when the train's whistle blew. He thought about jumping on the train without a ticket but he was too late, the train was already pulling away from the station. Not too late though, for a man with no luggage sprinting for the departing train which he caught with the help of the conductor. The man was smiling as he passed Wheeler and Daniel, and Lynch knew why.

They turned and left the platform talking to each other and Lynch followed them at a distance, his breath short and feeling a little faint from the shock of seeing Rafferty boarding the train. He doubted that Rafferty had seen him, but he was certain that Rafferty had recognized Daniel Shadlow. Rafferty was dangerous and he was stalking the Shadlows. Lynch had no time to waste.

Following Wheeler and Daniel discreetly, he watched them approach the train and enter a private carriage adjoined to the box car with the words "The Silver Queen" emblazoned on the side. Where the scruffy man had been pushed inside. The rest of the train was a string of unremarkable boxcars with numbers stenciled on them.

"Where is that train headed?" Lynch asked a worker pushing a squeaky, iron-wheeled cart.

"That one?" Pointing at the train carrying Daniel and Wheeler.

"It's going to San Francisco."

"Thank you," Lynch said, and quickly making his decision, he hurried off to purchase a ticket, but found a long queue. Struggling to keep his impatience in check while the customers ahead of him dithered and stalled he finally found himself at the ticket window.

"Where to?"

"Does the twelve thirty train to San Francisco stop in Kansas City?" The man looked at his schedule, taking his time.

"Yes, it does. But it makes lots'a stops. It's mostly a freight train. You wanna go to Kansas City?" Lynch nodded and hoped that he had enough for the train fare. He did, and after buying his ticket he raced back to the soon departing train. His belongings were lost to him now, but he smiled in the knowledge that he had his most important possessions with him. The warrant for Patrick Shadlow's arrest, and his pistol. He had all he needed.

Chapter 45

Harry was buoyed by the fact that they were heading west. Symbolically it signified that he was either moving towards a future he could enjoy, or a step closer to his grave at the hands of Hamlett Kincaid. Lying in his hammock swaying with the movement of the train, he wanted to again feel the hot wind on his face and the sweat run from his armpits. The very things that he had hated most about living in Utah were now a solace.

"What did you say, Harry?" Hamlett yelled down the train car. He had usurped the larger of the sleeping spaces where the small table and chairs were.

"Nothing," Harry replied, but heard the heavy footsteps approaching.

"The next time we get an opportunity to grab that little shit, I say we grab him. Are you listening to me, Harry?" Hamlett poked Harry with the barrel of his pistol. "I said, are you listening to me, Harry?"

"I hear you. Now leave me alone, I want to sleep."

"Just remember I have this gun, Harry, and I don't really care if I shoot you here, or don't. It's up to you." Hamlett turned away. "I doubt that your little friend will help you any more than Wheeler did, so don't go getting any ideas." Hamlett let out a laugh, more frightening than jolly. "I found you once, Harry. I'm sure I can find you again."

Hamlett's footsteps receded and Harry breathed easier. Living in such proximity to his executioner had hardened him so that the threats he was regularly receiving had less influence on him. There was a way out of this mess, he reasoned. He had only to wait for it to present itself.

Harry dozed, looking at the locked door that led to the adjoining train cars. He'd tried to open the door of course, but there was no escape there. He heard a cork being pulled from a bottle, a sound he was quite familiar with. Staggering and swaying along the narrow space between the cargo and the rough wooden wall of the train car Harry found Hamlett sitting in one of the chairs with his feet up on the table.

"Wheeler was good enough to give us some whiskey at least. D'you want some?" Hamlett held out the bottle to him. "Go ahead, Harry. You know you want it." Hamlett was correct in that Harry wanted to drown either his sorrows or himself in the tawny, fiery liquid.

"What's the matter, Harry? Go on! Have some! The condemned are always offered a drink before they die, you know." Harry's only pleasure was seeing Hamlett wince at the contraction of the burned skin around his mouth when he laughed. But he never took his eyes off the pistol lying on the table between them. "What did Wheeler say to you?" Hamlett watched Harry eyeing the pistol. "Harry!" he yelled. "I'm talking to you."

Harry snapped his head up. "Nothing, Ham. Nothing at all." Hamlett gave him the bent eye. "Honest, Ham. He just wanted to be cordial is all."

"What about your little partner? What'd he say?" Harry simply shook his head.

Wheeler, Harry remembered, had controlled from the start. "There's not going to be much talking, Harry," Wheeler had said gravely as Harry approached. "and I'll do all of it." Harry came no closer. "You're in a lot of trouble, Harry. And you're in deep it appears. You've only got one chance if you ever want to be rid of your partner." Wheeler flicked his eyes at Hamlett. "If so, then you'll do as I tell you, without question. Agreed?" Harry nodded, as would a chided child. "Now, get back on board."

"What about him?" Harry said under his breath, flicking his eyes at Hamlett. Wheeler tipped his hat to Hamlett, who touched the brim of his hat in return. Neither man smiled.

"Later, Harry." Wheeler said, dismissively.

Desperate, Harry dawdled, delaying his return to the train car. He'd been aboard the train less than two hours and already the small space was making him uneasy. There was nowhere to run, no escape.

Strangely, Harry was grateful that Daniel had said nothing. It was a relief since Harry had nothing to profess but excuses. Daniel had aged, but it was his look that disturbed Harry most. He had hardened. They had been friends once and Harry searched for a sign, any indication that there was even the slightest of a glimmer of hope of reviving their friendship.

But Daniel had offered none. Harry had seen similar looks before; written clearly on the faces of the women whose hearts he'd broken.

"He must 'a said something?" Hamlett snarled. "What did he say?"

Harry gave Hamlett a theater worthy shrug of innocence.

"Nothing, I tell you, Ham. Nothing! OK? He said that someone would come and take away the forms we had to sign. That's it." Harry turned away, headed back to the imaginary privacy of his hammock.

"Here. Take some food with you," Hamlett snarled, pointing at the food hamper. Harry opened and retrieved the remaining two sandwiches and one bottle of beer.

Hamlett pointed his pistol at Harry's head menacingly. "Don't you go getting any ideas during the night. Do you understand me, Harry?" Though the thought had fleetingly occurred to him, Harry shook his head in obeisance and retreated hugging the sandwiches to his chest. By sunset he'd eaten them all. Later that night as they crossed the plains Harry was positive the sound of his rumbling stomach frightened more cattle than the train.

*   *   *

"What will we do if there's someone at the station to arrest Patrick?" Red asked, quietly so that only Shirley heard.

"I don't know. How much trouble do you think he and Daniel are in?"

"I think more than they're letting on. I really don't know what to make of him, or his friend Gemma, either."

Shirley hugged her husband even more and smiled, resting her head on his chest. "I'm going to give them a chance, Red. They've been through a lot by the sounds of it." She looked up into Red's adoring eyes. "I can see a lot of pain there, Red. It's something that a woman in my line of business recognizes. Gemma might not be the one for him, but she's there for him now and that's probably enough for time being. At least until he and his family are out of danger."

"Have you noticed his teeth?" Red asked. Shirley sighed.

"I think it happened to him in prison." Shirley was quiet for a while. "It's sad. He was probably handsome once."

Patrick held his mother's hand through most of the night. An hour after their departure she had drifted off to sleep and he didn't have the will to wake her though his bladder was close to bursting and his buttocks ached. Megan and Gemma were also sleeping, their heads resting against each other's. Occasionally he looked across the aisle at Red and Shirley, Daniel and Kate and if Red noticed him looking at them, he would give back an encouraging smile.

The sudden discovery of Daniel's new family had been a surprise to Patrick and to them all. Already he had seen that Kate was very much like her mother, Shirley. Someone accustomed to ordering men around. There was a hardness to Shirley that he hoped not ever to see pointed in his direction. She was unlike any woman he had ever encountered. As tough as any man and wise as a mother. Whatever business she was in Patrick had no doubt that she was competent at it.

On the other hand, he was unsure of her husband, Red. He felt uneasy when Red looked at him, as if Red was looking for something inside him. He was friendly and cordial on the surface, but he was a suspicious man. Patrick had learned to read men quickly in prison and he had seen enough in Red's face to give him warning. Here was a serious man, one who had seen dreadful things, it showed in his eyes. That watchfulness, that mistrust.

Gemma stirred and smiled at him when she opened her eyes. Slowly sleep took her again and Patrick was left with his thoughts. The train rattled on through the night and Patrick eventually dozed. If he would have stayed awake, he would have seen a man in a plaid coat walk through the carriage casually inspecting the sleeping passengers. Red noticed him because when he saw Patrick, he smiled.

*   *   *

The seats had little padding, it was cold, constantly drafty and the smoke from the engine irritated the eyes. Every single moment was a mixture of clanging, banging, screeching, howling pained screams of tons of steam- driven iron hurtling across the plains. It was a hell on wheels, Lynch thought. Dante could not have been more correct. There were many layers of hell. Though this was one level he could not have imagined.

Sergeant Lynch was so hungry that his stomach's orchestral rumblings were no longer amusing. Nothing was amusing any more. His head ached and his clothes were beginning to offend even him.

Unclear of his final plan and running low on funds, he'd mailed Killeen a letter informing of his actions to date and of his progress. It was brief and concluded with a request for money to be forwarded to Kansas City, explaining that he would need the funds to buy several tickets back to England. It was becoming increasingly imperative that he apprehend Patrick Shadlow in Kansas City or risk losing them all for good. It would be his last, best chance.

There was also Rafferty to consider, and he was another problem entirely. What was he doing in Chicago and how on Earth did he follow them? There was no doubt what he wanted. But, was he prepared to kill again to gain the reward? Lynch had no doubts.

Chapter 46

It happened around dawn, at a water stop like many previous ones. It was good that the rest of passengers were asleep, fewer punters to interfere. Lynch eased himself out of his seat and walked quietly to the rear of the carriage.

Chilly air greeted him as he opened the door and stepped down off the train on the side hidden from the rough platform. Keeping to the shadows he walked along the train to Wheeler's private carriage. Taking the pistol from his pocket he climbed the metal steps quietly and placed his ear against the door. Suddenly, the door opened.

Daniel had seen a man's silhouette through the lace curtain and had opened the door expecting to see Wheeler. Instead, he saw the pistol and raised his hands when he recognized the man who was holding it.

"Where's the other feller?" Lynch asked, forcing Daniel back inside the carriage.

"Gone to the see the station master."

"Sit down and keep quiet."

"Who are you, and what do you want with me?"

Lynch was inclined to laugh. "I'm here to take you and your brother back to England. You're under arrest, lad."

They heard footsteps on the iron steps. Wheeler opened the door and smiled when he saw the pistol and the scarred face of the man holding it.

"Well, what do we have here, Daniel?" Wheeler came further into the small room. "Or should I say, who do we have here? My name is Jerome Wheeler," he said, holding out his hand. Lynch declined.

"I know who you are, Mister Wheeler. I read about you in the newspaper. My name is Lynch." Lynch kept his gun pointed at Daniel. "I have a warrant for this man's arrest, if you'd care to see it?"

"I would indeed care, Mister Lynch. Are you a bounty hunter?" Wheeler asked with a smile. "There are several others on board already, you see." Wheeler was watching Daniel closely, noting the fear in the boy's eyes. Lynch fumbled in his pockets, finally producing the warrant.

The train's whistle blew. The train car jolted forward, and Daniel fell into a chair while Wheeler gripped the window sill to stop from falling. Lynch pointed his pistol from one to the other nervously as the train began to move backwards. Daniel looked at Wheeler who smiled and winked mischievously.

"Putting on more rail cars, I imagine." Wheeler said, removing his hat. A picture of tranquility, he straightened his jacket and took a seat, motioning Lynch to sit across from him on the sofa. "May I see those papers please, Mister Lynch?"

"It's actually Sergeant Lynch, sir. Irish police, Dublin Constabulary."

"You've come a great distance, sergeant?" Wheeler took the papers and settled his glasses on his nose, "A very long way for two young boys, don't you think?" Wheeler watched Lynch over his spectacles. "Your government must want them very badly."

"They blew up a bank in Dublin and injured people. Me included," Lynch said. "Patrick Shadlow is a convicted terrorist who escaped from prison. He's wanted for another serious matter as well, I should add."

"And what matter would that be, sergeant?" Wheeler inquired.

Lynch looked sideways at Daniel. "He is wanted for the killing a man named Clive Reagan." Lynch saw Daniel's shock and inwardly smiled. "But sergeant, this warrant only names Patrick Shadlow." Wheeler placed the papers on the table between them. "Is this all you have?" Wheeler paused. Lynch remained mute. "If it is, then I doubt you have the justification to arrest Daniel Shadlow. You have the wrong man here."

Lynch straightened his shoulders and looked Wheeler squarely in the eye but kept his gun on Daniel. "There is an outstanding warrant for Daniel Shadlow as well, sir. I just happen not to have a copy of it at this very moment."

"Might I remind you that you're a long way from Ireland, sergeant? A very long way." Wheeler smiled; it was his most disarming tactic. "I doubt you'd know this, Mister Lynch. But where we're headed, most men have had a price on their head at one time or another."

"I'm not interested in other men, Mister Wheeler."

The train shunted again and moved in reverse. Lynch abruptly stood and pointed his pistol at Wheeler who, using his index finger, turned the barrel away from his face. "Please sit back down, Mister Lynch. You're making me nervous."

Lynch complied, though warily. The train shunted and stopped amid sounds of metal clasps making union. Then it moved forward again and Lynch relaxed, slightly.

"Daniel," Wheeler said, pleasantly, "would you make us some coffee, please?" Daniel stood and Lynch stood with him, pistol in hand. "Please, Mister Lynch, sit back down. He's going to make coffee. You might as well relax. We won't be arriving in Kansas City till noon."

*   *   *

At the Kansas City station, the Shadlows gathered their belongings and with brave faces prepared to take another step toward a hopeful future. Assembling on the station platform with Red and his family they were approached by a handsome young man dressed in a conductor's uniform.

"Are you Mister Corcoran?" he asked.

"Yes, I am," Red replied and the young man handed Red a telegram.

"What is it, Red?" Shirley asked. "Is there something wrong?"

"No," Red smiled, "Jerome wants us to wait here at the station.
He says he will arrive here around noon."

"There is a waiting room and restaurant inside the station, sir," the conductor said, helping them stack their luggage onto a cart. He pointed them toward the restaurant and restrooms and pushed their luggage cart into the station master's office, for safety, he said with a smile. The station restaurant was clean and bright with friendly staff that welcomed the weary travelers. They were seated at a large table covered in white linen and clean cutlery, a pleasant change from most of the places they'd eaten at along the way.

Megan excused herself to use the restrooms. She had washed her hands and turned to leave when she bumped into Gemma entering. It was an odd moment, and confusing. Gemma's face was flushed and she seemed surprised to see Megan. She quickly recovered, smiled at Megan and continued into the facilities. Though curious, Megan resisted the urge to mention it to Patrick.

*   *   *

Harry heard knocking on the door. At first, he doubted his hearing since the whistling of the wind and the clatter of the wheels drowned out most sounds. But when he heard the knocking again, he got off his hammock and put his ear to the door. Three knocks came again. Harry tapped back three times and the door opened to a rush of air. Wheeler stood in the doorway, motioning Harry to come outside onto the metal platform.

"Aw, Jerome?" Harry lamented, looking down at the pistol Wheeler was holding. Wheeler closed and bolted the door. "You're not going to kill me here, are you?" Wheeler laughed loudly.

"Harry, you are a treasure. No, I'm not going to kill you. We're friends, remember?" He urged Harry across the twisting metal bridge that connected the carriages. Harry paused, reluctant to cross, looking down at the ground rushing beneath his feet hoping he would never experience how it would feel to fall between the rail cars.

"When we go inside," Wheeler yelled over the wind. "I want you to play along with me for a spell." Wheeler placed the pistol into his coat pocket yelling in Harry's ear. "If you help me, Harry, I'll help you." Wheeler took another gamble and held out his hand for Harry to shake. Harry did so, though reluctantly.

"What's in it for me, Jerome?" Wheeler laughed at Harry's skepticism.

"Most importantly, Harry? You may get to live a longer life. Come Harry, I might even make you rich after all this is over." Wheeler laughed again. "If you live, that is," he added as he opened the carriage door and pushed Harry ahead of him. Lynch stood, his pistol pointing at Harry.

"You can relax, Sergeant Lynch," Wheeler said to him. "Mister Rich here is harmless. Aren't you, Harry?" Harry sat on the couch facing Lynch his hands resting on his knees. "It appears that you and Mister Lynch have something in common, Harry. Daniel Shadlow." Harry wrinkled his brow. Lynch remained impassive. "Sergeant Lynch wants to arrest Daniel and take him back to Ireland. Isn't that correct, Sergeant Lynch?"

Lynch nodded. "But there's a problem, Harry," Wheeler continued. "The sergeant only has a warrant to arrest Daniel's brother. So, I am sorry to inform you, that at the present time, there is no reward for Daniel. What do you make of that, Harry?" Wheeler waited for the information to sink in, observing with interest the various reactions. Daniel was relieved. Harry was confused, his mind swimming like a cat in a river. Lynch was unreadable.

"Daniel, would you please get Harry some coffee," Wheeler made a magnanimous gesture including Harry, "and could you bring the hamper in from the kitchen. We could all do with some nourishment." Daniel stood, Lynch raised his gun pointed at Daniel. Wheeler lifted his hand. "Relax, Mister Lynch, please. You're making me nervous again."

Lynch settled back in his chair eyeing Harry. "Who are you, then?"

Wheeler smiled. "Let me say that Harry and Daniel were partners once upon a time." Lynch gave Harry a quizzical look.

"Let me see if I've got this right. You," Lynch pointed his pistol at Harry, "and the lad were partners. And now you're turning him in for a reward?" A smile stretched the pale skin of Lynch's mouth. "And he knows about this, does he?" Lynch looked directly at Wheeler then at Harry and smiled. Wheeler smiled also.

"So, you can see, Mister Lynch, you have some competition."

"Is he the only one?" Lynch pointed his pistol at Harry.

"Oh, no," Wheeler laughed. "There's another one locked up back there in the other rail car. His new partner. Isn't that right Harry?"

Daniel overheard it all as he maneuvered the basket into the parlor.

Wheeler was smiling, enjoying Harry's disquiet immensely.

"Would you pass out the sandwiches, Daniel? Then you can take the hamper back to the kitchen." Daniel did as was asked. "Tell me again Harry, how much did you expect for Daniel's reward?"

"Five thousand dollars," Harry replied. Daniel handed him a sandwich hoping Harry would choke on it. He was lifting out a package of biscuits, sweet with dried fruit judging by the delicious smell, when his hand touched something unexpected. He looked up and saw Wheeler looking directly at him.

"That's what the other fellow said," Lynch was saying.

"What other fellow?" they all said in unison.

Lynch looked at them in turn as he chewed on his ham sandwich. "Rafferty, he called himself. He told me he was a Pinkerton's detective." Daniel carried the food hamper back to the kitchen as Lynch continued. "He's got a warrant too, so he said. Not for Patrick Shadlow but for Daniel Shadlow." Lynch looked up. Wheeler and Harry were looking at him intently.

"Do you happen to know where this Rafferty fellow is, Mister Lynch?" Wheeler asked, accepting coffee from Daniel's shaking hand.

"Yes, I saw him getting on the same train as the Shadlows." Daniel stopped pouring the coffee, alarmed. "Yesterday it was." Lynch continued, politely finishing his mouthful of sandwich before continuing. The silence was deafening but Lynch was oblivious. "He's dangerous too, from what I've seen of his mischief. He's wanted for questioning in at least one death that I know of. An old Irishman named Hogan." Daniel gasped. Wheeler gave him a warning look. Harry looked from one to the other.

"Maybe we could get this Rafferty to share living quarters with Ham." Harry said half joking.

"That's not such an outlandish suggestion, Harry."

*   *   *

"I heard you received a cable from your Sergeant Lynch?" Chief Superintendent Ivers said even before Killeen sat. Killeen handed over the cable.

"That's it?" Ivers asked in astonishment? "Just 'send more money'?"

"Well sir, in his defense, he does say that there is a letter following."

"How long will that take to arrive?"

"If it is coming from Chicago, which is in the middle of the country I believe, it could take two weeks." Killeen trailed off, gauging the disappointment on his superior's face. "He did say in the cable that the Shadlows are together and he will attempt to apprehend them both." Killeen offered.

"I'm wondering," Ivers said, absently, "how he intends to get them both back here."

"That could be the reason he's requesting more money, sir." Chief Superintendent Ivers considered Killeen's reasoning and put his index finger to his lips, pensively. "I suspect that the detective agency we've been using is uninterested in assisting Sergeant Lynch." Ivers leaned forward handing the cable back to Killeen. "We must have a copy of our contract with them here somewhere, Killeen. Find it and bring it to me, promptly."

"I'll get on it right away." Killeen hesitated at the door. "What about the money he requested, sir?"

"Send him 'alf." Ivers smiled. "I don't want him living the high-life on Her Majesty's coin. And tell him to keep us better appraised of his progress."

"What if he has them in custody already, sir?" Ivers looked up from his papers, considering the question.

"I would imagine that the local authorities would be more than happy to help if he were to ask them politely. Professional courtesy and all that, as they say in London."

Killeen left and strode down the stairs to his office. Seated at his desk he took the cable and studied it as if it would suddenly, mysteriously answer his dozens of questions. How would Lynch manage if he did indeed apprehend both Shadlows? Scenarios raced through his mind and situations that could present many obstacles. Did Lynch take handcuffs with him? Killeen tried to remember. Did he have his pistol with him still?

What would happen if Lynch was forced to use it?

Folding the cable and placing it in his pocket he took out the necessary request form and filled it out, making a copy for his own records. He was beginning to have serious doubts about this whole matter. What if Lynch was killed doing his appointed duty? What if an American citizen was killed during this arrest? That had never been considered as far as he knew. Suddenly he felt the physical, lower abdominal response to the alarm bells in his head. Did the British ambassador to the United States know about Lynch's mission?

Alone in the men's toilet he tried to clear his mind. Washing his hands under the thin stream of icy water, he looked at his reflection in the mirror and came to a disconcerting revelation. If the whole affair was to go into the toilet, it would be he, Killeen, who ended up buried deepest in the shit?

Chapter 47

Hamlett was in a foul mood. Mostly because of the now empty whiskey bottle that rattled about the wood floor under his hammock. Twice he'd tried to corral the thing, but both times he'd missed and once he'd almost vomited.

"Harry?" he called out to no response. "Are you dead yet?" He yelled again, laughing at his own joke. Still no response.

Curious, he eased his way between the crates and was surprised to find Harry gone. He pulled at the door but found it securely locked. He took off his hat and scratched his head. There was no sign of Harry, he'd vanished. Slowly, Hamlett's mind cleared and thoughts of mayhem refilled it.

He was halfway back when he clearly heard the sound of a key in the lock of the door. Someone was unlocking it, but his pistol was under his coat in his hammock, twenty feet away. The door creaked open a fraction and the wind whistled through. Hamlett saw his chance and rushed at the door crashing his full weight against it.

Outside on the twisting metal platform that bridged the gap between the rail cars, Wheeler was removing the key from the lock when Hamlett came crashing through the door, knocking Harry backwards into him. Wheeler fell sideways, knocked off balance by the opening door and if he hadn't grabbed the railing on the steps, he would no doubt have fallen off the speeding train.

Irate and wild eyed, Hamlett had Harry by the throat, choking him. Terrified, Harry pushed upwards on Hamlett's elbow but his grip on Harry's arm was unbreakable. "Gotcha, Harry," Hamlett snarled, pushing Harry backwards violently, pinning him against the iron railing.

Behind the open door and hidden from their view Wheeler was fighting for his life. Having lost his footing and rapidly losing his grip on the railing he was in serious trouble, and with no other option he let go of his pistol in order to grasp the railing with both hands. But still he was in serious danger. His strength was fast failing him and he was slipping further down the iron steps, one foot now hanging only inches from the sharp, gray rocks flashing under him.

"Help me, Harry," Wheeler shouted, panic in his voice, "I can't hold on!"

Still in Hamlett's clutches, Harry grasped Wheeler's outstretched hand and hauled him back on board. "Thank you," Wheeler gasped, clutching the railing as a saved sailor.

"Let go of me, Hamlett!" Harry screamed, his throat still gripped by Hamlet's powerful hand. "Let me go!"

Ignoring Harry's bleating, Hamlett reached out and grabbed Wheeler's coat, lifting him back up onto the train, then he pushed him against the door to his private car forcing Wheeler through it. Shoving Harry ahead of him, Hamlett followed them into the ornate rail car.

Safely inside, Wheeler regained his composure and faced Hamlett. "Well, there you are, Mister Kincaid. I was going to ask you to join us. Come on in?" Daniel stood just a few feet away and Hamlett smiled when their eyes locked.

"Ah, there you are, I've been looking for you." Hamlett said, and smiling, stepped further into the carriage. Suddenly a slender, dark object darted out from behind the door and struck Hamlett on the back of his head with such force that his knees buckled and he dropped face down onto the floor.

"Thank you, Mister Lynch." Wheeler said, gratefully. "You're quite handy with that cane."

"I've been watchin' you fellers out there and I detected some animosity. So I thought I'd put a stop to it." Lynch smiled his twisted smile. "I was thinking he might be another of them bounty hunters. I hope I was right. Wouldn't have wanted to injure an innocent man." Lynch took the pistol from his coat and pointed it at Harry. "Since you two seem to be such good friends, I'll give you the pleasure of tying him up. Take off his belt and use that, why don't cha'?"

"Well done, Mister Lynch. You appear to have solved one of our more pressing problems while presenting another. I must admit, I admire you." Wheeler loosened his collar and physically spent from his near demise, collapsed into a chair.

"Twist the leather," Lynch demanded. "Haven't you ever tied up a man before?" Harry shot him a pained look, receiving equal in reply.

"Better do as he says, Harry," Wheeler said. "He's the one with the gun."

"And don't you go forgetin' it," Lynch added.

"I might have underestimated you, Mister Lynch. Generally speaking, I quite like the men who torment Harry," he laughed.

Harry was unamused. "Alright, Jerome, you've got what you wanted. What about our deal?" Harry pointed his finger at Lynch. "And what about him?" Then, pointing at Daniel. "Or him?"

"Harry, sit down," Wheeler said, calmly. "I propose that we strike a bargain. If I lose, you can have the Silver Queen." Harry's jaw fell open. "But," Wheeler continued, "if I win, then you will be obliged to return with us to Aspen and tell a judge what you know regarding No Problem Joe's death. Is that fair?" Harry opened his mouth to speak. Wheeler stopped him with a serious look. "And, you never mention the reward for Daniel ever again." Harry mulled over the offer. "Plus, you promise never to return to Colorado."

Shooting Daniel fleeting glances, Harry listened to Wheeler while keeping a mistrustful eye on Lynch. It was unlikely that Harry would decline Wheeler's offer. He had little choice. It was his life and possible prosperity, or the prospect of becoming Hamlett's deceased victim.

It sounded like a reasonable offer to Daniel also. Except that it was his life and his family's future that were being bargained away.

All eyes on him, Harry mulled over the offer. What choice did he have? "What about Lynch here?" Pointing at Lynch. "Don't he want to take them both back where he came from?"

Wheeler pointed a warning finger at Harry. "That's none of your business, Harry."

"What do you want me to do with him?" Harry pointed down at Hamlett's unconscious hulking body. "Personally, I'd I wouldn't mind if he fell under the train wheels." Harry said, with a smile.

"That would make our deal irrelevant, wouldn't it Harry?" Wheeler said.

Harry knitted his brow in concentration. "Yeah, I guess it might."

"I guess we can let him rest with the Silver Queen," Wheeler suggested. "That way we'll know where he is." They rolled Hamlett on his side and checked his pockets. "Didn't you say he had a gun?" Harry nodded.

"He's an ugly fellow, isn't he?" Lynch said plainly, as he grasped Hamlett by his arms.

"Yeah, he is," replied Harry. Then realized who was calling the kettle black. He looked up and saw Lynch smiling.

"What happened to his face?" Lynch asked. Harry and Daniel looked at each other.

"Harry did that." Wheeler said, with a laugh. "You threw burning whiskey on him, didn't you, Harry? I know because it happened in my hotel." With a faint smile growing, Lynch considered Harry more closely.

Lynch stood and looked down at Harry. "Do you mean to tell me that you burned the hell out of this man's face, and he's your partner?" Shocked but amused, Lynch wore a look of disbelief as wide as the plains. "And this partner," he pointed at Daniel. "This one, you wanted to turn in for a reward?" Lynch looked hard at Harry. "What kind of a partner are you?"

Wheeler was still laughing as they hauled the unconscious Hamlett back across the twisting metal bridge and left him crumpled on the floor. "Where is his gun, Harry?" Harry pointed to the rear and Wheeler returned carrying Hamlett's revolver.

"That feller with the cane," Harry asked Daniel as they closed and locked the door on Hamlett. "Is he my friend now, or is he your friend?" Daniel shrugged.

"I have no idea, Harry." Daniel's smile faded. "I have no idea at all."

"Well gentlemen," Wheeler had regained his composure fully. "It seems that we have a few of hours until we get to Kansas City. How about we have ourselves a card game?" Wheeler opened a drawer in the coffee table and took out a deck of playing cards placing them on the table. "Do you know how to play poker, Mister Lynch?" Sergeant Lynch shook his head. "Well, now's as good a time as any for you to learn." Wheeler said, shuffling the cards.

"I have heard of the game, Mister Wheeler. It's a game of chance is it?"

"Generally speaking, it is." Jerome smiled at Harry while he shuffled the cards. "But, not always. Isn't that true, Harry?"

"What are we playing for, Jerome?" Harry asked petulantly. "I don't have no money and I doubt this feller has any either."

Wheeler finished dealing out the cards. "We're going to play for the Silver Queen, Harry. I'm going to put it up against Daniel's freedom." A hush fell. Daniel shivered.

"And what am I playing for?" Lynch asked. He had not yet picked up his cards and was waiting for an answer. Wheeler considered his cards and smiled at Lynch. "How about you and I play for Patrick Shadlow." Wheeler said it in a way that was neither joking nor a request. "Let's say, for the moment, his freedom for yours."

*   *   *

"Mister Corcoran." Red woke to a light tap on his shoulder and reluctantly opened his eyes. "I'm sorry to wake you, but Mister Wheeler's train should be here in twenty minutes." Red smiled his gratitude to the eager young man and couldn't help but notice how his gaze lingered on Megan's sleeping face.

"Alright everyone, time to rise." Shirley lifted her head, her hair pushed to one side and her cheek red from laying against Red's shoulder. "Where's Gemma?" Patrick asked sleepily, stretching his arms wide, looking around him. He hadn't heard her leave.

"She's probably in the toilet," Megan added. "Do you want me to go and see?" Patrick looked at her, his brow knit.

"No," Patrick said, easing himself away from the table. "I'll probably run into her."

Red stood and stretched. "I'm going to see which platform Jerome's train arrives at," he said kissing Shirley's cheek and pushing a stray strand of hair back into place.

Against the wishes of his cramped back and legs Red turned into the wind and briskly walked the length of the deserted platform. He was retracing his path when he saw the same man who had been watching Patrick on the train. He was walking on the platform across from him and when he saw Red watching him, he pointedly disappeared into the crowd on the platform.

Chapter 48

T he outskirts of Kansas City were sparse and preceded by large swaths of land scattered with cattle. Staring out at the cascade of open land Daniel felt mesmerized by the undulations of the great expanse as the train plowed across this great sea of grass, heading west. It was reassuring when he saw ranch houses and other signs of population.

Though there were possible bright and happy futures ahead for them all, his future was the one in the greatest jeopardy. Not one for playing cards, especially with Harry, Daniel had left the game with the excuse of checking up on Hamlett, finding him still unconscious on the floor. Even in his unconscious state the man reeked of anger. Daniel left quickly and paused for a moment on the open bridge between the carriages looking from one to the other. One held the consequence of his past crimes with Harry, and the other bore the results of his family's transgressions.

What was he to make of Sergeant Lynch, apart from the fact that he had almost killed him with a brick that fateful night? Technically he was in his custody but watching the sergeant playing poker, Lynch seemed more real, more human. When he laughed it was a good laugh, one of release, one of joy rarely found.

What was Lynch planning to do when they reached Kansas City? Daniel had not the slightest idea. Should he warn Patrick? Should he run and not stop running? How would Kate feel if she had to witness his arrest? How could he deal with being unable to see her and their daughter ever again?

The glass felt cold against his face. His tears hot. How had all of this come back to haunt him? It was all so far back in the past, so long ago. Couldn't they see that he was different now. He was a boy back then, a man now. He had a family. He didn't mean to hurt Sergeant Lynch. He took no part in his father's plans, couldn't they see that? He placed his hands flat against the glass, wishing he could somehow be on the other side, out there where the birds flew free.

They were nearer now, entering the rail yards, walking the gallows' steps. Daniel jumped when he felt Wheeler's hand on his shoulder. "Come into the kitchen with me." Lynch was watching them closely. "We're going to see how much food we have. Don't worry, Mister Lynch, we'll be right here," Wheeler reassured him as he urged Daniel along the narrow swaying corridor. "How's that Kincaid feller doing back there?"

Daniel smiled. "Still sleeping."

Wheeler took a deep breath and exhaled slowly. "Why would he strike an old man like Joe, I ask you?" Wheeler motioned Daniel closer. "Did you find the gun in the hamper?" Daniel nodded and lifted the napkin. Wheeler placed his hand over it. "I lost mine off the train back there but I have Hamlett's." He opened his coat revealing the pistol in the waistband of his pants. "Listen to me carefully, Daniel. I think I can persuade Mister Lynch to leave you be." Wheeler smiled briefly. The reassurance was fleeting. "But," he said, watching Daniel's smile fade. "But; I can't do the same for your brother." Wheeler considered Daniel and the despair that abruptly reappeared on his face. "Now, now," he said, "don't get yourself all down about it, son. Sometimes there are circumstances in life that you just can't change. It's a wise man who can recognize them and know them for what they are."

Daniel picked up the pistol and checked the cartridge chambers, all loaded. Wheeler placed his hand on Daniel's and touched his finger to his lips. "Not now," he whispered. "I want you to give it to Red." Daniel nodded. Wheeler turned and took down a bottle of whiskey from the cabinet before returning to the game.

"Ah, look what I found in the larder." Wheeler entered holding the bottle high in the air. "Sustenance!" he declared. Taking four fine glasses from a railed shelf he poured whiskey into all of them. "Cheers," Lynch said, raising his glass.

There came a series of shunts and bumps and eventually they moved forward again slowly as their train entered the station complex. When the platform appeared, Lynch became increasingly nervous. Wheeler noticed and so did Daniel. Harry was more interested in the contents of the whiskey bottle.

"Mister Lynch, can I have a word with you in private?" Wheeler asked. Lynch was skeptical. "I assure you that you have nothing to fear from me," he said, inviting Lynch to follow him back to the adjoining boxcar. "Come on, Mister Lynch, allow me to show you something that might interest you."

After he'd unlocked the door Lynch followed Wheeler into the boxcar that carried the Silver Queen, closing the door behind them. Hamlett was awake and stood when they entered but resumed his seat when Wheeler pointed his pistol at him. Lynch seemed unsurprised at the sudden appearance of a pistol in Wheeler's hand.

"Sit down, Mister Kincaid. It's not your turn to die quite yet." Hamlett reluctantly did as he was told but closely followed their conversation. "Did you see the Silver Queen at the Exposition, Mister Lynch?" Lynch shook his head no. "No, you wouldn't have had time, would you?" Wheeler trailed off, searching the stacked crates until he found a specific one. "Do you have your revolver with you, Mister Lynch?" Wheeler's pistol was casually pointed at Lynch.

Lynch reluctantly removed his heavy Webley revolver with a wry grin. "I do hope you're not planning on using that on me, Mister Wheeler."

"The thought never entered my mind, Mister Lynch." Using the butt of the gun as a hammer he hit the underside edge of the crate knocking the top loose. "Give me a hand on your end, will you?" Lynch took his pistol and did as Wheeler had done, knocking the wooden cover free.

Wheeler pulled back the straw and wood shavings exposing the solid gold figurine of a cupid holding a cornucopia of gold nuggets. In the twitching light of the slowly moving train, the glimmer of the light on the gold was hypnotic. The effect on Lynch was obvious. As if it was a sleeping baby, Lynch gently touched the face of the gold statue. "Is this real gold?" he asked. Wheeler opened the iron box that held the gold nuggets.

"Yes, it is Mister Lynch. Take one of the nuggets, why don't you?" Wheeler said, tempting the untemptable. "Go on, Mister Lynch. Take one. You won it fair and square. It's what we were gambling for. Take it, it's yours now."

Wheeler was closely watching the effect of the dilemma he had placed in front of this possibly honest man. He was confident that the result would be the same as it always was, as predictable as any of man's motivations. In some abstract way he relished that another man was caressing what had once held such importance for him. As if observing another man make love to his wife, as if he wanted it, as if he needed it to happen.

Sergeant Lynch ran his hands slowly over the surface of the statue, his fingers barely touching the glimmering sheen of the pale, gold. Could this be happening to him? Not some dream? Where, when he awoke, he would find himself back in his own bed. His own, cold, lonely bed. He gently lifted one of the dozen potato sized nuggets. It weighed more than a pound.

"One hand of poker, Mister Lynch," Wheeler cajoled. "I'll let you think about it awhile."

Lynch was emotionally disarmed. His barrier of righteousness had suffered during this long adventure and it had everything to do with the task itself. He was righteous and indignant that he had suffered so much at the hands of these two brothers. But, was it them or the father who was really deserving of the blame? When did this job, this purpose he had, when and where did it end? How far would he have to go to finish it?

Wheeler was holding Hamlett's pistol pointed casually at Lynch. Lynch acknowledged its presence but continued closing the lid of the cupid's crate.

"Are you planning on using that, Mister Wheeler?" Lynch asked again, watching Wheeler reversing his pistol and gently hammer the nails back into place.

"So, do we have a deal?" Wheeler pressed. Lynch sighed heavily.

"I'm afraid that the value of justice to me is far greater than this gold statue, Mister Wheeler." Lynch turned and pointed his pistol at Wheeler. "I'll take that, if you don't mind." Wheeler let Lynch take his pistol. "Perhaps this conversation should stay between us, Mister Wheeler. At least until I arrest Patrick Shadlow."

Keeping his pistol aimed at Hamlett, Lynch locked the door and motioned Wheeler across the gap between the cars. But, before they entered, he leaned closer to Wheeler. "Be calm, Mister Wheeler, and you might get your boy back." Lynch opened the door and pushed Wheeler ahead of him.

"There they are!" Shirley said, taking Kate's hand. "Aren't you excited to see Daniel again, Kate?" It was subtle, but Shirley felt Kate pull away. She looked at her daughter sternly. "Kate, there's nothing to be upset about. Well, actually there might be, but perhaps now is not the best time to pursue it." Shirley gave Red a look. He shrugged, understanding the difficulty of the situation.

Wheeler waved to them as the train came to a halt. He alighted with another man and together they walked to the front of the train to converse with the engineer.

Red noticed that it was John Carter, Wheeler's head engineer who was driving the train. He waved and Red waved back. Curious, Red watched the two men returning and noted that Wheeler was stone-faced. "Hello everyone," Wheeler said, his smile brief. "This is Sergeant Lynch." When Lynch pulled down his collar, someone gasped. "If you will all wait here, Mister Lynch and I will check in with the station master and then we will be on our way. Patrick, I trust you to stay here"

Patrick looked hard at Wheeler. Gauged him as he'd done to wardens in prison. Sergeant Lynch watched Patrick closely. Shirley and Kate sensed something wrong and Myra and Megan needed only to see Lynch's face to understand. Gemma squeezed Patrick's hand, fortifying him.

"I'll stay here," Patrick replied, not taking his eyes off Lynch.

Wheeler smiled. A train's whistle blasted the air.

"Good. I trust you, if you're half the man your brother is." Wheeler smiled, again making light of the situation. "Red, would you come with us please?" Wheeler, Red and Lynch walked to the station office and disappeared into the building.

"What are we goin' to do, Patrick?" Megan asked. Kate overheard them.

"Where's Daniel?" Shirley asked as the train puffed and hissed and pulled away from the station. They saw Daniel waving to them from the window of Wheeler's private car. Shirley's expression was far from jubilant seeing Harry standing next to Daniel at the window. The train picked up speed. He waved and she waved back.

"What's going on?" Harry asked, placing his hand on Daniel's shoulder. Daniel spun around, pushing the barrel of the pistol he had retrieved from the hamper into Harry's stomach. Hands raised Harry retreated a pace. "I can't believe you don't trust me, Daniel. After all these years?"

"Here they come." Megan said, pointing to the procession of passenger cars and gray boxcars, Wheeler's private car and behind it the Silver Queen.

It was a somber group that watched Red and Lynch return with Wheeler. Red motioned Patrick to join them.

"Patrick, I'm sorry to tell you this, but for the moment Sergeant Lynch is going to have to detain you." Patrick turned to run but Red caught him by the arm. "Patrick, stop!" Wheeler yelled. "Wait!" he commanded. and Patrick obeyed. "Listen to me for a moment. I've asked for some legal help to clarify the situation but for the moment, until Sergeant Lynch receives this clarification, you are his prisoner." Wheeler placed his hand on Patrick's shoulder to reassure him. "I will say that all this is a bit of a problem, but I'm sure that we will get it all straightened out."

Abruptly, Lynch stepped close to Patrick and took hold of his arm. "I haven't forgotten what you took away from me, Patrick Shadlow." He snarled. Both Wheeler and Red were surprised by the vehemence erupting from Lynch like a gunshot in the dark. Alarmed, Red stepped between them placing his hand flat on Lynch's chest.

"Alright you two!" Wheeler interjected, forcefully. "Enough said for now, I think. Red, why don't you and Patrick move the luggage into that rail car," he pointed to one of the passenger cars, "and once we're underway we can continue this conversation. It's a private carriage and I have plenty of food coming on board and someone to help. So, next stop, Denver in wonderful Colorado."

"What about you, Jerome?" Red looked concerned and tilted his head towards Lynch. "Will you be alright?"

"Don't you worry about us, Red." Wheeler smiled at Lynch who remained resolute. "We still have some business to discuss, don't we, Mister Lynch?" Wheeler cast a jovial look to Red, mainly for Lynch's benefit. "Then we'll see what happens, won't we, Mister Lynch?"

It was an odd situation. Between these two men there was an ocean of difference and a sea of inequity, yet, there appeared a momentary bridge of sorts.

"After you, Mister Lynch," Wheeler said, inviting Lynch aboard. "Red, would you come here, please?" Wheeler stepped out of Lynch's view and discreetly handed Hamlett's pistol to Red. "I'm still not sure how this is all going to turn out but I'd feel better if you had something to use in case things go bad."

Red slipped the pistol into his coat pocket. "I'd feel better, too."

"Look, Red, I didn't want to alarm you, but Lynch says that there's a bounty hunter out there following us."

"Out where, exactly?"

"Apparently, it's a man named Rafferty, or something like that who also has his sights set on the reward for Daniel and Patrick." Red chewed his lower lip at the news. "He might have followed you all from Chicago."

"What does he look like?" Red asked quietly, so not to be overheard.

Wheeler shrugged. "Lynch would know, I suppose. Now go on in there and settle everybody down. We have a double coal loader so we'll only be stopping for water until we get to Denver." Wheeler turned to climb the steps.

"Where will you be?" Red inquired.

"Mister Lynch and I have some unfinished business. We'll join you when we're done. Help yourselves to the refreshments," Wheeler said and disappeared into his personal carriage.

The whistle sounded and the train shunted and chugged, gathering speed and drawing stares from bystanders gawking at the short train with the gaily painted boxcar. Red pulled his hat down further on his head and holding onto it with one hand and the railing with the other he watched the platform trail away behind them, looking to see whether the man named Rafferty was attempting to board the train.

Satisfied that the train's speed would make jumping aboard impossible Red adjusted his coat and hoping for the best, opened the door. The train car was empty but for them. Perhaps it was the fact that they had never been on an empty train before, but the Shadlows were huddled together as were Shirley and Kate, expectantly, fearfully. Red felt the responsibility of a ship's captain whose courage would make the difference between safety and disaster and so save the day.

"Everything is going to be alright," he said to the expectant faces. "You can all relax. Daniel and Jerome will join us when they're done talking." Their trepidation was quite visible. "Shirley, Jerome told us that there's food back there if anyone needs."

"And there are blankets and pillows here too," Patrick added, putting words to their greatest desire, to sleep.

Shirley draped her arms around Red's neck. "I feel so safe with you," she said, looking up at him, kissing him lightly.

"You'll always be safe with me, Shirley Corcoran." Shirley smiled and pushed her hips against his.

"Perhaps," she whispered in his ear, "perhaps not. Maybe sometimes I don't want to be." His rumbling laugh tickled her belly.

Chapter 49

R afferty was not far away, drawing danger to him like a magnet draws scraps of iron. Not wanting to lose sight of his quarry he lurked about the station platform spying from afar what might be happening on the train bearing his targets. Anticipating that the Shadlows might leave the station on separate trains, he blended in with the assembled passengers ambling back and forth between the platforms finding places where he could observe their actions unseen.

Rafferty was surprised when Lynch emerged from the train with the older man in the tall hat. He'd no inkling that Lynch was so near. He watched as Lynch and the older man entered the station and returned moments later escorted by a porter pushing a cart bearing large woven baskets that he loaded onto one of the carriages.

It was the last carriage on the train that intrigued him most, the one emblazoned with the painted rendition of the Silver Queen. At the Chicago train station, he'd seen two men fighting on it as it left, and now he was very curious if anyone was still inside. Walking briskly, he circled the train and approached it from the opposing platform. Careful not to be seen, he raced across the train tracks and hid under the strangely painted carriage.

Hearing the sounds of feet approaching, he pushed his body up against the wheels of the train and out of sight. From underneath the train car he saw two pairs of shoes stop directly above him. One pair was new and freshly shined, the other pair well-worn and shabby. The new shoes stepped onto the iron steps.

"Well, Mister Lynch, let us go and continue that poker game, shall we?" The owner of the shiny shoes said as they climbed aboard. Rafferty was taken aback by the familiarity between these two. He sat back on his haunches to think but was almost killed when the wheel he was leaning against began to roll. Above his head iron axles screamed their tortured wail as the train cars took up their slack and the oily black wood ceiling above him moved forward.

There was no time to reconsider his plan as the rear of the train car passed over him leaving him exposed. Running in a crouch he chased it down, grabbed the railing on the Silver Queen car and swung himself up and onto the small platform. As the train cleared the station he passed several people. He waved to them, all friendly, and one of them waved back while the others scratched their heads.

Assessing his situation, he found the door to the train car securely bolted and the lock sturdy. Frustrated, Rafferty sat down on the iron steps and took stock of his situation. The only way he could see to get to the other carriages was either to wait for the train to stop or climb the metal ladder and walk along the roof.

The train's whistle screamed. Curious, Rafferty peered around the edge of the car and instantly pulled his head back as another train roared past in the opposite direction only feet away. Shaken, he sat on the hard metal ledge, pulled his coat closer about him and had a think.

*   *   *

"Did you see anyone tryin' to climb aboard?" Wheeler asked Red after he'd closed the door. Lynch also showed interest in the answer. Red shook his head.

"Did I tell you that I saw a man watching us back there?" Red said to them. Wheeler ceased shuffling the cards. Daniel watched Red like a dog waiting for food. "Around Harry's size. He was wearing a dark coat with a plaid collar."

"That would be him, then. That's Rafferty," Lynch confirmed.

"How is it that he's followed us so far?" Wheeler asked, his hands splayed. Lynch laughed.

"I think it was Patrick he's been following, Mister Wheeler." Lynch looked over at Daniel. "You're a tricky little bastard, aren't you?" Daniel shrugged.

"Mister Lynch, why don't you let the boy go back and be with his family? Red can join us."

Lynch looked around the room. Red was still standing, Daniel looked nervous and Harry dozed. "I can't see the harm." Lynch looked out at the rapidly passing landscape. "No man in his right mind would jump off a train at this speed. Off you go, then." Daniel stood.

"Don't go far," Harry said, laughing.

"Shut up, Harry," Wheeler barked.

After Daniel had left them, Wheeler placed the deck of cards on the table. "Cut the cards, Harry. Highest card deals and there'll be no cheating, Harry. Remember, this time your life depends on it."

"What about Hamlett?" Harry whined.

"You can take him some food later. Let me know if you want to ride back there with him." Wheeler laughed, placing the deck of cards on the table.

"How are we going to know who wins?" Lynch asked.

Wheeler reached underneath the coffee table and a drawer sprung out from which Wheeler withdrew a thick envelope. The drawer closed with a soft click and disappeared into the carved frame.

"In here gentlemen," Wheeler paused for effect, "are new Federal bills." Wheeler spread them out of the table fanning them. "There's fifteen thousand dollars, there." The effect was instant. Harry leapt forward in his chair, as did Red. Lynch, only slightly less. Wheeler divided the money into three piles of five thousand dollars each, keeping one pile and placing one in front of Harry and the last in front of Lynch.

"There in front of you, Harry, is the amount you would have received for turning Daniel in." Wheeler turned his gaze on Lynch. "And for you, Mister Lynch, there's enough money for you to either take Patrick Shadlow back to England or," Wheeler knew the value of a well-placed pause, "or, start a new life here in America. That will be up to you, of course."

"Not so quick, Mister Wheeler, not so quick."

"Call me Jerome."

"Well, Jerome," Lynch rolled the name with his heavy accent on the 'r' sound. "What you propose is extremely generous."

"Things are worth less than people, Mister Lynch." Wheeler said. "Not all people are equal," was his reply.

"Not all money is equal, Mister Lynch."

"Ahhh," Lynch laughed, "I now see what you're getting at, Mister Wheeler."

"Jerome, Mister Lynch, please."

"Then call me James," replied Lynch. "But I want to get this straight between us. I would be playing for Patrick Shadlow's freedom, if I lose. But if I win, I get to keep the money and take Patrick back?"

"Perhaps we would be playing for higher stakes than that, James. Perhaps, it has more to do with you returning to England with or without Patrick Shadlow." Wheeler gave Lynch a wry smile, easily translated. "Now let's play cards, shall we? Red will deal, five card stud poker. Bet as little or as much as you want, no limit. Once your money is gone, you lose. All bets are final once on the table. My word is my honor," Wheeler looked from one to the other, "and I trust that yours is the same." Wheeler stood and pulled the whiskey bottle from its nook.

"Let's have a drink, shall we?"

*　　　　　*　　　　　*

Daniel stood on the small space between the cars inhaling the smoke-laden air of freedom. Standing there alone with the devil behind and the devil ahead, he looked back into the carriage where he and his brother's futures were being gambled for. Strangely he felt a sense of relief. His life's story was finally out in the open, laid out bare for all to see. Well, most of it.

Chapter 50

"Do you think that all of this will get settled? I mean with Mister Lynch?" Kate asked.

Daniel smiled, mainly for the sake of his mother and sister. "I'm sure that it will." He squeezed his mother's shoulder more tightly. To his brother he gave only the slightest hint of his concern, but inwardly his fears were growing by the mile. "I'm going to sit with Kate for a while. Do you mind?"

Myra looked lovingly at her son and then at his wife, Kate. There were fewer dreams that bore more hope than that Daniel had found a wife and happiness. Myra let him go. He was a man with a family now and from where Paddy was, in heaven she hoped, he would be happy for them. Patrick and his friend Gemma were resting in each other's arms.

They could have slept on separate seats since there were no other passengers but they chose differently. She was pleased for Patrick. Happy that there was something other than the anger she saw blazing within him and considering what he had endured, she could never begrudge him whatever happiness he found in this life.

As she often did, she thought back on that night when she said goodbye to her husband, Paddy, for the last time. That same feeling of heat behind her eyes burned again as she remembered that last kiss. If she had known that there was a possibility that she would never see him again, she would never have let go of him that night. But it had all happened so quickly. So much had been beyond her control and once again circumstances were rushing along at a similar speed, as were her fears of losing her sons again.

Kate held Myra's gaze until Daniel sat down beside her. They smiled at each other, sharing their feelings in that special way that mothers and wives do. In a look, a gaze, a smile, it was enough said when she finally looked away. Her Daniel was back beside her and for the time being that was enough. Kate allowed him to place his arm around her shoulders. Shirley smiling at her and she smiled back.

Peace between them finally Shirley, was thinking, though she was not certain that it would be of the permanent kind. Kate, she knew, was still hurting from Daniel's supposed infidelity. Eventually, whenever it was that she broached the subject of Claire Cavendish, there would be fireworks. Of this she was sure. Kate was no less volatile than she when it came to an argument and if their marriage was to survive, he would have to pay a price.

Red was dealing the cards but not playing, content to monitor Harry and oversee his penchant for cheating. Harry was winning at this point in their game. So was Sergeant Lynch, who was a fast learner, or perhaps not. In a look between them Wheeler and Red both shared the suspicion that Lynch was a hustler and was already quite familiar with playing poker. Red also had a suspicion that Jerome was letting him win.

"Harry, do you want to go back and see if your friend is awake?" Red said. "Take him some water. He might need some food too."

Harry was stacking his money in front of him. "We'll be in Denver in the morning, won't we? He can last till then."

"Be nice, Harry. I'll go with you." Red said.

"Thanks, Red. He's not a very forgiving man when it comes to me."

"I can sympathize with him," Red said, smiling. "But, I doubt there'll be much to say. Come on, let's see what we can find to feed him with his hands tied." Harry followed Red like a beaten puppy returning with two sandwiches and a bottle of beer.

"Do you want me to come back with you?" Lynch asked.

"Thanks, Mister Lynch, but I feel safe enough with this." Red took the pistol from his pocket and pointed it at Harry, smiling at the surprised look Lynch gave him. "You carry the food, Harry. I'll carry the pistol." Harry nodded and followed Red across the swaying gap.

"I brought you some food, Hamlett," Harry yelled.

"Fuck you, Harry," came the reply.

Red smiled. "I think he misses you, Harry." Red nudged Harry forward with the barrel of his gun. Reluctantly Harry edged down the narrow space half expecting Hamlett to pounce on him at every step. Bumping and swaying down the corridor, Harry struggled to keep upright while holding the food and beer. Red was amused and unhelpful.

Hamlett was sitting on the floor with his back against the rear wall of the train car. He was hatless and angry, his face was contorted into a defiant snarl, a frightening grimace. Wind whistled through the grating of the small elongated windows of the car adding to the noise of the moving train.

"Look, Ham. I brought you some sandwiches and a bottle of beer." Harry yelled over the noise. Hamlett said nothing but only looked from Harry to Red with seething anger.

"I have to take a shit, Harry. What are you going to do about that?" Harry looked at Red for support but saw no sympathy there.

"I can't untie you, Ham." Harry replied. "Can you hang on until tomorrow?"

"Fuck you, Harry, and your smartassed friend, too. I hate you both."

Harry looked up at Red. "Can I untie him so he can eat his sandwiches?"

Red deliberated. "I guess so. As long as I keep my gun on him."

Harry helped Hamlett to his feet and sat him on the chair and placed the food on the small table affixed to the wall, then he untied Hamlett's hands. Hamlett stretched his arms and shook his hands to regain the circulation and inhaled the sandwiches and beer as a starving man would. Abruptly he stood up. In response, Red cocked his pistol still aimed at Hamlett's stomach.

"I gott'a pee," Hamlett said and turned to relieve himself in the bucket by the door. "So, you changed sides on me, did you Harry?" The sound of his stream echoed in the small space.

"I had to, Ham. They made me do it," said Harry and received a loud laugh from Hamlett in reply.

It was Hamlett's laugh that Rafferty heard from the other side of the train's door. Stiff and sore after hours of hunkering down in the lee of the wind outside on the small platform at the rear of the train, suddenly he was alert. Rafferty put his ear to the door and listened. He heard more than one voice.

Finished relieving himself, Hamlett was pretending to button his pants when he suddenly turned and made a grab for Harry's throat. Harry caught Hamlett's hand but not before he had been turned around and was being choked with such force that Harry's knees gave out.

Instantly Red was upon them and lashed out with his pistol at Hamlett's head, hitting him hard and forcing him to let go of Harry who fell to the floor grasping his throat and gasping for breath "Ha!" Hamlett said, smiling. "I almost got you, Harry." Hamlett felt the side of his head and his hand came away covered with his blood as he considered Red and the barrel of the pistol pointed at his face.

"Tie his hands good and tight, Harry. We want him in reasonable condition when he faces the judge."

"What judge?" Hamlett snarled as Harry turned him around and tied his wrists behind his back.

"We're taking you back to Aspen to stand trial for the death of No Problem Joe. Harry told us what you did to him."

"I had nothing to do with it," Hamlett yelled. "He was alive when we left him. Right, Harry?"

"The judge will make that decision, Mister Kincaid."

"Sorry, Ham," Harry said plaintively, backing away. "Really, I had no choice, did I?"

Hamlett spat a gob of saliva at him. "That's what I think of you, Harry Rich," he yelled at their backs.

Rafferty had heard only snippets of conversation coming from the other side of the door but had heard the bumping and thumping that befell Hamlett as he grappled with Harry. He did not relish the prospect of having to ride out in the open all night and doubted that he would survive. Cold, tired and hungry, his patience at its limit, he'd waited until dusk before deciding that it was now or never. Decision made, he rapped the butt of his pistol on the wooden door then put his ear to it and waited for a response. He rapped again, louder.

Hamlett was in his hammock when he heard the first tapping on the door. Righting himself, he put his ear to the door and waited. There it was again. "Who's there?" he yelled at the door. The tapping came again louder. "Who's there?" he yelled.

"Let me in," came the voice from the other side.

"I can't." Hamlett replied, curiously. "I can't open the door. I'm tied up."

"Stand back!" The voice ordered.

BOOM! Came the sound of a gun being fired and Hamlett dodged splinters of wood scattering in front of him. BOOM! More splinters showered him.

Chapter 51

Dawn was approaching. The rising sun gradually cast shadows westward across the plains ahead of them as one by one they awoke in various shades of discomfort, yawning and stretching.

The poker game had gone on throughout the night and when Red joined her Shirley asked as to the outcome. Red merely shrugged and then motioned Patrick and Daniel to join him at the end of the carriage where they spoke privately. Shirley watched them intently.

"What's going on back there?" Daniel asked. Red sighed.

"From what I can see it's not going well for either of you. Harry has won the Silver Queen and Mister Lynch has taken most of Jerome's money."

"What about us?" Patrick asked, anxiously. Beyond the windows of the train lay endless miles of nothing but grassland in all directions with no sign of inhabitants. He had already made up his mind to escape but to where he had no idea. That they had passed into Colorado territory had little import to him.

Patrick had slept little since Kansas City. Gemma had held his hand as she slept and he wondered if she would come with him when he made his run for freedom. What he could do to help his family in his present position, with neither money nor prospects, with no knowledge of the land and no skills, he was at a loss to say. Peering out at the dawn spreading across the boundless plains he saw himself as insignificant as the birds that floated in the morning airs. He envied them.

Hamlett threw his weight against the door and on the second attempt it gave way. An instant later he was falling over the railing and off the train. A hand reached out and caught him by his arm.

"Hello," said a voice from his left. Hamlett turned, the barrel of a gun appeared followed by a man dressed in a dirty plaid coat, his faced smudged with coal dust, his hat pulled down tight on his head. Rafferty backed Hamlett inside at the point of his gun. "I don't know who you are but I think we're on the same side," Hamlett said.

"Are you the only one here?" Rafferty asked. Hamlett nodded.

"Where are the others I heard?"

"They're in the other car, up front." Hamlett replied.

"That other feller. The one who looks like you. Is he in there?"

Hamlett nodded. "Why are you tied up?"

"They don't like me." Hamlett's attempted humor was unconvincing.

"I don't believe you. Sit down." Hamlett did as he was told. "Now, tell me why you're tied up."

"I'm trying to capture one of them fellers up there for a reward. I'll share it with you if you help me." Hamlett begged.

"Who?"

"You wouldn't know him. His name is Daniel Shadlow."

"Ha, ha, ha," laughed Rafferty. "Now that is a coincidence," he said, smiling. "So, we are after the same person it seems. Five thousand, dollar reward?" Hamlett nodded, tilting his head questioningly. "From Pinkerton's?" Hamlett nodded again.

"What are they going to do with you?" Rafferty asked, sitting on the hammock keeping his pistol pointed at Hamlett.

"They haven't told me," Hamlett lied.

"How many people are in the other carriage?" Hamlett shrugged.

"Do they have guns?" Hamlett nodded. "How many?"

"Untie me and I'll tell you." Hamlett smiled, slyly.

Rafferty spied the water jug and drank two cups quickly. "Got any food?"

"No. But they have some up there." Hamlett nodded forward. "I don't know your name but if you let me loose, I might be able to help you."

"Why would you do that?"

"I have my reasons. You can keep the reward for yourself. I don't care about that anymore."

The train was slowing. Rafferty watched Hamlett closely. "What did you say your name was?"

"Hamlett Kincaid."

"Where is this train going?"

"Colorado. Maybe to Aspen? You're looking at five tons of silver in here so they won't let that get far away from them."

Rafferty whistled, pushing his hat back on his head with the barrel of his pistol. "That's a heap of silver. Who's is it?"

"Belongs to Jerome B. Wheeler. He's in the next car. It's his."

"I'll make you a deal. I'll untie you, on one condition." Rafferty stood and motioned Hamlett to do likewise. "I believe there are two wanted men on this train and I'm going to need your help to capture them. What do you think about that, Mister Kincaid?" Hamlett's interest was piqued. "If you'll help me," Rafferty took his copy of the warrant from his pocket and held it in front of Hamlett at eye level. "I'll split the rewards. Ten thousand dollars. There's a Pinkerton's office in Denver. Five thousand dollars for each of us. What do you say to that, Mister Kincaid?"

"Then what?"

"I don't care what you do afterwards, Mister Kincaid. Do we have a deal?"

*   *   *

"Well gentlemen, I'm out of funds so I'm going to have to leave our little game," Wheeler said with a sigh. "Of course, you two can continue on if you wish. Please don't let me stop you." Lynch and Harry measured each other. "Are you happy with your winnings, gentlemen?"

Wheeler paid close attention to their reaction. He knew very well that a pile of money so large was a great temptation. "James, are you happy with our wager?" Lynch considered Wheeler then placed his gold nugget on the table.

"I can't be bought, Mister Wheeler."

"That's fair enough. Can't fault you for being a man of your word. What about you, Harry?" Harry was busy counting his money and arranging it in piles, smiling like a child at Christmas.

"It sounds good to me, Jerome." He had over six thousand dollars, more than the reward and hopefully enough to keep Hamlett from shooting him. He'd give it all to him if necessary. What Harry really wanted was to return to Aspen and retrieve the money from the bank robbery. He doubted Daniel knew who took it, or where it might be. But Harry knew for certain.

"It's probably time for you to feed your partner back there again, Harry. I'm hungry too." Wheeler was far happier than one would expect of a gambler who had lost fifteen thousand dollars and a five-ton silver statue. "Why are we stopping, Jerome?" Lynch asked, taking hold of his pistol.

"I don't know," Wheeler said, peering out of the window.

"Probably waiting for another train to pass, I suppose."

"Red, why don't you and Harry go and feed that feller back there?" Red nodded, sleepily. "Harry, see what we've got for him."

"Sandwiches is all that's left."

"Give them to him. I have plenty more food in the next car."

*   *   *

"That's not much of a plan. What did you say your name was?"

"It's the best I can do on short notice. The name's Rafferty."

"They have guns, you know?"

"Does that ugly Irishman have one?"

Hamlett touched his face unconsciously. "I believe so. But there's another feller in there that could be trouble."

"Big man with a wide, gray hat?" Hamlett nodded.

They heard the door at the front of the car being unlocked. Rafferty put his fingers to his lips and slipped out of the carriage, closing the door behind him. Hamlett sat back down on the chair and held his hands behind his back.

"Good morning, Ham," Harry announced as he approached, Red walking a pace behind, pistol at the ready. "Breakfast in bed for you today, Ham." Hamlett said nothing, shot daggers at Harry and Red.

"I gotta take a crap Harry. You gonna wipe my ass for me?" Hamlett laughed. Harry looked for sympathy from Red but found not a trace.

"Sorry, Ham, you're just gonna have to sit on it until we get to Denver." Harry was leaning down to feed Hamlett a sandwich when

Hamlett suddenly stood and wrapped his belt around Harry's neck catching even Red by surprise.

Harry twisted and turned but Hamlett kept Harry between himself and Red's pistol. Thrusting Harry ahead of him Hamlett released Harry and grabbed for Red's gun with both hands. Red dodged to his left but Hamlett caught Red's wrist and wrestled him for the pistol while Harry spluttered at their feet.

Hamlett had hold of Red's shooting hand and was twisting it downwards toward the floor with his elbow pushing on Red's throat. Red wrapped his arm around Hamlett's neck, choking him, and bracing his foot against a crate pushed with all his might, forcing Hamlett against the rear door of the carriage. Red thought he had Hamlet under control but the door swung open, sending them onto the narrow metal platform wrestling for his revolver.

Red saw Hamlett look to his right and smile. Then Red felt the cold metal of a pistol barrel pressed against his neck and heard the distinctive clicks of the hammer being cocked very close to his ear. Reluctantly releasing his grip on Hamlett, Red turned to face the man with the gun and instantly recognized him as the man he had seen on the station platform, the one Lynch referred to as Rafferty. Red raised his hands. Roughly, Hamlett snatched the pistol from Red's hand and pushed him out of his way, but Harry was gone.

"Harry, you piece of shit, you can't hide from me." Too late. Harry was opening the far door and Hamlett was hit by a gust of smoke that rushed at him through the train car like a hurricane. "Damn it!"

"Take off your belt," Hamlett said to Red, roughly turning him to face the wall while Rafferty held his gun on him. Deftly he tied Red's hands behind his back and then to the iron railing. "There, that should hold you." Hamlett smiled his twisted smile and punched Red hard in the stomach. Red's knees buckled. "I've been wanting to do that for years, Corcoran. I should throw you off and let you drag behind this train." He pushed Red's pistol under Red's chin. "I could've killed Harry Rich back then when I had the chance. But you? You had to go and stop me, didn't you? Well, we'll see how it goes for your friend this time."

Hamlett disappeared into the train car. Red twisted his hands but could not free them.

"Rafferty, you run up front over the roof and hold them and I'll come up from this end. Watch out for the old man."

Jerome was tired to his bones from the all-night poker game. Playing badly was against his nature and was exhausting. But, he'd cleverly not let on, and had achieved his objectives. Harry had the money he needed and Lynch had a mound of temptation to chew on.

"Here everybody, we have more food for you all," he said happily.

"Where did all of this come from, Jerome?" Shirley asked watching Patrick carry the hamper basket into the carriage.

"Just another of my little surprises." Wheeler was saying, but he stopped as Harry burst into the carriage, wild-eyed, red-faced.

"Hamlett's got a gun," he gasped, "and he's got Red too." Shirley jumped out of her seat and grabbed Harry by the collar of his coat. "Where's Red?" Harry pointed behind him. "How did this happen, Harry?"

Harry looked at the shocked faces of the women around him, seeing clearly their recrimination and fear. Daniel was already racing toward the rear car when Patrick caught him by the sleeve.

"Don't go," he said, "it could be a trap, Daniel." Daniel reconsidered.

"Stay here. I'll go and tell the engineer to stop the train," Daniel said, racing for the front of the carriage.

"Where's Sergeant Lynch?" Wheeler demanded, but no one knew.

With a loud bang, the door crashed opened and Hamlett barged in, pointing his pistol at Wheeler and then at Harry. Both Harry and Wheeler held up their hands.

Hamlett advanced slowly, his gun trained on Harry's forehead. "Ahhh, Harry, why did you run away from me?" His voice was a low rumble, loaded with menace. He grabbed Harry by the collar of his coat holding his gun next to Harry's cheek. "I was looking forward to throwing you off this train."

"Where's Red?" Shirley demanded, boldly walking toward them.

"Stop!" Hamlett demanded, but Shirley kept coming.

"I'm not afraid of you, Hamlett Kincaid," Shirley yelled. "Remember me? I used to mother you," she said, surprising them all. "For that miserable, lying piece o' shit you call your father. Do you remember that, Hamlett?"

Hamlett lashed out with his pistol, catching Shirley on the cheek and knocking her sideways onto Megan's lap. Kate leapt to Shirley's aid. Patrick lunged at him but Hamlett smacked him on the side of the head rendering him inert also. Myra screamed. All eyes were fixed on Hamlett.

Harry twisted and fought but Hamlett pushed the gun into his ear ceasing Harry's resisting. Abruptly, all eyes looked upwards at the sound of running footsteps coming from the roof above them. Suddenly, the door to the front of the train car opened and Daniel entered being held by the collar with Rafferty holding a gun in his back. He smiled wide when he saw Patrick unconscious on his mother's lap.

"Alright everybody let's settle down," Wheeler said loudly, hands held high, demanding calm. "Everything will be fine I assure you all." He darted a quick look at Daniel and mouthed Lynch's name, Daniel shrugged in reply. The same thought had entered Hamlett's mind also.

"Where's the old ugly feller?' Hamlett looked from one to another. Wheeler shrugged. Daniel shrugged also. "I have a score to settle with him. Come with me, Harry. Rafferty, stay here and watch 'em close. I'm going to find that other feller."

Hamlett's grip on his neck was unbreakable and Harry was forced back across the bridge to Wheeler's private car. Gripping Harry firmly in one hand and his pistol in his right he cautiously entered the carriage pushing Harry ahead of him. Holding the barrel of his pistol to the back of Harry's head they edged down the narrow corridor to the closed bedroom door.

"Open the door, Harry," he whispered. Harry shook his head. Hamlett cocked the pistol and Harry gripped the handle of the door, closed his eyes and opened it. Nothing. The small room was clearly empty. "You were lucky again, Harry." Hamlett said, pushing him along the carriage until they came to the rear door. The train was picking up speed again. "Well Harry, this time I think your luck is about to run out."

"I have money, Ham," Harry pleaded. "Look there's some in my boot and I won the Silver Queen fair and square in a poker game. It's mine." Hamlett reached down and pulled the money from Harry's boot and stuffed it into his coat pockets.

"We'll see about that, Harry."

Suspecting that Lynch might be inside, Hamlett fired two shots through the middle of the train door and kicked it open. Nobody there. Suddenly, with a rush of wind and a blast of its whistle another train flew past them going in the opposite direction.

Lynch had indeed been in the bathroom when Harry had first raced past, closely followed by Hamlett's heavy tread. Taking his pistol from his coat he'd backed into the water-closet and pulled the door closed, should Hamlett investigate. He waited five seconds and hearing nothing, opened the door and seeing Hamlett and Harry outside, he rushed back to the Silver Queen car.

"Mister Corcoran, are you here?" he yelled.

"Down here, Lynch." Red was still desperately trying to free his hands when Lynch came to his rescue. "Untie me quick. There are two of them now." Lynch nodded, untying Red's hands.

"Do you think you can run fast enough to get to the next carriage without them seeing you?" Red asked. Their train had slowed dramatically. A fast-moving freight train came hurtling past them and Lynch laughed.

"Best I get off the other side, eh?" Lynch swung down off the train and raced, hopped, skipped and almost fell beneath the train but with Red at his back they reached the platform to Wheeler's private train car.

Chapter 52

Rafferty was becoming increasingly anxious as to Hamlett's whereabouts.

"Where did that feller come from?" Rafferty asked.

Daniel was unable see who they were discussing but saw the expression on Megan's face. She was smiling and that was curious. "He came with the train," Wheeler replied.

Wheeler walked to the front of the carriage and a young man, who Daniel instantly recognized, stepped into view opening a basket and handing Wheeler wrapped packages.

"Why don't we have something to eat?" Wheeler said. "I think it will make us all feel better." He handed Daniel a package wrapped in clean white napkin.

Inside the package, on top of the bread, was half of a torn twenty-dollar bill. Daniel looked up at Wheeler, as he handed Kate a package also wrapped in a white napkin. A watchful Rafferty approached them.

"Sit on the floor," Rafferty ordered. "I don't trust either of you." Rafferty pointed to the young man in the conductor's cap. "You! Tie them up."

"Let them eat, Rafferty, or whatever your name is."

At the point of Rafferty's gun, Joshua did as he was told, using the sashes from the curtains to bind both Patrick and Daniel.

Out on the small, swaying platform between Wheeler's carriage and the Silver Queen, Harry was gasping for air and fighting to breathe. Hamlett was choking him by the collar and his life was in jeopardy. Smoky air from the locomotive clouded the air as Hamlett pushed his face up against Harry's, so close their breath mingled.

"This is it, Harry. You either tell me where the money is now, or I throw you off this train and let the buzzards finish you off." Hamlett was reaching for the handle to enter the Silver Queen car when the train lurched and bucked, throwing them both against the iron railings.

Momentarily freed from Hamlett's grasp, Harry turned, grabbed the barrel of Hamlett's pistol, twisting it away from him and punched Hamlett in the face hard, so hard he felt the middle knuckle on his right- hand break. But, wrestling for the gun, Hamlett's coat became entangled in the handle of the carriage's connecting mechanism and as they fought, he pulled hard on his coat, turning the crank and disengaging the cars.

They both felt a shudder under their feet and when Hamlett saw that the train cars were slowly separating, he ceased punching Harry's head. In that brief moment that Hamlett was distracted, Harry violently pushed upwards with the heel of his hand under Hamlett's chin, forcing him backwards. Refusing to relinquish his grip on Harry, Hamlett missed the top step, losing his footing and his hat. Driven by fear and fighting for his life, Harry did the unexpected. For all the times he had only ever dreamed of reversing the roles, he saw his chance and rammed his knee into Hamlett's groin with all the force he could muster.

Hamlett gasped and looked at Harry with the purest fury. But Harry still had hold of Hamlett's gun hand and hammered it repeatedly against the wall of the train. Hamlett managed to again grasp Harry's throat, pressing his face up to Harry's with a look of vengeance that withered whatever bravery Harry had in stock.

Unexpectedly, the train bucked crossing another set of rails. Not holding onto anything secure, Hamlett lost his balance again and let go of Harry to grab the railing. But his grip was unequal to his weight and he began slipping further and further down the stairs. A decision born out of desperation, he let go of the pistol and watched it bounce once before it disappeared under the train. With the looming realization that his situation was dire, he hooked his foot through the iron railing to brace himself. He was in trouble and Harry knew it. He grabbed for the railing again.

With a devilish smile Harry kicked him in the groin with such ferocity that all breath exited Hamlett and he fell even further down the steps. Hamlett knew he was fighting for his life and with renewed effort he clutched the railing with both hands trying to climb back on board but, as the seconds passed like days, slowly he realized it was futile. Harry saw the look of fear come into Hamlett's eyes. The tables had turned.

The train cars were separating inch by inch and were now a man's length apart. Red appeared but could only watch Harry's battle. Hamlett, he saw, was struggling to stay aboard but was gradually falling off the train. Red saw Harry stretch out his hand for Hamlett to take. But he saw that Hamlett's strength had gone from him. He lost his grip and fell back.

In horror, Harry and Red watched Hamlett's head bounce off the rocky rail bed and with a ripe melon-like sound, it burst with a bright red splash of blood as the passing rail ties took the rest of him away in pieces. First his head, then his arms and then sections of his torso disappeared, as if snatched away by hungry beast.

Harry watched this all happen just inches from his extended hand. Hamlett had made no attempt to grasp it and Harry looked down at his empty hand as if it was foreign. Why he had attempted to save his tormentor he knew not, but he had.

All that remained of Hamlett now was his left leg and rags of his pants flapping under the train. Then in an instant the shredded, blood-soaked material caught and was ripped away, taking the remnants of Hamlett's leg and foot with it. Gone. Just gone. All but for the empty boot. Harry and Red looked at each other in shock at what they had witnessed.

The distance between the carriages had now increased to twice a man's height and was no longer a space that could be crossed. "Leave it be, Harry. Let it go," Red yelled across the widening distance between the carriages. "It's not worth dying for."

"But I won it, Red. It's mine. I won it fair and square. I'm not going to just leave it." Harry yelled. Red shrugged, he knew better than to argue with a mad man. He had more serious issues to deal with.

With the greatest of caution, Red crept back along the corridor and quickly crossed to the next railcar. Removing his hat, he took quick peeks into the carriage. What he saw made him uneasy. Lynch was walking forward, holding his hands above his head. On either side, scattered about, were Myra, Megan and Gemma, but there was no sign of Shirley or Kate. No sign of Daniel or Patrick either, nor Wheeler.

Red then saw Rafferty, his pistol pointed at Lynch. Rafferty turned Lynch around feeling him for a weapon and Lynch saw Red peeking in the window. Wheeler stood, and following Lynch's gaze he also saw Red. Daring another quick look, Red saw a young man wearing a conductor's hat. Rafferty's pistol turned his direction. Wheeler shot Red a warning glance.

"Come here, Lynch," Rafferty commanded. Lynch took his coat from where he had been sitting and placed it on the seat next to Myra, smiling to her. She looked at him, confused but understood that Lynch's jacket held something of importance. Gradually, she gathered it to her and felt the weight of a pistol in the pocket. Lynch smiled and she smiled back as Rafferty patted him down.

"Well, Mister Rafferty," Wheeler said, gaining Rafferty's attention. "Now that you have us all here, what are you going to do with us?"

"I don't have all of you here. Where're the other two and where's the big ugly feller?" All heads swiveled with vacant looks.

Wheeler sat beside Kate and using his handkerchief helped staunch the bleeding from the gash on Shirley's head. He inspected the wound. "She'll be alright, Kate. And so will you, trust me." Wheeler smiled when she showed him the knife that had been concealed in the sandwiches.

"I'm curious, Rafferty," Lynch was saying. "We've travelled half way across this country trying to elude you. How is it that you keep showing up?"

Rafferty pointed his pistol at Gemma. She looked at him fearfully. He motioned her to come to him.

With his hands bound behind him Patrick watched as she slowly approached Rafferty. But for the sounds of the train, silence reigned. Rafferty smiled, not a pleasant smile, one that held mischief and danger. The closer she came to him, the more the danger loomed. They could feel it growing.

Rafferty roughly grabbed Gemma by the waist and kissed her fiercely. She tried to push him away, but Rafferty held the pistol close to her face and she ceased resisting.

"This is how Mister Lynch." His smile grew. He pulled Gemma closer, his smile menacing. "Gemma and I were close once, weren't we?"

322

"Ah," Lynch said, recognizing Gemma. "You, were the one in O'Malley's, weren't you?" Rafferty smiled. Gemma fought to push away but Rafferty held on tightly.

Rafferty pointed his pistol at Patrick. "She is how I found you."

Patrick's face was a palette of his emotions, a mix of anger, shame and hate. He'd been used. He knew it now. He was a mere puppy in this world of big dogs. He looked at Gemma with indescribable disappointment.

Gemma saw his pain and tried to go to him. But Rafferty held onto her tightly. She attempted to push away again, and in that moment, while Rafferty was distracted, Kate leaned forward and cut Daniel's bonds. Daniel held Kate's gaze and loved her more.

"Is this true Gemma?" Patrick was yelling. "Is what he's saying true? What about the priest?"

"Ah! Father John. The priest." Rafferty said, chuckling. "Ah, yes. Do you want to tell him Gemma? Or should I?" Patrick's face had flushed crimson with anger and betrayal. Gemma looked at him, sadness flowing with her tears.

"Go on, Gemma." Rafferty goaded. "Tell everyone that he's one of your brothers, why don't you?" Rafferty laughed, then savagely kissed Gemma as Patrick writhed on the floor trying to free his hands.

The door at the far end of the carriage burst open and Red entered, striding down the carriage with his pistol aimed at Rafferty. Wheeler jumped to his feet, his hands upraised.

"No, Red! This is not how it should end. Please lower your gun." He turned to face Rafferty, holding his hands out in supplication. "Mister Rafferty, I hope that you will do the same. You're making us all nervous here."

Red slowly lowered his gun as he walked down the rolling carriage. But, when he saw Shirley and the bloody gash on her head, he looked at Kate who inclined her head towards Rafferty. As in the old days, Red snapped his pistol upward and shot at Rafferty who dodged and fired back, missing Red but hitting Lynch who was standing behind him.

Myra screamed as Rafferty walked toward them, dragging Gemma. She felt found the pistol inside Lynch's coat and with some effort, pulled the hammer back.

"I wouldn't do that again," Rafferty said, letting go of Gemma but keeping his pistol pointed at Red. "If you do, I'll shoot your women. I mean it," Rafferty said menacingly, pointing his pistol at Shirley until he'd disarmed Red. Lynch slumped in his seat in pain. Myra gasped when she saw him and leaving the gun under his coat, she rushed to his aid.

Myra peeled away his jacket, gasping when she saw the ragged tear of the skin and the profusion of blood.

Wheeler stood to assist, but Rafferty would have none of it. Pointing his pistol at Shirley and Red, Rafferty failed to see Kate pass the knife to Megan. Gemma saw them but kept silent. She kept her gaze on Patrick, pleading in her eyes, scared as they all were.

"What do you intend to do with us all, Mister Rafferty? If that's your real name?" Wheeler asked.

"No. It's not my real name. It's the same as hers. We're cousins. Aren't we, Gemma?" Gemma's revulsion and disgrace took hold and she leapt at him trying to scratch his face but he grabbed her hair and pulled her head back cruelly. While Rafferty was torturing Gemma, Daniel showed Patrick that his hands were free. Patrick nodded back.

"I saw you at Hogan's house." Patrick said angrily to Lynch. "You killed Hogan, didn't you?"

"NO!" Myra cried out, recoiling from Lynch, making him wince painfully. He looked back at her plaintively.

"You're right, Patrick. I was there," Lynch said, through clenched teeth, pleading. "But I arrived after Rafferty had been there. It wasn't me, Myra, I promise you." Lynch looked at Rafferty. "You did it didn't you? Why? Why did you kill him?" Lynch asked. "Was it because he wouldn't tell you where they were going?"

Looks passed between them all. Shirley stirred and Red came to her side.

"Where are Harry and Hamlett?" Wheeler asked.

"Yeah. Where is my new partner?" Rafferty added.

"Which one?" Red prompted.

"I'll start with the ugly one. Where's he?"

"I wouldn't go counting on him. He won't be of any help to you." Red said blandly.

"Why?" Rafferty asked.

"Let's say that he's not on the train anymore and leave it at that." Rafferty bit his lower lip. "What about that other feller. Where's he?"

"I wouldn't know about that. Why don't you go on back and see?"

"No," said Wheeler. "I'll go." Wheeler stood and walked back to his private car and was about to open the door when he saw with a shock that the Silver Queen had disappeared. He turned and looked at Red, who simply shook his head. Lynch was watching them closely. A distraction was needed.

"What would it take for you to forget these two lads?" Lynch asked.

"A lot more than you have, I assure you." Rafferty replied. Gemma looked terrified. She looked to Patrick for compassion but saw none.

Painfully, Lynch withdrew the gold nugget from his pocket and held it up for Rafferty to see. "I know where there's more like this," he said, tossing it to Rafferty. It stalled in mid-air and seemed to float there. Captivated by the glittering object, Rafferty reached for the air borne nugget.

Seizing the opportunity, Wheeler leapt to his left and yanked on the emergency cord that ran the length of the carriage and instantly the train applied its brakes, tossing everyone about the carriage.

Rafferty fell backwards, losing his grip on Gemma who threw herself across Patrick, as Daniel pounced on Rafferty holding his gun down, pointed at the floor. But Rafferty was stronger and hit Daniel on the side of the head, stunning him. From behind, Kate flew at Rafferty and Megan came at him with her knife.

The gun roared and Gemma screamed. Kate had hold of the pistol's barrel, turning it away from them but Rafferty was far stronger and it discharged again. They heard another scream. Red arrived like a cloud burst and angrily pinned Rafferty to the floor as Daniel wrenched the pistol out of Rafferty's hand.

Gemma was laying on top of Patrick, face down, as if they were lovers entwined. With a gasp, Shirley suddenly saw that Gemma was wounded and though wounded herself, rushed to her side.

"Quick Kate, I need some bandages. Give me your petticoat." Blood was streaming from the wound in Shirley's upper arm but she ignored it. Kate hurriedly lifted her dress and quickly removed her under garments. "Tear it in strips," Shirley ordered.

Fortunately, for Gemma the bullet had passed through the fleshy part of her thigh and though it was bled profusely, Shirley reckoned that she would survive with prompt medical attention.

While Red and Daniel restrained Rafferty, and Kate and Shirley staunched Gemma's wound, Patrick looked on disinterested. Megan sat on the floor and took hold of Gemma's hand. Gemma never took her eyes from Patrick. But Rafferty wasn't done yet.

Chapter 53

Harry was drained, both emotionally and physically. His life-or-death battle with Hamlett had taken all he had and he sat on the iron steps of the boxcar, his hands trembling from fright. It was with a feeling of serenity that he watched Wheeler's train ascending the gentle grade and but for a trail of coal smoke, vanish from sight. As the Silver Queen boxcar slowed and gradually came to a stop his world slowed along with it.

It was tranquil and the gentle roll of the terrain was silent but for the whispering breeze. Absently, he looked down at the lone boot stuck in the steps and recounted what he had seen of his tormentor's demise. For once in his life he felt victorious. But there was more to it than simply killing the man who was planning to murder him. He had fought for his life and he had won. And he also had won the Silver Queen.

It was a slight movement at first, and it caused him no alarm, at first. Then came a lurch, and then another as the boxcar responded to the siren's call of gravity. Another screech of the iron wheels and then it began moving, rolling backwards down the track. Harry had presumed that boxcars needed to be moved by a locomotive and had no impetus of their own. He was wrong once again.

The boxcar was moving only at walking pace and it would've been easy for Harry to step off the train car in the hope that the next train would stop and pick him up. In Harry's thinking that next train would need to come to a complete stop or risk crashing into the Silver Queen. At which time Harry could lay claim to it in front of witnesses.

As was so often the case, Harry was again caught in a dilemma. If the other bounty hunter on the train, besides Lynch, actually had a legal warrant then he would never receive the reward money for Daniel, of that he was certain. But, if he abandoned the boxcar bearing the Silver Queen, would he be able to regain possession? He had no proof of ownership except Jerome Wheeler's word.

Slowly, his attention was drawn to the bank notes floating in the air, being scattered by the wind. He did entertain the thought of jumping from the train to retrieve them but chose not to risk his claim on the much more valuable Silver Queen to chase paper across the prairie.

He was ruminating on his situation when he saw splashes of red and body parts of his late partner as the boxcar rolled back over the stretch of track littered with his torn and tattered remains. Though gory in the extreme, Harry took some amount of pleasure in having had a hand in removing the blight of his tormentor from the Earth. No one would ever feel his indignities again.

Looking east through the rear door of the boxcar he saw something off in the distance. Something that gave him hope. A plume of black smoke from an approaching westbound train. He was saved.

*   *   *

"Tell me what happened back there, Red. With that Hamlett feller, I mean." They were standing together on the iron platform of Wheeler's private carriage looking at the tracks disappearing under their feet. The train's engineer had done as promised and was reversing the locomotive and its string of carriages down the long, fading slope, chasing after the Silver Queen. The runaway boxcar was much further down the track than they assumed.

Minutes passed while Red told his story. Red was detailing the events when he drew Wheeler's attention to the gory mess and scattered remnants of the late Hamlett Kincaid passing underneath them.

"No one must ever know about this, Jerome. It would not be good to have this connected to you. Most of all, the ladies must never know about it." Silently Wheeler watched the bits and pieces disappear. Red's advice was well taken.

"There it is!" Wheeler said, pointing around the long curve where the hills hid the tracks.

*   *   *

Harry saw the approaching locomotive as a savior of sorts. His new life beckoned, fortified with the knowledge he had both the Silver Queen and knew who had taken the money from the bank robbery. He could feel magnanimous regarding the six thousand dollars flying aloft on the prairie winds. It was of little concern to him now.

Without warning he shot backwards and fell to the floor. He was picking himself up when the jolt was repeated. Absorbed completely with his new-found wealth, he'd failed to see or hear Wheeler's train bearing down on him. Again, he was tossed about and caught a handhold to avoid being thrown off the train and onto the tracks.

Crawling on his hands and knees he righted himself and heard his name being called. He raced to the front of the carriage and was surprised to see Wheeler and Red motioning him across the gap between the cars.

"Put on the brake," Red yelled, pointing at the handle at Harry's elbow. Harry cupped his hand to his ear. Red pointed at the right-angled crank that Hamlett had unintentionally released during the fight. Comprehending, Harry grabbed the crank with both hands and pulled on it, but it refused to turn. Not an inch. Harry tried again, shrugged, appealing for help.

"Jump, Harry!" Red called out. Harry turned to see that the approaching train was no longer so far away. Accompanied by a loud screeching noise from the steel wheels the distance between Wheeler's train and his boxcar abruptly increased. The engineer, john Carter, having also seen the oncoming train, had applied the brakes. Harry looked at his friends plaintively, his salvation so close. But Harry dithered. There was all that silver and gold he would be leaving behind.

Wheeler and Red could see that Harry was frozen by indecision, and the distance between them was increasing rapidly. As their train slowed, Harry's boxcar continued to gather speed. With a screech of tortured metal on metal, Wheeler's train drew to a halt and immediately Carter appeared beside them also looking at the runaway boxcar.

"We can't catch it, Mister Wheeler. What do you want me to do?"

"Get us away from here as fast as you can, Mister Carter, and I think we should change our engine numbers at the next water stop."

Carter disappeared and soon the train began moving up the gentle incline.

"Where's Harry?" Daniel asked, joining them. Wheeler and Red pointed down the slope at Harry and the Silver Queen receding into the distance. "Where's the Silver Queen?" Daniel asked anxiously.

Wheeler turned and placed his hands paternally on Daniel's shoulders. "I wouldn't go worrying yourself, son. Both are replaceable." Wheeler winked at Red who had a sudden realization and laughed out loud.

"Well, I'll be damned, Jerome. You beat Harry at his own game, didn't you?" Red said laughing.

"Come on inside now," Wheeler said, leading the way. "Let's see if we can save you two dangerous outlaws from the law."

*   *   *

Unknown to them, back inside the carriage Rafferty was far from defeated. He lashed out and kicked Daniel on the side of his head stunning him and writhed out of Joshua's grasp. Squirreling around on the floor Rafferty found his pistol under the seat and pointed it at Joshua who backed away, his hands in the air.

Patrick was seething. Myra reached out for him but he pulled away and began to walk towards Rafferty, who lifted the pistol and pointed it at him. Unafraid, Patrick advanced, Rafferty pulled back on the hammer and cocked it. The two clicks were loud and dangerous. Kate jumped up and made a grab for Patrick's coat but missed. Gemma cowered as Patrick approached.

"It's not what you think, Patrick," she pleaded piteously. Patrick stopped. "I didn't want to betray you. I thought it was your brother he was after." Patrick looked at Gemma with unveiled contempt.

"And that's supposed to excuse you?" he yelled. "It was me or Daniel?"

"No! No, Patrick. I changed my mind. I love you, Patrick."

"I don't believe you, Gemma. You set me up. You're only in it for the money, aren't you?"

Rafferty laughed. "You're finally catching on now, aren't you? She was the one who told me where you all were heading." He turned the pistol on Lynch. "And you! You're always getting in my way. You're a problem."

"I'm not afraid of you, Rafferty." Lynch stood painfully and joined Patrick, now both allied against a common enemy. "You're a murderer and your loss would never be missed." Angered, Lynch was a force to be reckoned with and he knew that two of Rafferty's six bullets were gone. "What are you going to do, Rafferty? Or whatever your name is. Shoot us? All of us?" Silence fanned the tension. The embers of violence smoldered. Rafferty waved his pistol at them both.

"Is John Hogan truly dead?" Myra asked. "Did he kill him?" She looked from Patrick to Lynch and in their eyes, she read the truth. She rose from her seat, pointing Lynch's pistol at Rafferty's head. "I wish you dead," she said.

Suddenly the door at the far end of the carriage opened and Wheeler entered with Red close behind him. All eyes abruptly turned to the ceiling, to the sounds of footsteps running. Rafferty pulled Gemma in front of him straightening his shooting arm, pointing the gun at Patrick.

"What's going on here?" Wheeler bellowed. It was enough distraction. Lynch pushed Patrick aside and struck at Rafferty with his cane. The gun roared and glass shattered. Gemma bit Rafferty's hand and twisted out of his grip. The gun roared again. Daniel rushed at Rafferty grabbing hold of his collar pulling him backwards, wrestling to keep his gun hand pointed at the ceiling.

Another body fell on them. Joshua had hold of Rafferty's pistol by the barrel and was twisting it upwards but he lost his grip and the gun fired again. Patrick was raining punches on Rafferty, releasing his rage. Again and again he hammered on Rafferty's face until Red pulled him off. "Stop it!" Red yelled, and all became suddenly quiet. The smell and smoke of the gunpowder clouded the air. The train rattled onwards.

A groan here and a sob there; that's all the sound there was, barely audible over the noise of the train.

Wheeler was in shock. Shirley was holding onto her bleeding arm, Kate at her side, her eyes wide in fright. Daniel saw her fear and leaped over the prone body of Sergeant Lynch to comfort her. Lynch hadn't moved. Gemma had curled into a ball, pushing herself into a corner between the seats, sobbing.

Red had a firm hold of Rafferty and Joshua was tying his hands behind his back with Patrick's assistance. Red looked up and saw the fear on Kate's face, and the pain on Shirley's. He took Shirley in his arms and holding her tightly he pulled the bloody sleeve away from the wound.

"Kate, do you have something that we could make more bandages with?" Immediately a ripping sound came as Megan tore at her petticoat. She was handing it across the aisle to Kate when she looked down and screamed.

They'd not noticed that Sergeant Lynch was not moving and blood seeped from his shoulder pooling on the floor.

"Red, you see to Mister Lynch and I'll look after Shirley," Wheeler said calmly.

Daniel was already at Lynch's side, looking to Kate for inspiration. "Mister Lynch, we're going to turn you onto your back. This might hurt." No sound came from Lynch until they lifted his right shoulder and then he moaned loudly.

"Daniel, we have to turn him over," Red stated plainly. "Patrick! Come here and turn his feet while we turn his shoulders. Hurry!"

Patrick felt no need to answer and less inclination to help. His emotions roiled. He clenched and unclenched his fists and his breathing slowed. He'd found satisfaction in taking revenge in the past. It was all he was seeing in the present and a red tinge blurred his vision. He knew but one purpose.

"No! Patrick, no!" Megan yelled. Though no one else had noticed she had seen it building and she raced up the aisle climbing over Lynch in panic. Patrick was pointing the pistol at Gemma's head when Megan reached him.

"No, Patrick. This is not the way," she said gently, pulling at the pistol. Slowly his grip loosened.

Gemma had balled herself up into a corner, sobbing, covering her face. Slowly she lowered her hands and looked at him pleading through her tears.

"Patrick, please don't shoot me. I never betrayed you. I love you!" she cried.

"Patrick! We need you here!" Daniel called out. Patrick turned away for a second then returned his gaze back on Gemma. He let Megan take the gun from him, slowly releasing it, reluctantly letting go. Megan, watching them both as they wrestled with their roiling emotions, relaxed as Patrick walked away to assist Daniel and Red.

"Take his feet, Patrick," Red commanded, and together they turned Lynch onto his back. Myra appeared at their side ministering to the wound, lifting the clothing from it with obvious experience.

"Sergeant Lynch," she said, speaking calmly, taking his hand in hers. "We're going to take your coat off and it will hurt. Can you stand the pain?" Lynch nodded and smiled at her. Throughout the procedure, Lynch and Myra held each other's gaze, as if Myra's smile eased the pain and gave him solace.

"How bad is it?" Myra forced a smile.

"It could be worse," Myra said. "I think he'll live if we can get him to a doctor." She leaned down closer to him, her countenance soft and her voice soothing. "Don't talk, Mister Lynch. It'll do you no good. Just focus on me and staying alive."

Myra took the clothing that Megan had torn and more that Kate handed her and with competence she staunched the wound and bandaged it, fashioning a sling to support his arm and hold it to his side.

"You seem to have some experience with bullet wounds," Red said to her.

"Seen my share." She gave Red a glance and then returned her attention to her patient. "It's how I met my late husband, Paddy," Myra said casually. Daniel and Patrick exchanged looks with Megan. Lynch smiled broadly and winced in pain.

"This is a mess, isn't it, Jerome?" Shirley said, resting against Wheeler, something she had never done before.

"Nothing that money can't get us out of, I suspect," he laughed, making Shirley smile.

Chapter 54

"How do you all know each other?" Red asked.

Joshua looked about him, at the people he barely knew, the family he'd helped save twice. Myra sat by Sergeant Lynch while Red and Wheeler comforted Shirley. Megan held Gemma's hand for support while Patrick hovered over his mother protectively, closely watching Rafferty who sat on the floor with his back against the wall, his hands tied with his belt.

"It was Joshua's family who kept us safe when we were in New York. They took us in and hid us from these two." Daniel indicated Lynch and Rafferty.

"I'm sorry but I have to ask you. Why did you follow them, Joshua?" Wheeler asked.

"My father told me to. He said that I was to watch out for them."

Joshua grinned at Daniel. "He said that I needed to get my dreidels back."

Daniel reached into his pocket and took out the two curly locks of hair and passed them over to Joshua. "Thanks, Joshua. You've rescued us twice now."

"Why did you really follow us?" Megan asked. Joshua blushed and smiled at Megan.

"More importantly, I think, is how did you follow them?" Wheeler asked. "That's what's most intriguing to me." Wheeler's interest was written in the furrows on his brow. Joshua looked about him.

"We are Jews and my father has many friends. We know things and we tell each other when there is trouble." Joshua hunched his shoulders and splayed his hands as if there was nothing more to add.

Wheeler cleared his throat noisily, gaining their attention. "He came up to me in Kansas City, when we were attaching my locomotive," Wheeler was saying. "Asked me if we needed help on the train." Wheeler forwarded Joshua a smile. "I thought he was a bright young man, so I said yes. I had no idea that he was following you all." Wheeler reached out and patted Joshua on his knee affectionately. "I like your style, young man. Are you planning to return to New York?"

Joshua shrugged and looked at Megan. So much conveyed in a look. Shirley and Kate exchanged looks, as did Myra and Daniel.

"What are you planning to do with him, Jerome?" Red asked, pointing at Rafferty.

"Oh, yes. Well, I have a surprise waiting for him in Denver. First, we need to cover our tracks. I don't know what happened to Harry, but knowing him as I do, I'm certain we'll see him again."

"What about the Silver Queen?" Daniel asked the question on all their minds.

"Things are rarely what they seem in this world, Daniel. Would you all excuse us for a spell? Red, might I have a word with you?" Wheeler led them back across the gap and into his private car. Retrieving the whiskey bottle he poured himself a glass then passed the bottle to Red. "After what we've all been through this morning, I'm sure we could use some of this medication, eh?"

But Wheeler drank alone as he suspected he would. Red nursed the bottle until Wheeler retrieved it and refilled his glass.

"We do seem to have a predicament here, don't we? Two dead men. That is, if Harry refused to jump from the train. And three wounded. It's like a battlefield in there." Wheeler laughed a well-needed laugh, then turned serious again. "I think we were lucky, Red. Considering that mad man in there."

"Rafferty, you mean?" Red asked. Wheeler nodded. "What are we going to do about him, Jerome?" Wheeler smiled.

"A detective named Coleman from the Pinkerton's agency will be meeting us in Denver when we arrive. He met with Mister Lynch in Chicago and knows of his purpose but is not interested in arresting either of the Shadlow boys. Though, he is more than happy to arrest Mister Rafferty for several reasons. It seems that Rafferty is suspected of two murders in New York and," Wheeler paused for effect, "one of them was a Pinkerton detective. The other was your friend John Hogan." Wheeler smiled broadly. "So, I doubt we'll be seeing Mister Rafferty again after today."

"What about Lynch? Is he still of a mind to arrest Patrick?"

"I'm not sure. That's what I wanted to talk you about. For a start, I'm thinking that we should get out of Denver as quickly as possible so as not to draw attention. Lynch, Gemma and Shirley can get medical attention there and we can do that without fanfare if we move quickly. I'll discuss it with Carter when we stop for water." Wheeler took a large sip of his whiskey. "If we can keep ahead of the train behind us, we should be able to escape detection. My guess is that they will have to stop to deal with the Silver Queen." Red nodded his agreement. It made sense. "I can always say that it came loose, if anyone asks."

"What if Lynch still wants to take Patrick back with him to Ireland?"

Wheeler steepled his fingers. "He does have some recuperation ahead of him but it would appear that Daniel's mother is not averse to nursing him back to health. After that, who knows? I'm counting on him being a reasonable man who will make a reasonable decision, if a reasonable amount of money is involved. I hope he sees that there is more potential for a better life here than back wherever it was that he came from." Wheeler smiled for Red's benefit. "But there's no telling, is there?"

A somber scene greeted them when they rejoined the group in the carriage. Kate and Daniel attended to Shirley and she smiled bravely to Red when he appeared. Across from them, Sergeant Lynch rested comfortably leaning back against Myra, who seemed pleased at the situation.

Megan and Joshua had formed a wall of allegiance separating Patrick from Gemma who sat with her back to the window, sobbing, while Megan adjusted the bandages on her wounded thigh. Patrick brooded, eyeing Rafferty with a murderous look. Megan took pity on Gemma. She felt for her, for her despair, for her betrayal and for her bad decisions made under difficult circumstances.

But Gemma was closely watching Patrick, hoping for a sign that she was forgiven. None was forthcoming, her hope died. She looked up into Megan's eyes and more tears sprang forth.

"I love him, Megan. I truly do."

"You hurt him, Gemma." Megan both saw and felt her brother's pain. She herself had known so much of it in her life. So much of it had been showered on her family. She looked across at Patrick, sitting apart from them, from his family, from everyone and everything. An island of a man. Untethered, falling apart under the assault of life's breakers.

Perhaps, springing from her experiences as an outcast, an oddity, Megan recognized that these two broken people needed each other. As certain as the coming of a new day, she saw how these two lost souls fit each other and felt that their only chance at survival was based on a partnership.

"How is Rafferty doing?" Red asked Patrick. Receiving no reply, he glanced at Gemma huddled with Megan. "Are you both alright?" he asked. Gemma wiped away her tears and smiled at them in an odd way. Wheeler and he exchanged a look before he turned back to Shirley.

"How are you feeling?"

"Not bad, considering I've been shot. But thanks for asking." Shirley grimaced as she changed her position. "I'm sorry, Red, I shouldn't have said that. It was cruel."

"You've been worse," Kate added, smiling.

"Joshua, could you see if you can find us something to eat?"

Wheeler joined them. "Patrick, would you help Joshua, please?"

Patrick and Joshua stepped over Rafferty, hands bound and sitting with his back against the wall. Rafferty screamed when Patrick kicked him in passing, drawing an angry look from Wheeler, and from Myra, too. Wheeler motioned Red and Daniel to his side and spoke to Lynch in quiet tones. Lynch was in obvious pain but comforted by Myra who seemed a tonic to him.

"Mister Lynch, I would like to know what your plans are when we reach Denver? Mister Rafferty will be taken into custody and that leaves only you with a need to arrest Patrick. No doubt you have thought about that."

Lynch smiled, both at Wheeler and then, with effort, at Myra.

Daniel wrinkled his brow.

"I take it you have something in mind, Jerome?"

"Yes, I do, Mister Lynch, though I do wish this could be discussed in private. Here's my thinking. You still have your gold nugget, don't you?" Lynch nodded. Myra was holding it tightly. "And you also have the nearly ten thousand dollars that you won. So, let me ask you this. Why not consider settling in Colorado?"

Lynch pursed his lips. He turned with a grimace and looked up and into Myra's eyes. "I've caused you and your family a lot of pain, Myra Shadlow. I doubt you need more. But I'd stay if you would allow it?"

Daniel was so shocked he nearly fell over. He looked at Kate and Shirley and they were smiling.

"Well that's more like it, Mister Lynch," Wheeler said, smiling broadly. "Now where is Mister Rafferty's pistol, Red?"

The door opened and Patrick and Joshua entered carrying a wicker basket. Suddenly, Patrick dropped his end of the basket, racing forward.

"No! No!" he yelled. "Gemma, don't do it!"

Gemma had the pistol pointed at Rafferty and none of them were within range to stop her from shooting him.

Patrick stopped; his hands outstretched. "Don't do it, Gemma. Please, don't do this," Patrick begged her. "He's not worth it."

The train rocked and only the sound of its wheels disturbed the silence that had built around them.

"Go on!" Rafferty yelled back at her. "Shoot me, if that's what you want. I don't care. I fucked you and your stupid priest. Go ahead, shoot me. If you got the guts."

Megan and Kate both stood and each took tentative steps toward the shaking Gemma. The gun wavered but she did not. With difficulty, she pulled back the hammer on the gun and painfully took a step closer to Rafferty. Megan and Kate also moved closer. Patrick did the same. No one breathed. Lynch felt Myra squeezing his hand. He'd not noticed that before.

"Gemma! Listen to me. He's not worth it." Patrick's voice softened. "Don't let him come between us. He's not worth it. I love you. Don't let him pull us apart."

As if her world had upended, Gemma looked at Patrick and tears ran down her face. "I'm sorry, Patrick," she said, turning the gun and placing it under her chin. "Goodbye. I'm sorry."

Megan and Kate both leapt for the gun but Patrick arrived first, just as the gun discharged.

Chapter 55

"I see by the bullet holes that you had an exciting trip, Mister Wheeler?" Jerome surveyed the carriage noting the holes in the window and the roof from where narrow ribbons of sunlight shone bright spots of light on the floor at their feet. Scattered about were remnants of their journey; scraps of food in a wicker basket along with strips of clothing smeared with blood.

"Yes, it was, Mister Coleman. Yes, it was." They were alone in the carriage with Rafferty who was sitting on the floor, bound in handcuffs, still defiant. They looked at him without rancor or hate. Perhaps with distaste, but more simply indifferent to the man who had caused so much harm. John Carter entered and whistled at the mess.

"I've settled with the station master, Mister Wheeler," Carter said. "If we leave now, he'll say that we didn't stop and went on to Manitou Springs."

Wheeler nodded. "Well done, John. Do we have enough coal to get us there without stopping?" Carter nodded. "Very good. Let's get going then. As soon as Red and Daniel return, we'll leave." The quicker we're gone the better.

Coleman was in the process of lifting Rafferty to his feet. "I can take care of this from here, Mister Wheeler."

"Thank you again, Mister Coleman. I do appreciate everything you've done for me." They shook hands. "I have a little souvenir for you, if you'll accept it." Wheeler withdrew the one-pound gold nugget from his coat pocket and handed it to Coleman whose eyes lit up when he held it in his hand. "Think of it as a gift from Sergeant Lynch." Wheeler winked. "Will you keep me appraised of this case as it progresses, Mister Coleman?"

"I will most certainly do that, Mister Wheeler. It will be my pleasure, I assure you." Coleman pushed Rafferty out of the carriage where they were met by a large, muscular man dressed similarly to Coleman. Together, holding Rafferty's arms securely, they escorted him along the platform toward the exit, passing Red and Daniel returning to the train.

"How is everyone, Red?" Wheeler asked as they joined him in the carriage. "Daniel, would you tell Mister Carter that we would like to get going." Daniel left and ran up to the locomotive. The train choofed, the wheels turned and momentarily, Daniel was back on board. "This place is a mess," Wheeler said absently, observing the obvious. "Let's retire to my private car. We can have our talk there," Wheeler said, leading them back to the rear carriage as the train pulled away from the station.

"Sit down you two, we have some decisions to make." Wheeler poured himself a hearty dose of whiskey. "So, is everyone being taken care of, Red?"

"Thanks to you, Jerome, they are," Red stated. "Your doctor friend has assured us that the wounds to Shirley and Gemma are not life threatening and they should be able to travel soon. Perhaps longer for Mister Lynch."

"What has Mister Lynch said about his intentions? Anything?" Wheeler asked, looking intently at Daniel.

"Your guess is as good as mine."

"And what of your brother, Daniel?" Wheeler asked. "Has he run off, as he probably should? What about his friend, Gemma?" Red and Daniel passed a look.

"She'll be fine, Jerome," Red added. "But we're fortunate that Patrick pulled the gun away from her before she could do herself any harm. It was close." They shared a moment of reflection, each reviewing the attempted suicide from their individual perspectives.

"I've made arrangements for them all to stay at Senator Cavendish's house until they're ready to come back up to Aspen," Wheeler said. "But I was wondering if they all should just stay here in Denver permanently? They would be the subject of scrutiny up in Aspen and I'm sure there would be questions asked. What do you think, Daniel?"

Daniel's face flushed knowing that Kate was possibly aware, if not certain, of the affair with Claire Cavendish. He shrugged and looked down at the floor. When he looked up, he saw was being watched closely by both Wheeler and Red.

"I'm not sure, Mister Wheeler, but I think that Mrs. Holland would put my family up at her boarding house for as long as needed. She knows me."

"Well, that's a start. I'm hoping that we can keep this messy business out of the newspapers and placing them under a senator's roof is as good a protection as I can imagine for the time being. Keep them all out of sight for a while. What about that young Joshua fellow? What's he going to do?"

Daniel smiled. "I don't know if he will head back to New York right away. He's fond of my sister it seems. I gave him the directions to Mrs. Holland's."

"Personally, I hope he decides to stick around. I like him. There's a need for his kind out here in the west. No one like him is going to make any money in New York. Especially since he's Jewish." Wheeler laughed. "Are we going directly back to Aspen, Mister Wheeler?" Daniel inquired. Wheeler laughed. Red smiled.

"No. We're heading south. I have some played-out coal mines down near Pagosa where we can hide the Silver Queen. Then we'll head on back to Aspen. I don't think I want the Silver Queen anywhere close to me for some time. If I get asked about it, I'll say it was stolen."

"I thought the Silver Queen was back out there on the plains," Daniel said, "with Harry?" Wheeler and Red exchanged knowing glances. "I have not the slightest idea what has happened to our friend Harry Rich, but I do know where the Silver Queen is. It's right where it always was, here on my train."

"How can that be, Mister Wheeler?" Daniel asked, looking confused.

"Daniel, there were two Silver Queens, you see. Both of their boxcars were painted, but only on one side. When the real one was turned around in Kansas City it appeared from the station as a plain boxcar." Wheeler and Red laughed. "It was not too difficult to trick Harry and that other fellow. Oh, that gold nugget was real. It's now in the possession of Mister Coleman. A souvenir from Mister Lynch, you might say."

"So, the Silver Queen is safe?" Daniel asked. "Yes, it's safe. It's my insurance."

*   *   *

Daniel's house was cold and empty when he arrived home. Maisie and Rachelle had pressed him and Red for information but the story they had concocted about Shirley and Kate remaining in Chicago to shop for clothes made perfect sense to them.

The following morning Red had arrived early to roust Daniel and together they sat in Wheeler's office drinking coffee until he arrived. Wheeler was less than jolly as he tossed the newspaper onto his desk.

The headline in the paper blared out the foul news from Washington that the Sherman Silver Purchase Act had been repealed, sounding the death knell of Wheeler's industry in Aspen. "Silver is a thing of the past," it blared to them unnecessarily.

The report of a train crash had been relegated to the second page. The story in the newspaper stated that a westbound freight train had collided with a mysterious boxcar in a desolate part of northern Colorado. Also, it stated that least one person was killed in the collision and that the accident was under investigation by the railroad authorities.

Finished reading the story, they looked at each other with a mix of humor and dismay. They were all aware of Hamlett's demise, but was Harry also deceased? They had no way of knowing.

"There's something else, Daniel." Red took two envelopes from his coat and passed them over. "No Problem Joe asked me to give these to you."

"Do you want to read them in private?" Wheeler asked. Daniel shook his head no.

"I think it best if we all knew what is in here. Joe might have been murdered for it."

They watched in silence as Daniel opened the first letter. It was Joe's will. After reading it he handed it to Red who passed it over to Wheeler.

"I'm not surprised that Joe would leave his stable to you Daniel," Red said with a smile. "He was always on your side. You knew that, didn't you?" Daniel nodded and opened the second crumpled envelope. It was crushed and misshapen as if it had been rolled into a ball. Daniel's eyes filled with tears.

"Now, now, son. Don't go on about it," Wheeler interjected. "Joe is in a better place, I suppose. Hamlett got his just reward, and apparently Harry did as well. No loss there, and it saved us the expense of a murder trial."

Daniel tore the remaining envelope open and emptied the single content on Wheeler's desk. It was a key. One single key. One that would fit a sturdy lock judging by its size. They all looked at the old key lying on Jerome's walnut desk, as if it would tell them its secret.

"Do you have any idea of what this unlocks?" Wheeler asked Daniel.

"I'm guessing that whatever it fits is most likely in Joe's stable. I suggest we go and see." Wheeler grabbed his coat and hat and followed Red and Daniel out into the street and together they headed to Joe's stable.

"How are they all doing in Denver, Daniel?" Wheeler enquired.

Daniel was reluctant to respond, having heard nothing from Kate.

"They're doing fine, Jerome," Red said for him. "Mister Lynch is out of the hospital and they are all staying with Daniel's friend, Mrs. Holland." Red smiled. "Shirley's doing fine but I'm not so sure that Kate is very happy to be living in the same house as Claire Cavendish."

Daniel stopped walking, stunned by Red's remark. "Why do you say that, Red?" Wheeler and Red swapped looks and began to laugh. "Why are you laughing?" Daniel said petulantly, suddenly worried.

"There's a lot to life, isn't there, Red?" Red nodded sagely. "There's danger at every turn. Risks to be taken daily. And then there's women." Wheeler laughed loudly, patting Daniel on his shoulder. "What I've gleaned is this, young man. They know every move we make and still to this day I don't know how they do it. It's a complete mystery to me, and to all men I'd imagine. But what I've learned to do is to own up to whatever misbehavior it is that you're being accused of. Apologize profoundly." Wheeler looked sidelong at Daniel. "Then do whatever you want to do."

"Why do you say that, Mister Wheeler?"

"Daniel, Bill Cavendish and I are old friends. He and his wife are not." They were approaching Joe's stables. "What she did to you she's practiced before. Make no mistake about it. Bill knows. He also knows that she would use your dalliance to protect him. Or cause you harm if ever she felt so inclined. It's how she is. How they all are, I'm guessing. Remember I told you that, eh? Ahhh. Here we are. No Problem Stables."

The old wooden building looked much the same. Much like the late Joe Bolon, weathered and gray. But, even from the road Daniel felt the difference. As if it had lived for Joe, it seemed to have died along with him. Perhaps it's the souls of the occupants that give a house a personality? Noticeably, to them all, whatever you called it, it was no longer present.

"Would you rather go in alone?" Red asked. Daniel looked at the building, the vacant corral, the fences that needed repair just like his marriage. He looked from Wheeler to Red and shrugged. They knew of his past now, and of his most recent unlawful pursuits. He could think of nothing more they could discover about him.

"No," Daniel said, and headed for the small side door.

He knew Joe's stable well. It had been where he had kept his horse, Marigold. Sunlight shone through the eastern window making the dust motes glow as they danced in the still air. The smell of new hay was noticeably absent and that brought on his sadness again. Breathing a sigh, he looked at the key in his hand and walked into Joe's room. It was neat and tidy now and Joe's things where Joe had left them. It was Joe's absence that was the difference.

With the key in hand Daniel walked back into the stables looking about him for a clue to his mystery. The stalls were empty, the lonely pot-bellied stove that was always lit was cold. His eyes roamed the roof of the barn, following the beams and joists that he had never paid any attention to before. He'd always assumed that the eye-bolts and hooks in the beams were for lifting hay up to the hayloft but now he noticed that their separation was odd, they were too close to each other.

He looked for a ladder, could see none, then remembered the one lying against the outside wall next to Harry's sled. They followed him outside and when Red saw his intention, he grabbed an end of the heavy wooden ladder and with some effort they freed it from the entangling weeds and together carried it back into the barn.

"Where do you want it?" Red asked, as Daniel inspected the beam above them.

"Let me go up and have a look here." Daniel climbed the rungs quickly. On top of the cross beam he found lengths of chain neatly laid out so that they could not be seen from below. When he saw what Joe had done, and realized their purpose, he began laughing.

"What do you find so funny?" Wheeler asked testily, as Daniel climbed down. Daniel was smiling broadly.

"Red, help me put the ladder against the wall." Together they leaned the ladder up against the place where the beam and the wall met. As Red steadied the ladder Daniel climbed up and at the top uncovered Joe's secret.

The hidden lengths of chain that ran along the beam were attached to the wall with a large iron lock. Taking the key from his pocket he inserted it into the lock. It fit. The lock held the ends of the chains to the wall of the building, and once he unclasped it, the chains fell noisily to the floor forcing Wheeler and Red to jump out of the way or be felled by the swinging chains.

Descending the ladder Daniel inspected the base of Joe's iron oven closely. Neither he nor Red had noticed the flanges on the feet of the oven before, and only did now when Daniel cleared away the dirt. With Red and Wheeler watching in fascination Daniel passed the chains through the eye bolts, then threaded the chains through the flanges and attached the ends above the oven using the lock.

Climbing the ladder again he passed the loose end of the chain through an eyebolt and then to the wall, through an old wooden block and tackle and back down to the floor. Descending to the ground he cleared away a pile of clutter and found a second block and tackle attached to the wall behind a bale of hay and threaded the chains through it.

Standing back and appraising the contraption for a moment he then took hold of the chain and pulled on it. Nothing happened as the slack was noisily taken up. He pulled again and to Wheeler and Red's astonishment, the heavy iron oven lifted out of the ashes and rose up six inches. Daniel pulled again and it rose another six inches.

Wheeler and Red looked at each other, surprised by Daniel's discovery of Joe's wizardry. A few more pulls on the chain and the oven had lifted several feet off the floor. Daniel wrapped the chain around a post and silently, almost reverently, all three of them looked into the hole at their feet.

"Well I'll be damned," Wheeler said.

Daniel got down on his knees and pulled away the canvas covering what was hidden underneath. But the canvas was too heavy to lift so Daniel climbed down and pulled the cover back. They all gasped.

There, under his feet was the money that he and Harry had stolen from the Leadville bank. Some was still in the bags from the robbery and some was in an old army sack. Daniel dropped to his knees and tears welled up in his eyes. So much came into focus, all in a rush. Here was their stolen money, which meant that it was Joe who had burned down Harry's cabin the day he was married.

Daniel then began laughing. So, did Wheeler and Red as it dawned on them that Joe had tricked them all. Joe had probably imagined the worst possible consequences when he heard Harry gave his cabin to the newlyweds. What might have happened when Kate moved into the cabin was anybody's guess. But it could have sunk any possibility of a successful marriage if Kate had discovered his past exploits with Harry. Daniel then recalled that Joe had joined the wedding party late, but he had made nothing of it at the time.

"I knew that old coot had my money," came a raspy, familiar voice from behind them. "I just knew it."

"How are you Harry?" Red asked, without turning.

"Why the sudden concern, Red? You're a changed man." Harry continued, "Shirley's the cause I bet." Harry laughed. "Don't turn around fast. I have a gun."

Red and Wheeler watched Daniel's expression and were not emboldened by it. His jaw was clenched and his face bright red, his breathing forced.

"Hand up the money, Daniel." Bag by bag, Daniel lifted the money bags out of the hole and placed them at Harry's feet. "All of it!" Harry demanded in a tone foreign to them. Red and Wheeler exchanged looks. "Now get out." Daniel did as he was ordered and joined the others facing Harry.

"You got here quick, Harry," Wheeler said. "I didn't expect you so soon," he said, pleasantly.

"I bet you didn't, Jerome. I bet you thought that I was marmalade out on the northern plains. Me and your Silver Queen."

"Well we're glad that you're in good health, Harry. That's all that counts, isn't it?" Wheeler gave Red a skeptical look.

"Not in my reckoning it isn't. You tricked me, Jerome, and you're going to pay for it. I'm going to tell the world that your precious Silver Queen was nothing but a hoax. You'll look a fool and a fraud when I tell them reporters."

"What reporters, Harry? The reporters who will be at your trial for Joe's death and the death of your friend Hamlett Kincaid? You participated in both of them Harry." They clearly saw the effect this had on Harry.

"I don't think you'll do that, Jerome." Harry said, pointing his gun menacingly at them, each in turn. "I think you're going to want to keep this whole business private, Jerome. Just between the five of us. Well four, now that Hamlett has met his maker. I doubt you'll want them reporters asking questions about that fellow Lynch or Daniel's brother."

Wheeler and Red exchanged looks. Wheeler nodded and turned back to Harry. "You can't possibly get away with all of this money without help from us, Harry. How about we make a deal?"

Harry laughed loudly. "Oh, no you don't, Jerome. I'm through making deals with you. That money I won off you is floating all over the northern plains and your silver statue was nothing but plaster and sand. It was worthless. You cheated me, Jerome!" Harry screamed Jerome was laughing hard. So hard, that he had to hold onto Red's arm to steady himself. Finally, he gathered himself. "Will you tell us what happened out there on the plains, Harry, please? I'm dying to know."

"You can laugh, Jerome, but I nearly died out there. I thought I was going to be a rich man. Then I thought I was going to be a dead one.

That train had a full head of steam going when it rounded the corner. The engineer was asleep I'm guessing because he didn't even put on the brakes."

"What happened?" Daniel asked, honestly concerned. Wheeler's face was flushed and Red was struggling to hold in his laughter too.

Harry seemed lost in thought as he relived the moment when the train collided with the Silver Queen. "I saw it coming and tried to signal them but they didn't see me coming down the hill, fast like that. So, I jumped off before the train hit. I thought all that silver would stop the train, but it didn't. All it did was make a hell of a noise and disappear in a cloud of dust.

Wheeler had fallen to his knees, on his knuckles, laughing so hard he was crying.

"Oh, it's funny to you, Jerome, isn't it?" Harry said, decidedly unamused. "No silver. No gold. Just sand and rocks flying all over the place. I could've been killed, Jerome," Harry screamed loudly, in frustration.

Wheeler relapsed into another fit of laughter. "I want my money, Jerome. All of it. Or I'll kill this little bastard." Harry said pointing his pistol at Daniel. Daniel put his arms up in the air. Red gently lifted Wheeler back to his feet.

"Put your arms down, Daniel," Wheeler said. "Harry's not going to shoot you. He's not going to shoot anyone, are you, Harry?" Harry looked at the faces of his jurors in turn. He knew Wheeler was right. Harry was many things, but a killer he definitely was not.

"Listen to me, Harry. We know you tricked Daniel into helping you rob the bank," Red said. "You could've gotten him killed back there; do you know that? Or he could have ended up in prison because of you. The boy was an innocent until he met you, Harry." Harry's arm wavered, the gun barrel lowered a fraction. "Then, years later, you come along and try to turn him in for a reward? You're despicable, Harry." Harry was weakening. His attention wandered, his jaw clenched then relaxed, his anger ebbed.

The hole between them could have been a canyon, but in a flash, Daniel flew across it and grabbed Harry's pistol. Red charged in from the left and grappled Harry to the ground. Seizing the opportunity, Wheeler joined in and pinned Harry's hand with his boot and retrieved the pistol, pointing it at Harry, quieting what fight he had left.

Slowly the mangle untangled. Daniel and Red released Harry and stood over him. Harry rested on his elbows breathing hard and looking close to tears, fake of course.

"Get up Harry!" Wheeler demanded. Harry staggered to his feet.

"You look a mess. How did you get here so fast?"

"When the train stopped to see what had happened, I climbed onto the caboose before they saw me. They walked the tracks saw what was left of Hamlett and scratched their heads. I rode on the roof to Denver then caught a train here." Wheeler was no longer laughing.

"You know you can't leave here without someone seeing you carrying all this money anyway." Harry looked up and chewed his lower lip. "So, here's what I think I can do for you, Harry. I can get you out of here on my train if you leave now."

"What about the money?" Harry nodded toward the stack of money. "It's mine." He gave Daniel barely a glance.

"Not all of it, Harry," Wheeler said. "Your partner is entitled to half of it. If Daniel was going to jail because of you, you can at the very least share your plunder equally. Don't you think that's fair? How much money is there, Daniel?" Wheeler asked.

"Around thirty-two thousand dollars," Daniel replied, his participation in the robbery now an open secret.

"Well, here's what I suggest, Daniel. Give him half. If ...," Wheeler held Harry's attention "if Harry will agree never to bother you, or any of us again." Wheeler paused and watched them both, appraising their reactions as Daniel and Harry warily eyed each other suspiciously. "Is that fair enough for you, Harry? Do you agree to the terms? If you do, I'll get you and your loot out of town unseen."

His greed and his proximity to the stolen money made Harry's face come alive. Where prior, his smudged, bearded face held naught but anger, there was now a sublime smile of acceptance and supplication to the god of money laid at his feet. Realizing that he had been beaten, Harry simply nodded.

"If we're all in agreement?" Neither Harry nor Daniel dissented. Alright then, let's get all this money divided and packed up and then we'll wave you off for the last time eh, Harry?"

*   *   *

Jerome's locomotive chugged off into the distance headed north toward Glenwood Springs. They stood close together on the wooden platform, three men watching the reason they all knew each other disappear down the tracks.

"Does Kate need to know about the money, Mister Wheeler?" Red looked over at Jerome, also curious as to the answer. Wheeler shrugged.

"I don't see why," Wheeler said sagely. "In my experience, the less your wife knows about your financial dealings, the happier you both are." Wheeler laughed, slapping Daniel on his shoulder. "I do believe that we've seen the very last of Harry Rich and that's a cause for celebration in my books. I think a drink is in order, don't you?"

The Saloon Bar at the Hotel Jerome had never seemed more welcoming.

THE END

Perhaps.
But not quite yet.

EPILOGUE

The Ogallala Indian Reservation, 1893.

The wind flew across the wide expanse of grassland. Cottonwood trees huddled in the river bends while crows and buzzards circled and cawed. A small band of Indians sat on their horses outside of the trading post. Only one of them dismounted and entered the rough wooden building.

"Howdy chief, what can I do for you today? That's a mighty fine hat you got there." The reservation sheriff asked. The chief's hat was overly large and covered his ears.

"Yes. It is a good hat."

"Where did you get it?"

"Near the iron rails where the trains go. I found these boots too."

He held up one large-sized boot. "The other boot had a foot in it."

"Anything else?"

"I found a belt buckle." He handed it over to the man behind the desk. It was a large buckle with the word Tabor in raised letters. The man turned it over, "Leadville, Colorado," he said to himself, reading the inscription.

"So, is that all you found?"

"I found this money too." The chief opened his pouch and the sheriff whistled.

"That's a lot of money you have there. And you say, you found this out on the prairie, near the train tracks?"

The chief nodded. "The buzzards and coyotes ate the body but he was a big, white man.

"Can I buy these things from you, chief?"

"Why you want them?"

"Curious, I guess. I want to find out who this man was."

To be continued. Maybe.